A YOUNG MAN'S FANCY

Susan Pleydell was the *nom de plume* of Isabel Senior, née Syme. She was born in 1907 into a well-to-do farming family at Milnathort, near Kinross. They moved to Dollar when she was in her teens, and later to another farm near Rumbling Bridge. She had great musical ability, inherited from her mother, and after a local education was sent to the Royal College of Music to study the piano. Later she taught at a girls' school in Bexhill at which time she was introduced to Murray Senior, then head of History at Shrewsbury School. They married in 1935. He had two headmasterships in the 1950s, one of a grammar school near Manchester until 1956, the other in South Wales. She taught the piano at Shrewsbury and for some years afterwards.

She had always been well read and having long had an urge to write began in earnest in the mid 1950s. It took a lot of effort to reach publication, but the first novel, *Summer Term,* eventually appeared in 1959. It makes full use of her experience in schools, as does its sequel, *A Young Man's Fancy* (1962). Her other eight novels, the last published in 1977, benefit from her experience in music, her Scottish background – and, of course her own imagination, sympathy and powers of observation.

She died in 1986.

By the same author

A YOUNG MAN'S FANCY

SUSAN PLEYDELL

Greyladies

Published by
Greyladies
an imprint of The Old Children's Bookshelf
175 Canongate, Edinburgh EH8 8BN

© Susan Pleydell 1959

This edition first published 2011
Design and layout © Shirley Neilson 2011
Preface © Claire Smerdon 2011

ISBN   978-1-907503-10-8

Set in Sylfaen / Perpetua
Printed and bound by the MPG Books Group.
Bodmin and Kings Lynn,

Preface

Does anyone actually read introductions? When I was asked to write an introduction to *A Young Man's Fancy*, the second book by Susan Pleydell to be published by Greyladies, I was very pleased. I had read Pleydell's earlier book, *Summer Term,* with pleasure and looked forward to reading the sequel. But when I mentioned this honour to a group of book-loving friends, I was somewhat disappointed (shattered) to hear that while they had all read and thoroughly enjoyed *Summer Term*, not one had bothered with the introduction. "They always contain spoilers," one complained, while another felt that she "didn't need somebody to tell her what to think about a book" and *if* she read an introduction at all it was only once she'd finished the book and *then* only if it was written by somebody "reputable." Ouch ...

In *A Young Man's Fancy* we are reacquainted with some of the engaging characters we met four years earlier at Ledenham School. Again the story centres on Headmaster Hugh Fielding, known to and his family as Beak, his wife Hester, whose absence formed the basis of the plot in the earlier book, and youngest daughter Alison. Alison has just returned home following her domestic science training which she chose only because "any mutt could do it," and is in no hurry to find a job. She plans to spend the Spring Term catching up with her old friends and enjoying herself as much as possible. In the intervening years, the community has witnessed three weddings (one most unexpected) and while many of the individuals introduced previously still grace the Masters' Common Room, new colleagues have joined them and some that played a minor role in *Summer Term* now take centre stage. Due, at least in part, to Alison's effervescent personality, the Ledenham young people find many opportunities to enjoy dinner parties, dances and impromptu gatherings despite the dreary weather and the school's remote location.

In the opening pages, two unrelated events—t he death of an elderly School Governor and the sudden illness of the Beak's ever efficient secretary Miss Wills—throw the well-ordered machine that is Ledenham off its usual path, with far-reaching consequences. Pleydell tells us that Miss Wills "ranked with the river and the School clock; a familiar part of life, impersonal, unchanging and, as far as could be seen, eternal." Even as she is being bustled into an ambulance, the competent Miss Wills suggests employing a trained secretary who lives nearby. This young woman is hired and once again Pleydell shows us the devastating effect that outsiders can have upon a closed society. Other outsiders also make their way into Ledenham society, causing disruption and ill-feeling through their unsympathetic ways. Turmoil and confusion also arise from misunderstandings between old friends and a pall is cast over Alison's exuberance by the homesick Norwegian *au pair,* Marthe Jensen, who initially seems as wet as the weather.

Once again automobiles play a significant role in the plot. Recognising the need for her characters to be able to escape from the remote community of Ledenham, Pleydell provides them with an array of vehicles, from Angus Cameron's car, "elderly and given to freakishness," to Sir

Arthur Hinton-Brigg's gleaming Rolls and Land Rover, which are cared for by the ambitious chauffeur Eric. Cars provide not only freedom but also create rumours and misunderstandings when the "wrong" characters are seen driving together, demonstrating the far-reaching effects gossip can have in a closed society.

I think one of Pleydell's greatest skills is demonstrated by her deft descriptions of the homes of her principle characters—in just a few words she sets the scene, painting a vivid picture of the room or building thereby providing a wealth of detail about the inhabitants, their personalities and preferences. While imbuing her main players with distinct personalities, she also shows great affection for her minor characters, giving them a life off-stage. As readers of *Summer Term* will notice, she allows her people to grow and change; some that begin almost as caricatures reveal unexpected depths.

While few boys appeared as individual characters in *Summer Term,* we now meet several boys in person, in the classroom, on the playing fields—and in the Headmaster's Study—where they play a significant part in the events of the term. At the other end of the spectrum, we also see the inner workings of the Board of Governors and its vital role in the operation of a large public school, which, I was surprised to read, is nearly four hundred years old. I think that because Pleydell concerns herself more with the Headmaster, his family and their friends, I have never had a true sense of the age and traditions of the school itself. And while the school forms a most necessary background to the story, I would expect that *five hundred* boys would be more present—or at least noisier!

The book opens on a gloomy note: "It is the season of dark mornings, unspeakable weather, epidemics and catarrh." The inconsistent weather of the Spring Term at Ledenham School reflects the ups and down of the events that take place over the course of the story, from depressing mud and slush to gleaming brilliant snow, with the characters either invigorated or depressed by the weather. The story is certainly *not* gloomy but the cold wind and incessant rain serve to reflect the difficulties encountered by the young people in their relationships, the uncertain situation in the Headmaster's home and the tensions in the Masters' Commonroom. I *hope* I do not give anything away by saying that eventually spring arrives, the sun shines and Matron puts away her remedies, thus marking the end of the Spring Term.

Despite knowing that none of my friends are likely to read this introduction, I have done my best not to spoil the plot, ruin any surprises—or to tell you what you should think about the book. I will say that while many of the characters appeared in *Summer Term*, I think it is entirely possible to read and enjoy *A Young Man's Fancy* on its own merits. The book does not include any real spoilers for events that happened previously. And when I asked Shirley about any more books by Susan Pleydell, she smiled enigmatically. I wait in hope.

Claire Smerdon
Edinburgh 2011

A YOUNG MAN'S FANCY

1

NOBODY connected with a school can regard the spring term with anything but repugnance. There is something to be said for the other two. In the autumn there is a new start, a clean slate and rather nice weather, and it is quite a long time since one last saw boys or colleagues; the summer is the summer, more eventful than the rest of the year and getting to the end of it. But the best thing about both the summer and the autumn terms is that they are not the spring term for which there is nothing to be said at all. It is the season of dark mornings, unspeakable weather, epidemics and catarrh. Every part of school life is a struggle against fearful odds and the worst of it, perhaps, is that the struggles are successful and the term goes on.

Ledenham took a morose pride in its spring terms. People in the south, it felt, hardly knew what a spring term was and certainly the School and its surroundings made no bones about the fact that it was winter. The buildings, though well-heated did not look it, being of a grey stone which on the hottest day looked cool. Beyond the playing-fields with their bare trees were the hills on which snow fell early and lingered while the river, so kindly a friend at other seasons, was bad-tempered and hostile. There was, of course, another side; brilliant exhilarating days which made winter seem the best of seasons, tobogganing when the snow came, skating on the tarns, immense quantities of food and a great deal of cheerful, talkative fug; but these alleviations were in the nature of surprises. They were not to be counted on, not even looked forward to, and the day before the spring term was one on which misfortune seemed peculiarly appropriate.

For the Headmaster the day before any term begins is one of intense pressure and this was rendered hideous to the Headmaster of Ledenham by the departure of his son Michael whose school was starting term a day earlier than Ledenham. Michael was nearly eighteen and the youngest of four so that Mr. Fielding had been seeing his children come and go for years, but he had only got used to it in the sense that the ache of their going was familiar. The effort of putting it aside and working with his usual speed, concentration and equability was considerable but it also was familiar and only an uncommonly sharp eye could have observed it.

After breakfast he waved cheerfully as his son was driven away rather fast by Mrs. Fielding, who did everything briskly on these occasions, and when he went to his study it was no surprise to hear a piece of bad news from his secretary. Old Canon Harris, Miss Wills told him, had passed away.

"Oh," said the Headmaster. "Well—it's not surprising, I suppose. He must have been about ninety."

"Eighty-nine," said Miss Wills placing the paper on which she had transcribed the telephone message before him. "The funeral on Tuesday. In the morning. Your Greek set—"

"Yes." Mr. Fielding glanced at the message and part of his mind considered his Greek set. The first period with them this term—undesirable to set written work or tell them to read on. Switch to the afternoon—"Message to Mr.

Clayton," he said.

Miss Wills scribbled busily. "The flag?" she suggested.

"Yes—Tuesday. Tell Hacket."

"And a wreath?"

The Headmaster assented to the wreath and the business of the death of a Governor had been dealt with. On Tuesday he would attend the funeral, the School flag would fly or droop at half-mast and that, so far as Ledenham was concerned, would be the end of old Canon Harris who had been a Governor for fifty years and had not attended a meeting for twenty. Not, therefore, a figure who would be greatly missed in the life of the School, but behind the Headmaster's calm face there was uneasiness and a desire to swear while Miss Wills, who knew everything, mingled a certain decorous awareness with her tidings-of-death expression.

She made the required notes and went away to telephone the order for the wreath, assembling, as she went, her private notes in her orderly mind. It would be necessary to keep the time of the funeral before her so that no confusion should occur in the Headmaster's appointments and it would be necessary to remind the Headmaster about it on Monday afternoon. Monday would also be the time to tell Hacket, the porter, about the flag. If he received instructions too soon he was apt to forget

In her own small office Miss Wills sat down at her table and reached for the telephone. As she lifted it an expression of acute apprehension broke the imperturbability of her face and she replaced it and drew back her hand. Pain began as though somebody put a match to a well-laid fire. Agonizingly it throbbed and mounted and gasping she bent

3

forward over the table. Its climax forced a groan from her, then it receded slowly, leaving her trembling and cold. In a moment she sat up. A drink of water would be welcome, it might relieve the nausea, but she decided against crossing the passage to get it. This had been a bad attack. However careful she was about what she ate the pain was coming more frequently and more severely. She really must, thought Miss Wills reluctantly, go to the doctor and get something. She straightened her back cautiously, put up a hand to smooth her hair and reached again for the telephone. "The Headmaster of Ledenham's secretary," she said firmly and selected white chrysanthemums and tulips for Canon Harris's wreath.

Miss Wills had been established in Ledenham as Headmaster's secretary long before Mr. Fielding's appointment and she ranked with the river and the School clock; a familiar part of life, impersonal, unchanging and, as far as could be seen, eternal. As the clock lived in the turret affair on Main School Miss Wills lived in the cubby-hole next door to the Headmaster's study. As information was obtained from the clock so was information, more extensive and on the whole more reliable, obtained from Miss Wills—provided the enquirer was entitled to receive it. Her efficiency was such that when the Headmaster and his wife had words Miss Wills was a knockout. "You know perfectly well that if it wasn't for Miss Wills you couldn't run the School for a fortnight" was final and Mrs. Fielding used it only when she was hard-pressed since cordial agreement from her adversary usually brought the encounter to an abrupt and unexhilarating close.

It was many years since her employer had consciously

seen Miss Wills, and when she came in response to his ring to take the letters he did not look up. His mind was on the correspondence he hoped to get out of the way before the first of the day's appointments and he was also finding it difficult not to think about the probable effect of Canon Harris's death on the School's affairs and his own.

"What is the date of the Governors' meeting?" he asked.

"The 25th," was the prompt reply.

Mr. Fielding scowled for a moment, waving his spectacles thoughtfully by the leg as he contemplated the probabilities, while Miss Wills with a grey face sat beside him listening to the threatening murmurs of pain.

"Right," he said, thrusting on the spectacles with one hand and picking up a letter with the other. "Dear Colonel Pratt, I have had a talk with your boy's Housemaster who agrees with me that there is little point in his thinking of university. We suggest—"

Miss Wills' pencil flew. It faltered a little and with an effort went on. It faltered again and stopped and as the Headmaster looked up it fell to the floor and she bent forward, groaning and clutching her notebook to her. Mr. Fielding, after a paralysed second, sprang to his feet and she made a feeble gesture to fend him off.

"Quite all right," she gasped angrily. "Don't—don't—It'll pass. Indigest—" the voice trailed away and her head sank down on to the table.

His finger was already on a bell and events moved fast. The house man appeared with a startled face and vanished again as the Headmaster called the doctor's number. The white-overalled figure of the matron dropped a pile of sheets and raced from the top of the house. Fifteen minutes later the doctor's car drew up at the door.

By the time it drove away again with the patient protesting and Matron providing a soothing obligato, a goggling queue had formed of people to see the Headmaster. He had just got rid of the last of them when Mrs. Fielding returned, late for lunch.

The news met her at the door and she went straight to the study which still seemed to vibrate with the activity of the morning.

"Hugh," she said, "this is frightful. How bad is she?"

"I really don't know," replied the Headmaster. "Baddish I think. Miles thought probably appendix but he couldn't be sure."

"What on earth will you do?"

He lit a cigarette and leant back in his chair looking a little hopelessly at the papers which had accumulated on his desk in the course of the morning. The difficulty of running the School even for a day without Miss Wills was apparent.

"An agency, I suppose," he said. He had never needed to engage a secretary. "The Bursar will know. It isn't going to be a matter of days whatever it is."

"No. Matron went with her, you said? She'll be all right then," said Mrs. Fielding with perfect faith. "They'll ring up from the hospital as soon as they know anything but you can't wait. You'll have to—"

There was a tap on the door and Matron herself appeared, her cap crisp and unruffled, the situation in hand.

"Acute appendix," she announced to their anxious faces. "They'll do the op. this evening. She's been having pain for

6

some time but of course," her tone was resigned, "she never said anything. We just got a few things together for her and the ambulance came right away. She wrote a note for you, sir."

She handed an envelope to the Headmaster and while he opened it Mrs. Fielding went on talking about Miss Wills. "Was she in pain all the time, Matron?"

"Well, she was, Mrs. Fielding, but Doctor gave her something. She wasn't too bad. Really," Matron laughed a little, "she was angry more than anything. And of course," with a glance at Mr. Fielding, "it *is* awkward for the Headmaster."

"It'll work out," said Mrs. Fielding. "Miss Wills mustn't worry. What about your lunch?" Mrs. Higgins would have it ready for her, said Matron, and she would hurry upstairs now and get on. Mrs. Fielding nodded. A major crisis inevitably brought its train of minor crises and the disruption of Matron's beginning of term preparations was one of them. "I'll send Alison to give you a hand," she promised and as the door closed turned back to her husband.

Miss Wills had been very ill, in pain and greatly agitated, but she had done her best for her employer. The note contained a brief apology for human frailty, some vital information—"Appointments on office desk—Masters' meeting 8-30—New boys in top l.h. drawer—Canon H. Tuesday 11-0—Holy Trinity—Flag." And a substitute.

"She says there's actually a trained secretary free in Ledenham now," the Headmaster said incredulously. "Girl called—" he paused and looked again at the paper in his hand, "—could it be Oonagh?"

"Oonagh? Of course!" Mrs. Fielding's expression had changed from controlled despair to hope. It now displayed a lively exasperation. "It would be Oonagh—what's her name?"

"Hepburn. You know her then?"

"Yes and so do you. She was the girl in the Meadows row."

Mr. Fielding remembered. "Oh—that girl. So she was. Still—it's a long time ago. She must be flying higher than schoolboys now. Miss Wills says she wouldn't recommend her—the girl—as a permanency, but she hopes to be back herself in a few weeks and she thinks she—the girl—would be all right as a stop-gap."

"I'll bet," said Mrs. Fielding relaxing momentarily, "that she—Miss Wills—didn't say that."

"No," agreed her husband, "she said it better but longer. She says the girl is competent. It would save a lot of trouble."

In one way, of course, it obviously would save a lot of trouble. The question, Mrs. Fielding felt, was what other trouble might it bring? She had quite a lot of faith in human nature but she by no means swallowed it whole and she had a vivid recollection of the girl who had been at the bottom of the Meadows row several years ago. The leader of a giggling party which lurked hopefully round the fringes of the playing fields—

"Why isn't she in a job?" she asked crossly. "She's been at home for ages."

Mr. Fielding referred to Miss Wills. "Her mother isn't strong."

"Oh," said Mrs. Fielding.

8

Her tone was eloquent and the Headmaster himself felt a certain reluctance as he recalled Oonagh Hepburn to mind and thought of bringing her in to the very centre of the School. "I think I must give her a trial, you know," he said. "After all she's here and it's fairly urgent." He looked again at the papers on his desk and his wife looked with him.

"Yes," she said. "Of course. You could go and see her after lunch and she might start at once. She's probably flying at commonroom level now but that's their look-out."

"It's not impossible," observed the Headmaster, "that the commonroom—or some of it—is already aware of Miss Hepburn, wouldn't you say?"

"Very likely," his wife agreed and sighed. "I don't really mind about the girl so much as her mother. I've been fending Mrs. Hepburn off for years and now they'll be in. However—it's a crisis. I'll put up with it."

"You can freeze them out later."

"Very difficult and not a thing I'm good at. Never mind. Come and have lunch and then go and rout the creature out."

As they went along to the private side of the house the Headmaster's mind reverted to his other troubles.

"Mike go off all right?" he asked. Mrs. Fielding replied flatly that Mike had gone off all right and he slid his arm through hers, there was no need for words. "Canon Harris is dead," he said, recalling the secondary depression which had been with him all morning.

"Is he, poor old thing?" said Mrs. Fielding. "He won't be much of a loss."

"He leaves a gap, however."

She turned a startled face to him and stood still. "Good

9

grief, Hugh!" she exclaimed. "Sartha?"

"I'm afraid so," said the Headmaster and they looked at each other for a moment and then went silently in to lunch.

Alison, who was to be sent to help Matron, was the third of the Fielding children, a long-legged girl with an active grace of movement which was athletic rather than seductive and a lively expressive face. Her clear grey eyes were like her father's, they were gayer and more trustful than his but they could, on occasion, display the same penetrating, rather disconcerting intelligence; her warm colouring and abundant brown curls were her own. She was waiting in the dining-room with commendable patience and no surprise for, since she had been no more than three or four years old when her father became Headmaster of Ledenham, she was accustomed to lateness for meals and abstraction on the part of her parents and she had heard from Mrs. Higgins, the cook, about the current crisis. She was very sorry indeed for Miss Wills, who to her was something between an old friend and an old pest, and she had a fairly shrewd idea of the difficulty confronting her father. Starting term without a secretary, or at best with a stand-in, would be no joke and she was quite as sorry for him as for the patient; but she was also the only person in Ledenham who was looking forward to the term with unqualified pleasure and cheerfulness kept breaking in.

"Darling, you shouldn't have waited," her mother, coming into the room at last, spoke with absent-minded remorse and an air of being considerably harried. "You've heard about poor Miss Wills?"

10

"Yes, Mrs. Hig told me." Higgins the houseman, who cruised about in the course of his duties and Mrs. Higgins tied to the kitchen were equally gifted as pickers-up and spreaders of news and it was assumed that by now most of Ledenham would have the details of Miss Wills' collapse. "I'm terribly sorry," Alison went on, "but I find it difficult to take it in. I mean—who'd have thought she had anything to operate *on?*"

"Repairs would be more credible, you feel?" suggested her father.

"Well—yes. Re-wiring or some small replacement. Isn't it a pity I didn't do secretarial instead of domestic? They were equally repulsive and I could have stepped modestly in and saved the School. What are you going to do, Beak?"

Ledenham Headmasters were by tradition 'the Beak' and Mr. Fielding was no more perturbed by his children's direct use of the title than by the knowledge that everybody else used it indirectly. He explained about Oonagh Hepburn and Alison rolled expressive eyes from him to her mother and back again.

"Well, well," she said. "That'll make a change for you."

"Is she an acquaintance of yours?" he asked, amused.

"Not to say an *acquaintance.* We smile, knowing each other well by sight. She's different from Miss Wills in many ways, you'll find."

Her father laughed. "Any change must be for the worse," he said, "but any secretary—almost—is better than none. If you want to save the School, Alison, go along to the office after lunch and tell everybody I'll be back as soon as I can. Take messages whenever possible."

"I told Matron you'd give her a hand," said Mrs. Fielding.

"Will you when you've finished in the office? She's a bit rushed because of going with Miss Wills."

"Leave everything to me," responded their daughter soothingly. "Which Governor is it who's died?"

Both her parents looked startled and then resigned.

"Was that Mrs. Higgins too?" asked her mother.

"No—that was Higgins. He only knew it wasn't Lord Leyburn or the Bishop—Canon Harris? Never heard of him."

"Nobody's heard much of him in your lifetime," said her father. "He was very old."

"That'll mean a new one," said Alison chattily. "I wonder who it'll be. How do you *get* Governors?"

"This one will be nominated by the Mayor and Council of Snaydon," she was informed briefly.

"So nobody knows who they'll pull out of the bag?"

"No," said the Headmaster, "nobody knows," and Mrs. Fielding changed the subject.

Alison was one of those girls for whom no obvious career presents itself. Her scholastic record was unimpressive, she had no particular bent and no ambition. Her choice had finally fallen on domestic science on the grounds that people always have to eat and any mutt could do it, but when she finished her training she was in no hurry to begin. As she left college an opportunity was offered to her to go abroad and now she was home and intending that a judicious choosiness about jobs would keep her there for some time. The School House at Ledenham was a very good home and in her view she had not had nearly enough of it.

After lunch while the Headmaster drove off through the main gates in pursuit of Oonagh Hepburn and Mrs. Fielding

12

in her smaller car headed for Leyburn, the nearest sizable town, to see Miss Wills in hospital she went along in excellent spirits to hold the fort in the deserted office. The School House was a very large building. In one end of it the private side was a pleasant and commodious dwelling for the Headmaster and his family; the other end contained dormitories, changing rooms, dayrooms, studies and dining-hall for nearly a hundred boys, with rooms for Matron and the assistant housemaster. Between were the kitchens which served both family and boys, the Headmaster's study and the secretary's office.

Alison reached the business area by going through a baize door and walking a short distance along a passage. The study came first having, so to speak, a foot in each camp and Miss Wills' office was strategically placed so that nobody approaching from the outer door beyond could get at the Headmaster unobserved. The office was small but it was interesting. Alison, who had never been let loose in it before, could have had a pleasant experimental time among typewriters, duplicators and rubber-stamps but as she opened the door the telephone rang, footsteps could be heard in the passage and exclamations of; "Good lord! What are *you* doing—Where's Miss Wills?" began.

Most of the callers were geared to the beginning of term and though friendly did not linger; they left a message or said they would try again and hurried away. But a different note was struck when, after the customary respectful knock, a red head appeared round the door.

"Good lord!" came the inevitable exclamation. "What—"

"Angus!" shrieked Alison leaping to her feet. "You're back! I *am* glad to see you—what ages it's been—"

"Aye," the newcomer came right in and beamed at her, "it has that. I mind ye fine though."

She chuckled, delighted by the assurance that she had not been forgotten and the instant resumption of intimacy brought about by Angus's holiday Scots. He was an immensely tall young man, magnificently built, whose nationality could never be in doubt for a moment. There was the hair, neither auburn nor sandy but uncompromisingly red, shrewd pleasant eyes behind solemn spectacles, high cheek-bones with a freckle or two; and the correct English which was his everyday speech was not as the English speak it.

They shook hands, beaming joyfully at each other and Miss Wills' office temporarily disappeared, giving place to a confused but pleasing conglomeration of past scenes. The first, so to speak, human word addressed to Angus Cameron in Ledenham had been spoken by Alison, then a leggy schoolgirl of 17, in an attempt—vain but no less friendly— to soften the severity of Miss Wills. In two weddings of unusual interest to both of them they had, as bridesmaid and usher, supported each other. At Alison's first ball and at subsequent balls there had been Angus and like a backcloth for such pageantry were hills they had climbed, golf-courses round which they had hacked their hilarious way and the mud and heavy breathing of mixed hockey.

Alison perched herself on Miss Wills' table, Angus sat down on the discouraging chair provided for visitors and they proceeded to catch up.

"Angus," Alison began at once, "d'you know I'm going to stay at home for quite a long time?" Angus hadn't known and expressed satisfaction. "Of course," she went on, "I'm *looking* for a job, but I've been told there's no absolute rush and I'm going to be very, very choosy. Everybody says I'll soon get bored with Ledenham in winter but I won't."

"Of course you won't," said Angus. "Not at all. There's any amount to do."

"I don't know that I'd like to go on for *ever* being a daughter at home but just for a while—it'll do me."

"Fine that," Angus agreed again. "It'll be a relief to stay put for a bit I would think. How did you like it? Get any climbing in Switzerland?"

They moved to the Alps. Alison had not been lucky enough to do any climbing but she had had some ski-ing and agreeable suggestions were thrown out regarding opportunities for enjoyment in the near future if the snow came. Then they remembered where they were and Angus asked what had happened to Miss Wills.

"Ill!" he exclaimed as astonished as everybody else. "Good lord! Poor thing. What's happening then?"

"A girl called Oonagh Hepburn we *hope*," Alison held up crossed fingers. "Beak's hunting her out now. Have you ever come across her?"

Angus looked a little reserved. "Yes, I do know her, as a matter of fact," he admitted and Alison laughed and was beginning to tell him that her brother Richard had once met Oonagh at a dance when more approaching footsteps caused her to revert hurriedly to business.

"Beak should be home any minute but he'll be pressed," she said. "Any message?"

"Oh—no. No need to bother. Probably see him later. Spot of awkwardness about the Sevens," Angus explained lucidly as he prepared to depart. "Any chance of seeing you before the rush? Could you come and have tea?"

"I'm going to tea with Frances," said Alison regretfully.

"So will I, then," said Angus. "Might have a drink, perhaps, later. What do you drink nowadays? Still on squash?"

A knock sounded and there was no time to raise her eyebrows and speak loftily of Italian wines. She made a face at him and hissed 'shandy' as the door opened.

"First wee step on the downward path," muttered Angus and then greeted the newcomer. "Oh it's you, is it. Alison, you probably don't know Tim Selby, do you?"

Alison did not know Tim Selby, who had joined her father's staff while she was abroad, but she had heard of him. A commonroom needs its scholars, its athletes and an artist or two; it needs its revered elder statesmen and it also needs its quota of young, even irreverent bachelors and Tim Selby was the latest of these. She had recognised the expression with which her mother spoke of him—Mrs. Fielding liked irreverent young men if they were of good quality in their irreverence—and her cousin Frances, who was married to one of the staff, had quoted Tim with amusement. Tim Selby, now shaking her cordially by the hand, was a very good-looking young man, dark and unusually elegant, with bright alert eyes. He was also a good physicist but that did not concern her.

"Welcome home," he said. "This is a pleasant beginning to a lousy term."

"Miss Wills, do you mean?" asked Alison.

"Miss *Wills?* Certainly not. There's nothing pleasant about Miss Wills' misfortune for her or—"

"I thought you meant it in, *here's* a nice thing, sort of way."

16

"A pretty kettle of fish? No. I wasn't referring to Miss Wills, nor did I speak paradoxically. I—"

"He means," said Angus kindly, "that he's pleased to meet you but he's polysyllabic by nature. Likewise he shows off. Otherwise not a bad chap if kept in his place."

"Quiet, Cameron," said Mr. Selby. "Now you've put me off. I had a nicely turned phrase with which to greet Miss Beak. Gallant, yet respectful; conveying pleasure and admiration delicately combined with the deference due to the Headmaster's daughter." He looked sadly at Alison. "Gone."

"Might it come back, do you think?" she asked hopefully.

"Not that one I'm afraid. You've missed it. Chalk it up against Angus."

"You'll hear plenty more," Angus assured her.

"What's going on here anyway?" demanded Tim attacking. "What would Miss Wills think if she saw her office now? A young lady sitting on her sanctified table hob-nobbing with a ton of Scotch beef—"

"I am dealing with the Headmaster's business for the present," said Alison having a shot at Miss Wills' quelling tone. "He will be back," she glanced pointedly at her watch, "at any moment."

"I'll push off," said Angus. "See you at tea, Alison."

"Will you tell Frances I might be a bit late?" she called after him. "I've got to go and stooge for Matron."

"Are you both going to tea with Frances?" said Tim. "Hi—Angus! It isn't a party, is it?"

"Not as far as I know," said Angus and to Alison. "They'll be a bit late themselves I expect. They've gone to play golf."

He went away and the two left in Miss Wills' office

looked at each other with the slight alteration in expression which comes when there is no third party present. Tim Selby's grin was a comment on his own nonsense and Alison, disposed to like him, responded with a direct and friendly smile.

"Beak—my father really will be back in a minute," she told him, "but it's a bit of a crisis. Can you leave a message?"

"Well actually," said Tim, "I knew it must be a crisis and I came to say I can type. Quite accurately and quite fast. But if you're coping—"

"Oh I'm not coping. I can't type. That's very good of you—I'll tell him—but he hopes he's got a stand-in."

"Already? Quick work."

"It's a girl here. Oonagh Hepburn—"

"Oonagh?" The lively face looked surprised and then greatly amused. "Good God!" Alison laughed and he said: "Do you know her?"

"Only by sight."

"Well, well," said Tim as she had said herself but he went on to add: "What a piece of goose for Oonagh."

Alison, much intrigued, began an encouraging "What do you mean?" but the door of a car slammed outside the window. The Headmaster came in with a rapid step and a lissom figure in a striking coat scurried after him with the short steps and wobbling ankles of tight skirts and stilletto heels.

"Ah, Selby," he said. "You've met my daughter, I see. Miss Hepburn, Alison. Mr. Selby—"there were constrained murmurs for which he did not wait. "If you want me, Selby—"

"No, sir," said Tim quickly. "I only came to say I could do

18

some typing if it would help, but I see you don't need it."

"Thank you," Mr. Fielding could be cordial even at his most brisk. "A good offer, but I think we're all right," and as Tim got himself neatly out of the room he was going on: "Alison, if you'll show Miss Hepburn where—a—everything is we'll get on. Have you any messages for me?"

He took the messages Alison had for him and went away to his study. Alison turned to meet a pair of large eyes, interested and excited.

"Did we come a bit too soon?" asked Miss Hepburn chummily. "Tough."

2

THE founders of Ledenham School would have been a good deal surprised if they had seen it in its mid-20th century form. The original School was still in use as a library but the 'master's house', in which a few boarders had been received at the cost of £10 a year for each lad had long ago disappeared. The buildings themselves and their apparently random placing told the story of nearly 400 years of growth, good buildings and bad buildings, varying widely in style, but since nobody had made the mistake of departing from the grey local stone there was a satisfactory unity about the whole. Land had been acquired in the course of the centuries, pushing the boundaries of the School further and further out from its centre, but playing-fields for 500 boys occupy a large acreage and the School had also pushed its way into the village. The boarding-houses, of which there were now nine, had begun with School House inside the grounds, others clustered near the gates, occupied a conveniently placed country house or two and at last appeared here and there in Ledenham itself as suitable sites were found.

Just outside the main gates a tall, functional looking house known as the Zoo provided accommodation for the bachelor masters. The married men found homes where they could, the majority of them in houses built by their predecessors in more spacious days. In these, even in the thirties, young couples with incomes in the region of £400 set up house with a resident maid—a second maid being commonly added with the second baby—and gave dinner parties; now most of them were rather amateurishly divided and the young couples with incomes at least doubled in name lived in parts of them. Help, when there was any, consisted of a char once a week and an elaborately organised system of baby-sitters, but they still entertained boys and each other to very much the same kind of meals though finger-bowls were out and the effort was greater.

Holly Lodge had not been divided. It was a solid, comfortable house of medium size and in it lived Patsy Henderson, his wife Frances and his son John; and, temporarily, a young Norwegian, Marthe Jensen, who was studying English and helping in the house. Patsy Henderson was in his middle thirties and he was an out-standing schoolmaster, good academically and a distinguished athlete, who knew boys thoroughly and handled them with understanding which never overflowed into fuss or verbosity. Twelve years or so ago he had been one of the valuable young bachelors, not of Tim Selby's sprightly kind but economical in speech and movement and casual in appearance, with direct eyes which revealed directness and integrity of mind. Now he was one of the most influential men in the School; his wife, who was the Headmaster's niece, was thought by many people to confer upon Ledenham the distinction of owning the most beautiful schoolmaster's wife in England, and to their house above all others visitors dropped in. Patsy was large, calm and comfortable, Frances lovely to look at and never put out and there was always plenty of tea at any reason-able hour of day or night.

Tim Selby left School House grinning at the incongruity

of Oonagh Hepburn in place of the rigid propriety of Miss Wills. Recalling the young lady's exultant face he thought that the ill wind which had blown Miss Wills to hospital had done nicely for Oonagh but he hoped that the Beak would lock up his private papers. The Beak, however, he reflected comfortably, was not easily deceived and he turned his mind to his own immediate affairs, which were centred on Holly Lodge, and walked home to the Zoo considering tactics.

If Patsy and Frances Henderson had gone to play golf as Angus said, it meant that Marthe Jensen would be out with the baby. Tim had no experience but from observation he calculated that on a cold winter day like this babies were taken in by half-past three. If, therefore, he went along to Holly Lodge soon after that he would have a chance of some time with Marthe before the hosts and the tea-party arrived. He established himself at the window of his study, which was upstairs and had a good view of the road, and presently a girl walked past pushing a pram. A few minutes later he opened the door of Holly Lodge and went in as she carried the baby, a jovial ten-months-old boy, downstairs.

At first sight Marthe Jensen did not look the sort of girl for whom Tim Selby would lie in wait. Tim might possibly be an unstable young man, he was certainly not a simple one and his appearance and manner suggested that his tastes would lean towards the glamorous beauty. Marthe was not glamorous. She was a thin girl, a little angular in build, with dark hair cut very short, straight eyebrows above deep-set eyes and a mouth which closed firmly. Her skin was clear and colourless and she wore a pleated skirt, a jersey of the fisherman type and no make-up. A closer scrutiny showed that the unpadded bones were beautiful, the eyes, which were rather hidden by the depth of their setting and the closeness of brows and eyelashes, were almost sea-green and her face, though it was reticent was expressive and, when she smiled, illuminated. Tim had fallen in love with the smile which had suggested sunshine on clear water to his imagination and she did, in fact, look a creature of water and mountains and dark conifers. He received a medium smile as she came towards him down the stairs, better than polite but reserved, while the baby stared and then grinned affably.

"Hullo, Marthe," he said. "Happy new year. Hi, John." He held out his hand and kept hers while he stroked the baby's cheek with a finger. "Did you have good holidays?"

"Very good," she answered readily. "John was astonished by Christmas. So many things coming out of a sock."

"His sock?"

"No," the best smile appeared briefly. "His father's sock was more convenient. And you? I hope you had nice things in your sock?"

"A few," said Tim. "I've come to tea. Is it all right?"

"I'm sure it is all right. Alison Fielding is coming and Nick. Angus too perhaps. But you are too early."

"Yes, I know. Patsy and Frances are playing golf. I'll help you get it ready."

"Oh—it is ready," she said. They were still standing in the hall, though she had recovered her hand, and as she spoke she led the way into a large sitting-room, pleasantly untidy with books, toys and knitting, and put the baby down on the floor. He crawled off rapidly to his toys and she stood watching him, looking a little uncertain.

23

Tim was not at ease either. He tried ordinary conversation but he couldn't manage it. It was stilted and unreal and at last he turned to her to say what he had come to say.

"Marthe," he began, "are you still adamant?"

She glanced at him. "Adamant? I don't know what that means."

"Unyielding."

"Oh—then yes. I am adamant."

Even at this difficult moment he smiled at her immediate adoption of the new word, but it was a very brief smile. "Have you thought about me at all in the holidays?" he went on. "Have you remembered that I want you to marry me?"

"I remembered you said so," the reply was given unwillingly. "I would like not to talk about it again."

"But I can't not talk about it," said Tim. "I'm in love with you. I can't just drop it with a light laugh. Marthe—why won't you marry me?"

She made a small gesture of distress. "Oh Tim—there is only one reason for marrying anybody. All the others are reasons why not."

There was a pause. "This scene isn't going well," he said. "We're getting nowhere."

"No," said Marthe. "It is better to stop." She went across and picked up the baby again. "You want your tea, don't you?" she said to him. "We'll go and put the kettle on so that there is no waiting when they come in."

Tim said: "Marthe—please wait a minute," and took the baby from her, removing her barricade. John Henderson was used to being passed from hand to hand. He leant a nonchalant elbow on Tim's shoulder and looked on benevolently while Tim with his free hand caught one of Marthe's and held it. "Now," he said, "please don't just brush me off. Do you dislike me?"

"No, not at all," said Marthe.

"Do you believe that I love you?"

She hesitated. "I think I am a Norwegian girl and a little different from English girls and so for a time I am—interesting—"

"No," said Tim. "It's nothing like that. Marthe—you must know it. How can a man do more than ask a girl to marry him?" There was no answer to that and after a minute he went on: "I can only tell you again that I love you. I'll always love you. You're the girl I want for my wife—to love and to cherish—"

He stopped and Marthe glanced up at him and away again, catching her lower lip between her teeth. There could not be a more honest, more manly declaration of love and the lively face was serious. She could not but be moved, speech was impossible, but she shook her head. There was a tense little silence and then Tim said:

"Well—that's that. But you don't dislike me. Will you at least come out with me sometimes? Let me see you and—give me a chance?"

"No," said Marthe unhappily. "It is better not."

"Why? You go out with the others. Nick and—"

"But don't you see," she cried, "with the others it means nothing. To them and to me only a little pleasure. If I go out with you after you have—said this, it means what I don't want. Besides I don't like to—"

A wail from the baby interrupted her. He had been still

long enough and their unhappy faces and voices were frightening. Tim let Marthe's hand go and put his up to hold the struggling little creature.

"All right boy," he said gently, "it's all right," and gave him back to Marthe. "That's the end then, is it?" he asked her. "I'm completely and finally ditched?"

Marthe's English was very good but it was not her native tongue. She could find no words, but she knew what he meant—or near enough. She nodded and turned to go out of the room.

"You needn't go away," said Tim. "I'm going. You needn't say I've been here—" But he was too late. The front door was flung open and the hall was suddenly full of people and cold air. He had an impression of faces in the doorway staring at him; Frances in a red hood, her eyes and cheeks bright with air and exercise—Patsy behind her— Nick Vincent—There was, in fact, no moment when they stopped to stare but nobody could have missed the signs of crisis. Tim was pale and silent, Marthe pale and confused, not far from tears, and the baby rather overdid his welcome to his mother.

"Tea," said Frances loudly. "We won't wait for anybody—"

Tim wondered if even now he could make his escape but it was too difficult. Better to sink into the background than have the fuss of explaining an unexpected departure. There was a short period of pandemonium in which, mercifully, nobody took any notice of him. The baby, restored to joviality, surged about the floor, encouraged by Nick Vincent, a fair, squarely-built man who was the assistant housemaster of School House and a close friend of the

Hendersons. Chairs and tables were placed in a wide fireside circle and Tim went to the kitchen and silently took a laden trolley from Marthe and wheeled it in. The front door opened and shut noisily and Angus appeared, immensely large and cheerful. It opened again to admit Alison, rather out of breath, and the baby who was now confined in a small chair raised his voice above all the other voices in a long "M-m-m-m-m!" of famished impatience.

They were at last seated and John fell upon his honey sandwiches and was no more heard, but peace hardly prevailed.

"I sometimes wonder if fireside tea is such a good idea," Frances remarked. "No sugar Alison, Nick—and you, Tim? No-sugars coming up—"

"Of course it's a good idea," said Angus, hacking substantial slices of bread and passing them round speared on the knife. "There's nothing so comfortable. Psst! Alison—catch." He lobbed a piece of bread over to her and she caught it with a slightly dangerous grab.

"Whoops!" she said. "Thanks. Rough and ready as ever, I see."

"Allow me to offer you the butter," said Nick Vincent. "This must be a sad change, I fear, from the urbane courtesy of Italian gentlemen."

"Indeed yes," she accepted the butter, sighing and smirking regretfully. "One is a little spoilt, perhaps. Such polish—so suave—"

"And all about five-foot-two, I suppose," said Angus.

"Well—compact. But every inch cultivated. None of these vast empty spaces."

"Oonagh installed?" asked Patsy before the theme could

27

be further developed.

Yes, Oonagh was in, said Alison. "Complete with smell," she added. "The office is a different place already."

Marthe, who was sitting beside the baby lending a hand when required, looked across at her with a flash of laughter and Patsy asked: "What sort of smell?"

"Oh—Nights in Paris, perhaps, or one of those with a number. *Numero cinq.* Anyway not coal-tar soap."

"I must drop in," said Patsy into the general laughter and Frances cried: "Oh *poor* Miss Wills!"

"She can disinfect, you know," Nick pointed out reassuringly.

"How heartless we all are," she said. "Is there any news of her, Alison? Did Aunt Hester see her?"

"Yes," said Alison. "She was pretty dopey but still angry, Mummy said. They're doing it about 5 o'clock. Any minute now, in fact," and feeling sobered about Miss Wills and rather guilty about Oonagh she added: "Actually, Oonagh seemed to be taking hold very well. Bit of luck she was available. Even though," to Tim, "you can type."

"Oh Oonagh will be all right," said Angus. "She's quite a nice girl, really, isn't she Marthe?"

"Oonagh?" Marthe, who had been perfectly silent since tea began, looked a little startled. "Oh—yes. She's very kind."

"Oonagh," Frances explained to Alison's surprised face, "has been around quite a bit lately." Her tone was noncommittal but Alison decided against telling the story about her brother Richard meeting Oonagh at a dance and Frances went on to a new subject. "Did you see Clare and Nevill, Angus?"

Angus had had supper with the elder Fielding daughter and her husband who lived in Edinburgh and the conversation became intimate. Tim, who had not been contributing much anyhow, lapsed into complete silence and felt himself an outsider. The Hendersons, Nick Vincent, Angus and Alison were all old friends. Marthe, the foreigner, a temporary sojourner in Ledenham, had apparently spent the month of the Christmas holidays playing around with the young Fieldings and had been drawn in to the intimate circle. She had gone to a hunt ball as Richard Fielding's partner. There had been a dance at School House.

"I suppose," said Angus bitterly, "you had to have it in the middle of the holidays."

"Of course we did," retorted Alison. "As you know. We had to have it when we were all at home," and as though she felt that Tim was being left out, she turned to bring him in. "It's one of the snags of School that people go away in the party season. There's never a date when everybody's here."

Tim murmured a polite response and remained outside, inclined to agree with Angus who observed with offended stateliness that her line would be more convincing if absent friends, however remote, had been given the option. It was the last straw to hear that while he, as he felt now, had done nothing for that month but think of Marthe she had been dancing and enjoying herself without a thought for him. Everything was off-key. A bitter boredom isolated him. They were all—the lovely Frances, with whom, like most of the Ledenham young men, he had been for a time agreeably and harmlessly in love; Alison, warmly pretty

29

and gay and the three men—they were all unreal. Their voices and laughter were loud and meaningless and Marthe, who was real, was infinitely remote. He got up as soon as he could/

"Will you excuse me if I push off, Frances?" he said abruptly. "I've got rather a lot to do."

"Yes, of course," said Frances and in the general movement of clearing up which had released him she followed him out of the room. "Tim—"

"Yes?" he was already at the door and turned to her unwillingly. "Tim, dear," she said hesitantly, "I don't know if I ought to pretend to see nothing, but I'm—I feel responsible for Marthe—"

"Marthe is in no danger from me," said Tim shortly.

"No," her colour deepened but she went on: "not danger, I know. But—don't pester her, Tim."

Frances was—with doubt and reluctance—giving him a gentle friendly hint. Tim, who would have died, he felt, quite cheerfully, to keep Marthe safe from harm or unhappiness, was angrier than he had ever been in his life.

"You—and Marthe—can make your minds easy," he said. "Good-bye, Frances. Thank you for the tea—for many teas," and he went out and shut the door, leaving them all warm and cheerful in that friendly room.

The cold wind was blowing flakes of snow about and he walked quickly along the road, past the Chaplain's house which looked as if it had fought a losing battle for years against its encroaching shrubs and creepers, to the Zoo where open doors, trunks half-unpacked and heavy feet tramping to and fro told of the bachelors' return.

"Hullo, Tim," shouted somebody, "meeting's 8-30, isn't it?"

"Yup—8-30," he responded briefly and raced upstairs to his own room to finish unpacking, to turn his mind as far as he could to the work of the term and to contemplate with sinking heart the unspeakable term itself stretching endlessly before him.

The inevitable lack of privacy in such establishments as the Zoo is not felt as a disadvantage when all is going well but in Tim's present state it seemed intolerable. By the time he went down to dinner he had pulled himself together to the degree necessary for life to go on. He knew, that is to say, that he could do his work and that nobody who did not know him very intimately would see anything unusual in his face or bearing. But he had no desire at all to meet the six men with whom he would eat his meals for the next eleven or twelve weeks. Nick Vincent, though his rooms were in School House, ate his dinner in the Zoo and he and Angus Cameron could hardly have failed to see at Holly Lodge that something was up. Then there was Burgoyne, a Lancastrian with a long comic face and eyes which missed nothing, and Willie Munro who was a trial at any time, a youth overflowing with hearty piety and constantly amazed by the obvious. Richards and Lawson, who lived, each in contented solitude, on the top floor were more detached. Richards was devoted to music, always listening to some inner fount; Lawson was engaged to be married and lived mostly by post.

Willie was already in spate when Tim entered the dining-room. "Poor thing! It's absolutely rotten for her," he was saying. "Oh hullo, Tim. I say, have you heard about Miss Wills? She's having an operation—at least I suppose she's had it now. I wish there was something one could do.

Would one go and see her?"

"Give her a chance to get a bit of strength back," said Tim nastily and the bland eyes of Mr. Burgoyne rested upon him briefly.

"That's right," he agreed. "You're a fine upstanding young fellow, Willie. You might be an agitation rather than a comfort. Leave it to Hum."

Hum, or Mr. Perry, was the School Chaplain and Nick Vincent said: "Even Hum would be an intruder. Miss Wills is the vicar's dish. I don't think she's ever been in Chapel."

Willie looked solemn. "That's rather sad, I think."

"Why?" asked Tim.

"She's a pillar of the parish church you know," said Nick.

"Oh, I'm sure she is," Willie hastened to proclaim his faith in Miss Wills. "But she's one of the School community. It seems such a shame that she's separated from it in worship. I don't know," with a shade of severity, "who draws the line about who goes to Chapel and who doesn't."

"Got to consider the size of the building," said Angus. "Anybody else want the last drop of soup?"

"No thank you. Yes, of course one has to consider the size of the building; but people who serve the School as she does—"

"Did anybody ever draw the line at Miss Wills?" enquired Mr. Burgoyne, mildly bored.

"Almost certainly not," answered Nick. "She simply lives in the village and comes into School for business hours. Chapel, as you ought to know, Willie, is for the people who live in the School."

"Yes, but—"

"Oh *lord!*" said Tim.

"Mun-ro," begged Mr. Burgoyne, "drop it. The fare provided in Chapel isn't any better than what's dished out in any other place of worship—C of E. But I'm willing to bet," he glanced round the table, "that the congregation will be up one—no, two probably—on Sunday. Any takers? Half-crowns."

Nick laughed aloud. "No. It's a certainty. Poor Mrs. Beak!"

Mr. Munro looked pained and then puzzled and gave up. He changed the subject. Alison Fielding was at home, he told them. "She's terribly pretty," he said, "and awfully nice and jolly. No—*you* know—side about her at all. Actually," he simpered happily, "we're rather friends—"

"How?" demanded Angus staring at him.

"Well—I mean I've seen quite a lot of her. Dances. Living near has its advantages you know. I was at their dance. Gosh!" he looked round at his unresponsive colleagues. "Honestly, the girls were marvellous. They really were. And knowing them all so well, you see— Frances always looks super and Marthe, well Marthe came on like anything, but Alison—"

His voice trailed away. Looking lamentably sentimental he was lost, it seemed, in his memories. On one side of the table Angus's hackles were up, on the other Tim showed his teeth. Mr. Richards was listening to some distant strain, Mr. Lawson was with his heart in Nottingham. Mr. Vincent and Mr. Burgoyne exchanged resigned glances. The term was getting off to a promising start.

"What have you done about Secker?" Burgoyne asked Angus loudly.

"Out," said Angus.

Willie looked up. "Oh dear," he said before anyone could stop him. "P-S will be terribly cut up, I'm afraid. I mean—I know your reasons; Secker's been incredibly tiresome. But he's the fastest man we've got. P-S'll feel it."

"Can't help it. I'm not having the Sevens wrecked. Chap's a ruddy nuisance."

"Couldn't you talk to him again?"

"No."

"I mean, poor old Pearson-Smith—"

"Pearson-Smith," said Tim, "is also a ruddy nuisance. Chuck your plates along, will you? Richards—wake up."

"Oh—sorry," said Mr. Richards passing plates, and having been roused he looked round rather uneasily and made an announcement. "I say, I hope none of you mind. I'm taking up my flute again this term."

It was well after 11 o'clock when the Headmaster wound up the masters' meeting and went home. For something like sixteen hours he had been doing his job; dealing with people and with crises, taking decisions—all of them important to somebody—and carrying in his mind as he always did the affairs and personalities of the six hundred or so individuals for whom he was responsible.

"Quite a day," his wife remarked as he sat down beside the drawing-room fire. "I brought in the whisky."

"Well," he said, feeling for his pipe, "—yes. It rates a whisky, I believe. Thanks." He looked at her companionably as she put the glass beside him and sat back with deliberate relaxation.

"The doctor rang up," said Mrs. Fielding picking up her

knitting. "They're quite happy about her—it was perfectly straightforward."

The Headmaster, recalling the events of the morning said: "Good."

"How was the meeting?"

"Fairly bad-tempered."

"Spring term."

"True." He lit his pipe and smoked in silence for a moment. Then he went on: "There's a bit of a row on. Pearson-Smith is pale with fury because Secker has been dropped from the seven-a-sides."

"He's a very tiresome boy," said Mrs. Fielding severely.

"But a very good wing."

She stopped knitting and stared thoughtfully at the fire. "It's an odd thing," she said, "how all P-S's top boys get slightly spoilt. I suppose you backed Angus?"

"Oh yes. Henderson and Vincent agree with him. There's no question about the decision."

"No wonder P-S is pale."

"No." Mr. Fielding scowled into space recalling the commonroom scene as he went into it and the faces of the men waiting for him. "I fancy," he said, "that Selby had exacerbated matters. He had the look of a man who'd let fly and P-S looked as if he'd been flown at. Hester—" he paused for a moment with an expression of calculation and then said: "Seventeen years. We've been here for seventeen years and I'm fifty-seven, is it? Or eight?"

"Seven," said Mrs. Fielding, rather startled. "What on earth—?"

"Well—we might retire in a year or two, mightn't we? It would automatically come up for consideration when I'm sixty, but Mike's nearly through with school. We needn't wait."

She looked at him aghast. "Good gracious, Hugh!" she exclaimed. "You aren't ill, are you? The bad tempers are nothing—Miss Wills will be back—It's only the spring term."

"Oh yes," he brushed these routine trials aside. "I can cope with all that."

"Then—I suppose you're brooding about Sartha. I'd forgotten about him, as a matter of fact."

"I don't think I've forgotten him completely at any moment of the day," confessed the Headmaster. "You'd better stop 'Sartha' and practise Sir—Arthur with deference and precision. You'll be seeing quite a lot of him I expect."

"He wouldn't notice. At least—he might, of course." Mrs. Fielding dropped her knitting into her lap and contemplated Sir Arthur Hinton-Brigg. The threatened Governor was self-important, interfering and bombastic but—"Aren't you rating him too high—or low?" she asked.

"I don't think so."

"After all, he'll be new. Things are going perfectly smoothly. Need he be much of a nuisance?"

There was no reply for a moment. Mr. Fielding took off his spectacles and waved them gently, frowning with an effort of concentration. "What's that fish," he demanded suddenly, "that they put into tanks with other fish? It chases them about. I forget why. Keeps them awake or from getting too fat or something. What *is* it?"

"I have no idea," said his wife. "At least—" her brows also drew together in a frown,—"yes, I do seem to—What *is* it? Do carp come into it?"

"I thought carp rang bells when they wanted food. That needn't necessarily rule them out, perhaps." He looked across at her and laughed, abandoning the search into his subconscious memory. "Anyway—I don't want to be chivvied round the tank by Hinton-Brigg."

Mrs. Fielding began to roll up her knitting. "At the end of a long and tiring day," she said kindly, "it's not uncommon for the imagination to get a little over-heated. How did you get on with Oonagh?"

He groaned. "Splendidly," he said gloomily. "Remind me every morning to be thankful for small mercies."

"She's a small one, is she?"

"Rather small," said the Headmaster.

3

ON the following afternoon 500 boys came pouring into
Ledenham and the buildings which had stood empty for a
month were filled with life, noise and vitality. Ill-temper,
so far as it prevailed, the sorrows of Tim Selby and the
shadow of Sir Arthur Hinton-Brigg were unknown to
Alison and an inch of slushy snow did nothing to daunt her
spirits. She was delighted to see the boys back. For the first
time for years their coming did not herald her own
departure and she rejoiced as hurrying figures multiplied in
the grounds and sounds of bustle and loud, cheerful voices
came through from the boys' side of the house. Though the
Fieldings were quite well insulated they were not cut off
from the hundred or so people who for the greater part of
the year shared their home. They felt restless and uneasy
for a day or two at the beginning of each holiday in the
sudden, almost eerie quiet of the great bulk of empty house
and they were correspondingly aware of its fullness at the
beginning of term. It was not particularly noisy; the half-
broken voices—always the loudest, banging doors and
occasional strains of music were all fairly distant and so
much part of normal life as to be scarcely heard, but even
during the hours when the boys were out of the building,
in School or on the playing-fields, their presence was felt
like a strongly beating pulse and to Alison it was an
exhilarating part of home.

She was very content on Sunday morning in Chapel as
she listened to the familiar roar of the School's singing, Mr.
Perry going out of tune in the usual places and her father's

brief, crisp sermon. Oonagh Hepburn was sitting in the part of Chapel reserved for School wives and children, accompanied, obviously, by her mother. Nearly everybody came on the first Sunday of term when good resolutions were new and the hen-coop, so called, was on the small side. Surprised, resentful glances were cast upon the Hepburns, and the latest-comer, who happened to be Mrs. Pearson-Smith, looked questioningly at Mrs. Fielding and made her way, admirably dignified, to the visitors' pews at the back.

Even on a cold January morning people paused for a few minutes after the service to exchange greetings and news. Alison's presence was news, Miss Wills' progress was of interest, though it was general rather than personal, and Mrs. Fielding and Alison stood in the centre of a changing group while masters passing raised their mortar-boards and boys, wearing the blank look which misses nothing, raised a finger to the lobe of the right ear. Alison was talking to Frances Henderson when Angus Cameron and Tim Selby walked quickly past. Angus grinned and hailed them cheerfully, Tim raised his cap without a glance and Frances gave a small, exasperated sigh.

"What's the matter with—" Alison began, but it was not the time or place for explanations.

"Alison!" cried a high, uninhibited voice and a smiling energetic lady, very smartly dressed, bored her way through the crowd talking as she came. "My dear! *What* a ray of sunshine! A gleam of light in this horrible term— isn't she, Mrs. Fielding? I hope you're keeping her here for a nice long time?"

Alison said: "Till I get a job," rather guiltily, and her

mother laughed.

"Don't encourage her, Annette," she said. "Nobody was ever less enthusiastic about her career."

"I'm so immature," pleaded Alison.

"Of course you are," agreed the newcomer promptly. "Utterly unfit to go out into the world—much better at home. And then," the voice was dropped and eyes rolled significantly, "where would you find better opportunities? We all know about girls' careers—"

A nasty swipe, thought Alison, taking it on the chin with a light laugh. She met a gleam of amused understanding before her cousin Frances turned away and the gay voice went on, rising and falling as the nature of its words and discretion required.

"We must have a party," this was loud and clear, "I've been planning it—*not* during your father's sermon," it dropped again though Mrs. Fielding's attention was directed elsewhere, "his are the ones I listen to. We'll have a picnic supper and dance and we'll have it at once so that everybody realizes you're home."

Alison was delighted. She had had rather too much commiseration about being in Ledenham for the dreariest term of the year and Mrs. Courtney's constructive approach was welcome. Also she gave very good parties and when she made a plan she carried it out. Her husband, who was less ruthless in making his way through a crowd, now joined them and she was already informing him as he approached of the treat in store for him.

Mr. Courtney was an exquisite gentleman of beautifully preserved middle-age and he was smiling and bending courteously over Alison's hand as he listened to his wife.

"Splendid!" he said dutifully. "How very nice to see you, Alison my dear. When did you—"

"Friday?" his wife cut him short. "Plenty of time. I'll ring everybody up."

"I'm sure Friday's all right," said Alison. "Isn't it, Mummy?"

Mrs. Fielding, who had been with them intermittently, said: "Perfectly," and was going on; "It sounds—" when she was interrupted.

"Good morning, Mrs. Fielding," a new voice broke in and she turned to find Oonagh Hepburn standing meekly beside her, her mother two paces in the rear. The eyes of the mother and daughter, now fixed on her, were exactly alike. They agreed that they were fortunate in these features and as features they were good; large and widely open, nicely set beneath well-trimmed brows. As windows of the soul they were less impressive. Very little soul was revealed and that little, taken in conjunction with small, rather tight mouths, did not altogether inspire confidence. "This is Mummy," Oonagh was saying, the eyes beseeching. "I hope it was all right, us coming to Chapel. We thought—"

"How do you do, Mrs. Hepburn," Mrs. Fielding shook hands smiling pleasantly.

"Oonagh was full of doubt," said Mrs. Hepburn, mother to mother, "but I told her you would *expect* to see her in Chapel. After all, she is one of you for the present and the religious part is *so* vital I always say. Wasn't it *providential* for your husband that she happened to be free?"

Attentive ears surrounded them. Mrs. Fielding replied moderately that Oonagh's freedom was convenient. "I can't say," she went on, "that we expected to see her in Chapel, but if she likes to come sometimes while she is doing this job it will be all right. You notice I expect, that our part of the Chapel is rather small? But there is usually room in the visitors' pews at the back."

Mrs. Hepburn drew herself up. "Oh, of course," she began, "if that is—We had no intention of intruding—" "Of course not," said Mrs. Fielding cordially. "Since there were no other visitors it was a most natural mistake."

The listeners relaxed. The words 'visitors' and 'mistake' had been said. Mrs. Hepburn's eyes, not quite pleased, moved on to rest thoughtfully on the smart, compactly corseted figure of Mrs. Courtney to whom Alison was introducing Oonagh.

"Another pretty girl," cried Mrs. Courtney good-naturedly. "The School's looking up. It's so sad about poor Miss Wills—not that I know her in the least—but then she'll get better. Now—Oonagh, is it?—Oonagh must come along to our party, Alison."

There were glad cries from Oonagh, murmurs of contralto joy from her mother and anguish on the face of Mr. Courtney. Mrs Fielding removed herself and Alison rather hastily. Henry Courtney was a perennial source of surprise to her and a recurring source of amusement. For many years he had been a somewhat trying part of Ledenham, a good assistant master and passionately devoted to the School but richer than his colleagues and inclined to superiority. Four years ago his Ledenham career had been interrupted by a piece of folly so crass that it had, for a time, removed him from the scene and the surprise lay in the fact that he had come back. Love for the place, combined with inability to make himself at home in other places, had carried him over the hurdle of his return; the amusement was caused by the effect on him of the lingering uneasiness and of the lively and determined wife he had brought with him. For most of the community Henry was so familiar a figure that they had almost forgotten he had ever been absent, but Henry himself was not quite the man he had been. Clipped wings were apt to come to mind.

"Darling," he said as he started his car a few minutes later, "that was *rather* unfortunate," and it was clear that he was, like a kind husband, making as little as possible of a serious error on the part of his wife.

She raised her eyebrows higher than seemed necessary and said: "What was?"

"That girl," he began, half-laughing since he was playing it lightly.

"Girl?" said Mrs. Courtney unhelpfully. "Are you talking about Alison Fielding or the other one—Oonagh what's-her-name?"

"Oh—not Alison of course. The—er—Hepburn girl. She—well, it wasn't a very good idea asking her to this party, I'm afraid."

"Why not?"

The car halted at the School gates and Mr. Courtney looked carefully to the left and then to the right before he drove out on to the empty road and replied: "For the intimate kind of party you have in mind, darling, I think it's really better to keep to our own set."

"Our own set is very short of girls. And there's nothing particularly intimate about the party I have in mind."

"Still—I hardly think—"

Mrs. Courtney turned and stared at her husband. "What *are* you trying to say, Henry? The people don't keep a shop or anything," her tone was mocking. "You aren't trying to tell me the girl is a what-we-mustn't-mention are you?" Greatly shocked he denied anything of the sort and she went on: "Well, even in a crisis I wouldn't expect Mr. Fielding to employ anybody who wasn't respectable—that is if he knew."

"No doubt she's perfectly *respectable*," Mr. Courtney feeling that he was being unjustly heckled spoke less genially. "There are plenty of respectable people whom one doesn't ask to one's house. There was some trouble a few years ago with that girl. Er—one of the boys—You are still comparatively a newcomer, my dear, so you don't quite see it all, but in the School we do have to be rather careful. And one has one's standards. I don't think Miss Hepburn will be a very happy addition to your party, I must confess, and in my opinion she is of a type it's better not to encourage. I'm afraid they'll take advantage—Still—" he turned in at his own gate and glanced round with a forgiving smile, "—the invitation has been given. It can hardly be withdrawn, I suppose."

He pulled up at the door and Mrs. Courtney prepared to alight. "Not unless there's strong evidence that the School will suffer seriously from Oonagh Hepburn coming to the house," she said giving the word 'school' a peculiar inflection suggesting inverted commas. "One's standards will have to take their chance. Ugh!" She stepped out into the slushy snow. "How foul this is. Why am I not in Bermuda?"

44

Henry was silenced. He drove round to the garage feeling very ill-used but aware that nothing more would be said about Oonagh Hepburn by him. He was happily placed in the world. He was a master in his old school because he would rather be that than anything else; his salary was comfortably supplemented by an ample inheritance and he had a wife who was not only attractive but even richer than he was. But there were drawbacks. If Annette felt like going to Bermuda there was nothing to stop her. She could book a seat on a plane any day and he would dislike it very much. For one thing he would miss her; for another he was sensitive to speculation in the eyes of his colleagues.

In the days since Miss Wills' collapse the Headmaster had been assiduously grateful for the small mercy vouchsafed him. Oonagh was, as Miss Wills had said, competent. She was well-trained, intelligent enough to do the essential work which was all that he gave her to do and she did not irritate him more than he had expected. There was at first a good deal of girlish appeal. Was she doing things exactly as he liked them done? He would be sure to tell her if she wasn't, wouldn't he? And, "Oh Mr. Fielding, *please* call me Oonagh. Miss Hepburn sounds so stiff"

"I'm afraid I shall probably call you Miss Wills," —he had replied truly and his tone and involuntary gleam of amusement brought that to an end. He felt mildly guilty— after all she was young and he didn't want to hurt her feelings, but he did not re-open the subject.

He readily acknowledged that he was spoilt by Miss Wills but the acknowledgment did nothing to lessen the nuisance of being without her. She was like a mechanical extension of himself. If he asked a question out came the answer. If he stretched out a hand the relevant paper was put into it. And in all the business that went through his hands, the confidential matters, the delicate matters; the private affairs of boys and masters, awards and punishments, Miss Wills' discretion was so complete that she never even gave a sign that she was aware of them. Day after day, year after year, she came into the study, a quiet, almost invisible figure, bending slightly to the left by the filing cabinet, slightly to the right by the table, with an undisturbing clump of rubber soles. Oonagh tacked in by unpredictable routes with a fussy clicking of high heels, tight, brightly coloured garments which caught the eye and scent which made him long to throw the windows open. And when she brought him the letters to sign she stood close by and fidgeted, looking over his shoulder at whatever papers were lying on the desk. On the first Monday of term she not only fidgeted, she failed to go away when the letters were signed.

"Yes?" he said absently, his thoughts having already moved on.

"Oh Mr. Fielding," it was the pleading voice, "*do* you think I could speak to Alison?"

He glanced up. "Certainly. At least—I don't know if she's in. You'd better go along and see."

People were always going along to see if the Fieldings were in but Oonagh, perhaps unaware of it, expressed glad surprise. "Oh—can I really? Oh—*thanks,*" and she scampered away on her clicking heels.

Mrs. Fielding was out and Alison, having tea by herself very comfortably with a book by the drawing-room fire,

46

was not particularly pleased to hear a knock on the door. But she was used to knocks and shouted "Come in" quite cordially.

"Oh—hullo," she added when Oonagh appeared.

"Your father sent me along," said Oonagh. "I say!" observing the comfortable arrangements of tea and book, "Nice to be some people."

"How long were you living at home in idleness before you took on this job?" Alison enquired with spirit. "Because I've only had about three weeks so far. Is there a message from my father?"

"Oh no." Oonagh let the subject of living at home in idleness slide. "Actually I wanted to speak to you about the Courtneys' party and he said to come and find you. What are you wearing?"

"Oh—a dance frock," said Alison. "The men will be in dinner jackets." She hesitated and then politeness triumphed. "Would you like some tea?"

Oonagh said she would love some tea and hitching her skirt up sat down in the armchair opposite. "I've got a duck of a white," she went on, "—ooh, toast! Lovely. Thanks. It's *short* but it's strapless. Would it be too—you know—smart? It won't be a big party will it?"

Alison did not think that it was possible to be too smart for Annette Courtney's parties and said so. She herself meant to wear her best frock which was not only strapless but long.

"Oh," said Oonagh and thought about it. "I'll wear my white," she decided and smiled. "I must say I'm looking forward to it quite madly."

"So am I," Alison said returning the smile and they

settled down to their tea.

As a means to getting on in the world Oonagh Hepburn believde in being all things to all men. Not gifted with subtlety of mind she was liable to over-act and slow to observe the effect of her performance but she was industrious. Mr. Fielding—girlish helpfulness; Mrs. Fielding—wistful sweetness. Any young man—hep and pep. Girls were sometimes allies, more often enemies and feeling her way with Alison Fielding she began with candid chumminess.

Alison found her better company than she had expected. The girlishness which had nauseated her the day before was not in evidence and the memory of it was overlaid by an entertainment value which she later summed up as being quite high on a low level. And she was competent. The secretarial competence for which Miss Wills had cautiously vouched meant nothing to Alison but competence as a girl did impress her and Oonagh, in her own way had it. Alison admired the eyes, she admired—with reservations—the *élan* of clothes and skilfully bleached hair and most of all she admired the confidence, the enviable air of success.

They talked about Alison's experiences in Italy and Switzerland and the sort of jobs which enable girls to get about the world. Thye talked about Oonagh's jobs which had been numerous; all too boring to be tolerable or alternatively rendered impossible by people who were jealous. Then they drifted back to Ledenham. The School was a never-failing topic of interest and gossip in the district as Alison, of course, knew, but as one of the Headmaster's family very little of it came her way and to hear it reflected, not too indiscreetly, by Oonagh amused her. Then it became more personal. Oonagh, it seemed, knew everything about everybody in the School. She talked familiarly of masters, and of their wives when they had wives, by Christian names or nicknames; and in ever-narrowing circles she drew closer and closer till Alison began to feel herself subjected to a squeezing process designed to produce a kind of extract of Alison to be placed along with all the other information in Oonagh's store.

One by one the bachelor masters were dangled invitingly before her and the handsome eyes watched for reaction. Nick Vincent. Oonagh always thought he was terribly nice and why had he never married? Burgoyne. Willie Munro. Lawson was engaged, of course; Richards a bit wet. Tim Selby was introduced with a look which hinted at amusing private knowledge. Angus Cameron came last and was unmistakably pushed. Angus, Oonagh said, was sweet. She supposed Alison knew him pretty well? But of course she had been away for a long time and things never stood still did they—It was all, Alison felt, rather off-key but it appeared to be good-natured and harmless enough. She parried questions and sidestepped suggestions with what skill she had and her lack of response perhaps got through for Oonagh reverted to the Courtneys' party and her pleasure at the invitation.

"I believe Little Campion's absolutely marvellous inside," she said. "I've never been in. Of course I've always known them by sight, but I must say," there was a glance of amused resignation, "the School people are pretty slow about getting together. I've always thought Mrs. C. looked nice—she's lots of fun, isn't she?—but Mr.! Stiff isn't the word—he never sees me, of course. Quite honestly it makes me hoot, remembering the toss he took over your cousin Frances."

"What?" cried Alison, really jolted.

"Well goodness," Oonagh laughed at her, "that's no news to you, is it? I mean everybody knows he made such a fool of himself about her that your father threw him out. Then she married Patsy Henderson and Courtney married Annette and came back. Gosh, Alison, surely you knew that?"

Alison had never been very fond of Henry Courtney, he was almost the only person in Ledenham whom she had consistently dodged from her childhood up, but on this occasion she was on Henry's side. She could see no obligation on him to seek out Oonagh Hepburn and draw her in to the circle of his friends; and she was stirred to lively resentment by this complete outsider's familiar use of her cousin's name and rather too accurate knowledge.

"Somebody's been feeding you a lot of boloney," she said.

"Oh it's quite true," was the unshaken reply. "I got it all at the time from Roddy Meadows. Did you know Roddy?"

"No."

"He was in old P-S's House," explained Oonagh looking amused and reminiscently smug. "I saw a lot of Roddy at one time. Quite sweet but just a wee bit wet, really," she dismissed Roddy Meadows. "So I got all the dope. Was it kept from your innocent ears?"

It seemed to Alison that a good thumping lie was the only course open to her. She achieved an amused laugh. "Poor Henry!" she said. "It was quite ordinary—he was invited to go to America for bit and went. But I know there

50

was the usual crop of rumours. Boys are great scandalmongers, you know." She smiled kindly at Oonagh, pitying the simplicity which swallowed what the boys were saying and got up to put a log on the fire. "How long have you been living in Ledenham?" she asked, changing the subject as she sat down again.

Oonagh looked resentful. She had skidded and been snubbed and she was not quite sure about a come-back. "Oh," she said flatly, "five or six years."

"Do you like it?" persisted Alison.

"Well—it's not exactly my dream. Actually," there was a faint return of animation, "it's been quite a lot of fun since Marhet came."

"Marthe?" Alison was surprised and Oonagh in her turn smiled kindly.

"It's always easier for two girls than one, you know," she explained. "Marthe and Tim Selby ganged up, see, and Tim introduced me to Angus. We have quite a merry time." She laughed "Quite frankly I'm thrilled to bits the holidays are over. Have I missed them! You might come along sometime if you like. Of course I don't know how you're placed— Gosh!" she looked at her watch and got up. "I must fly. Ta for the tea—been fun. See you—"

"Friday, I suppose," Alison, a little uneasy about the snub, mustered cordiality and Oonagh paused at the door and looked back.

"Oh yes, Friday," she said. "Who are you going with, if you don't mind my asking?"

"I'm not going *with* anybody exactly. It's a private party," said Alison, the cordiality slipping. "Nick Vincent is transporting me because we set out from the same base.

51

Why? Do you want a lift?"

"Oh no, thanks awfully." Oonagh gave another of her conscious little laughs. "Angus will be taking me."

It was Mr. and Mrs. Fielding's custom to lunch in the House dining-hall during term as regularly as their engagements permitted, taking with them any members of their family who happened to be at home and any guest who was not liable to be unnerved by the experience. Alison did, at first, find it a little unnerving. She had been in the House very little since she grew up and the boys were strangers to her, but it was familiar ground and two days after her tea with Oonagh she was no longer conscious of eyes as she followed her mother between the rows of decorous backs.

"Benedictus—" her father began grace briskly when they reached the high table and it was followed by immediate uproar as a hundred chairs were pulled out and a hundred people sat down and conversed in reasonable voices.

"Isn't it a pity about the snow?" Alison remarked to the sturdy prefect on her right. "We might get some more, though, with this wind." A downpour of rain had dealt with the inch or two of snow the day before and a withering wind was now dealing with the rain.

"You want snow, do you?" said the prefect with polite surprise.

"Well—yes." Higgins placed a substantial helping of stew in front of her. "Thank you. I think it would be nice to have some snow. Don't you?"

The more aesthetic looking prefect opposite passed the potatoes and smiled. "Not Butler," he said. "He's one of those fanatics who's miserable if he can't play ball."

"Don't exaggerate," said the sturdy one mildly. "I'm not as bad as that. You forget what's at stake," and leaning forward a little he addressed Nick Vincent on Alison's other side. "Mr. Cameron says the field's okay, sir. At least—it'll do."

"Oh good," said Nick. "You're going on this afternoon, are you? I'll come and have a look at you."

"What's this?" asked Alison.

"The most savage game yet invented," said the aesthetic prefect, "—with the possible exception of ice-hockey."

"I thought that was Rugby League. Don't tell me you've taken to—" Several voices told the aesthetic one to cut it out and assured her that Ledenham had not taken to Rugby League. The game in question was seven-a-side Rugby which was not savage though undoubtedly very fast.

Alison said: "Oh yes. I did hear somebody mention it. But it's new, isn't it? We never used to play seven-a-sides." The 'we' was entirely unconscious and nobody thought it at all unnatural.

"You're very badly out of touch," said Nick. "This is the—is it the second or third?—third season. It's Mr. Cameron's baby. We're taking it quite big."

"The tournament thing and all?"

He laughed at her. "The tournament thing! Certainly. We went in last year and did quite well. And we're getting better. Ask Butler."

"I'm sure I'm very sorry to be dropping bricks," said Alison to the sturdy one who was grinning cheerfully, "but if friends and relations fail to keep you informed when you're not in the midst what can you do? Here's another—

53

I've never seen it played."

Nick said: "T's, t's, t's," and half of the table embarked on a course of instruction which lasted for what remained of the stew and throughout the jam roll.

"Very well," she said as they got up, "I'll come and watch this afternoon. The Old Level, did you say?"

"It's quite good to watch, really," said Butler encouragingly.

Alison had no doubt that he was right, provided one enjoyed watching boys' games which she did; but she was not perfectly sure that she wanted to watch this one.

"Are you going over?" she asked Nick as they left the hall.

"Yes—about 2.30. Coming?" he said and she felt better. Oonagh's parting words on Monday had left her with an uncomfortable hollow feeling in the region of the solar plexus. It was not a large hollow; she was not simple enough for that, but it persisted because it was difficult to know how much weight to attach to the confidence with which the words "Angus will take me" were uttered and the smugness of the accompanying smile. She and Angus had been friends for years but, as Oonagh had observed, it was a long time since she had seen much of him and no friendship between a man and a girl can survive unchanged if either falls in love with someone else. It would, Alison thought, be pretty awful but bearable if Angus fell in love with a girl like, say, Marthe. It would be unbearable if it was Oonagh and, though she couldn't quite see him falling for Oonagh, there was the confidence and the smile.

It was the first day since term began that the ground had been in playable condition. Nobody was very fond of going for runs, though there were certainly many days ahead when running would be the only practicable form of outdoor exercise, and the School swarmed happily over the fields as Alison walked across with Nick to the pitch known as Old Level. There were several games of hockey in progress, Willie Munro vociferous in charge of one of them, Mr. Burgoyne economically caustic with another, and a more distant view of the running track and practising athletes.

"Nick," said Alison, "you look quite middle-aged strolling gently along in an overcoat."

"Well, I'm getting on, of course," said Nick, "but I've always strolled in the spring term. I have nothing to contribute to hockey or athletics."

"Don't you help Angus with his Sevens?"

"No. Angus looks after his own Sevens. Patsy and I take a kindly interest and lend tone—and occasionally support."

"Aye aye," the voice of Angus hailed them and he trotted up, vast and cheerful in shorts and sweater with the lesser form of Tim Selby beside him in a track suit.

"Alison," he said, "I was hoping you'd be out. Will you come to tea? It's Wednesday and therefore a half as you may remember and I've got a cake."

Alison's hollow feeling lessened. She said she would be delighted to eat his cake.

"Are you asking anybody else?" asked Nick hopefully. "What kind of cake?"

"Nobody else. It's just a small cake."

"Chocolate, though," Tim put in. "Very rich. Leads to biliousness and spots if eaten in the quantity you seem to envisage."

"We'll leave you a bit," said Alison stepping on to the duckboard at the edge of Old Level. Boys were already on the pitch punting the ball about and the three gentlemen looked at them appraisingly.

"Not bad," said Nick. "Pity about Secker though. You could do with his speed."

"But not with his temperament," said Angus. "Tim's going to make a sprinter of him. He can be as much of a ballerina as he likes on the track—as we know." He began pulling off his sweater, revealing an old Scottish jersey, the thistle still flowering bravely on its faded dark blue.

"Here's a treat. The fancy haberdashery," observed Tim in return for the ballerina. "For whose benefit? The spectators or your performing fleas?"

Angus emerged. "Morale," he said. "Gor—it's cold!" He looked at Alison and held the sweater out. "You'd better have this—"

"Thank you," said Alison accepting pounds of warm wool. She threw it round her shoulders and Angus ran out on to the field, both of them serenely unaware that the state of Angus's heart was now revealed to his friends Vincent and Selby.

Fourteen boys took up their positions. Angus looked them over, glanced at his watch and blew his whistle. There was the exhilarating thump of the kick-off and everybody raced into action.

"Lumme!" said Alison happily.

"Good afternoon, Alison," said a slightly petulant voice beside her and they were joined by a lean elderly man whose appearance, though the hat he was raising was not a deer-stalker, was reminiscent of Sherlock Holmes. He wore a meagre overcoat of snuff-coloured check which had been part of the Ledenham scene for nearly forty years and he looked chilly.

"Good afternoon, Mr. Pearson-Smith," Alison responded nicely. "What a fast game this is, isn't it? I've never seen it before."

"Ah," he said in comment and vague agreement. "It's a new thing here of course. Indeed it's really only come up in the last few years. One never used to hear of it. I'm not sure it's such a good idea. In my opinion we were better as we were, confining football to the autumn term. The athletics too—we never used to take them so seriously. The spring term was the hockey term and it seemed to me to work very well."

"Hockey was never so generally popular as rugger, of course," said Nick soothingly, "and Cameron has got them very keen on this ploy."

"And at least," added Tim, not so soothingly, "it disposes of the worst of the toughs. And athletics," he added, "are much in vogue. There's Secker sneering on the touchline. I'd better go and take his mind off it."

Alison following his glance and conscious of tension saw a tall boy in a track suit watching the game, every line of his drooping form redolent of victimization.

"There's no need," Mr. Pearson-Smith said icily as Tim moved away, "to be unpleasant to the boy."

"I hope not," said Tim.

It did not appear that he was unpleasant to the boy. They stood together for a moment talking about the game but when they walked off towards the running track Mr. Pearson-Smith peered after the upright back and the sulky one worriedly, like a mother who watches her unwilling child carried off to play. He sighed and grunted a little, a demonstration directed, presumably, at Nick; but Nick's eyes were on the game and a promising passing movement on the part of the backs.

"Very nice," he remarked genially.

"I suppose," said Mr. Pearson-Smith, glancing doubtfully at Alison and then deciding to ignore her presence, "one must assume that Cameron is to some extent justified in his treatment of poor Secker since you and Henderson have supported him. It was a very severe blow to the boy."

"Of course it was," Nick agreed, while Alison's flesh crept uneasily on her bones, "and we all regret it. But none of us had any doubt. He had really been behaving very badly, as I know you agree, P-S."

"Boys frequently behave badly. Secker, of course, is not without flaw. But what troubles me is that this particular punishment seems not only excessive but destructive. No appeal to the boy. Simply dropped without a word."

"He had plenty of warnings you know."

"He may. I can only say—and as his Housemaster I know him better, possibly, than others know him—that it came to him as a complete shock. Most damaging, in my opinion."

"I'm afraid," Nick sounded sympathetic but inflexible, "it's the unfortunate Housemaster who takes the rap on these occasions. A boy who feels he's got a grievance is the worst of all nuisances in a House. But Secker's got another season in hand. If Selby gets him going on his running and he does as well as he's capable of doing in cricket next term he'll come up all right. It'll do him no harm to think a bit less of himself."

"It's very hard to see," Mr. Pearson-Smith pronounced gloomily, "what may be the effects of such a shock to a boy's confidence. I confess I am doubtful about the value of Selby's influence. Good afternoon, Alison."

He raised his shabby hat and walked away and Alison slid a cautious glance at her remaining companion who responded with a discreet wink.

"Man is born to trouble as the sparks fly upwards," he observed philosophically and returned her attention and his own to Old Level.

4

AT the end of the game Angus, having reclaimed his sweater and told Alison that if she followed slowly he would be ready by the time she arrived, ran off towards the Zoo, his long strides carrying him out of sight at great speed. Alison strolled after him, parting from Nick as she paused to watch hockey, exchanging greetings with one person after another. Willie Munro, who was, she knew, ready to attach himself if given the slightest encouragement, walked a little way with her, telling her that they would meet at the Courtneys' on Friday. Then he pounded on in case, he said, he got chilled, and Tim Selby said "Hullo, Miss Beak," and fell into step beside her.

"You look very clean and comfortable," she said, glancing at his track suit.

"Oh, we're very gentlemanly on the track," he said. "Trouble is the games types always make me wait for the bath. Angus is too big to argue with and Willie makes such a fuss it isn't worth it."

"You're coming to the Courtneys' I suppose?" Alison, remembering Oonagh's gossip, looked round at him and smiled. If he and Marthe had 'ganged up' he would be looking forward to the party and, liking Marthe, she was ready to extend her friendliness to him. But he was not responsive. He did not return the smile and his expression was indifferent.

He said: "Oh yes. Nobody ever refuses a Little Campion invitation. The food's good, the drink's good, Annette's good and one puts up with Henry."

"Poor Henry," said Alison. "You're very hard on him. He's a good host."

"Oh thoroughly conscientious," Tim agreed laconically. "Is he a friend of yours?"

"Well—a lifelong acquaintance."

"You must have a very loyal nature if you can stick up for him after a lifelong acquaintance. How's Miss Wills?"

"Fine, I believe. Doing as well as can be expected."

"I bet your father'll be glad to see her back. She's a wonder, that woman."

"Is she a friend of yours?" she echoed his question with amusement but he was more cordial about Miss Wills than she had been about Henry Courtney.

"Rather," he said. "I think a lot of Miss Wills. How's our lovely Oonagh making out?" Alison said the report was the same; doing as well as could be expected and he went on: "Do you see much of her? She also is booked for the Courtneys' I hear."

"Yes, she is. I don't see her much but she came and had tea with me the other day. I didn't know her before."

They had reached the Zoo and Tim, opening the door, said: "She's quite good company, is Oonagh," and added casually as she went past him into the house: "Provided you remember she's a liar."

"A *liar?*" Alison turned and looked at him to see if this was a rather ill-natured joke, but though there was some amusement in his face it was certainly not jocular.

He said: "I fear so. She makes use both of the whopper direct and the whopper implied. But it's fairly harmless so long as you know what to expect. Arm yourself with plenty

61

of salt and enjoy the fun." A cheerful sound of whistling was heard from above, one of Angus's tunes: "O-oh whistle an' I'll come tae ye, my lad," and he gave her a sudden friendly grin. "Sounds happy, doesn't he?" he said. "I expect you know your way. I hope he hasn't used all the hot water in his enthusiasm."

Alison had known Angus' study when it belonged to Patsy Henderson and it had not changed much. Neither had felt the urge to express himself in artistic decor. The dingy assortment of furniture was the same, the golf-clubs and cricket bats, boots and books, the scarf—apart from its colour—and the single inexplicable grey sock might have been the same and it was still, as it used to be, notable for hospitality and the convenience of its arrangements.

The fire blazed generously and a small meat-dish stood in the hearth, its contents covered by a bowl. The tea-tray was on an upright chair drawn close to one of the armchairs, the cake was on the mantelpiece within easy reach and there was a biscuit tin, also within easy reach, on the floor. The host, though tidily dressed, looked a trifle damp and smelt of soap.

"Dear, kind Delia," he said, referring to the bachelors' cook and indicating the meat-dish, "has made anchovy toast in your honour."

"I'll tell her how good it was when I go down," said Alison who knew what was expected of her.

"Will you pour out?" asked the host courteously.

"No fear," replied the guest with decision.

"It's the thing, you know, for the lady to do it."

"One of the things devised by gentlemen in their own interest. You carry on. I'll sit back and watch, taking my ease."

"Well unless we shift everything you'll have to take your ease in the not-so-good chair. Still—if that's the way you want it—No sugar, I believe. Dig in."

"Angus," said Alison when the toast was nearly finished, "why have you been so unkind to poor Secker?"

Angus looked a little surprised and then said: "Poor Secker my foot. I saw P-S on the touch-line—beefing to Nick, I suppose?" She nodded. "That's a nice thing," he went on bitterly, "scaling on a chap before the general public."

"Out of a full heart the mouth speaketh. What happened?"

"Och," it was a disgusted sound, "the silly chap wouldn't do what he was told. Perfect nuisance."

"So you flung him out?"

"Just that."

"Never stopping to think, of course, what you were doing to the poor boy's psyche. Undermining his confidence—"

Angus laughed heartlessly. "Nothing that I know of could shake that poor boy's confidence. I tried everything. In the end we got rid of him before the rest had decided between mutiny and assault but it was a near thing."

"Mr. Pearson-Smith seems to see it differently," said Alison. "He's hurt."

"He'll get over it. He's always very touchy about his House, you know, but he comes round all right given time."

Alison knew about Mr. Pearson-Smith's touchiness. One of the hazards of Ledenham which every new master had to learn to negotiate was that any complaint about a boy in his House, unless handled with consummate tact, brought forth only cold, incredulous indignation.

"I can see why he's huffing at you," she said, "but why is he so down on Tim Selby? He wouldn't come in to it."

"There's quite often somebody down on Tim," said Angus. "He's what you might call outspoken—if you were being charitable—and he doesn't suffer his elders and betters gladly."

"He likes Miss Wills."

"Does he? Yes—I dare say he would." Alison wanted to know why Tim should like Miss Wills who, though highly respected, hardly seemed to her a subject for either liking or disliking. "She's never woolly," Angus offered as an explanation. "She's got a good grip on essentials and she doesn't flap. We get a few flaps in commonroom," he added with a faint grin. "Small things get inflated. They subside again."

"But Tim doesn't wait?"

"No, Tim's apt to crack in." His grin widened. "Poor old P-S grieving about Secker said he hadn't slept since he heard about it and Tim said—" he broke off suddenly, laughing outright, and then glanced at her apologetically. "Sorry—I don't think I can tell you what Tim said."

"Go on," said Alison but he was firm.

"No, it isn't suitable. It wasn't suitable then either, as a matter of fact. Aroused ill-feeling. Ready for cake?"

He reached up a long arm to the mantelpiece and Alison said "Please," rather absent-mindedly and thought about Tim Selby who was good-looking, amusing and provocative; who found Miss Wills likable; who was impatient with inflated grievances; who had, for some reason, given her a deliberate warning about Oonagh Hepburn.

"I like him—I think," she said a little dubiously. "Gosh! You've given me about half the cake. Thank you."

"Mostly fluff," said Angus. "Yes—you'll like Tim. He's all right under the—" he paused for a word.

"Fluff?" she suggested.

"Well, I was going to say prickles but it isn't exactly that either. It's more uncompromisingness. Bit too damned honest. As a matter of fact he's having a baddish time just now." Alison said "Marthe?" and he looked up quickly. "Did he tell you?"

"No. Oonagh said something about him and Marthe."

"Oh—Oonagh," said Angus flatly. "Well yes, it's Marthe; but it's off." There was a short silence and then he went on: "I think he was too outspoken there too. Marthe seemed to like him all right."

"There's a lot of difference between liking a person all right and being in love though," said Alison and at once regretted a remark so trite and so unnecessary.

"That's true enough," he agreed and a heaviness descended upon them. "More tea?" asked Angus politely and she passed her cup feeling that they had had enough of Tim Selby and his troubles. It was time they changed the subject. "Oh well," she said, dismissing it, "it may come right. I hope so. But after all that's *them.*"

"True again," said Angus and as he passed back her cup his restored cheerfulness was so noticeable that she was surprised and faintly abashed. She wondered uneasily if he had resented anything she had said or if he was simply bored, as men often were, by talk about people. Whatever the cloud was it had passed and he was smiling at her. "Are you booked for anything this evening?" he asked. She wasn't. "Well, as you're here, what about a flick and food in Leyburn?"

"*Food?* You can't possibly be thinking of more food—"

"Not immediately. The form is—flick first and then Molloy's Steak Bar. Have you been to Molloy's? Then you haven't lived. Come on," said Angus.

The blossoming of a friendship between a man and a girl into love is so commonplace that it arouses no surprise and little interest in anyone except the principals themselves; but every time it happens is the first time, fresh, new and miraculous and not, as a rule, devoid of awkwardness. The friendship between Angus and Alison had been unemotional, an affair of shared tastes and activities, liking of an undisturbing kind and a more than ordinarily good companionship. That evening they stepped towards a new world but it was a tentative step. They hardly knew, indeed that they took it but things were not quite what they used to be; for Angus as a natural result of seeing the girl he had in a genial, possibly slightly condescending way, been fond of transformed into grown-upness, for Alison because of the push administered by Oonagh.

In the matter of how she was placed she had had to confess to herself that she had counted on Angus as, in a way, her property; an escort, a sharer of jokes, the best of friends, though not what Oonagh would call a boy-friend. There was nothing about him which endorsed the suggestion that he now occupied the position of boy-friend to Oonagh, no evidence but that he was delighted to see her, Alison, back and had every intention of carrying on their ancient alliance from where it was interrupted more than a year ago. The mere thinking about it, however, the

66

realization of how awful it would be if Oonagh had stepped in made her look at him differently and brought about her part of the change.

Nothing, in the technical sense, was said. In the course of a particularly good evening at the cinema and Molloy's Steak Bar they talked in lower tones than had been their custom, in the cinema Angus leant towards Alison to catch a remark and stayed where the leaning took him and when, as they set out for the drive home, he dragged an old Cameron rug from the back of the car and tucked it round her Alison's comfort was disproportionate to its dingy folds.

"Nick's driving you to Little Campion on Friday, isn't he?" said Angus as he drew up at School House, his tone implying that, of course, there was nothing in that. "I'm ferrying Tim and Oonagh," and there was nothing in that either. Two short drives, less than a mile all told. But there was a great deal in the evening—with dancing—which lay between.

Alison said she was looking forward to the party and thanked him for his hospitality and, as she spoke, Angus was suddenly aware that for her as well as for him the undisturbed companionship was altered. He hesitated. It seemed almost inevitable that now, at this moment, he should put his arms round her and kiss her. But not quite inevitable. He said they must go to Molloy's again soon and adding a hearty good night departed without further delay.

Back in the Zoo with a feeling that it would be a good idea to resume contact with reality he dropped in on Tim. The room was full of smoke and the subdued sound of a dance band turned low and Tim, his hair on end, was at work on a pile of corrections. Angus switched off the dance

67

music without ceremony and a tentative, breathy tootling took its place.

"Take your choice," said Tim without looking up.

Angus listened. "It's not very *loud*," he said fairly.

"No. He doesn't give it much juice. I'll be glad when he gets a new piece though." Upstairs Mr. Richards' flute pursued its cautious way through 'Sheep may safely graze'. "This boy's halfwitted," said Tim and slashed a red line across the page in front of him.

Angus fished for his cigarettes and sat down. "How did you get on with Secker?" he asked.

"Oh—Secker," Tim flung down his pencil and turned to the fire. "Well—he's maintaining his sulks. He's a nice mover, I must say, but I don't suppose he'll bother to train."

"He might. Give him a new chance to show off. Cigarette?"

"Thanks—I doubt it. Encouraged by his Housemaster, who came to mourn in a most helpful way, I fancy he's set on martyrdom. How the hell did anybody come to give P-S a House?"

"I dare say he wasn't so bad when he was younger," said Angus. "Come to that he could be worse now. He's just a bit soft."

"He's exactly like a hen," said Tim and a little cheered by the thought of Mr. Pearson-Smith in feathers and a comb he turned to other matters. "Enjoy the pictures?"

Angus keeping his eyes on the fire said: "Not bad."

"Willie's on your trail—scout knife in hand."

"Willie? How the—Oh, Delia, I suppose."

"Delia couldn't wait to let the news slip out," Tim said with relish. "Mr. Cameron's taken Miss Alison to the pictures. A-*ha*, we all said. Except Willie who was—for once—dumb—"

"Shut up," said Mr. Cameron. He felt the colour rise in his face and saw Tim grin. "Hell! You can't turn over in bed in this place without somebody making a broadcast feature of it."

"Don't let your feelings run away with you," said Tim. "Why grudge us our vicarious thrills? If you've nothing worse than that to put up with you'll do. She's a very nice girl, Miss Beak."

"She's all that," Angus heaved himself to his feet. He opened his mouth to assure Tim that there was nothing in it, of course, and then shut it again. It wasn't true and Tim wouldn't believe him anyway. "It's absolute hell," he said instead with sudden sharp resentment, "feeling that—a thing like that's being pawed over and nattered about."

Tim laughed. "Cheer up, Angus," he said. "We all love you."

Henry Courtney had not married till he reached the age of forty because his bachelor state was so comfortable. He and his mother, pooling their very considerable resources, lived in one of the best houses in Ledenham and did much for Henry's old school by maintaining its traditions—the traditions, that is to say, of the 1930s when Henry attended it as a boy. In Little Campion if nowhere else things were done properly, standards were upheld and lines were drawn. The Headmaster, the Housemasters and senior members of commonroom with their ladies came to dinner; the rest of the commonroom, the doctor and the bursar were asked to sherry parties and the matrons came once a year to a terrible tea-party. Mr. Courtney felt, quite genuinely, that he was keeping alive a small part of a social system which was of value, but in this his wife did not give him much support. Parties at Little Campion in Lady Courtney's day had never allowed guests to forget that there is no greater mistake than to imagine that the rich regard you as their equals. Annette's parties were merely for fun; generous, extravagant affairs which she and her guests enjoyed hilariously. But though she made fun of Henry's little snobberies and laughed at the Public School Spirit she was not without snobbery of her own. She was not much interested in unattractive girls and she expected men to wear the right clothes and have plenty to say.

Nice-looking, charming, or rather pretty were the labels usually attached to Alison Fielding but as she entered the Courtneys' drawing-room on Friday evening she was beautiful. She had been delighted when Annette proposed the party but in the days since then, and especially since Wednesday, it had grown in importance. It had, as she looked forward to it, a shining quality, and though she was unable, or unwilling, to analyse the shine too closely it made her very happy. Enjoyment began as she dressed, everything went so well. Her hair was docile which was not always the case; the springy brown curls were apt to defy her but tonight they almost arranged themselves. The long, full-skirted dress of corn-coloured Italian silk was lovely in itself and she could see as she looked in the mirror that it was quite startlingly becoming. Frances, who was an expert, said sometimes that a dress or a hat did or did not do a lot for its wearer. Alison, looking at herself, thought that the Italian frock was doing surprising things for her.

Her grey eyes, which she had compared unfavourably with Oonagh's best feature, seemed larger and brighter than usual, her hair and warm skin glowed and she smiled, half amused and wholly pleased that she could look like this.

She picked up her coat and ran downstairs as Nick Vincent came into to the hall to fetch her.

"Ready?" he said looking at her as she came towards him with his cheerful semi-avuncular grin. Then he looked again. "You're very beautiful."

"It's a good frock, isn't it? You haven't seen it before." She spread out the wide skirt to show him.

"It is," said Nick, "but I was referring to the girl. I feel all thrown out. Trembly in the knees and damp about the hands."

Alison regarded him fondly. Nick as house-tutor had been almost part of the family for years. His square figure and ruddy, cheerful face were connected with many of the young Fieldings' best times and enough hero-worship lingered to make his approval peculiarly exalting.

"Fancy!" she said. "But aren't you making too much of it? Am I all that up?"

He laughed at her as he took her coat. "At the *moment* you're breath-taking. In you get," he put her into her coat. "I suppose you've just grown up and I hadn't seen it coming. There will have to be a bit of advance booking, I fancy, if elderly friends are to have a look in when the band strikes up."

"Oh Nick," said Alison. "Life's really rather nice isn't it?"

"Not bad at all," said Nick.

Other people too were startled by Alison's radiance. Henry Courtney's urbane greeting was tinged with surprise. One or two were moved to a kind of compassion, it spoke so plainly of a lovely ephemeral phase of life, and Angus suffered a searing and illuminating agony, but Annette only saw Alison Fielding looking gratifyingly attractive and surged forward to tell her so.

"My dear," she cried, "how glad I am that I thought of having this party! You look—" her gesture was eloquent, "—delicious. Now tell me," lowering her voice, "just so that I know where I am—is all this glow for somebody special or—?"

Alison who was feeling pleasantly uppish answered quite truthfully that she was full of good will towards all men and her hostess responded with a gurgle of plump laughter.

"I'm not sure I believe you. But—look round. We have some nice young men in stock. You know everybody, don't you?" It was not a large party, between twenty and thirty people, and Alison knew them all. "Keep off Cubby Lucreton," hissed Annette with a little giggle, indicating a stoutish youth with a formidable moustache, "he's ear-marked for Julie Hinton-Brigg. It almost comes into the alliance class, doesn't it? But anyone else, my dear—except Henry, of course—The evening is yours."

"Annette," said the voice of Tim Selby, "you're running on. A queue of polite guests is trying to say how do you do to you. How do you do? What a charming party this is— Miss Beak—I'm at your feet."

"Miss Beak? You impertinent boy!" shrieked Annette, delighted. This was the sort of thing she liked to hear. "Alison—have nothing to do with him. There isn't a scrap of sincerity in his nature and what a *naughty* roving eye—"

"Hul-*lo*, Alison!" Willie Munro added himself to them. "I

say—isn't this marvellous? It's just like the holidays, isn't it? You had that frock on at—"

There seemed to be a pleasant conspiracy to make much of Alison. She stood enjoying her moment, the centre of a cheerful, delightfully admiring crowd, aware of Angus on the edge of it biding his time. Then with a sudden commotion a figure in white pushed its way between the black coats and a compelling arm was thrust through hers.

"Alison, darling!" cried Oonagh. "Oo—aren't you *gorgeous!* You make me look like a 'ickle girl in my short frock."

She looked round with embarrassing roguishness and to the startled Alison, feeling like Alice in Wonderland in the Duchess's grip, came the recollection that it's easier for two girls than one. A gleam in the eye of Mr. Selby said plainly, "Hit her on the head," and recognising social blackmail when she met it she would have liked to follow his advice. But there are things a lady cannot do. She laughed at the roguishness and with good grace welcomed Oonagh in to the circle.

Mrs. Courtney, however, was a competent and sharp-eyed hostess. Oonagh as a stranger rated special attention, being present in the teeth of Henry's opposition she rated more and she would get it, but the high voice and the dash for the centre were not lost upon Annette. She avoided a meaning glance from her husband and sailed in, smiling and cordial, to restore order.

"You haven't had a drink yet," said Angus's voice above Alison's head as Oonagh was detached and absorbed and it went on gravely in broad Scots: "I doubt pop or shandy'll hardly be the tipple for ye the nicht. Come awa' and try a wee cocktail in a quiet corner."

Alison was neatly cut out from the crowd and led away to the Courtneys' impressive bar. "Angus," she said, her dignity a little impaired by laughter, "I must ask you to alter your tone. My pop-swilling days are long past."

"I suppose so," said Angus, reverting to English. "It seems a pity in a way—Cocktail? Henry's special. Quite a test. You wouldn't like an extra cherry? No—of course you wouldn't. Sorry—"

He gave her a glass and raised his own in salutation. It was not in Angus to tell any girl that he was at her feet and if his life had depended on it he could not have said any word to Alison now that might sound in the slightest degree personal. But his face was not quite so reticent as his tongue. He did not do badly.

"*Supper,*" cried Annette. "Dining-room, everybody."

Her picnic was an elaborate meal which began with bouillon in gay, very contemporary cups and proceeded exquisitely through lobster mousse, but it was picnic-like in the sense that people moved about and helped themselves and each other and Angus had gone foraging for orange water-ices when Alison was joined by Julie Hinton-Brigg.

The two girls had met each other at parties, pony club and dancing classes from the age of four and a certain limited intimacy existed between them. They never met except on social occasions but these, particularly in early youth, are revealing and Alison, at any rate, knew a good deal about Julie who plunged without preamble into the subject which, for the moment, interested her.

"Alison," she said, "who's *that*?"

Alison, recognizing the purposeful stare which used to be

fixed on the cake of Julie's choice, followed the line. Under the fluffy prettiness there was will-power of the bull-dozing type and it was seldom worth while to get in its way but there was a temptation to do a little harrying at the start. She looked blank and said: "Who?"

"That one," said Julie. "The dark one being jolly with Annette."

"Oh," Alison was still rather slow, "perhaps you mean Tim Selby."

"Tim Selby? School, is he?"

"S'right."

Julie went on looking at Tim for a moment while Alison finished her first ice and received the second, exchanging wordless comments with Angus on the pirating of his chair. Then she spoke again.

"I must say he appeals. Quite strongly. Any just cause or impediment, do you know?"

"Well," said Alison, "I really can't tell you. He hasn't been here long so I hardly know him. And then, of course, they all lead a double life."

"A *double life?*" the round eyes looked startled.

"They're here in term time but nobody knows where they go or what they do in the holidays. He looks as if he might have several impediments, don't you think?"

"A girl in every port, you mean? Well, he does," said Julie seriously, "but then, if there are a lot none of them matter. Be a pal Alison, will you?"

Tim could doubtless look after himself and Julie would get to know him anyhow. "All right," said Alison, "but I'm not going to whistle him over now."

"Oh no," Julie was not impatient provided she saw her

way. "That would be crude."

Recollection stirred in Alison. "I thought I heard you were engaged?"

Julie, spooning up ice cream shook her head vigorously.

"Don't you believe it," she said. "That's Pop, blast him. He wants me to marry Cubby Lucreton. Do you know Cubby? That's him gnawing his moustache beside that Dutch girl who's with your cousin."

"Norwegian," said Alison and looked across the room at Marthe talking politely to the stoutish young man. Marthe was like a dryad in a curiously becoming cloud-grey dress, her black hair the only definite colour about her, and as she looked particularly ethereal beside Cubby Lucreton so she emphasized his stolidity. Julie was going on to explain.

"Cubby'll be Lord Lucreton one day, you see, and of course there's skads of money—"

"I thought you'd got plenty."

"Well nobody ever has *plenty*. I wouldn't mind being Lady L. in some ways but it's priced a bit high in my view. Anyway I'm not going to be married off by Pop. Would you?" Alison said she couldn't imagine the situation arising. "No—I dare say you couldn't. It's feudal. Victorian. Who's the girl in white?"

"Oonagh Hepburn. She's doing a temporary secretary job for my father. She lives in Ledenham."

"Never heard of her." An appraising stare took Oonagh in. "Not bad. Bit cheap," was the verdict. Oonagh was in a group which included Annette, Angus and Tim. Alison, again following the line of Julie's stare, looked at the duck of a white, which was a good frock, and the play of the handsome eyes and wondered about her own reaction to

76

the personality which was a strong desire to dodge. "She seems to be gunning for both blokes," observed Julie interestedly. "But I would say more likely to bring down your red-headed giant than my—what's his name?—Tim."

"She's attractive," said Alison fairly but there was no response. The face beside her had melted into a dimpling smile and Tim detached himself and strolled unhurriedly across the room towards it. She made an unnecessary mutter of introduction and got up. Cubby Lucreton was walking away from Marthe and she went over to join her, feeling ruffled.

Marthe had turned Tim down and therefore, of course, Tim was free to flirt with any girl he fancied: but as she looked at Marthe's curious loveliness, which seemed at that moment to make Julie, Alison herself and every other girl in the room look as crudely colourful as a bad oleograph, she was angry with him. A man who could appreciate Marthe's quality should not waste anything of himself on Julie Hinton-Brigg. And there was a faintly forlorn look about Marthe before she looked up and smiled.

"You are a kind of queen this evening," she said. "Or princess, perhaps is better. It is very becoming."

"You make me feel like the traditional dairymaid," said Alison and explained; "Red-cheeked and substantial."

"Oh—" Marthe laughed. "No—that isn't at all how you are looking. You mean I have no colours? I think when that is so it is better to stay plain."

Alison said: "I wouldn't say plain. Are you happy? Do you know enough people?"

"Plenty of people and they look after me very kindly," said Marthe. "Who is the young man with—" a neat gesture sketched a moustache.

"Cubby Lucreton. Christened Cuthbert. Did he have anything interesting to say?"

"Only that he likes Switzerland better than Norway. He is very gloomy I'm afraid. He—"

"Coffee, ladies," Angus appeared before them with two cups. "And stay where you are, if you don't mind. Annette's getting restless and I don't want to lose sight of you, Alison. You haven't forgotten you've promised me the first dance?"

Alison had not forgotten. It is very agreeable when the young man by whom one wants to be sought out makes clear his intention of doing it and she wondered who would seek Marthe out.

"What are you talking about in your girlish huddle?" Oonagh's voice demanded playfully as Angus went away. "Tan Oonagh tum and hear secrets?" Alison, again seized in an affectionate grasp, stiffened in spite of herself and Marthe gave the impression of withdrawing cautiously into a shell. "I say," the voice went on with a change of tone, "haven't you lost grip, Marthe? I doubt me if you're going to see much of Tim tonight. Look!" She rolled her eyes towards Tim and Julie, who were giving a spirited performance of hitting it off, and rolled them back inquisitively. "Come to think of it, why haven't I seen you lately? You haven't washed it up, have you?"

"Poor Marthe," said Alison without much hope. "How on earth do you expect her to cope with that kind of English?"

"Oh Marthe can cope with most kinds of English when she likes," was the reply. "Are you and Tim finished?"

"There was nothing to finish," said Marthe. "A few times to the cinema or dancing only."

"But have you had a row?"

"Oh no. Not at all."

"Well, quite honestly," said Oonagh, "I think he's behaving pretty scurrilously. That girl he's with is Julie Hinton-Brigg. You introduced him, didn't you?" to Alison. "I suppose she's a friend of yours."

"Bonk!" was Alison's thought as the shot got home but there was no need to reply.

"Come on, everybody," came Annette's rallying call. "Pick up your partners and let's get dancing."

"And here," said Oonagh complacently, "comes Angus."

Dropping Alison's arm at last she took a step forward to meet him and there was a confused moment in which several things happened at once. Alison saw Nick crossing the room and had time to wonder if he expected to have the first dance with her since he had brought her to the party, but Nick winked at her cheerfully and went straight to Marthe. "Dance, Alison?" cried Willie Munro advancing hurriedly with outstretched hand and Oonagh, a confirmed taker of arms, raised her hand to take Angus's.

Alison was dumb. She looked helplessly at Angus and opened her mouth with no idea what ought to come out of it. But Angus didn't hesitate. His arm was not there for Oonagh's hand and he took the muddle in a kind of flying tackle.

"Sorry, Willie. You have to book early . . . Coming, Alison? Press on everybody—"

"I *say*," began Oonagh—

"Oonagh," the voice of the hostess cut her short, "have you got a partner, dear? Willie—you know Oonagh, don't you?" and they were hustled, resentful and sadly resigned respectively, into the stream of traffic moving to the drawing-room where the carpet was up and Henry already switching on the music.

In that small party it would have been anti-social—and conspicuous—for a couple to dance together too frequently, and though Alison danced with Angus more than with other men it was not, she hoped, noticeably more. She danced with Patsy, an experience so comfortable that she was tempted to put her head on his shoulder and go to sleep, and she had several with Nick, whose dancing her sister Clare had described as a poem. Tim, who was also a very good dancer, was excessively gay and insouciant and she had rather more than she wanted with Willie, whose manner was portentous and his hand a trifle damp. Henry Courtney—she noticed that he was increasing in girth—steered her round the room asking if they had heard from Clare lately and how her brothers were getting on, and the future Lord Lucreton danced in morose silence, broken only by occasional brief questions.

"Dance much?"

"Not an awful lot."

A silent round. "Know Julie well?"

"Oh yes we've always known each other."

"Believe Hinton-Brigg's a Governor of the School now, isn't he?"

"Is he?" Alison was surprised. "I didn't know."

"So he told me. Some old buffer's died and he's taken his place. Not much in it, I shouldn't have thought but," a faint gleam of amusement appeared and vanished again, "he likes that sort of thing. So does my old man."

Another silence and then another interjection, half

question, half statement. "Red-haired chap's Cameron the Scotch Rugger international, isn't he?"

"Yes."

"Athletic types drift into schools, I suppose. Henderson used to play Test cricket, didn't he?"

"Yes."

"What's this fellow Selby? He anything special?"

Alison said that so far as she knew Selby was nothing special and the dance was over. "Thanks very much," said Mr. Lucreton and resigned her with a polite bow to the red-haired Cameron who wanted to know what was funny.

There was no opportunity to tell him, no chance in that small convivial gathering for any confidential word, especially with a partner ten inches taller than herself. But it was not an occasion when words were of paramount importance. It was, for Alison, that memorable party which as a rule comes only once. She was a success, she was in demand, she was in tearing spirits; and beyond all this there was Angus seeking her out with unobtrusive zeal and ingenuity. Their conversation was of the frothiest but as the evening went on the rest of the party grew indistinct. Dances with other men seemed a waste of the time that was left and she saw almost nothing of what went on around her. After the last dance she felt his reluctance to let her go and saw her own small shock of desolation reflected in his face. The party was over, Nick would take her home, not Angus. They were parting now.

"A heavenly party, Annette," she said, taking her leave. Annette said: "My dear, I'm *so* glad you enjoyed it," with what seemed immoderate significance and amusement and Alison, responding with a vague smile went upstairs with the other girls.

In the midst of their babble of talk she came to. Julie, excited and pleased, pounced on her with an invitation. Marthe she noticed looking more than usually remote and rather tired and the gay, serene Frances was cross. Oonagh was noisy and aggressive and pointedly ignoring herself; a polite remark when they were for a moment next each other was met by deafness and a deliberately turned back.

"Oh damn!" cried Oonagh loudly and affectedly. "Lost my powder. Frances—lend me yours, will you? I *must* have powder."

Frances snapped. "Powder and cotton wool on the dressing-table," she said pointing. "My puff smears no face but my own."

When Alison went down, glad to be turning her back on them all and the strange atmosphere of irritation, Angus was waiting for her by the stairs.

"I wish I was taking you home," he said quietly.

"Yes," she said. "But it's only a minute . . ." and she pressed on with something she had to tell him. "Angus, Julie Hinton-Brigg has asked us to lunch on Sunday, but—"

The rest of her sentence was lost. Nick, suddenly close, cried: "Ready? Come on, then." "Angus!" roared a voice from the door, "for Pete's sake move your ruddy vehicle—" and Angus's head was too far above hers for anything but a bellow to reach him through the uproar. She looked at him anxiously.

"*Here* I am, Angus," shrieked Oonagh. "We're holding everybody up, darling—"

"All right Alison," said Angus. "Good night," and he caught her hand quickly and was gone.

5

IN the county of Ledshire there was no man so generally disliked as Sir Arthur Hinton-Brigg. Ledshire itself was small and almost entirely agricultural but big industry was not far off and the county kept a particularly nervous eye on the town of Snaydon which was just over the border and maintaining a steady growth. Snaydon was full of factories, bustle and brass of all kinds and Sir Arthur was the spearhead of the Snaydon advance.

He was not a clever man. The prosperity and the knighthood had come to him through efforts and achievements which were not his own. His maternal grandfather was, so to speak, the first Hinton, his father the first Brigg and it was their energy and ability which had made the firm of Hinton Brigg Ltd and a fortune. The knighthood was in the nature of a posthumous award and it had been a great help to Sir Arthur in his own work in life which was the pursuit of grandeur.

From his public school days he had pursued it assiduously and with success. As a boy he was handsome, athletic and rather too well-mannered. As an undergraduate—entrance to the universities was easier in those days—he spent a good deal of money, never imprudently, and was seen in the right places near the right people. As a young man he married the daughter of a Ledshire landowning family and soon after the war he bought Thaxley Manor, his wife's old home, and moved into the county. He was still as he had been at school, handsome, elaborately courteous and disliked, but there was no resisting him. He bored his way to the forefront of Ledshire affairs, carrying, like a personal standard, the prestige of the fine old family to which his wife belonged, carrying her, it might almost be said, as a shield; and Ledshire sighed and suffered, laughed in private, and in public concealed its feelings under uneasy heartiness and let him get away with it. Like his daughter Sir Arthur was of the bulldozer type. Almost nothing was worth the fatigue of argument with him and if argument went too far or led to action he was a ruthless—and dirty—fighter.

On the day of the Courtneys' party when Alison Fielding met Julie Hinton-Brigg, Alison's father encountered Julie's father, not in the flesh but in the form of a growing cloud on the horizon. It was the day of the first Governors' Meeting of the year—there were normally three—and before the meeting Mr. Fielding, as his custom was, lunched with his Chairman, the Earl of Leyburn.

"I suppose," said Lord Leyburn, "that when you heard poor old Harris had gone at last you had the same premonition as I had." The Headmaster thought it very likely and the Chairman said: "Well—it's happened."

"Already?"

"Yes—and no. Snaydon have written begging to nominate Sir Arthur Hinton-Brigg and I must say they've been uncommonly smart about it. Poor old Harris is hardly cold and he'd been a governor so long and inactive so long I expected them to have forgotten they have a nomination. Indeed Craig said something about reminding them presently." Mr. Craig was a Leyburn solicitor and Clerk to the Governors of Ledenham.

"I'm rather hazy about these nominations," said the

84

Headmaster in a conversational tone, as if diverted for a moment to a subject of academic interest. "Are you bound to accept them?"

"I wouldn't like to say that," Lord Leyburn was similarly chatty. "Craig would know the ins and outs. I've never, myself, known the governors refuse a nomination. It would be an extreme thing to do. I had thought in this case we might ask Snaydon for another clergyman. We're not by any means overloaded with clergy and they're quite good Governors as a rule. However, I was too late. And in any case," returning to reality, "it probably wouldn't have worked." He put a large forkful of beef and vegetables into his mouth and chewed vigorously, his rather prominent blue eyes staring straight before him.

"I hoped," said the Headmaster, "along, I know, with many of the Governors, that your son would fill the next vacancy on the board."

Lord Leyburn put down his knife and fork and pushed his plate away. "Snaydon wouldn't have nominated him though."

"Wouldn't they? He'd be an excellent nomination. He has his business connections in Snaydon—"

"Oh yes—reg'lar job. Doing quite well. But they wouldn't like it, y'know. Wouldn't feel he was their man. Besides—*I* couldn't have suggested it. Neither could Craig."

"So you'll bring Hinton-Brigg's nomination before this meeting?"

"Yes. Have to do that."

There was a pause. The beef was removed, cheese was placed before them and they both crunched biscuits.

"It's at the May meeting, isn't it," said the Headmaster,

"that questions of retirement and new elections come up?"

"Er—yes," said the Chairman and there was another pause, full of thought. "Yes it is," their eyes met with a flicker of hope and then it died. "Coffee? I think we're bound to have the fellow, y'know. Have a brandy."

"Thank you," said Mr. Fielding gratefully. Of course they were bound to have Sir Arthur Hinton-Brigg. He had never doubted it from the moment Miss Wills told him that Canon Harris was dead and he had said all that he intended to say. The time had now come for acceptance. "He's an experienced man of standing," he said. "There's no reason at all, sir, why he shouldn't be a useful member of the Board."

"There are plenty of reasons," Lord Leyburn corrected him. "But," gloomily, "not a tittle we can use. All the same," he straightened his shoulders and thrust out an authoritative chin, "I'm damned if we'll have him before we must. We elect in May. He must wait for it. And that means we don't see him till October—here. See plenty of him," he added, despondent again, "elsewhere. Terrible fella. Absolute pest on the Bench. Can't persuade him his opinion isn't law. He'll be a nuisance to *you*, y'know." The prominent blue eyes were suddenly direct and shrewd. "Busybody if ever there was one."

"I can put up with a good deal," said the Headmaster.

"And at least," concluded the Chairman, "we've got a respite. We'll hold him till October."

But though October looked a nice long way off to the Governors who would only be harried thrice annually and might forget about Sir Arthur in between, the Headmaster's case was different. For some years there had been signs that

Sir Arthur was prepared to take an interest in the School and Mr. Fielding, as he drove himself home after the meeting, reflected that the interest would now be taken. There are no rules to which Governors are bound to adhere in their behaviour. Those of proper feeling behave properly, but when there is improper behaviour the Headmaster can only hope that the offender will learn and Sir Arthur was not an educable type. He would descend majestically on the School in and out of season, wasting time and patronising the assistant masters. He would invite boys to lunch at Thaxley and pump inaccurate information from them. He would offer to present a flight of hurdles or a new squash court and thereafter use his generosity like a pistol. At all school functions he would be an embarrassment.

All this Mr. Fielding anticipated as a certain perennial nuisance, but more serious and less predictable was the long term effect of a trouble-making Governor on the School. During his seventeen years at Ledenham the Governors had been a friendly, reliable party, united by a Chairman whom they trusted and who knew his job. But Lord Leyburn was growing old.

"I can only hope," he said to his wife that evening, "that Leyburn will last my time. In fact I'm determined that my time won't outlast his."

"Ledenham will survive," said Mrs. Fielding, "even if— which heaven forbid—it gets Sartha as a Chairman."

"Oh yes," her husband agreed, "Ledenham will survive. He may rock it but after four hundred years of ups and downs it would take more than Sir Arthur to knock it off its perch. He could easily knock me off mine though."

87

On the following day the Fieldings left home for a brief weekend visit to another school where Mr. Fielding had an engagement to preach on Sunday. Alison felt it to be a misfortune, a minor one but not negligible, that it happened to be this weekend for she was still suffering slightly from the abruptness with which the party had come to an end the night before. She had been swept off by Nick and Angus had gone to ferry Oonagh and Tim when the few minutes of going home would, if they had gone together, have wound the evening up. And she wished that she could be sure she had remembered to tell him she was going to Stoneleigh so that he would realize why she had had to refuse Julie's invitation to lunch. There was nothing to be done about it. Angus was in School before she could ring him up in the morning and he was still in School when she was driven away; but fortunately he was not the kind who went in for misunderstandings.

"How was the party?" her father asked over his shoulder and she leant forward and gave them the news, telling them what there was to eat, of Henry's increasing corpulence, Annette's gay kindness and who was there.

"I didn't know Sartha was a Governor, by the way," she said. "When—"

"*What?*" cried her father. "Who told you that? Julie?"

"No, it was Cubby Lucreton," she said, surprised. "He said Sartha himself told him and is very bucked about it. Why did you shout at me?"

"I didn't shout at you. I shouted because he isn't a Governor. He's nominated but he won't be elected till May."

"Oh. Cubby must have heard wrong."

"Why should he confide in Cubby Lucreton?" Mrs. Fielding wondered but Alison knew the answer to that one.

"Because he's trying to marry Julie off to him. Julie's very embittered about it."

Her father laughed. "She may be embittered but I expect she'll be Lady Lucreton yet."

"You don't know Julie."

"No. I do know Sir Arthur."

"Tough, is he?" said Alison. "I must say he looks it. Well—it may be a case of Greek meets Greek but I'll back Julie."

The Headmaster thought of offering to bet on it but deciding that it would be unseemly drove on without comment, wondering if the Lucreton boy had got it wrong or if Sir Arthur had.

Angus was quite as badly frustrated as Alison by the abrupt ending to the party. The distance between Little Campion and School House was short. Even at 2 a.m. it would not be appropriate that his car should stand at the Headmaster's door for any length of time and he did not think, he was almost sure, that he would not have kissed Alison or said anything special. He was strongly of the opinion that Tim's disaster was the result of speaking to Marthe too soon. In love as in other matters Tim had been precipitate and he was determined not to make the same mistake. But it had been a wonderful evening. The few minutes alone with Alison would have consolidated the past and given him a chance to make arrangements for the future. In short, he would have liked to take her home.

"My new friend Julie," said Tim as they went into the

Zoo after dropping Oonagh at her house, "has asked us to lunch on Sunday. Can do? Miss Beak, you, me."

Perceiving that after all there was a future, Angus cheered up. "Oh yes," he said. "Alison said something about it. Yes—that'll fine. I'll fix it with her."

On Saturday afternoon he had a very muddy seven-a-side practice and was not altogether sorry that Alison had not turned out to watch. When he was clean again he went round to School House, hoping he might be asked to tea, and rang the private side bell. The outer door was closed which was unusual, though it was cold, of course, and it was a long time before Higgins opened it.

"Miss Alison?" he said looking surprised. "She's away from home, sir."

Angus exclaimed: "Away?" and Higgins became sympathetic and greatly interested.

" 'Fraid so, Mr. Cameron. Didn't you see the Headmaster's notice? They're all away till late tomorrow night. We don't expect them back not before eleven."

"I see. Thanks," said Angus composing himself. He had known and forgotten that the Beak was to be away but it had never occurred to him that Alison would be going too. He had assumed that she was telling him that she had accepted Julie's invitation; she must have been trying to tell him she couldn't. But—now what? He must find Tim and clear it up.

He went back to the Zoo but Tim was out. It was past midnight when he came in and Angus pounced.

"Where the hell have you been?" he demanded angrily.

"Sh-sh," hissed Tim. "Don't bellow."

"Come in here," said Angus and scooped him into his

room. "There's been a mistake. Alison's away. She—"

"Yes, I know. Julie told me."

"You mean—You've been out with her?"

Tim frowned and lighting a cigarette strolled over to stand near the remains of Angus's fire. Angus was looking unnecessarily surprised and very severe.

"We had a flick and a steak," he said carelessly, unaware that Molloy's Steak Bar had become holy ground, "and she said Alison couldn't go. She'd fixed it with me first, you see, and there was no chance to consult. Then she caught sight of Oonagh and thought—A, she'd do instead and—B, would tell us."

"*Oonagh!*" said Angus. There was an unpleasant silence. "Well, why didn't she tell us? Plenty of time in the car."

"Your guess is as good as mine."

"It was deliberate."

"Probably."

"She meant us to think Alison was going till it was too late to do anything about it," said Angus in a muted shout. "Well—it isn't too late. You can do as you like; I'm not going. I'm not going to be diddled that way."

"Oh God!" said Tim. "How tired I am. I exhaust—" he collapsed into a chair and closed his eyes. Angus regarded him coldly.

"Naturally you're tired. Chasing off to Leyburn after—"

"I chased much further than Leyburn. I chased to Thaxley; Leyburn; back to Thaxley; home."

"More fool. It isn't even as if you liked the girl."

"Well," said Tim, "I wouldn't say that. My lower self likes her and it's time it had a run." There was snort of disgust from Angus and he opened his eyes and smiled sweetly then closed them again. "Angus, are you engaged to Alison?"

"No," snapped Angus. "I'm not. Get up and go to bed."

"I only asked," explained Tim soothingly, "because if you aren't, why should you back out of Thaxley tomorrow? It's only a lunch."

"Because I don't choose to be diddled by Oonagh."

"Looks rather a give-away don't you think?"

"Who's to look at it?"

"Well—there is Oonagh. Does Angus go nowhere unless Alison goes too? Would Alison cut up rough if he did?"

Angus looked taken aback and then swore profoundly. Of course if he cut, that was the sort of thing that would be said. Not by Tim, but by Oonagh and the other girl; and it was the sort of thing he was damned if he would allow. If he could prevent it.

"I suppose I'd better go," he said gloomily and added as Tim at last got up from the chair; "Blast you."

"I'm sorry Angus," said Tim. "I really am. I was so mad with that little bitch Oonagh when I heard it that I nearly scrubbed it then and there. And then I thought it was such a hell of a fuss to make about going to lunch. At least we can lush up the new Governor."

"Governor?"

"Hinton-Brigg's just joined, Julie says."

"Gawd!" said Angus staring at him. "That chap? Never!"

Tim, surprised, said: "Why? do you know him?"

"Know him? Everybody knows him. He's mixed up with every ruddy thing in the county. Rugger—cricket—He's the lousiest man I've come across in all my puff." He paused and looked at his astonished friend. "You'd have thought twice about running after Julie if you'd seen her old man first," he told him grimly.

"Help!" said Tim.

But he was not destined to be terrified by Sir Arthur Hinton-Brigg on Sunday. After a ten-mile drive, with Oonagh very gay beside him in the front of the car and Angus very dour in the back, they reached Thaxley to find that Sir Arthur and Lady Hinton-Brigg were away from home and Julie was making the most of it. Nameless orgies, her manner implied, lay before them.

A cynical manservant took their coats and she swept them through the hall, which was very warm and heavily scented with hyacinths, to a large hot room filled with the sound of jive. The room and its furniture were old and beautiful, the gramophone throbbed, mimicked and crooned incontinently. Julie, jiving as she went, hastened to dispense cocktails, whose mighty kick Angus ascribed to a lavish dollop of brandy. A sensation of nightmare seized him. They had come in from fresh, cold air and country roads and without a moment of transition plunged into Bedlam at one o'clock on Sunday. It could not be real—

"Drinkies!" cried Julie and jiving, glass in hand, sang: "Drink up—*d'da*—d'da—d'da—d'da—*d'da*—Drink up— d'da—*d'da*—"

"Yippee! *D'da*—d'da *d'da*—"responded Oonagh joyously.

"You know," Julie paused as a thought struck her and stared round-eyed at Angus, "I never thought you'd come. Aren't you Alison Fielding's boy-friend?" Angus said no. "Aren't you? I thought on Friday at Annette's—"

Angus felt his colour rise and was dumb. Tim opened his mouth to speak and Oonagh gave a little trill of laughter.

"There was some rough work at Annette's," she said, glancing meaningly from Tim to Julie. "But actually, the reason Alison isn't here now is that she's gone to see her boy-friend."

"They've gone to Stoneleigh," Tim said quickly.

"Cubby was at Stoneleigh," observed Julie unheard.

"I know they've gone to Stoneleigh," said Oonagh, greatly amused. "The Beak's preaching. But quite frankly, can you imagine a girl going sixty or seventy miles to hear her father preach?"

Julie said, quite frankly, she couldn't imagine going a yard to hear anybody preach and Oonagh laughed.

"Stoneleigh," she said, "has its attractive young masters too, I expect. At least I know it has one—" a telephone conversation overheard had leapt into her retentive memory, complete and ready for time, "—Martin Sykes. Does that ring a bell? He was here—School House. Did you know him, Angus?"

"Before my time," said Angus woodenly.

"Was he? Yes—I suppose he would be. I just remember seeing him about. Terribly good-looking chap. Even then everybody knew he and Alison—"

Tim looked up sharply. There was an increase of certainty in her voice when she heard that Angus didn't know Martin Sykes and she was being a little careless.

"Quite a nursery affair," he remarked pleasantly. "Alison would be what? Thirteen—fourteen? A little early for everybody to know—"

Julie picked up the cocktail shaker. "More drinkies— Let's drink to Alison. I like Alison. She was looking jolly attractive at Annette's but I thought," nodding at Angus, "it was you, if you get me. Alison!" She held up her glass.

"Alison, by all means," said Tim, holding up his, "with or without Sykes. You didn't," he added, smiling affably at Oonagh, "ask me if *I* know him."

Oonagh hesitated but she held on to her own amused smile. "You couldn't have known him *here*," she pointed out. "And I don't suppose he goes about telling everybody. But it's quite true—she wasn't so young as all that—"

"Well," said Julie, "I'll ask Alison next time I see her," and she dismissed the subject of which she had had enough. "Drink up, my hearties—"

"No thank you," said Angus to a third dynamic cocktail, but the second was doing him good. He was less ready than Tim to assume that lies were being told and Oonagh had undoubtedly given him a shock. It could be true that there was something between Alison and Martin Sykes, who was remembered at Ledenham as an exceptionally good chap. He had never heard anything to suggest it, but then— would he? He had no right to feel that he knew all about Alison. He wondered if Sykes had been at the Fieldings' Christmas dance; if Alison had looked then as she had looked on Friday at the Courtneys'.

Julie had returned to her purpose of having a riotous party. In Angus's view she was quite a pretty little thing, extraordinarily silly but not so depraved as, perhaps, she hoped and it was uphill work. Time, place and people were against anything in the nature of orgies, except that there was every opportunity to get extremely drunk. With her third cocktail in her hand she was setting, so to speak, at Tim, her round eyes narrowed and fixed on him with all the sultriness at her command. Oonagh, with a look of vague, soaring gaiety, was advancing on himself.

"Darling," she said in a tender murmur oddly unconnected with her expression, "have I nipped a little flower in the bud? I had to, you know. It wouldn't have been k-kind to let you go on not knowing the truth. But you hadn't got far, had you?" Her tone had become more practical and she peered at him, focusing with a little difficulty, to see how she was getting on.

"Dear Oonagh," he responded, "let me take your glass," and he removed it from her hand and placed it out of reach.

"Lunch is served, miss," announced the cynical man, glancing round to see what they had been up to.

Angus was looking forward to making a few trenchant observations to Tim when, if ever, they got safely back to Ledenham. If this was the sort of thing his lower nature fancied the sooner he got his higher self back in the saddle the better; and in future he would kindly refrain from involving him, Angus, in his dubious arrangements. But as they ate their excellent lunch in the Thaxley Manor dining-room his wrath abated, as his wrath against Tim usually did abate before he got the good of it.

Tim might be impetuous and not always so steady as he should be but there was never any doubt about his quickness of wit and he took charge. He talked unceasingly and his compelling eye mobilized Angus in support. He cowed the cynical manservant so that the drinkies went round more slowly than the hostess intended and it was so skilfully done that the girls were perfectly happy. They were both rather high, to put it mildly, but that was a negligible misfortune; an advantage indeed, since it prevented dissatisfaction with the line taken and the resultant drowsiness enabled the sober section of the party to organize an early escape.

"In you go," said Tim to Oonagh, opening the back door of his car.

She blundered in and he tucked a rug over her. "There you are, nice and cosy," and he shut the door.

"Hi!" shrieked Julie from the steps. "She's all by herself! Poor girl—she's all by herself in the back of the car!" and pointing at Oonagh she fell into a fit of laughter which looked as if it might be difficult to stop.

"Angus!" cried Oonagh as her solitary position suddenly came home to her, "aren't you coming—? *Well!* Quite honestly, I think you're the rudest—"

"Don't untuck the rug," called Tim cheerily.

"I'm cold. This car's perishing."

"Wrap up and drop off for a bit. Sober up before you get home to mother."

"*Really!*" said Oonagh, but as the car moved forward she lost her balance and with much commotion she flounced into a corner, muffling herself ostentatiously in the rug.

"Well," said Tim addressing the windscreen, "at least we did come out by that same door wherein we went."

"M'h'm," agreed Angus. "Mind—you took us in; but you've brought us out in fair order—considering—so I'm not going to give you the hammering I intended to give you. Cigarette?" He lit cigarettes for them both.

"*I* want a cigarette," cried a plaintive voice from behind but they ignored it and went quietly on with their conversation.

"Did your lower nature enjoy itself?" asked Angus.

"No," was the regretful reply. "Pity. It can do with quite

97

a lot of silliness but there's a limit. Especially when there's nothing else."

"So you're through?"

"I'm afraid so. I promised to go to a dance next Friday—some show in Snaydon—and that'll see me out. Cubby can do a comeback. Angus," there was a change in the muttering voice, "you do know, don't you, that we have with us a most consummate liar?"

There was a pause and then Angus asked: "*Do* you know Sykes?"

"No. But—"

Angus interrupted with a note of finality. He had no desire to discuss the matter. "I don't just see," he said, "how this creature would know anything about it, but the thing itself isn't impossible—or unlikely. I don't mean it's likely that 'everybody knew' while he was at the School."

"I think the whole thing's impossible," said Tim. "Phoney."

"Ah," said Angus, grinning faintly, "but then, like our friend behind, how would you know?"

They drove on in silence. Behind them Oonagh fell asleep and when they drew up at the Hepburn residence they had to wake her. She crawled out of the car, dazed, dishevelled and very cross, and as Tim on one side and Angus on the other put out steadying hands and rallied her with encouraging voices, Frances Henderson walked past pushing her baby in his pram.

"Let *go*," snarled Oonagh shaking herself free and, not without a hint of a stagger, she hurried up the path and into the house.

"Oh Gawd!" groaned Tim. "What will mother say? Could

we have done anything? I don't think so—Ass!" They got back into the car and passing Frances he tooted his horn. Angus waved and a hand in a scarlet glove was lifted in unsmiling response.

Tim's usually pale face flushed angrily. "I'm sorry Angus," he said. "I'm afraid that didn't look so good. An ill-fated expedition."

Angus said nothing. He was suddenly furiously angry; with Tim, with Oonagh, with himself, with Frances. He strode upstairs when they went in to the Zoo and banged his door to shut out everybody. He didn't know how he was ever going to recover from Frances' cut—for from her to him that unsmiling gesture was no less. Tim had been an ass but he had been genuinely misled about this damned lunch. Oonagh was Oonagh, practically sub-human. He himself had also been misled and had acted for the best with no anticipation of pleasure and Frances, knowing him as she did might have given him—and Tim too—the benefit of the doubt. Uneasily, along with the memory of what Frances had seen came the memory of Julie who was sure he was Alison's boy-friend. If she thought so from seeing them on Friday evening, Frances—and doubtless everybody else—must have spotted what he was feeling about her. To see him two days later, helping to decant a thoroughly sozzled Oonagh Hepburn from a car was not a thing that Alison's cousin could be expected to like. He considered going round to Holly Lodge to explain and at once rejected the idea. To explain why he was explaining would be almost like a corroboration of the boy-friend idea and God knew he didn't want that.

He went restlessly to the window and stared out,

wondering what Alison was doing at Stoneleigh now. On Saturday when he had got over the dismay of finding her gone he had told himself that he would see her on Monday, tomorrow, and with luck make up for the loss of the consolidating drive home from the party. Now it was different. If he told her about Thaxley she would understand his and Tim's predicament and laugh at it; but there was Sykes. It was at least odd that Oonagh had got hold of the fellow's name. He would go to School House tomorrow afternoon anyway, thought Angus, because he must find out about it if he could, and he observed the weather from the angle of seven-a-sides. It was very cold and the sky was heavy with dark clouds which had a faint, menacing tinge of orange in the grey. Snow coming. It looked as if he could count on a free afternoon and hoping that the Fieldings would get home all right he turned from the window to make himself a cup of tea. In a tin he found a remnant of chocolate cake. He looked at it speechlessly for a moment and then threw it violently into the fire.

WHILE Angus stared out at the lowering sky and wondered what she was doing Alison at Stoneleigh was talking to Martin Sykes. She was having one of her usual difficulties about Old Ledenhamians whom she had not known particularly well; since it would no longer be suitable to address him as Sykes should she go for his Christian name—she did know it, which was not always the case—or would Mr. Sykes be more polite? He was having the same difficulty about her but they had quite an agreeable conversation. The weekend altogether was quite agreeable but she was very ready to go home and on Monday morning her thoughts ran on much the same lines as Angus's thoughts had run before he had heard of Martin Sykes and been cut by Frances Henderson. She and her mother congratulated each other at breakfast that the snow had held off till they got home, but since they were back without mishap or delay she welcomed it, and thought happily of a good fire in the old nursery which was the family's refuge from public life.

"Damn!" said her father from behind a newspaper.

Mrs. Fielding looked up from Michael's Sunday letter. "What?"

"This moron! This unspeakable puffed-up fool!" burst from the Headmaster. He paused and looked at Alison. "You have no ears."

"Okay," said Alison obligingly and he went on:

"What can you *do* with a man like this? Look here—" and he handed the paper to his wife, pointing out a small headline.

The paper was the Snaydon daily, which kept him abreast with local affairs and the headline announced: "New Governor for Ledenham School". Sir Arthur Hinton-Brigg, Mrs. Fielding read, had accepted an invitation to join the Governing Body of Ledenham School in succession to the late Canon Harris. She skipped a few valedictory remarks about old Canon Harris, curled her lip over Sir Arthur as a distinguished Old Boy of a school which she rated rather lower than it would have liked, and smiled at Athletic Successes and airy references to the University Career. Her eyebrows went up as she read of Sir Arthur as an Authority on Education on the strength of the above, and when the article concluded by congratulating the School on the acquisition of a Governor who would confer upon it new life, new strength, new hope, she passed the paper to Alison in silence.

"Quite a puff," said Alison. "Who would write it? I thought you said he wouldn't be a Gov. till May."

"He won't," her father told her. "He wrote it himself, I imagine. And there's this," he added to his wife.

'This' was a letter dated from Thaxley Manor on Saturday. "My dear Headmaster," Sir Arthur had dictated, "You have doubtless been informed that I have accepted a nomination to the Governing Body of Ledenham. I think it best to make plain from the beginning that I never assume responsibilities of this kind lightly. When I consent to serve on a committee I do so with the intention of taking my full share in the work and authority of that committee.

I should be glad to see the School and have a talk with yourself as soon as possible. Either Wednesday or Thursday of this week would suit me and I shall be delighted to

102

lunch with you and Mrs. Fielding.

Perhaps you will be good enough to let me know immediately which day will be convenient as I have many calls on my time.

Yours very truly,"

The signature was illegible but dashing.

"How graciously he asks himself to lunch," remarked Mrs. Fielding. She raised her eyes from the single page and she and her husband looked at each other. Alison looked at them both. She was curious and she hoped for some degree of enlightenment but there were occasions when it was better not to be told. Information picked up when dropped was one thing and didn't count; anything you were told was knowledge and could be awkward. Her mother was frowning, her father wore his dead-pan face and she wished she knew more about how Governors worked.

"And how do you propose to deal with this?" asked Mrs. Fielding.

"I propose to tell him," the Headmaster replied promptly, "that we'll be delighted if he and Lady Hinton-Brigg will lunch with us. I will add that though, of course, his election in May is a formality it is not possible for me to receive him as a Governor before it takes place. If he likes to come and pay us a private visit he can."

Mrs. Fielding nodded. "That should hold him," she said. "Put in a few flowers."

"Oh I'll do that." He got to his feet and gathered up his letters.

"Are you remembering we've got people to dinner?" she asked in a tone of routine reminder. Yes, he said, he hadn't forgotten.

"How they'll hate turning out in the snow, poor things," he said on his way to the door and as he opened it he paused and looked back at her. "*Carp,*" he added significantly and went away to his study to finish reading his letters and then to put on cap and gown and walk through the snow to Chapel.

As he went the baize door squeaked and thudded and Matron appeared. A boy in the House had gone down some days before with flu. He had come back to School late because of a wedding in his family and Matron made no secret of her belief that the whole affair had been arranged on purpose to start an epidemic in Ledenham. It was asking for trouble, in her opinion, to get married at the beginning of the spring term.

"Good morning Mrs. Fielding, good morning, Alison," she said sombrely. "Two more. Evans and Crofts have both got sore throats and temps and Baker's temp is up again. Morris has been sick. He's got a slight rash."

Mrs. Fielding groaned. She hated rashes and spots. "He was all right yesterday?" she said. "Then it can hardly be measles. German measles, do you think? They aren't chicken-pox spots?"

"No," said Matron and relented slightly: "I think it's something he's eaten, but I've put him in the isolation room till Doctor's been. It's all I can do."

"Very well, Matron," said Mrs. Fielding, registering the fact that there was more than flu and spots on Matron's mind this morning. "I'll come up and have a look at them— Yes, Mrs. Higgins?"

Mrs. Higgins had come to report that one of the veg women was off. Flu, she *said*. And Elsie wasn't too keen on

104

doing the extra. Higgins appeared behind his wife. Perks on the phone and he couldn't get ducks after all; would chickens do? Mrs. Fielding's day had begun.

"I'll come through and speak to Elsie," she told the cook. "No, Higgins, chickens won't do. I'll ring Perks myself in a minute." Food for the dinner-party had first priority. She went briskly to her desk in the drawing-room and took out a large notebook. The Claytons, Pearson-Smiths and the Chaplain—she turned over the pages. She had once heard of a Headmaster's wife who provided mutton cutlets for prefects' supper-parties with such regularity that the ceremony was known as 'mutlet' and she had taken the story to heart. It was an extreme case, of course, but there was no doubt that when she considered what to give her guests to eat the first thing that suggested itself was what they had had last time.

"Beef-olives," she said, putting the book away. Nobody had had beef-olives for at least two years. She picked up the telephone. "Three pounds of steak, cut thin—yes, beef-olives—nicely trimmed. Yes, for dinner, but Mrs. Higgins is short-handed so she would like it early. Yes, very cold. Good morning—Mr. Perks? Yes, it is a pity you can't get the ducks—No thank you, I won't have chickens— Perhaps you will be able to get what I *order,*" not too much emphasis, "next time—Yes, it is cold. Good—"

"Mummy," said Alison, "these flowers have had it. Shall I see if Smith's got anything?"

"Yes, but he hasn't much left," said Mrs. Fielding, putting down the telephone. "You may have to try the shop and goodness knows what *they'll* have." She was moving on, her thoughts going ahead of her, but Alison had more to say.

105

"There's nobody coming to tea, is there?" she asked.

"I don't expect anybody. Why? Did you think of going to Frances?"

"No. But there won't be any games, I think Angus might drop in."

Mrs. Fielding said: "Well, that'll be all right," and they parted. She looked after her daughter, whose back view as she ran upstairs was exceedingly cheerful, and for a moment Sir Arthur Hinton-Brigg and the demands of Ledenham receded. Alison's bloom had not escaped her parents and Mrs. Fielding hoped that it really was a good idea letting her stay at home for a time instead of bundling her into a job at once. The child's longing to stay had moved both herself and her husband, partly with a sense of guilt; they had so little time or thought to spare for their children during term. But Alison's looks implied something more than the happiness of being in a well-loved home after a year's absence and in the pressure of the job it must not be overlooked. She was young for her age in some ways; Angus, Mrs. Fielding smiled slightly, was fairly guileless too and in her view a modicum of guile was necessary to the successful conduct of a love-affair in such a close community as a school. If, of course, it was a love-affair. But there was no time to brood over the possibility of anything so painful as that thought suggested. She dismissed her daughter from her mind and went to the kitchen where her next task was to ensure by a judicious mixture of scolding and cajolery that, despite the absence of the flu victim and the resentment of Elsie, the boys would be fed.

It was about an hour later that she went through to the

106

boys' side and climbed the stairs to visit the sick. Three of the four beds were occupied in the first of the sick-rooms. In one only a tuft of mouse-coloured hair was visible and she went over quietly and looked at a flushed, sleeping face; Baker with a considerable fever. The other two patients, propped uncomfortably on their elbows, grinned cheerfully and assured her in hoarse whispers that they weren't too bad.

In the small isolation room Morris, who was thirteen and new last term, came to attention in bed and smiled nervously.

"This is a nuisance for you," said Mrs. Fielding. "Are you feeling better?"

"Oh yes, thank you, Mrs. Fielding." The smile widened confidingly, "I felt better as soon as I'd been sick."

"It often happens. Let's look at your rash—" A skinny chest was exposed. "Oh, I don't think much of that."

The boy, tucking in his chin, squinted down and said it seemed to have faded a bit.

"Good," said Mrs. Fielding. "But don't go wandering about till the doctor has seen you."

"Oh no sir," said Morris and blushed rosily. It was a relief to him, as he slowly relaxed after the strain of the visit, that Mrs. Fielding hadn't noticed the slip.

Mrs. Fielding was frequently addressed as 'sir' and she never did notice; but she was smiling a little as she went down to Matron's room. She had dealt with huffs and grumbles in the kitchen; she was now on her way to find out what—to put it crudely—was biting Matron and deal with that; and floating above such routine tasks was the consciousness of Sir Arthur Hinton-Brigg poised for a plunge into the Ledenham tank. But her life was volcanic by nature. In compensation it was never dull and seldom short of comic relief and if at times she thought favourably of peaceful retirement a glimpse of a passing boy was enough to restore her contentment. That schoolboys as a class have their faults she knew as well as anybody, and inside the class she could, after years of experience, sum up the individual with penetrating shrewdness; but the operative fact was, she liked boys.

In Matron's room she accepted a cup of coffee while they exchanged views on Morris's rash and Baker's temperature and then the cause of the cloud was revealed.

"There was quite a little scene in Chapel yesterday," Matron began with elaborate chattiness. "Have you heard about it yet?"

"No. What was that?"

"Oh—well, it was silly, really, but everybody felt quite annoyed. Oonagh Hepburn and her mother came again and they went and sat in your place."

"I suppose," said Mrs. Fielding, "that Oonagh, knowing we were away, just thought they wouldn't be turning anybody else out."

"You told them last Sunday about the visitors' pews, Mrs. Fielding," Matron said indignantly. "They shouldn't have come to the hen-coop at all, and nobody *ever* sits in your place. It looked terrible. Mrs. Pearson-Smith went and said something but they didn't move."

Mrs. Fielding laughed. "Well it doesn't matter," she said. "I don't mind who sits in my place. It was rather stupid, perhaps, to go to the hen-coop again but it's no worse than that."

Matron, however, was not prepared to dismiss the offence so lightly. "I don't suppose you do mind, Mrs. Fielding," she persisted, "but it was the same as if Higgins or somebody went and sat in the Headmaster's stall and—"

"It isn't really the same, you know. There's nothing official about my place."

"It's the position," said Matron. "When I saw that girl sitting there and remembered how she used to carry on—"

"That's a long time ago," Mrs. Fielding said quickly. "She is really doing a useful job—and it won't be long till Miss Wills is back. How long, do you think? They're keeping her in hospital for a fortnight."

Matron, successfully deflected, became professional. "It was the day before the boys came back—the Thursday," she said and counted on her fingers; "Friday, Saturday, Sunday—This is the eleventh day. Well—I should think she'd be all right in another two weeks or a bit more."

"We mustn't let her start too soon," said Mrs. Fielding getting up to go.

Matron said "No," rather reluctantly as she also stood up and added, "Of course she'll be fretting to get back—" She hesitated and her eyes met Mrs. Fielding's. "I don't want to fuss about Oonagh Hepburn, Mrs. Fielding," she said, apologetic but unconvinced. "It sounds silly, I know, but people did feel it."

"I know," said Mrs. Fielding. "One does dislike it. But it isn't for long, and," smiling, "it's the spring term, remember."

"That's true," said Matron and laughed.

That cloud had passed, reflected Mrs. Fielding as she went back to the private side. Matron's clouds always did pass as soon as she had said what she thought, but it was extraordinary what passionate hatred was aroused by people who pushed themselves in where they didn't belong. It was one of the School perquisites, of course, that one had rights in it which other people hadn't, and a School peculiarity, or perhaps a more general one, to resent those who refused to stay in their proper places.

As she went through the baize door with the usual squeak and thud, Alison came out of the pantry carrying a tray and said: "Coffee?"

"Well—I had a cup with Matron. Yes, I'll have another."

Alison, pouring out coffee, enquired if Matron's equanimity was restored and then reported: "Mrs. Clayton rang up. She said would you ring back *if convenient.*"

"They aren't cancelling dinner, are they?"

"No, they're looking forward to it." The telephone rang. "Perhaps that's her—"

Mrs. Fielding carried her cup to the telephone and sat down, but it was Mrs. Pearson-Smith's voice which came over the line.

"So sorry to be a nuisance," it said, "but I've forgotten what time you said for this evening."

"As usual," said Mrs. Fielding; the time for School House dinner parties never varied. "Seven-fifteen for seven-thirty."

"Oh—good. Thank you," there was a slightly uneasy laugh. "By the way—have people been getting at you yet about the scene in Chapel yesterday?"

Mrs. Fielding's eyes slid round and saw that Alison was reading *The Times* which she had spread out on the floor. "Chapel?" she said to the telephone in a tone of mild enquiry.

Mrs. Pearson-Smith's voice quacked busily and the Hepburn delinquency was again unfolded. "We were all absolutely taken aback. Nobody really knew *what* to do; whether to ignore it—But we all felt that something should be said—*some* protest—and they—well *I* went and spoke to the woman."

"Oh? And did they move?"

The voice at the other end of the line became impassioned. "*Move!* Indeed they didn't! She—Mrs.—whispered something about disturbance and *knelt down."* Mrs. Fielding bit her lip and there was a short pause. "Annette Courtney," the voice resumed, "wanted something said after the service but," said Mrs. Pearson-Smith impressively, "I said no. In my opinion, I told them, this is a matter for Mrs. Fielding to deal with—or even the Headmaster himself. After all, you did speak to them last Sunday and everybody knows the Chapel isn't for the public."

"Yes," said Mrs. Fielding, dealing with it, "it is tiresome. But the thing is, just for this short time they feel they aren't the public, and the girl is really helping us out. It won't be for long. I think it's better to take as little notice as possible."

The telephone was silent with profound disagreement. "Of course," it said at last, "we all know what the girl is *doing.* Worming herself in—She's wanted to for years and now she's making the most of this very unfortunate—" there was a slight hesitation and then a change of tone. It became almost a mutter. "You know I never repeat gossip, Mrs. Fielding, it isn't my way. But I feel you ought to know—She—the girl—was seen yesterday afternoon being taken home in a car by Angus Cameron and young Selby—" the voice dropped even lower, "—*quite drunk.*"

"Dear me," said Mrs. Fielding. "How did you—?"

"It was my matron. She was visiting her sister-in-law who lives opposite. They saw the whole thing. I don't know where they had been—"

There was always somebody who lived opposite or just happened to pass. Mrs. Fielding said levelly: "The Hinton-Briggs had a young lunch party at Thaxley yesterday. Alison was asked." She felt Alison's head come up from *The Times* as she went on: "If it was as you say, the child may have miscalculated—or simply overdone it. So many of them think it's clever—" She changed her voice, giving it a sound of conclusion. "As to the other business I really think it's best to leave it unnoticed. I doubt," drily, "if the religious fervour is of the lasting kind and it would be a pity to fan the flames."

There was a pause and then she smiled as a chuckle came over the wire. "How true," said Mrs. Pearson-Smith. "The dull thud—no reaction—"

"I think so," said Mrs. Fielding.

She immediately went on to call Mrs. Clayton's number. Alison got up and left the room, glancing significantly at the cooling coffee and received a resigned lift of the eyebrows in response. Mrs. Clayton wished to dissociate herself from any protest about the invasion of the hen-coop. She had, she confessed, resented it at the time, but her husband had laughed immoderately and said that the hen-coop was well named. Everybody, she thought, was probably beginning to see the episode in that light. Mrs. Fielding agreed that they probably were; but before she

112

could rise from her chair the telephone rang again. Mrs. Courtney wanted, she said, to apologise. She felt—and Henry had duly rubbed it in—that she had made a serious mistake in asking Oonagh Hepburn to her party.

Her disconsolate voice made Mrs. Fielding laugh outright. "Really, Annette," she said, "I don't think you need take on. Why shouldn't you ask her? It was very nice for her."

"That's what I thought," said Mrs. Courtney. "But you see, they *are* tiresome people and my kind thought let them get a foot in the door—They've asked us to a sherry party. I would just go and ask them back once but Henry *won't*; so I have to tell a lie and leave them brooding over their well-founded suspicions. The girl was rather a trial on Friday, as a matter of fact. Did Alison tell you?"

"No. In what way?"

"Oh—nothing specific, you know. She got a bit high and was a little embarrassing," the voice held distaste and a slight reluctance and then it changed. "I dare say," it added with Mrs. Courtney's plump chuckle, "Alison didn't notice. Her attention was fairly localized. She looked quite enchanting, Mrs. Fielding, and so happy—"

"She had a wonderful party," Mrs. Fielding cut in before any more could be said and when she had replaced the receiver she murmured: "Oh damn—" very quietly, staring out of the window at the thick, swirling snow. How insensitive—indelicate was the out-moded word—could nice, kind people be? She drank her cold coffee and got up as a knock came to the door.

"That pipe in the changing-room, Madam," said Higgins with ghoulish satisfaction. "Frozen again. Solid. I told the

113

Bursar last year *and* the year before, it's false economy, I told him, leaving that pipe the way it is—Should I ring the plumber?"

"I'll do it," said Mrs. Fielding, adding pointedly that it would let Higgins get on, but the telephone rang again before she reached it.

"Mrs. Fielding?" She could not identify the voice immediately. "Leila Hepburn here. It seems we gave great offence to some of your ladies yesterday. It was really rather an unpleasant experience, but I do want to apologise to *you.*" Mrs. Fielding said, "To me?" and the voice flowed on, well rehearsed. "To you. Last Sunday we saw with dismay that we had turned Mrs. Pearson-Smith out of her place, but we thought as you were away—Not realizing, of course, that your place is officially reserved—Quite *royal.*"

"It isn't officially reserved," Mrs. Fielding explained rather coldly, "but it has been the custom for many years for the Headmaster's wife to have that place and we do provide places for visitors."

"Yes, you mentioned that, but—" there was a little laugh, "—the visitors pews! *Rather* bleak and conspicuous—and we're hardly visitors, are we? Oonagh—she was really terribly upset, poor child, and it *was* rather hurting—"

Profound boredom had descended on Mrs. Fielding. "I am sorry," she said, "if Oonagh felt upset, but you know the School Chapel is private and this temporary work she is doing doesn't take her out of reach of her own parish church."

There was a pause. "I am afraid I assumed," said Mrs. Hepburn, "that as she is helping your husband out of a difficult predicament the School would be only too pleased

114

to welcome her. But I know that—well, to *me* friendliness is everything, but I suppose it's a mistake to expect everybody to have the same feelings."

"I think it is a mistake," replied Mrs. Fielding flatly, "to regard the School Chapel as anything but the place where the School meets for worship. But I hope Oonagh has met with no unfriendliness."

She said good-bye and rang off feeling ruffled and dissatisfied with herself. True, she had made only one crack and that quite a small one, but she had failed to smooth things over, and however trifling or even meretricious things were it was usually better to deal with them smoothly. To avoid, in fact, fanning flames.

"I've made an enemy," she told her husband when they were in the drawing-room after lunch and exchanging their first words since breakfast.

"I should have thought," said he realistically, "that you'd rather have Mrs. Hepburn as an enemy than a dear friend. I have been very disagreeable to her daughter this morning so enmity was inevitable anyway, if that's any comfort to you."

"Good," said Mrs. Fielding relieved. "What were you unfriendly to Oonagh about?"

"She was late. Rolled up nearly half an hour after I got back from Chapel. Said she was feeling poorly, which would have touched me more if she hadn't been getting steadily later for the last week."

His wife said: "Well, she may have been feeling poorly, according to Mrs. P-S—"

"Yes," said the Headmaster when he had heard what Mrs. Pearson-Smith's matron saw, "now I think of it that's

115

rather how she looked," and as Alison came into the room carrying the coffee tray he added: "Mr. Barker is away for the night."

This remark was familiar to Alison and it always made her laugh; it expressed with such economy her father's resigned attitude to School gossip and was a relic of his first meeting with it. A very new assistant master in his first job he had been dining with a senior colleague whose wife, as they sped the departing guests, had stared with startled eyes at the house opposite and exclaimed: "Good heavens! Mr. Barker is away for the night!"

"What a long time since I heard Mr. Barker," she said. "I've forgotten how she knew."

"I never discovered," said her father. "I think the landing light was off. Or it may have been on."

Alison spent the early part of the afternoon laying the table for dinner and she was lingering over the finishing touches, since it kept her between dining-room and pantry within certain sound of the door bell, when her mother, pen in hand, came out of the drawing-room.

"Darling," she said, "I can't remember whether the Hinton-Briggs are asked for Wednesday or Thursday. Can you?" Alison didn't think Beak had said which. "Well, will you nip along and ask Oonagh? If it's Wednesday I'll have to cut a meeting."

"All right," said Alison. "Where will you be?"

Mrs. Fielding, faintly surprised, said she would be in the drawing-room of course; she was writing letters; and Alison, satisfied that the bell would not ring unheard, pushed her way through the baize door and went briskly along the passage as the clock struck three.

It was some days since she had been in the office and it struck her that it showed signs of deterioration. So did Oonagh. The room was untidy, less business-like; Oonagh looked bored and slack. She was sitting at the typewriter but there had been no sound of typing.

Alison said "Hullo" and asked her question. Oonagh without a word got up and reaching for an engagement pad licked her thumb and turned over the pages.

"Thursday," she said.

"Thank you," said Alison and, feeling that she could hardly bolt without some further exchange, asked: "Did you enjoy the party?"

Oonagh stared at her coldly. "D'you mean the Courtneys' or yesterday?"

"I meant the Courtneys'. I didn't know there was one yesterday."

"Well, quite honestly I didn't have an awful lot of fun at the Courtneys'," said Oonagh in a disillusioned drawl. "Considering the School owes me quite a lot I don't care to be called 'Miss Er' by Henry Courtney."

This seemed to Alison a minor drawback to an evening's entertainment and she said so, adding encouragingly: "He always sounds rather snooty and nobody could be friendlier than Mrs. Courtney."

"*Mrs. Courtney,*" the words were heavily weighted, "was certainly friendly enough to ask me. I must say I was pretty low on her list when I was there. And I won't say what I think of your cousin Frances Henderson's manners. Everybody makes such a fuss about her looks. I don't see that she's anything special."

"There's nothing wrong with *Frances'* manners," Alison

117

used a little emphasis herself, feeling that she had had about enough of the complaining voice, and Oonagh, who had not sat down again but stood drooping against the table, drew herself up.

"Thanks very much," she said. "My manners get by all right everywhere else." Her face sharpened and became ferret-like and after a brief hesitation she attacked. "Of course," she returned to her drawl, "you were busy weren't you? You and Julie Hinton-Brigg."

"What do you mean?" asked Alison sharply and Oonagh, warming to her theme, went on with an enigmatic smile:

"You wouldn't know, would you. *I'm* all right. When we were at Thaxley yesterday a certain person was asked straight out if he was your boy-friend and there was no hesitation about his reply. I must say I'm sorry for Marthe, but still—That's life, I suppose." She shrugged her shoulders and sat down, summing up inevitably: "When all's said and done it's a rat-race."

Alison, looking at her steadily, said: "You must know perfectly well that you're maundering."

Oonagh, smiling, replied: "Well, dear, we'll see, shan't we?"

There was neither pleasure nor profit to be gained by prolonging the conversation. Alison went away. The baize door squeaked as she pushed it open; as it thudded shut Angus entered by the business door at the far end of the passage behind her.

The snow-storm had got well into its stride. Games and runs were impossible and Angus, with a free afternoon, calculated that 3 o'clock was the best time to go and see Alison. If things went well he could be asked to tea; if they went badly he would have plenty of time to get away.

As he walked across through the snow, it occurred to him that he would rather not ring the private side bell and encounter Higgins again. He had a small but genuine matter to place before the Beak and he could then take the private side on the flank. He plodded on head down, past the private side and entering by the business door called at the secretary's office to make the usual preliminary enquiries.

Oonagh received him coldly. Angus said "Hullo," and yielded to temptation.

"How's the head?"

"I don't know what you mean."

"I was asking kindly if you've got rid of your hangover."

Oonagh was very dignified and much offended. "I would never have believed if anyone had told me, Angus, that you and Tim would ever have behaved like you did yesterday. *Shoving* me into the back of the car—accusing me—Quite honestly I can't forget it. Of course, I know you were both high."

Angus with moderate apology said they had thought she would be more comfortable in the back and passed over the counter-accusation.

"Headmaster in?"

"No."

"Any idea where he is or when he'll be back?"

"I don't know that where he is concerns you. He won't be back before half-past six."

"I might see him in the evening perhaps," said Angus, whose business with the Headmaster was not urgent.

"There's a dinner party this evening."

"Oh—blast. Oh well. Alison in, d'you know?"

Oonagh looked up. "Why ask me? Why not ring the bell and ask Higgins? That's what private visitors do."

"I will," said Angus, regretting the flank attack.

"Actually," said Oonagh, "you'll be wasting your time. Alison's gone with the Beak." She regarded him with unkindly glee. "Seeing her wouldn't get you anywhere, you know. I told you—"

Angus departed, banging the door and she went to the window and watched him trudging past the private side and on towards the gates.

Alison spent the rest of the afternoon beside the good fire in the old nursery listening with lessening hope for the bell. She remembered Tim's strange warning that everything Oonagh said and still more everything she insinuated should be taken with a large pinch of salt, but she could not entirely ignore her. And though the snow meant that Angus was free till tea-time he had not come to natter about Friday, tell her about Sunday at Thaxley and hear about Stoneleigh. She, Alison, had had a grand party on Friday. Doubtless everybody had seen her having it. Nobody must see that she had been simple enough to imagine it meant more than a grand party; and she was not going to join Oonagh in the ranks of girlfriends competing for Angus's favours.

The dinner-party that evening consisted of Mr. Clayton the senior assistant master and his wife, Mr. and Mrs. Pearson-Smith and the Chaplain to balance Alison. The Rev. Humphrey Perry was elderly and rotund with thick spectacles in a strangely twisted gold frame and he was capable of balancing anybody of any age and either sex with equal dexterity. Alison, brought up in a house where visitors were of well-nigh daily occurrence, was aware that social enjoyment may be found outside one's own age-group as well as in it; she could hobnob pleasurably with a 13-year-old new boy or, at the other end of the scale, Lord Leyburn. But this evening Mr. Perry did more than amuse her. He did that certainly—indeed it was all amusement—but as she laughed and talked the uneasy, muddy feeling which she had brought away from Miss Wills' office with Oonagh in it, cleared, and she got up from the dinner-table with restored confidence in honest friendship and good manners.

She too had contributed something to the party, which was one of those routine gatherings, not particularly exciting in themselves, which give people who are working together an opportunity for leisured and sometimes valuable talk, and as she followed her mother out of the room the four men looked after her and smiled.

"She has grown up very nicely," said Mr. Perry and Mr. Clayton remarked that he had never expected her to be so pretty.

"Would it be indiscreet among old friends," enquired Mr. Pearson-Smith, "to speculate on Cameron as a follower? There was something which suggested it to my mind—Ah! Yes, I have it. I went to look at his unnecessary seven-a-sides the other day and Alison was watching, muffled in his sweater. Not entirely without significance, I thought."

Mr. Fielding was used to keeping his reactions to himself. He laughed easily. "She's been muffled up in Cameron's garments on so many occasions," he said. "Their friendship has been too long and too noisy for romance, I fancy."

"She's like Clare was," said Mr. Perry comfortably, "and your Valerie," to Mr. Clayton. "Great friends with them all and very nice it is. I love to see it."

"I thought that was out of date," Mr. Pearson-Smith, having no children of his own, regarded the matter with academic interest only and not very much of that, but he was a relentless talker and went on, solemnly facetious: "I must say it seems to my old-fashioned mind more civilized—and, on the whole, more amusing—than the premature, experimental couplings of the present day. I don't know," glancing at Messrs Fielding and Clayton, "if this instance of survival is to be attributed to superior wisdom in the male parents."

"I don't think the male parents have much to do with it," confessed Mr. Clayton mildly. "Being brought up among boys they're used to them and regard young men as fellow-creatures rather than prey."

The Headmaster merely passed the port without comment and Mr. Pearson-Smith moved on from the modern young woman to the modern young man. Talking of regarding the opposite sex as fair prey, he said with a greyish twinkle at his own wit, little Selby seemed to have the makings of a carnivore.

"Last term I understood him to be devouring that young Swedish girl the Hendersons have with them but I hear that Hinton-Brigg's girl is now the quarry." More than one of the gentlemen listening marvelled anew, less at the efficiency of the grape-vine than the interest aroused in unexpected bosoms by the tit-bits it circulated. "I cannot," he was going on, "bring myself to like that youth."

"Now I do like him," said the Chaplain.

"But then, my dear Perry, it's your professional duty to like him."

"No it isn't. My duty—and yours—is to love him, which is different."

"He's a good physicist," said the Headmaster and Mr. Clayton, a little indignantly, added:

"He's a good appointment. No trouble with discipline; gets on well with the boys and his athletics are useful—"

"He's bumptious," pronounced Mr. Pearson-Smith.

"What were you like at that age P-S?" asked Mr. Perry innocently. Mr. Pearson-Smith joined readily in the laughter.

"Opinionated," he confessed. "But I *think* less vocal. It is, on the whole, a blessing," he went on, ostentatiously addressing nobody, "that appointments rest entirely with the Headmaster. How quarrelsome we should be if we were empowered to discuss the matter and decide it by vote. Autocracy is really very restful when one accepts the judgement of the autocrat."

"I won't say it's restful for the autocrat," said the Headmaster, "but it has the virtue of saving time. Will you help yourself and pass the decanter?"

"Talking of autocrats," said Mr. Perry significantly and there was immediate response. The commonroom had been tearing the Snaydon daily's article to shreds all day. Mr. Clayton said:

"I was afraid of it as soon as I heard old Harris was gone, but he can't be elected yet, can he? I thought May—"

"The significance of election seems to have escaped him," said the Headmaster.

123

"Possibly he thinks of it as a ceremony resembling coronation," Mr. Pearson-Smith suggested. "King Sartha from the moment poor old Harris pegged out; crowning postponed till the better weather. When is he taking over, Headmaster?"

"He proposes Thursday. I explained that it would be as much as my place is worth to treat him as a Governor before he is one, but he—and Lady Hinton-Brigg—are coming to lunch. I thought we'd have a bachelor to round off the party." His glance rested on the Chaplain, who said hastily: "No, Headmaster," and he laughed and said: "Vincent, then."

"Excellent," said Mr. Pearson-Smith with relish. "Quite excellent. A gentlemanly young usher and yet nobody in particular—to the lay eye. Then he can leave early, and if that doesn't work he can come back with an urgent message and rid you of the incubus—for the time being. I am really quite glad that the time of my retirement is near."

"I'm afraid," the Chaplain said sadly, "he'll be a very great nuisance."

"I can't understand," burst from Mr. Clayton, "why that man is allowed. He has no ability, he's disagreeable and his name means nothing, and yet he's getting a position in the county second only to Lord Leyburn. Why? How does he do it?"

Mr. Fielding smiled. "I'm not quite sure," he said getting to his feet. "Shall we go into the drawing-room? No doubt we'll discover."

"I can tell you now, Clayton," said Mr. Pearson-Smith as chairs were pushed back. "His method is simple. He is without scruple or bowels and he can spit further than other men."

7

THE SNOW was sufficient to turn the thoughts of Ledenham away from games and athletics but for a day or two it was tantalizingly undecided. Toboggans and skis were dragged out from store and hopefully examined on Monday only to be thrust back on Tuesday after a night of rain. Tuesday itself was a horrid mixture of frost and thaw with sleet driven by a vicious wind and in the morning Alison, feeling virtuous and tough, went out to fetch fresh supplies of gargle and aspirin for Matron.

It was in this kind of weather at this time of day and this stage of the week that the drawbacks of an indefinite stay at home with nothing particular to do became apparent. The only satisfactory way of getting through cold, wet Mondays and Tuesdays is in doing a job which has to be done and there was no such job for her in Ledenham. Matron, who had thankfully heard Morris pronounced pure and returned him to circulation, now had six mild cases of flu and Baker rather less mild but drove her firmly away from risks of infection. Offers to help with the veg were turned down by her mother on the grounds that the kitchen could manage perfectly well with one short and if given help now would be deeply injured if it was not forthcoming in all similar circumstances in the future. Fetching the gargle and aspirins being the limit of her usefulness, therefore, she was in no hurry to go home and she turned instead into the teeth of the wind and went to have elevenses at Holly Lodge.

Frances' welcome was not, at first, cordial either.

"Haven't you got measles?" she demanded, barring the way.

"No," said Alison. "Something had merely disagreed. He's up."

Frances relaxed. "That's all right then. Come in. I'm in the kitchen."

"Silly mutt," said Alison rudely. "It would have been all right anyway. I don't even know what the boy looks like and I've had all the plagues. It's no good being a fussy mother in a school."

"I'm not fussy at all," retorted the mother with dignity. "Of course John will get all the diseases but I see no point in inviting people to blow germs at him while he's still a baby. Coffee?"

"Please. Where is John? We have got flu in the House."

"He's up in the nursery with Marthe. I don't really mind about the flu," said Frances, confessing to a certain lack of logic. "It's in all the Houses more or less and Patsy is more likely to bring it than anybody—but I'm scared of spots. You make the coffee. I want to get these cakes in."

She turned to the kitchen table and the materials for the excellent substantial fruit cakes which were always ready for droppers in, and Alison took her coat off and set about making coffee.

"Good weekend?" asked Frances and they were off on the intimate, casually allusive talk of cousins who live in the same place and know each other well. Proceeding backwards through the weekend they arrived at the Courtneys' party, but there the conversation took an unexpected turn. Alison, though conscious that she had, perhaps, overestimated the party, still thought of it as an exceptionally good one; Frances, it appeared, did not.

"Not?" said Alison surprised. "Why? What was wrong with it?"

"Well," began Frances, "it was very silly of Annette to ask Oonagh Hepburn—as she now realizes, I may say. And I'm really angry with Tim Selby."

Alison blinked and made a grab at the saucepan as the milk rushed upwards. "Sorry," she said and went to fetch a cloth. "I don't see why Oonagh shouldn't be asked."

"My dear Alison—"

"Wait a minute. I say—I really am sorry about this mess. Are you all right for milk?"

"Perfectly. It doesn't matter. But—"

"Wait," begged Alison and having got the milk under control turned her own mind and Frances' to a serious consideration of Oonagh. "I don't *like* her," she said, "and obviously you don't either; but she lives in Ledenham and she's helping Beak. Why shouldn't she be asked to parties? You couldn't very well *not* ask her could you?"

Frances glanced at her curiously. "You've evidently been giving Oonagh some thought."

"Yes I have," said Alison and there was silence for a moment while Frances pushed her cakes into the oven and set a timing gadget to ring in an hour and a half. Then she sat down beside her cup of coffee and lit a cigarette.

"You said yourself," Alison reminded her, "that Oonagh's been about a lot lately. She knows Marthe and Angus and all of them quite well."

"Yes, I know," Frances agreed. "They're pretty short of girls to run about with and Tim—blast him—dragged her in to make up parties when he was rushing Marthe. Angus," she added a little reluctantly, "seemed to be allotted to her quite often."

"I don't know why you're so furious with Tim," said Alison ignoring Angus, "but one thing at a time perhaps. Let's finish Oonagh off."

"I rather wish we could," confessed Frances. "I'm not quite clear in my mind about this because I dislike her so much but I think the nub is that it doesn't much matter if she runs round with the Zoo boys—they know pretty well how she rates—but if we ask her in it makes her a friend of ours and that, if you get me, alters the rating. She's a horror, Alison. So is her mother. Did you hear about them in Chapel on Sunday?" Alison hadn't and the scene was described to her. "It was too ludicrous," said Frances. "It would have been far better to take no notice but Annette got in a state about it and everybody was hissing—Then Mrs P-S tried to move them—" she stopped and laughed.

"And did they move?"

"Not on your life. Mrs. H. said in a sanctified whisper that it would mean disturbing everybody and sank devoutly to her knees. Poor Mrs. P-S! Routed by piety—" They both laughed and then Alison said:

"I'm surprised that Annette minded. I thought public school snobbery was one of her best jokes."

"So it is, but this isn't snobbery. She doesn't like butters-in any more than the rest of us and she's kicking herself because she says she's pulled Oonagh in boots and all by having her at that party and now we'll never get rid of her without turning her into a martyr."

"Is she really a horror, or just non-likeable?" persisted Alison.

"I think," said Frances, "that she's quite a lot more than

128

non-likeable. If you're worrying about fair play for Oonagh, Alison, don't bother." She hesitated and then with rather an anxious glance at her cousin she went on: "This sounds a loathsome bit of dirt. Perhaps I shouldn't say anything about it, but you might hear it from someone else. I had John out on Sunday afternoon and as we came past the Hepburns' house Tim and Angus were yanking Oonagh out of Tim's car. She—well, she looked disgusting. Tight and a wreck. I don't know where they'd been."

"They were at Thaxley Manor for lunch," said Alison. "Julie asked me and as I couldn't go I suppose she got Oonagh to make the numbers even."

"But—she couldn't have got like that at Thaxley."

"Well she told me yesterday they'd been there."

Alison's voice was expressionless and Frances got up to pour out more coffee. "It looked pretty squalid, I must say," she said without turning round. "I'm afraid I more or less cut the whole party. But there's no use making too much of it. I mean, Angus and Tim were all right and if Oonagh got high at Thaxley they couldn't help it. They'd have to get her home."

"Yes," said Alison. "Well, that seems to conclude Oonagh. What's wrong with Tim?"

"Oh—Tim," Frances shrugged a shoulder and returned with the replenished cups. "When my daughters grow up," she announced unexpectedly, "I intend to chaperone them properly."

Alison exclaimed: "Gosh! Poor things!" and laughed; but though young Mrs. Henderson in her slacks and tartan shirt looked very unlike the conventional picture of a chaperone she was unmoved.

129

"Not poor things at all," she said. "The last thing I want to do is to spoil their fun; I'll simply look after them so that it *is* fun." She sat down again and addressed her cousin earnestly. "As soon as Marthe came in September Tim fell for her. He was always in and out of the house, he kept taking her out—mostly in parties with Oonagh—and by the end of term he was pressing her hard to be engaged to him—"

"And?"

"Well, I think she liked him quite a lot but she was nowhere near ready for that. And I think if they'd been meeting in chaperoned parties it wouldn't have boiled up so fast. If it had—in Victorian days—Patsy would have told him to pipe down for a bit. I did say something to him and he took umbrage. He's never been near us since, and on Friday he bestowed flashing smiles on Marthe and me and went and roared about with Julie Hinton-Brigg."

"Angus told me Marthe had turned him down," said Alison. "He says he's very cut up."

"I'm sure he's cut up. So am I and so is Marthe in a way. But what can one do?"

"It seems to me you'll have to get the subject up before you begin chaperoning the girls."

"Oh I know the subject. The trouble is, one chaperone in the world isn't enough. But you must admit, Alison, that it isn't much fun for a girl to be monopolized by a man so that everybody else is driven off and everybody sees it; then it's over and everybody sees that too."

Alison was uneasily ready to admit it; but she could see no solution to the problem except, as they were talking in Victorian terms, prudence on the part of the individual.

And that was not so simple as it sounded.

"Did you miss being chaperoned?" she asked.

"No, I don't think I did," Frances replied honestly. "But I was mostly in London. It's so conspicuous in a place like this. One thing I *can* say—the gossip never coupled Patsy and me till we were engaged. But that was Patsy—It's much nicer when nobody is watching all the ups and downs."

"So I should think," said Alison.

"I don't quite know what Marthe's feeling," Frances went on after a pause. "She doesn't say anything, but it's a bit drab for her. Patsy and I are going out to dinner tonight; could you come and spend the evening with her? Patsy'll fetch you."

"Of course I will," said Alison.

She said it with genuine pleasure. She had seen a good deal of Marthe in the few weeks since she came home and they had liked each other immediately. There was much to be said for forgetting young men and emotions from time to time; and if she could enliven what was perhaps a drab time for Marthe, Marthe could provide for her a companionship which would be stable in the shifting sands which threatened her footsteps. When she left Holly Lodge the evening with Marthe was pleasantly in her mind, but she was thinking of the shifting sands as she walked along the road towards the Zoo and saw Angus come out.

Angus had had a free period and he was now on his way in to School for the last lesson of the morning carrying a load of notebooks. His headgear was a shabby square, the plywood protruding at the corners and the tassel meagre, and over his mackintosh he wore his gown like a gigantic black muffler. He smiled at Alison over the voluminous folds as he went forward with his customary greeting, but there was a note of question both in the smile and the tone of the "Aye, aye!"

"Aye, aye," responded Alison with great heartiness and the smile gave way to concern.

"What's the matter?" he demanded.

She looked at him and laughed weakly. The shifting sands seemed so unreal, so theatrical and silly in connection with the familiar solidity of the oddly dressed figure before her. "Nothing's the matter, Angus," she said. "I was temporarily in a different world. Frances says she's going to chaperone her daughters when they grow up."

It was one of those careless remarks with which one laughs lightly and which sends the conversation off on gay, inconsequent lines; but in this case it was not successful.

"Oh," said Angus shortly. "Why?"

But Alison was already regretting the remark and was evasive. "Part of a general reconstruction of the social set-up," she said and they walked on.

"Her daughters might have different views, I would think," said Angus, but the bell would ring in a couple of minutes and he had no time for Frances' daughters or the social set-up. "I've been trying to get hold of you ever since Friday," he went on, doing his best to keep any shade of reproach from his voice. "I called on Saturday and had an awful jolt when Higgins said you'd gone—"

"But I told you," said Alison. "Didn't I? I thought—"

"It didn't penetrate. I thought your last words were that we were going to Thaxley on Sunday."

"Oh—" she turned to him, "I'm sorry, Angus. I was afraid

there might be a muddle. There was such a racket going on."

"Well, never mind. It wasn't your fault."

"And you went, so—so that was all right?"

"We went," he agreed. "I wouldn't say it was all right, but at least it cured Tim of your friend Julie."

"She's not a *friend,*" protested Alison, rather nettled at having Julie, of whom it was good that Tim should be cured, pinned on to her in the same breath.

"Your acquaintance then. So then," Angus passed on, "I thought I'd see you yesterday, but you were out."

"Out? I wasn't out. When?" They looked at each other, pausing in their walk.

"In the afternoon. About three."

"But—I was in. Did you ring?"

"No, I didn't ring," he gave her a glance half amused, half sheepish. "Fact was, I didn't want to face Higgins again. I thought I'd get at you sideways. I had a little thing to see the Beak about so I went in that way and Oonagh said you'd gone somewhere with him."

"But," said Alison again and stopped. She remembered the School clock striking three as she went through the baize door after talking to Oonagh but at the same time it occurred to her that it might be better to let it pass. "She must have got it wrong," she said flatly. "Another muddle."

"She was quite definite," said Angus but he too felt that the episode was better left unprobed. He had now resumed contact with Alison and after this curious confusion his object was to get back on the rails, more or less at the point they had reached on Friday, though with caution because of Sykes. "Well, now," he said cheerfully, "the snow. Is it, or isn't it? I think we'll get it. Skis handy?"

"Within reach—not exactly out."

"No good being premature. And another thing—d'ye mind the Ledshire Reel Club?"

"Aye," said Alison, "I mind it fine." Ledshire had succumbed to the prevailing enthusiasm for Scottish dancing just before she went abroad and a growing society met in a regular round of village halls, schools and, occasionally, a large house.

"It's in our gym on Saturday," Angus told her. "Can do?"

She hesitated and hedged slightly. "Have you been going regularly?"

"Oh yes. Hardly ever miss."

"Do you go in a party?"

"Sometimes. A lot of us go. As often as not we just drift in. I'll come for you of course."

"Does Oonagh go?"

"Lord, no! I can't imagine Oonagh—" he stopped suddenly and turned on her. "What's all this, Alison?"

They had reach the point where she went straight on to School House and he turned right to his classroom. They both stood still, unconscious of the cold and of the snow falling on them and Alison was nervously aware of Angus's eyes. Unlike those of the Hepburn ladies they were negligible as features and normally they twinkled, glowed or looked solemn behind his spectacles, pleasant eyes but unobtrusive. They now felt like searchlights. She looked down and drew a pattern in the snow with a foot. The torn black cloth of Angus's cap stirred in the wind.

"Well," she said uncomfortably, "it's only that I've heard you've been taking her to things and I—" this was horrible,

"—well, it would be hard luck if she was left out."

There was a short pause. "How did you know I went to Thaxley?" asked Angus suddenly.

"Oonagh told me yesterday afternoon."

"H'm. Did Frances tell you she saw us bringing her home?"

"Yes, Angus," Alison looked up quickly. "She said she cut you and Tim and now she's sorry."

"Is she? She needn't be; it was pretty squalid. Alison—you and I have been good friends for a long time haven't we?"

"Yes, very good friends," she said without hesitation.

"You'll believe me then, that Oonagh isn't and couldn't be a friend. I've been in parties with her and danced with her. I owe her—absolutely nothing. Do you believe that?" For the third time Alison said "Yes" but Angus went on; "What about Saturday, then? Okay?" and she was back in the shifting sands. Everybody sees—Julie asked straight out if he was your boy-friend and—It's *awful,* cried Alison's heart, when people watch—

"Angus," she said miserably, "I think I won't. I might—might just turn up. Marthe might come—"

Angus was looking at her steadily. "Alison," he said, "what *is* this? What have I done? Is there somebody—"

The bell burst out in violent, intolerable clamour. Suddenly boys were everywhere, running through the snow from Main School to science block, to the library. She shook her head hopelessly. Angus raised his battered cap and plunged into the crowd.

Alison went home. Presently she trailed after her mother into hall and took her place at the high table. The aesthetic

135

prefect who usually sat opposite had vanished—to the sick-room, Butler told her and as she struggled with the excellent boiled beef he glanced at her plate and said: "You're not getting flu, are you, Miss Fielding?"

"Oh no," said Alison, stiffening her spine, but she felt that it wouldn't be a bad thing to get flu. To go to bed with a good excuse to be miserable—

"Are you all right?" asked her mother after lunch. "You're not flu-ish are you?"

"No," she said again, and added truthfully: "I got cold coming home." Her mother said: "Is that all?" and Alison, meeting her look, said: "Actually I met Angus and we had a bit of a—a sort of quarrel."

"I didn't think you and Angus ever quarrelled," Mrs. Fielding's voice was matter of fact. "What got into you both?"

"Well—it was a muddle," said Alison, "rather long and involved. The snappy bit was because he asked me to go the Reel Club and said I wouldn't."

"But why not? I should have thought you'd like to go. It's here isn't it?"

"Yes, and I would like to, but—" she stopped and caught her lip between her teeth then she glanced at her mother and said: "*Mr. Barker.*"

"Oh—" Mrs. Fielding's comprehension was swift and it did not underrate Mr. Barker. "Yes," she said, "it can be a great trial. Very muddying."

"I believe," said Alison, "it might not be a bad idea to press on with the job-hunt."

"Well," said her mother, "of course the job-hunt was going to start anyway. But I think, you know, that it's

136

making too much of Mr. Barker to let it influence your plans or actions—provided there's no other reason for altering them, which I'm sure there isn't." She looked at her daughter's downcast face. "Don't take it too seriously, darling," she added and smiled. "Daddy at his very lowest level said once that 'the Barker's worse than the bite'."

"Haw haw," Alison responded, appropriately hollow.

Angus had swept into School and taught his Upper VIth set with great speed and what seemed to him at the time extraordinary brilliance. He restrained himself from clouting the heads of two worthy youths who failed to keep up; and later, with even greater effort, refrained from assaulting Willie Munro at lunch.

"Angus," Willie began, "are you taking Alison to the Reel Club on Saturday? It's here, you know." Angus barked a negative and with his eyes on his plate went steadily on re-fuelling. "*Aren't* you? I thought you were sure to—Oh *well,*" hope sprang, "I think I'll ask her to come with me."

"Why on earth should she go with you?" demanded Tim.

"If you ask me, Mun-ro," said Mr. Burgoyne, benignly paternal, "you shouldn't venture."

Willie's face fell. "But—why not? I mean—I *know* her well enough—"

"It's not the occasion," Mr. Burgoyne explained. "Alison will roll up to the gym on Saturday—weather permitting which I doubt—escorted by Nick and three or four School House prefects. And I," he continued, "shall immediately rush up and book her for Hamilton House for which I need a reliable partner."

"Whereupon," Tim put in promptly, "you will find that she has already promised it to Butler and intends to devote her evening to boosting the prefects' social morale. It's a black date this."

"Well of course it's very *nice* for the boys being allowed to come," said Willie loyally.

"But even nicer if a squad from some ladies' seminary was imported to balance."

"Ah well," said Mr. Burgoyne, "perhaps in time. We progress, though slowly."

Angus, as soon as the meal was over, marched upstairs to his study and seized the telephone. "Miss Alison," he said firmly to Higgins and waited.

"Hullo?" said Alison's voice at last, rather bleak.

"Alison," he said, "Angus here. Look—I'm sorry. You were quite right about Saturday and I was an ass." There was no reply and he went on anxiously: "Alison—is it all right? I mean—do you accept my apology?"

There was a faint giggle. "Mutt!" said Alison. "Of course," pompously, "I accept your apology. It didn't rate one. But—do you see—" she stopped and he said quickly.

"Yes—I do," and went on: "I hope you're coming on Saturday. Burg wants to book you for Hamilton House. You'll be coming over with Nick and the boys, won't you? Okay?"

"Yes," said Alison. "Okay."

And that, thought Angus as he put down the telephone, was about as good as he could expect. He lit his pipe and sat down in his armchair feeling exhausted and still seething with wrath. His up-bringing in a Scottish manse had not only ingrained in him the habit of telling the truth himself but also the assumption, which was even more of a handicap, that other people would tell it. Experience had soon taught him that it was not a safe assumption but the remnants of it made him, and he recognized it, slow off the mark and proportionately angrier when he arrived. He felt a fool when he remembered how meekly he had allowed himself to be bamboozled by Oonagh yesterday, but though he had never thought very highly of her it surprised and shocked him that she should have lied outright and on such a scale. And why? Vengeance might account for yesterday's whoppers—and if that was her object she had achieved it— but why the Martin Sykes story? If it was a story; she had got hold of the name. And God knew, he concluded gloomily, what she had thought up to tell Alison about him.

At three o'clock he woke up with a start as Tim came into the room.

"Aren't you going over to the gym?" he asked. "Your chaps are there now—Been asleep, have you?"

Angus, looking at his watch, swore and struggled to his feet. "Hell! How did I go right out like that? I'll get over now—"

"No hurry," said Tim. "The Sergeant's there."

"Have your lot done their stint?" Strenuous circuit training in the gym was a means of keeping footballers and athletes in condition when the weather made outdoor exercise impossible and as Angus supervised and encouraged the footballers, Tim urged on the athletes.

"Some of them," he said now, rather glumly. "Secker didn't turn up—in fact nobody from Pearson-Smith's. This voluntary training isn't such a good idea in my view."

"I don't think you could make it compulsory," said Angus. "It usually works all right—Seckers don't crop up so often."

Tim said: "In that case I'll try school-mastering a little longer. Did I see you talking to Miss Beak this morning? Any echoes from the past?" Angus told him. Frances, though shaken at the time, now pitied more than she blamed them. "And Miss Beak?" Tim's tone was studiously careless.

"Oh Alison's all right," said Angus flatly.

Just before seven that evening Patsy Henderson called for Alison with his car.

"You shouldn't have bothered," she said, climbing in. "It's no distance."

"Far enough to get wet," said Patsy. "Don't stir till we get back and I'll bring you home. We won't be late."

"Where are you going?" Alison asked carelessly. "I see you're dressed up smart."

Patsy's reply was equally casual: "Going to the Bishop's," but it struck her that there was more than his usual economy of speech, and she refrained from further questions.

"I've never got as high as dinner," she remarked, "but their parties were always very lavish. They might have asked you at more clement season," and they went on to talk about the roads.

Frances was ready, also smartly dressed and also, Alison noticed slightly preoccupied. "Make yourselves comfortable," she told the girls. "Remember the sherry, Marthe," and they drove away at once.

"And now," said Marthe, smiling, "we also have a party."

When she had joined them in the kitchen that morning after the baby had gone to sleep, Alison had thought that

140

she looked as if she was having what Frances called rather a drab time. It was always a composed face and always a pale one but both the composure and the clear skin had altered a little, as though the sun had not shone on her lately. This evening she was alight again, as pleased to have Alison's company as Alison was to have hers.

"I thought it would be nice," she was saying, "—Frances thought you would like it—to have supper in here by the fire. So I have made us a meal almost like Norwegian."

"Lovely," said Alison and was moved to quick compassion by the 'almost like Norwegian', "Oh Marthe, do you get homesick? I was *terribly* sometimes in Italy."

"Sometimes, yes. It must be," said Marthe. "They are so kind, Frances and everybody. It is very good to be here. But—"

"You want your own people from time to time."

"Yes—it is very far. Sherry for you?"

Alison said "Please" and went on talking rather hurriedly. "I don't think I've ever drunk sherry—or any other intoxicant—with just another girl before."

"No? I think for me too it is the first time," said Marthe. "It is very—what is this word?—mancipated?"

"Emancipated. It's a wonderful thing," said Alison idiotically, "to be a woman of the world. Travelled— Experienced—"

"Yes indeed," agreed Marthe and held up her glass. "*Skaal!*"

"Cheers," responded Alison.

There are not many greater pleasures than a good, long, uninterrupted talk in comfortable circumstances with a congenial member of one's own sex. They took two and a

141

half hours over their supper. Still talking they carried the things to the kitchen and washed up. Marthe lifted the sleepy baby and dealt with his needs while Alison looked on, and when he was in his cot again they trailed back to the sitting-room and went on from where they had left off. Nothing had been said of immediate personal concerns till Alison asked: "How long are you here for?"

"I came for one year," Marthe replied and frowning a little went on hesitantly: "But—I am not sure—I think perhaps I go home before. After half a year perhaps." She stopped and sat looking at the fire but Alison had an impression that she did not want to close down on the subject; that she would like to talk about it if she could find a way to begin.

"Homesickness?" she suggested, knowing that it could not be the only reason. It was bad enough sometimes but it was not a reason for a girl like Marthe to cut her time in a household as friendly as the Hendersons' by half.

"That a little," said Marthe and then looked up. "But no. It not true to say that. It is that I have been very mistaken."

"Mistaken?"

"That is the wrong word perhaps? I mean I have not been clever."

Alison thought it would be best to plunge. "Do you mean about Tim Selby?" she asked.

"You have heard it, then?" Marthe looked rueful. "I suppose everybody—"

"Frances told me a little," Alison said quickly. "And Angus, who is a very old friend and a friend of Tim's too. That was all. Angus just said that you had turned Tim down and Tim is very cut up—I mean unhappy about it."

142

"Oh—" said Marthe. She made a small, hopeless gesture. "It was too difficult. I would like to tell you—"

"Tell me anything you like. I'm quite safe."

"I am sure. You see Tim was very kind, very friendly, at once when I came. I liked him very much. But then he began to say he was in love with me, and that I did not like."

"You mean you didn't think you were going to be in love with him?"

"I mean that I think he is one who likes being in love."

"But I think he meant it."

"Well—he said so. He asked me to marry him. But I am nineteen and in a foreign country; it is not time for me to think of marrying. And he asked would I go out with him sometimes and I said no. If I go out with him alone it means too much," said Marthe as she had said to Tim himself; and then added something she had not said to him: "Before you came home there was no other girl here but Oonagh. Tim would ask her so that we could have parties— sometimes Angus would come or Willie. But I don't like to go any more with Oonagh. Always she is pretending we are going out to make love. It never happened," added Marthe drily, "but always, I suppose, she hopes."

Alison laughed and made a face of distaste. "So—you cut it out?"

"Yes, I did. So cleverly I did it that Tim did not understand at all and is angry, not with me only but also with Frances. I don't know why."

"It was very difficult for you," said Alison. "I don't see that you could have done any better really." She stopped. Both of them were staring at the fire, both of them

143

thinking how frighteningly easy it is to say or do the wrong thing; how well-nigh impossible to know what is the right thing. "*I* think," Alison went on at last as if they had discussed the matter thoroughly instead of sitting in silence, "that it's best to go straight on and take no notice of muddles or quarrels. Tim is a nice person. I'm sure he doesn't want to make you miserable." She thought of Julie and her voice trailed away.

Marthe looked too as if she might have Julie in mind for a moment, then her face cleared. "It is very nice that you are here," she said and added with her gleam of amusement. "Perhaps after all I do not go at once to look for a boat."

Alison laughed and quoted Oonagh. "It's always easier for two girls than one."

8

ON THURSDAY Sir Arthur and Lady Hinton-Brigg came to lunch at School House.

"I suppose," Mrs. Fielding had suggested without much hope, "it would hardly do to take them into hall."

Her husband shuddered. "It would not," he said. "The chap would get up and make a speech." So the party was arranged with a view to amiable flatness which it was hoped might prevent Sir Arthur from getting steam up. Alison would be there—of right—and her presence and that of Nick Vincent, who was not only a gentlemanly young usher but an astute aide, should ensure freedom from attack at any rate during lunch. That an attack was inevitable Mr. Fielding had no doubt; the declared purpose of the visit was to break in to the School and its affairs; but every moment's delay in the launching was something gained.

More snow fell on Wednesday and Mrs. Fielding's hopes rose. But it was reported on Thursday morning that they were managing to keep the roads fairly clear and a few minutes before 1 o'clock a chauffeur-driven Rolls Royce drew up at the door and the Hinton-Briggs alighted. The Headmaster never hung about waiting for arrivals. Mrs. Fielding did the hanging about, not without occasional complaint, while her husband went on with whatever he was doing till he was informed that guests were actually in the house and did not always hurry then. The Hinton-Briggs, therefore admitted by Higgins were received by Mrs. Fielding and Alison and had begun drinking sherry before the host appeared.

Sir Arthur was a large man whose well-made body had thickened with the years in so uniform a fashion that he was still shapely; a fine, if beefy, figure of a man. He had been fortunate too in keeping his hair—somebody had remarked spitefully that there was plenty of muck below its roots—and as he had never suffered from any kind of doubt, confidence clothed him, an impenetrable armour The only sign of mortality and a lifetime of doing himself too well was in his complexion which at its best was dusky red with a network of veins and at its worst a terrifying navy blue.

Lady Hinton-Brigg also had her armour but it was less easy to define. She was a pale, slender woman with well-bred face and hands and a sleek patina of expensive upkeep which in itself made her beautiful. Her clothes were exquisite and her jewels magnificent, but no woman ever grudged Lady Hinton-Brigg her clothes and her diamonds when they looked at her controlled face and small rather friendly smile.

The Fieldings and the Hinton-Briggs met from time to time at county functions or in other people's houses but Mrs. Fielding' contacts with Sir Arthur had hitherto been limited to the V.I.P. handshake which moves you on to make way for the next in the queue. Now, as his hostess and with no more important lady present she was accorded all his attention; the bend, the smile—gracious but rather vaguely aimed, the courteous murmur. Alison received the handshake, unleavened.

"It's years since I saw the School," Lady Hinton-Brigg with her smile said to Mrs. Fielding. "A family of cousins were here and we used to come to things then. You really have a delightful house."

"Charming," pronounced Sir Arthur, inspecting the School House drawing-room. "Furnished by the Governors, I suppose. What is the financial arrangement? Do you pay rent?"

The furniture, Mrs. Fielding replied politely, was their own and she was relieved from the necessity of explaining the nature of the financial arrangement by the entrance of her husband.

The Headmaster greeted Lady Hinton-Brigg and turned to shake hands with his embryo Governor. He was as tall a man as Sir Arthur but he had grown thin instead of thick and he stooped a little. His hair, whatever the reason, was less and spectacles with heavy horn rims made it difficult to read his expression.

"Very good of you to come over in this weather," he said to Sir Arthur. "How are the roads?" and he pursued the snow till Nick Vincent appeared and was presented.

Sir Arthur stared at the young man as though mystified and rather offended by his presence and as the young man received a glass of sherry from Alison and joined in the ladies' conversation, he turned to the Headmaster.

"I—a—You understand, of course, Headmaster, that I am here in order to have a talk with you—a—officially?" Mr. Fielding replied genially that he was looking forward to their talk but geniality was not enough. He was drawn aside. "I have no doubt you understand me. When I undertake new responsibilities I always insist on being given the picture fully and at once. I am a busy man as you know, but I am never an inactive member of a committee.

Of course most of your Governors are well known to me. Leyburn is an old friend. Leyburn and I are very intimate."

"You have seen Lord Leyburn since the nomination was made?"

"No. No, oddly enough I haven't. I—a—he's away, I fancy. I think he told me something was coming up in the Lords. Something he's interested in. I saw Craig. Craig is—naturally, I suppose—very important about the election formality." There was an amused, slightly pitying smile. "One expects one's Clerk to be punctilious. He makes a great thing of it—nonsense, of course."

"Well," said the Headmaster, "it is largely formal but there is a certain reality about it. You are not, in fact, a member of the Governing Body until they have elected you."

"Oh yes," said Sir Arthur. "I am appointed by the Snaydon people. Their nomination is decisive. You're wrong. Just as Craig is. However I told Craig I intended to go ahead and get the data. One can do nothing without the data—and he referred me to you. Said you could tell me more about the School than anybody."

Mr. Fielding, duly chalking it up against his friend the Clerk, replied readily. "Certainly," he said, "I can tell you a great deal about the School."

"Shall we have lunch?" said Mrs. Fielding.

It appeared to Alison that very little would be required of her at this party. Conversation, if not general, would fall into two sections between her mother and Sir Arthur on her left, Lady Hinton-Brigg and her father on her right with Nick, who was seated between the two ladies, giving a push where required. But they had hardly begun their soup before disaster befell her.

"Julie was so delighted to meet you again at the Courtneys' the other evening, Alison," said Lady Hinton-Brigg smiling at her across the table. "She tells me you've been abroad."

Yes, said Alison, she had been abroad and she had, of course been delighted to meet Julie again.

"And it was so nice," added Lady Hinton-Brigg, "that you were able to come over to lunch with her on Sunday. I hope—"

"But—I wasn't. I mean—" Alison, aware that she was yammering, coloured, "Julie asked me, very kindly, but I couldn't go. I—"

She was about to embark on explanations about Stoneleigh but Sir Arthur beside her flung up his head and stared at her and Lady Hinton-Brigg cut in.

"Oh—of course," she was saying lightly, charmingly apologetic. "Julie did tell me. She'd asked you and you couldn't. Another girl—I've forgotten for the moment—"

Alison, still feeling hot, perceived with a further rise in temperature that Julie's mum was gagging. She said: "Oonagh Hepburn," quickly and Lady Hinton-Brigg neatly picked it up.

"Yes—Oonagh came instead—"

"What's this?" demanded Sir Arthur. "A lunch party on Sunday? I heard nothing about it."

"Didn't you?" said his wife. "I thought you were there when Julie was talking about it—In any case," she smiled again at Alison, "it wasn't very important."

"Who was there? Was Cuthbert—?"

The blood of the Fieldings and Nick ran cold. Sir

Arthur's tone was formidable; there was a threat, unmistakable and terrifying, of a marital row. But Lady Hinton-Brigg maintained her poise. She gave a little laugh and said, again, addressing Alison;

"I've made one mistake, haven't I? I'd better confess frankly that I'm not sure now who did come. I expect Cubby was there—" and she added to Mrs. Fielding: "You probably find too, there are so many young creatures coming and going—"

Sir Arthur turned to Alison. "Do you know who did me the honour of lunching at my house on Sunday?" he asked. But Alison had recovered and, no longer abashed, she was resentful.

"I wasn't there, you know," she explained clearly. "Julie invited me and I couldn't go."

"I think I heard," remarked her father in his genial social voice, "that two of our young men were of the party." He smiled at Lady Hinton-Brigg. "We are always delighted when we hear of invitations for them from our neighbours and at the same time we feel complacently that we do confer some benefit on the neighbours. They are, taking them by and large, agreeable young men. You agree, Vincent, don't you?"

"Certainly," said Mr. Vincent promptly. "At least, sir, I agree whole-heartedly with the first part. It would hardly become me to do more than simper with regard to the second."

Lady Hinton-Brigg laughed. "I assure you both," she said, "that Ledenham's agreeable young men have always been appreciated to the full in Ledshire society."

"I am not aware," said Sir Arthur, "that I am acquainted

with any of them. I know Courtney; but one could not call him young."

When the lunch-time hazards had been more or less successfully negotiated Sir Arthur reminded the Headmaster that they had important matters to discuss. "You will excuse us, Mrs. Fielding, I am sure," he said, turning courteously to his hostess. "A man as busy as I am can very rarely escape from the pressure of affairs. Now, Headmaster, we'll just—"

They withdrew. A few minutes later Nick and Alison followed them from the room, parting in the hall with a silent pantomime of shattered nerves, and the two ladies were left to a gentle, impersonal *tête-à-tête* which they both found more than tolerable.

In the study the interview went, at first, very well. Sir Arthur had eaten a good lunch, he was smoking a good cigar and he sat in a comfortable chair listening with glazed eyes while the Headmaster recited Ledenham's entry in the Public Schools Year Book. There were at this date 514 boys in the School, he said, and went on to give the number of assistant masters and the height to which the fees had regrettably risen. Nicely into his stride he described the curriculum and the organization of forms and subjects. "The scholars and the brightest of the non-scholar entry go straight into the Vth and take Ordinary Level at the end of their first year. Normally in eight or nine subjects. From there they go to the Remove and—"

But this was not, apparently the kind of data for which Sir Arthur thirsted. He grew restless. "Quite so," he said, stirring in his comfortable chair. "All that, of course, is your province. It does not—at present—concern me. Perhaps it

151

will save time if you give me the answers to a few questions. The number of boys tells me nothing. Is the School full?"

The Headmaster replied that the School was full and its waiting list healthy. Then that his staff of assistant masters was satisfactory and the School's record in scholarship and games reasonably good. Sir Arthur expressed gratification and passed on.

"You have been here for a good many years, I understand. Nearly eighteen? Yes—I suppose you would be unlikely to find anything much better. What is your salary?"

Mr. Fielding looked at him and smiled. "Nothing on earth," he said, "would induce me to speak of that with any single Governor, Sir Arthur."

There was a slight gaping pause. "But they must all know it."

"No doubt they all know it."

"Then I can't see your objection. Naturally your own salary and those of the assistant masters are matters upon which I expect to be informed."

"That information will be given you by Lord Leyburn. Or," the Headmaster remembered his debt, "the Clerk."

"I have already told you that the Clerk referred me to you. That, I take it, is tantamount to instructing you to answer any questions I may ask you."

"The Clerk never sends me instructions. I am most ready to tell you anything which I may properly tell you, but salaries are—"

"I think," said Sir Arthur, "that you may leave it to me to judge what is proper."

"I am afraid," returned the Headmaster, "that with all respect I may not."

There was a short disagreeable silence. Sir Arthur's face grew dark and he thrust his chin forward aggressively.

"Do you mean to say," he began, but Mr. Fielding interrupted him. He would give away no confidential information but he did not intend, if he could avoid it, to quarrel with Sir Arthur.

"I am sure you understand my position," he said and was about to enter into some explanation of his position when it occurred to him that it would certainly be difficult and that a meaning glance might suffice. He added the meaning glance. Sir Arthur received it blankly, but as he groped for understanding the pressure eased a little.

"Er—of course," he said. "As one of your Governors I fancy I am entitled to require full co-operation from you but these matters—Matters of finance are hardly your concern."

Mr. Fielding, meekly accepting this view, hoped that the meeting was drawing to a close but he was disappointed. Sir Arthur wished, he said, to make a very thorough inspection of the School; and he wished to meet—inspection was again implied—the assistant masters. It would be best, he suggested, that the Headmaster should arrange a sherry party, or perhaps two, for this purpose. The Headmaster gave himself a little time for reflection by pushing the cigars across to his visitor and lighting a cigarette. Only a fool could go so far in misinterpreting his own position as this. Such inflated self-importance was almost pathologically foolish. And yet nobody could be more dangerous than a fool.

"Sir Arthur," he began carefully, "I cannot, of course, speak for all schools but I can tell you the customs of this one and of its Governing Body. Any Governor is a welcome guest at any time. They are invited as a matter of course to all School functions and I am glad to say they come when they can. But there has never been anything in the nature of an inspection of the School by a Governor and it is quite contrary to custom to assemble the assistant masters especially to meet one Governor. The May meeting takes place in the School and you will meet the staff at tea on that day."

"I have never," replied Sir Arthur deliberately, "been a sheep. I use my own judgement. I go my own way. The habits of other members of the Governing Body do not greatly concern me."

"Then I can only say with regret that I can make no departure from the normal practice without authority from the Governing Body through the Chairman."

Sir Arthur in his turn took his time. He allowed his displeasure to be felt but he contemplated his newly lit cigar with a faint smile which put the gentleman who defied him in his place.

"Mr.—a—Fielding," he said, "you don't, as yet, know me very well. I am not accustomed to having my decisions questioned nor my wishes set aside. However, matters will no doubt be adjusted. Now there is one further point. Mr. Secker, who is a Director of one of our subsidiary companies, informs me that his son has, in very peculiar circumstances, been displaced from one of the School teams. The XV I think I am right in saying. Possibly you have some satisfactory explanation?"

154

"I think so," said Mr. Fielding. "Did Mr. Secker intend to make a formal complaint? He has said nothing to us."

"Formal?" Sir Arthur pursed his lips. "Well the complaint was not submitted to me in writing. Nothing of that sort. But I certainly took it as having been made with sufficient formality and I assured Mr. Secker that I would deal with it."

"In that case," said Mr. Fielding briskly, "perhaps you will be good enough to let me have the details in writing." As he spoke the telephone on his desk buzzed discreetly and he picked it up. "Yes?" he said. "Yes—in five minutes." He glanced at his watch and smiled at his guest. "I'm afraid that—"

"Good God!" Sir Arthur consulted his own watch and the engagements of Headmasters were as naught. He struggled up from the comfortable chair and surged along the passage to the private side. His farewells were brief. He was displeased and he was making no secret of it. "Is Sharpe there?" he enquired very loudly of nobody in particular, and hustling his wife before him he entered the Rolls and was driven away.

In the car Lady Hinton-Brigg leant back in her corner and looked straight before her but she was perfectly conscious of storm signals by her side. Her husband sat bolt upright and there were movements which were familiar; thrustings forward of the chin, easing of the neck as if from a too-tight collar.

"That man," he said at last, "has been there too long. And old Leyburn's past it. Lost grip. There will have to be changes, as I fancy," with a short laugh, "they foresee. This fellow—like Craig—was in a great hurry to inform me that

I am not yet a Governor."

"Well," said Lady Hinton-Brigg, "you aren't, are you?" At the Fieldings' table her voice, when she spoke to her husband, had been not absolutely conciliatory, perhaps, but certainly soothing. Now it was merely cold. "I don't see," she added, "how even you can be a Governor before you're elected."

"My dear Cynthia, you know nothing about it," was the reply.

"You seem to be in a minority of one in your interpretation."

"Wha'? Nonsense! It's perfectly clear. I shall see Leyburn. They will find that I know my way about. Now—perhaps you will explain this luncheon affair of Julie's. Why was it kept from me?"

Lady Hinton-Brigg, ignoring his accusing stare, took out her cigarette case. "Nothing was kept from you, Arthur," she said and flicking on a little gold lighter she lit her cigarette and inhaled deliberately. "Julie simply had a few youngsters to lunch."

"Fielding said two of his men, and there was this girl—who was *she?*"

"I really don't know. Somebody she met at the Courtneys'."

"That means Cuthbert Lucreton was *not* there."

"Very likely not."

"I simply cannot understand you," declared Sir Arthur, almost more puzzled than angry. "You know my wishes. You have always known my intentions in the matter of this understanding with Cuthbert Lucreton. It has been—virtually—settled for a very long time. Lucreton approves—naturally. More than approves. Cuthbert himself is anxious for the marriage—"

"But Julie isn't."

"Julie is an idiot. She doesn't know what she wants."

"She knows what she doesn't want, though," said Julie's mother. "She doesn't—at present—want to marry Cubby. And I don't see that you can make her marry him. It would be quite wrong to try. Leave her alone and—"

"Leave her alone? That is exactly what's wrong with the young people of today. Parents have abdicated. They shirk their responsibilities. As you are doing. I am not prepared to abandon my proper authority."

"All the same," Lady Hinton-Brigg moved a little to reach the ash-tray, "you can't—in these days—force a girl into a marriage she doesn't want. You'll make a great mistake if you try it."

"You're quite wrong," said Sir Arthur. "There is no question of force. Cuthbert is a thoroughly acceptable young man. His position is excellent. If you will only do your duty as her mother Julie will give no trouble. I expect your co-operation. Am I to have it?"

There was no reply for a moment. Lady Hinton-Brigg sat looking with unseeing eyes at the smart young chauffeur's ears, smoking her cigarette and thinking about her husband and her daughter. There was very little to choose between them in the matter of obstinacy or of egotism.

"I ask you again," said her husband, "do you intend to co-operate with me?"

"Yes," she turned to face him. "On the whole—yes, I think so. Julie," drily, "is quite alive to the advantages of the marriage and I should say she likes Cubby as—"

"I wish you wouldn't use that absurd nickname."

"—Cuthbert, then, which is even more absurd—I should say she likes him as much as anybody. But I must say, Arthur, that she would be more likely to marry him if she thought we were against it. You'd better leave her alone."

"You're quite wrong," said Sir Arthur with finality. "I shall see her at once."

He did not see his daughter at once because she had driven her own small car to Snaydon which contained friends and cinemas, but the interview took place that evening. Julie was determined but when she was tackled about the Sunday lunch-party she was handicapped by her uncertainty as to the extent of her parents' knowledge. She did her best, however, fighting every step of the way.

"I thought," said Lady Hinton-Brigg, whose tone was almost casual, "that Alison Fielding was coming—"

"How did you—"

"—but we were there today and she told us—"

"Oh, I see. Well I *asked* her and then she—" She tried a last-minute cancellation by Alison but finding that untenable fell back another step. "You see the thing was, I'd got Tim Selby and Angus Cameron coming—as a matter of fact *I* thought the Cameron was her boy-friend but it seems he isn't—well, and so I thought I'd better get hold of another girl and I saw this Oonagh Thing and asked her. That's really all."

"Why did you ask these young men in the first place?" demanded her father who had been listening with suspicion to the rather garbled explanation. "We don't know them. Why not Cuthbert and some of your friends?"

"Why not ask them?" Julie countered with spirit. "Why

should I always be stuck with Cubby and that lot?"

"Because," he explained patiently as to an idiot, "however worthy and respectable these young people may be they are not of our own class. Furthermore, Cuthbert has a right to object to your entertaining other men in his absence."

Julie flung up her head, an inherited gesture. "Cubby Lucreton has *no rights over me,*" she cried loudly. "I've told you before. I *hate* Cubby." She took a deep breath. "I'm going to marry Tim Selby."

9

A PASSING Roman Catholic who had lived in the Zoo for one term had left his mark upon it in the form of fish for lunch on Fridays. Friday. Lunch? Fish, stop, ran Delia's mind. Then moving on; Dinner? Poor things they had fish for lunch; and liver and bacon with syrup tart to follow adjusted the balance. But on the Friday following the Hinton-Briggs' visit to Ledenham while his colleagues tucked in to liver and bacon, Tim Selby was setting out to drive to Thaxley Manor, resplendent in white tie and tails.

He was rather reluctant and very empty. His appetite for pleasure, healthy and appropriate to his age, had lost its edge since Marthe Jensen turned him down. He could still smile and talk, he could flirt with Julie Hinton-Brigg and he could eat and drink and smoke; but he had been given a new view of pleasure, a glimpse of a new heaven and a new earth, and had little zest for many things that had pleased him well enough before he saw Marthe. He seemed, too, to have lost the first ebullience of youth. Hitherto, no matter how hard his day's work he had had energy for a strenuous evening—he had never even thought about it. To-night he was conscious that Friday was the heaviest day in his time-table and he resented the snowy, treacherous roads as peevishly, he told himself, as an old man.

He pushed his car along as fast as conditions allowed. Ten miles to Thaxley, five miles on to Snaydon; not too much time and in any case he couldn't catch up with dinner too soon. Melancholy rumblings already threatened and, embarrassment apart, the inner gentleman must have sustenance before anything convincing in the way of social merriment could emerge. The car skidded unpleasantly at the gates of the Manor and, muttering crossly about sand, he turned in and bumped and slithered up the drive which had been imperfectly cleared.

"Good evening," he said rather crisply to the cynical manservant who opened the door. "Is Miss Hinton-Brigg ready?"

"If you will come in, sir, I will enquire," was the reply, very smoothly uttered and he was ushered into the hall. It was very hot and the scent of the hyacinths, which was oppressive, reminded him sourly of Sunday. If Julie kept him waiting more than two minutes his collar would subside into a clammy rope round his neck and he was already feeling that he could quite easily be sick if he thought about it.

"Perhaps, sir, I should take your coat," suggested the man. "Miss Julie may be a little time and I believe Sartha wishes to see you."

"Very well," said Tim and as he yielded up his outer garments he met an eye in which expectant and inquisitive glee was not altogether concealed.

He was shown into the drawing-room. "Mr. Selby, m'lady," announced the butler, if he was a butler, and Lady Hinton-Brigg, who was alone in the room, got up from a chair beside the fire and came forward.

Tim had never seen either of Julie's parents before. Her mother's unmistakable air of breeding surprised him slightly and he knew enough to appreciate the elegance of the slim black dress, the pearls and the perfection of finish. She was holding out her hand to him with her small friendly smile.

"How do you do, Mr. Selby," she said. "What a horrible drive you must have had. Come and have some sherry— And a cigarette?"

"Thank you," said Tim. He was not sure if the sherry was altogether a good idea in view of his emptiness and the drive to Snaydon ahead, but it might placate the ravening wolf within and he had seldom wanted a drink more. One glass—He accepted it thankfully and lit Lady Hinton-Brigg's cigarette and his own.

"Mr. Selby," she began immediately and rather hurriedly, "I'm afraid Julie is a very naughty girl." He looked at her questioningly and she went on: "The truth of the matter is that she is more or less engaged to Cubby—that is Cuthbert Lucreton. I think you met him at the Courtneys'—"

"I did meet him," said Tim, "but—"

"Yes. Well—Julie is—has been rather silly and—and quarrelsome lately and I'm afraid she has, quite unforgivably, made use of you to irritate Cub—Cuthbert. I can't tell you how ashamed of her I am, and I'm sure she will be ashamed of herself when she comes to her senses."

Lady Hinton-Brigg stopped, sounding a little as though she was short of breath. They had not sat down and Tim placed his glass, hardly broached, carefully on the mantelpiece.

"I don't in the least mind being used," he said, "but I didn't know that Julie was engaged. If I've irritated Lucreton it was unintentional. I had no idea of getting in his way."

"Of course you hadn't," said Lady Hinton-Brigg. "It is entirely Julie's fault. As I say, she is really being very

162

naughty and tiresome. But—of course—"

"I suppose this evening's—" he boggled equally at the words engagement and date which were the only ones that occurred to him and she went on:

"I'm afraid—yes. This evening's off. Finish your sherry, Mr. Selby, won't you? Let me give you some more."

He thanked her and drank the sherry but refused to have more. "It will be some time before I eat," he said, and remembering about food he realized that he really was far away from it, both in distance and time. The Hinton-Briggs might have rung him up and saved him from discomfort and bad roads. Lady Hinton-Brigg looked as if the same idea might have crossed her mind.

"My tiresome Julie!" she said apologetically. "I really am so very sorry, Mr. Selby. I'm sure the kindest thing I can do is to send you away at once to have your dinner and—if you can—forget this annoyance. My husband thought he ought to see you, but I don't think—"

Tim was quite sure there was no need for him to see Sir Arthur; at dinner the night before Nick Vincent had been eloquent about the newly nominated Governor. And he would prefer not to encounter Julie. She had rung him up yesterday afternoon and the enthusiasm which had reached him over the wires made it clear that the motive power for this broken date was not her own. There was a feeling of bread and water about, and if a thwarted Julie broke loose she was capable of creating on a formidable scale. He thanked Lady Hinton-Brigg and said that he would not trouble Sir Arthur.

"Then I won't keep you another minute," she said. "Good-bye, Mr. Selby. Thank you for being so charitable."

She held her hand out again. "You have my most profound—"

The door opened and she broke off, dropping her hand, as a woman burst in; not Julie, as Tim had instantly feared, but an elderly woman, eager and clumsy. She had a large face with a vague, underhung jaw, and her hair, her dangling earrings and her beads had a look of the raffish twenties, greatly decayed. But over these and a lamentable flowered silk dress she wore triumphantly the mantle of Sir Arthur's grandeur.

"Sartha will see the young man now, Lady Hinton-Brigg," she announced, tremendously important.

"Oh—I don't think there's any need," said Lady Hinton-Brigg's light voice. "Tell Sir Arthur Mr. Selby is just going, Miss Foley. I have explained—"

"Sartha's waiting, Lady Hinton-Brigg."

Sir Arthur's wife gave up; surprisingly, Tim thought. Why didn't she bite this hag? "Very well," she said and turned away. He bowed, and following the plunging figure of Miss Foley glanced back from the door, but he saw only a rigidly upright back.

"Mr.—Selby, is it?" said Miss Foley sharply as she led the way across the hall.

"Yes," he snapped, full of hatred, and caught sight of the cynical man hovering.

Miss Foley's movements, as she approached the presence, became cautious. She crept up to the door, keeping an eye on the handle in case it should squeak as she turned it, and edged in to the room, beckoning Tim in with her.

"Mr.—Selby, Sartha," she murmured reverently and tip-toeing across the room left it by another door which she closed noiselessly behind her.

Sir Arthur took no notice. Except for the excessively efficient heating the library at Thaxley Manor was just as it had been in the days of Lady Hinton-Brigg's father; even the large, flat-topped desk at which the present owner now sat had been written on by him when writing was unavoidable. It was, like the drawing-room, beautiful, a dignified, gracious room; and it was very quiet with only a purring from the log fire and the subdued tick of a fine old clock to give comfort to the silence. The master of the house was in a dinner-jacket and sat smoking a cigar and staring at the papers in front of him.

Tim, observing him curiously and with no lessening of hatred, used the word staring deliberately. Nobody, he thought, looking at that face could imagine that the man was reading. Mental age six with a low I.Q. was his assessment and he was now witnessing a Great Man Act, crude in conception and in performance pure ham. Sir Arthur raised his cigar to his lips with a large hand and lowered it absently to the desk again. Tim looked at the clock, looked at his watch and moved towards the door. The great man lifted his head briefly and said: "Wait."

Sir Arthur Hinton-Brigg's rudeness was exceptional and notorious but a good many men feel that they may be as rude as they choose to a man who is young and in the main the young men display a surprising degree of well-mannered self-control. Tim thought of asking "Why?" and departing on the tag, but upbringing prevailed. He paused, the paper was—presumably—read, and Sir Arthur leant back in his chair ready to deal with him.

"Your name's Selby, I believe."

165

"Yes."

"Master at Ledenham, aren't you?"

"Yes."

"Anybody ever teach you to say 'sir'?"

"Certainly," said Tim. Upbringing was all very well.

"Very well," Sir Arthur's tone said that insolence had been noted. "One of the new type of masters, I take it. In my opinion the public schools should keep to public school men. However—I understand that you had arranged to dine and dance with my daughter this evening. The arrangement is cancelled."

"So Lady Hinton-Brigg told me."

Sir Arthur had a way in conflict of pausing for a moment, assembling his greatness so that he was almost visibly inflated. By some people it was observed with terrified dismay; Mr. Fielding observing it had reminded himself that nobody is more dangerous than a fool, but Tim, quick to see the folly, was not experienced enough to be aware of the danger. The crack about public school types had rather cheered him and he did not try very hard to control his expression.

"Now," said Sir Arthur, "I don't propose to keep you long but it is necessary that you should understand the position."

"It isn't very difficult, is it?" said Tim injudiciously. "Your daughter arranged to come out with me. She is not coming. That's all, I think."

"Not quite, Mr. Selby," Sir Arthur's face had darkened. "You would be well advised to keep your temper and hear what I have to say. Miss Hinton-Brigg is engaged to be married to the son of a very old friend, Lord Lucreton, whose name you may possibly know. I do not intend that

166

Lord Lucreton and his family or my own family should be annoyed by your attempts to pursue Miss Hinton-Brigg. Wait!" Tim had opened his mouth to speak and the large hand was raised. "I have very little more to say. Simply this. You will make no further attempt to see Miss Hinton-Brigg. I shall have a sharp watch kept on you and if there is any more of this annoyance I shall know what steps to take. That is all."

Tim knew that the wisest thing he could do was to leave the room and the house without another word, refusing to let the episode touch him. He had no feeling for Julie, indeed he had already made up his mind to see no more of her, and the threats were absurd as well as empty. But they were threats and Sir Arthur, back in his act, was returning to his papers with elaborate unconcern. He had dealt with a nuisance and forgotten it. It seemed to Tim absolutely wrong, unthinkable, that a man should get away with that degree of bullying folly.

"Sir Arthur Hinton-Brigg," he said, "you are offensive." The head was flung up. "You owe me an apology and I hope you will make it. I have had a slight, agreeable acquaintance with your daughter, no more, and I resent extremely your allegations of misbehaviour." He stopped and, as he stood returning his accuser's stare, part of his agile mind sniggered at him that he had caught the infection of pomposity. The pure young man, erect and proud in the face of injustice.

Injustice rose slowly to its feet, a massive six foot two.

"Mister Selby," said Sir Arthur, "do you know who I am?"

Tim was conscious that he was three inches short and a

167

ton or so light if physical violence broke out but that part of him which was watching the scene was overcome by its absurdity. Outraged dignity advanced towards him and he laughed aloud.

There was an incredulous pause then a short bellow of rage. Sir Arthur plunged at his desk and began ringing bells. The door on the far side of the room flew open to admit Miss Foley swooping and clucking, and at the other door the manservant appeared, startled out of his cynical decorum.

"Whatever—oh goodness!—oh Sartha—are you—" gabbled Miss Foley.

"Pigeon!" roared Sir Arthur. "Turn this man out of the house. Instantly. I have never heard such insolence— *You*—" turning savagely on Tim, "—you'll hear more of this. Do you know that I am a magistrate? Do you know that I am a Governor of the School? I will have you dismissed—"

"You would be well advised to keep your temper," said Tim and left the room.

The hall seemed extraordinarily quiet and the drawing-room door was shut. The cynical man, still a good deal shaken, brought his coat.

"It don't do no good to cross Sartha," he said, looking at the young fool with bolting eyes and added severely: "and it's not right as he should be crossed. Not in his position."

"I dare say not," said Tim. "Thanks. G'night."

It was snowing heavily, fine, hard, determined snow. He had been in that horrible house, he supposed, for less than an hour but his car was white. He got out a pair of old gloves and a leather and cleared the windscreen while the

168

snow drove against him stinging his face; then he set off cautiously to drive the ten miles home to Ledenham.

Two and a half hours later he stumbled into the Zoo.

"Oh hullo!" said Willie, whose study commanded the door and who was a popper-out by nature. "It's you, is it? I thought you were at a da—"

"Go away," growled Tim struggling out of his coat.

"Good Lord! You're wet—you're soaking! You haven't had an accident, have you? You're shivering."

"So would you be shivering if you'd been crawling through a blizzard on an empty stomach."

"Haven't you had dinner?"

"Nothing since the fish."

"Good lord! You'd better have some whisky and I'll get you something." Everybody in the Zoo bought whisky for use in emergencies but when emergencies arose Willie was the only man who ever had any and there were times when his eagerness to do good to his fellow men came in handy.

"Bovril would be better," observed Mr. Burgoyne who had come out of the other ground floor study to see what the commotion was about.

"Grrrrr!" said Tim.

"Bovril *would* be good," agreed Willie. "I'll get it. Better have some whisky first though," and he bustled away.

Angus joining in from above advised a hot bath. "Water's boiling," he said. "Come and eat in my room. I'll make the fire up—"

Twenty minutes later Tim, in his dressing-gown with Angus's—a hairy affair in some obscure tartan—on top, was seated beside a roaring fire and since Willie had trustingly brought the bottle everybody was having a spot of emergency whisky. Willie appeared, his tongue out, and carefully put down a loaded tray.

"Cup's a bit too full," he said. "Oh—sorry. It has slopped a bit I'm afraid. I've made you an omelet. Three."

"Every home should contain a boy scout," said Mr. Burgoyne, lounging comfortably against Angus's table with a noisome pipe in his mouth. "One, not more."

"What's the top mark for scouts?" asked Tim gratefully.

"Oh—rot," said Willie.

Angus put the kettle on to brew up the inevitable tea and they all watched while Tim rapidly disposed of the bovril, the omelet and a large hunk of pork pie, throwing out instalments of his story as he ate. "Couldn't see a yard. Didn't actually stick—Off the, road twice on the flat bit— Ten miles an hour—Gor—that man!"

"Unpleasant," said Burgoyne, "but you may as well forget it. You don't feel that something rare and wonderful has passed from your life, do you?"

"Meaning Julie? No." Finished with the solids Tim lit a cigarette and leant back, a steaming cup of tea beside him. "But all the same I don't know about forgetting it." He hesitated and looked sternly at Willie. "Now look here, you're not to go babbling this all round the place."

"I don't babble," protested Willie, stung.

"You babble."

"Not when I know it's private."

"Well—mind you don't. This swine—he'd have the law on me if he could. I don't know if you can be had up for cheeking a knight and a magistrate and a Governor."

Burgoyne laughed. "Could Eton have him up for likening one of its alumni to a grammar school type? Don't be an ass.

The chap may be a swine—in fact it's common knowledge—but he won't be such a fool as to—"

"All I can say, Burg, is—you're not acquainted with him."

"No, thank God. But—"

"I wouldn't think," said Angus, "that there's anything in the law idea, even for that chap. He might bung in a rocket to the Beak."

"Yes," said Tim. There was a short silence.

"It's a pity you said anything really," Willie said sadly.

Mr. Burgoyne took his pipe out of his mouth and looked at it. "It's almost always a pity to say anything," he remarked, "but—"

"All right, Burg."

"—but the Beak's a man who makes his own decisions. He can estimate the relevance of a rocket from Hinton-Brigg at least as well as you can."

Tim said, "I suppose so," and Angus picked up the tea-pot and refilled cups. He was concerned for Tim but he could not see that it would do any good to burke the facts. Tim had said too many things that would have been better left unsaid and though nobody denied that he was, or would be, good at his job several people had reason to resent his unguarded tongue.

"I don't know," he said woodenly, "if the Beak has to take any notice of Governors if they complain."

Nobody knew much about Governors. Burgoyne, who was older than the others and the only man present who had taught in another school before coming to Ledenham, hazarded a guess.

"So far as I know the Govs have nothing to do with the

staff. The Beak's entirely responsible."

"But in the case of a specific complaint?"

"That I wouldn't know. All I can say is—the Beak can tell a hawk from a heron and he's a very fair judge."

Tim sighed. "Well, that's something, I suppose."

"It's a great deal."

"You just keep your mouth shut till the end of term, Tim," said Angus.

"Why limit it to the end of term?" enquired Burgoyne, heaving himself upright. "Cheer up," he added more encouragingly to Tim. "You're quite a good little physicist and any scientist has some scarcity value in these days. All is not lost. Go to bed."

Willie Munro got to his feet and as a matter of course collected Tim's supper things and carrying them downstairs to the kitchen washed them up and put them tidily away. From one of the top floor rooms came the sounds of a flute played softly; in the other Mr. Lawson wrote to his girl. Outside the snow grew deeper in a curious, rather sinister silence. Tim, warmed, fed and cared for, lay in bed, too tired to sleep at once. When he closed his eyes he still saw his headlights against the thick wall of driving snow and felt himself peering and straining.

He had, he thought dejectedly, made a hell of a hash of Ledenham. It was true, as Burgoyne said, that the Beak was a just man and a shrewd judge and he, Tim, still couldn't accept the possibility of saying nothing and letting a bully ride over you. But there it was—the bully was a Governor, powerful and a fool, and for the first time he saw the danger of fools. And it wasn't as if the unspeakable Sartha was the whole of it. Of course he had been quick to mock people who didn't like being mocked, careless and conceited in common-room affairs; a good enough physicist and a failure as a man living with other men. A failure, too, in the thing that mattered most. Against the insistent snow he saw Marthe's face as she declared that she wouldn't even go out with him any more, and he rolled over in bed and let despair close over him.

Like Tim Lady Hinton-Brigg was over-tired. As his closed eyes went on peering through snow, her ears still heard in the silence of her bedroom the clatter and uproar of the scene which had followed his departure. Julie sobbing and storming, shrieking defiance to over-top Sir Arthur's furious shouts and, until Lady Hinton-Brigg herself got rid of her unsuitable presence, Miss Foley yapping like a Pekingese on the edge of the scene.

She drew a curtain aside and with hands cupped like blinkers looked out at the snow. Thaxley's geographical position made it easily isolated by a snow-storm, a circumstance which Sir Arthur's power had so far failed to rectify, and she wondered what the effect would be if they were snow-bound now. She was not very hopeful. Her husband's wrath was never cooled by time. It stayed at its original heat till the object of it was removed or punished. And Julie would not slacken in her efforts to get her way till she got it, or, alternatively, till something new distracted her attention. All the same, thought Lady Hinton-Brigg, it would be a lull. The prospect of being cooped up with her infuriated relatives did not trouble her. Julie would stay in her own rooms with television and glossy magazines, her husband would dictate endlessly to Miss Foley and for herself she valued nothing more than solitude.

She had not yet reached the stage when she could be still and she lit another cigarette and walked about her warm, luxurious room. She had liked the look of Tim Selby and she wondered if he had got safely back to Ledenham, and, putting aside the thought of what her father would have said about a hungry boy being sent away from Thaxley unfed to drive ten miles through a blizzard, she wondered what this ludicrous business would do to him. Arthur would undoubtedly carry out his threat to write to the Headmaster and probably the Governors. She paused in her walk and staring at the fire saw first the calm, authoritative face of Mr. Fielding and then the bristling terrier-like figure of Lord Leyburn. Separately and together they were a tough proposition and she sighed, seeing a time of noise and disturbance ahead.

But she did not dwell on it for long. It was not her custom to discuss her husband even with herself. She would have a hot bath. With leisurely care she took off her jewels. She hung up the slim black dress and thought of a visit to London, Paris too, perhaps, to see about clothes for spring. She went through to her bathroom and deliberately enjoyed the hot water, the scent of her bath-salts and then the soft warm towels. The brushing of her hair, the ritual care of her face and hands absorbed her and then there was her bed. She made sure that everything she might want was on the table beside it; books, cigarettes, hot milk in a thermos jug. There were sleeping tablets too but she hardly expected to need one. The clamour and the shouting had, for the time being, passed. Soothed by her solitude and her exquisite comfort, Lady Hinton-Brigg got into bed.

10

NEXT morning the snow lay deep and crisp and even over Ledshire. The sun came out with coy, self-conscious smiles, adding sparkle to the scene without warmth to blur the precise tracery of the trees or unburden telephone wires, and Ledenham looked very beautiful. It had been, on the whole, a good-natured storm; there was no drifting to speak of and the roads, though difficult in places, were nowhere impassable, but even the most amiable fall of snow emphasizes the gulf between those who are responsible adults and those who are not. The Ledenham masters were not indifferent to beauty and there would be, for some of them, fun to be had with the snow but that would come later. The boys were demoralized. Even sensible persons who could normally be counted on to behave with sufficient decorum went suddenly wild, using the edge-and-trip technique to send their brethren headlong into the snow, snatching the odd handful to throw or thrust down unguarded necks; and authority's task was to keep its thumb on the bottle, to control the effervescence till the morning's work was done and it could be given its head.

"Thank God," said Nick Vincent as he entered the common-room at break, "we're more than half through. Lunch fifteen minutes early, chaps, and they can go and get it out of their systems."

"It won't be much good," observed Angus who was pouring coffee from a huge steaming jug. "Too soft. Here—"

"Thanks," said Nick accepting a cup. "I don't mind whether it's soft or hard so long as they get rid of their lunacy." He drank some coffee and lit a cigarette and became more charitable. "They're not doing too badly I suppose. Good, clean fun—Hullo! Anything wrong?"

Mr. Richards had come in to the room looking startlingly pale and trembling visibly. Heads turned and Angus hastily poured another cup of coffee.

"Here you are," he said. "What's up, Rick? Got flu?"

Richards sorted out his breathing. "Had a b-bloody riot," he muttered and horribly conscious that the attention of the common room was on him he took the cup from Angus and put it down hurriedly before his shaking hand spilt its contents. Nick asked "What happened?" and he went on: "My lower VIth set—They were all sniggering when I went in—had trouble with them before—been bad since the beginning—Secker started whistling 'Sheep may safely graze' and—"

The inmates of the Zoo bit their lips but their amusement was involuntary and passed when the voice of Mr. Pearson-Smith was instantly raised. It was one of his boys who had been named.

"Of course it's a grave offence to whistle in School," he said humorously. "But there is the snow, and if they are going to whistle it is, perhaps, less offensive to whistle Bach than pop."

"But," cried Willie Munro, wide-eyed and indignant, "you don't understand, P.-S. 'Sheep may safely' is Richards' *piece*. I mean," explaining it fully, "it's what he always plays on his flute."

"Oh I *see*," Mr. Pearson-Smith was greatly entertained.

"But they wouldn't know that. Richards'—a—performances are private, I take it. They wouldn't mean it personally—"

"Even I, with less than *one* year's experience, couldn't swallow that one," said Tim.

Mr. Pearson-Smith's amused smile faded. "There is no evidence at all," he began coldly, but Richards, reminding everyone that even a worm will turn, attacked.

"I don't know what you mean by evidence," he said with the courage of despair, "but I've been taking that set for two terms and I know what it's like. Of course it was personal. It's always personal. And I've reported Secker to you before. If *you* won't deal with him I'll—I'll go to the Beak. I won't go on like this."

"My dear Richards," Mr. Pearson-Smith's tone changed again, this time to patience and formal apology, "I am extremely sorry that a boy in my House should be troublesome to you. The fact is, of course, that Secker, poor lad, has had a very bad blow and, quite naturally, he is trying—without being conscious that he is doing it—to assert his individuality. To reassure himself. They don't always," with an understanding smile, "choose the best way of doing it, but he's really a very nice boy. I'll speak to him and I'm sure—"

"I wouldn't have thought," observed Angus at his most wooden, "that even his mother would have found Secker a very nice boy at present."

"I agree," said Tim. "I also take Secker—both for physics and athletics—and I have also reported him to you, Pearson-Smith, more than once. The time for 'speaking to him' is past, in my view."

"Your complaints, Selby, have mostly been concerned with his failure to attend for circuit training. May I remind you that it is a voluntary activity?"

"It's voluntary in the sense that he needn't undertake it," said Nick before Tim could reply. "As he arranged with Selby to do it he must turn up. That's accepted, isn't it—?" he glanced round, "—in every voluntary activity from the choir down. You can't have people drifting in and out."

"I can only say again," said Mr. Pearson-Smith stiffly, "that I am exceedingly sorry that Secker is being troublesome. It does not surprise me and I am confident that the phase will pass if I am permitted to handle it as I, knowing the boy, think best."

There was a pause into which burst the clamour of the bell.

"I am now going to take Secker's set," said Tim before anyone else moved. He picked up his books. "And I declare before you all that if he tries anything on with me I'll act."

A dull flush stained the pale scholarly face of Secker's House-master. "If you touch that boy," he said furiously, "or any other boy in my House, I shall report you to the Headmaster instantly."

"And I'll report," retorted Tim, equally angry, "that if a Housemaster won't discipline his boys other people must."

"I'm out this period," said Richards suddenly. "I'll go over to my room for a bit," and he followed Tim out.

"*Really,*" exclaimed Pearson-Smith as they went, "they're very poor quality these young men. All this cry for discipline—it's simply a confession of weakness—" he looked round the men left in the room and met the eyes of Patsy Henderson.

"I don't think," said Patsy, "that they're much different from any other young men. If I were you I'd beat Secker for this Richards episode."

"I have no intention of beating him, I assure you."

"Well, somebody will lay violent hands on him if you don't." Patsy collected his books and on his way to the door paused. "Bad thing," he said, "for a chap to take a swipe at a boy. Give him six P.-S., and there'll be no more trouble."

But even if the advice would have been taken, which was unlikely, it was too late. Secker was enjoying a gratifying success in his rôle of nuisance. The baiting of Mr. Richards had provided really ripe comedy; the whistling of 'Sheep'—a work so frequently rendered in various arrangements by various incompetent musicians that it was funny anyway; the sharp rebuke; the elaborate apologies; the voice from the back—"Sir, would you say the flute is a *difficult* instrument?"—the mounting row—Secker felt himself inspired. Selby was admittedly a tougher proposition than the soft-voiced flautist but Richards had really been too easy. As Mr. Selby entered the laboratory he smiled at his friends and addressed him sunnily.

"Sir," he held up a large, dilapidated bun, "will you excuse me if I eat this now? I just got in a short circuit during break—" There was a sound like a pistol shot. Secker's eyes filled with tears of pain and astonishment.

"Get out your notebooks," said Mr. Selby into the silence.

At Thaxley Manor the gulf between the responsible and the irresponsible seemed to the chauffeur to yawn between himself and his employer. Though the roads were not impassable no experienced motorist went out unless his journey was really necessary and when he was ordered to take out the Land Rover and drive to Ledenham to deliver a letter to the Headmaster he did not mince his words.

"A letter!" he cried, staring incredulously at the plump envelope in Pigeon's hand. "A *letter!* I ask you! Invitation to tea, I suppose Why the . . . couldn't the . . . old so-and-so ring up? Wires ain' down."

"Yours not to reason why, Eric," replied Pigeon, rather pleased than otherwise that his colleague should be subjected to hardship "What's in that little billy-doo would just about fuse the whole system if I mistake not. The Foley played it on her machine fit to bust. Quivering all over, she was, with the expression she put into it."

"What's cooking, then?" asked Eric, interested in spite of himself.

Pigeon smiled. He liked an audience. "Young Julie," he explained, "is having an affair de coor with one of the school-teachers. Smart little cock—came over here last night and cheeked Sartha; dunno who he thinks he is, I'm sure. So this here what you've got's a complaint to his boss. You're to bring back an answer, and if you ask me the lad's had it. The Swan's a decent enough house if you've long to wait—"

"Gor!" said Eric and trudged off to shovel the snow away from the garage doors.

Sir Arthur provided a smart uniform—a livery, he liked to call it—and he believed that his well set up young chauffeur wore it at all times when on duty; but he was wrong. In Eric's opinion a Rolls demanded a uniform, nothing else looked right, and in a different way Sartha and her ladyship also demanded it, but he was not in favour of it for its own sake. When the Land Rover drew up at the sight of the porter's uniform at the Ledenham School gates it was not a neat peaked cap which he thrust out of the window but a round one, knitted in red and white with an exuberant pom-pom on top.

"Got a letter for the boss," said Eric. "What do I do with it?"

Hacket did not approve of easy-mannered young chaps with pom-poms but they are among the things we have to put up with today. "The Headmaster," he said, just giving a hint of the proper way to talk, "is in School at the present. He won't be out—" he took his watch from his pocket, "—let me see—Saturday—not for another hour. Not long gone in to tell you the truth. Take it to that door," he pointed to School House, "not the near door, the fire door. Go in, turn right and you'll see a door marked 'Enquiries'. Seckertary's office. She'll see he gets it."

"Ta," said Eric and drove on.

Life had been very stale for Oonagh for the last week. She was not, as the Headmaster had observed, a stayer. When the novelty of a new job wore off she flagged and the high hopes with which she had embarked on this one were not being fulfilled. Her mother, she considered, had muddled things so that it was hardly worth while going to Chapel any more and in any case though Chapel had paid one dividend in the form of the Courtneys' party, it had done nothing for her since. She was, in fact, merely the temporary secretary.

The Headmaster's correspondence, however, provided occasional interest and it had sent her along to the private side in search of Alison this morning as soon as Alison's father was safely in School.

"The Reel Club is in the gym tonight, isn't it?" she began. "Do you mind if I go along with you? Or—who are you going with?"

Considering the tone of their last conversation and the machinations subsequently revealed Alison thought this was rather much. Fortunately there was an easy way out.

"I'm going across with Nick and the boys," she said. "Are you a member of the club?"

"No, but—"

"Neither am I. I'm going as a guest myself so I'm afraid I can't take you."

"What about those boys?" asked Oonagh sharply. "Are *they* members?"

"No. The club invites them when it meets here."

"Then I don't see—Who *are* members? Angus is, isn't he?"

"You could try Angus."

Oonagh hesitated. It would be nice to know if Alison and Angus had got together and sorted Monday afternoon out, but Alison's face and voice gave nothing away. It might be worth while to draw her fire. She assumed a look of amusement and her drawl.

"I quite thought," she said, "that Angus would be taking you to *this*. Is it," she laughed, "all over between you?"

She succeeded in drawing fire but not the shot she expected. Alison met her eyes.

"One thing is over anyway," she said coolly, looking a good deal like her father. "I'm rather busy. And aren't you meant to be in the office?"

Oonagh grabbed at the tail of her mistake. "Oh Alison!"

she cried. "Don't be so—Can't you take a joke?"

Alison apparently couldn't. Oonagh went back to her office and was brooding over the scene when Eric knocked at the door.

"Come in," she shouted crossly.

Eric padded in and her eyes widened. As the message of the pom-pom, the sheepskin-lined wind-cheater and the flying boots got home they widened further and the corners of her tight little mouth rose slowly.

"Hullo—*ullo,*" said Eric. Responding to the wide eyes he swept the cap off and attractive ridges of hair were revealed. "Been wondering all along the road what I was coming for," he said. "Now I know."

"And who," demanded Oonagh, smartly on her cue, "might *you* be, may I ask?"

Eric said he was the man she had been looking for all her life and then thought it best, before the scene went further, to produce his employer's letter. "Brought despatches for your boss, before I forget," he said and handed the plump envelope over.

Oonagh looked at it. "The Headmaster, Ledenham School," Miss Foley had typed, and then, *appassionato;* "URGENT. From *Sir Arthur Hinton-Brigg. By hand.*"

"It says urgent," she said, "but he won't be back for—" she glanced at Miss Wills' clock but as she never remembered to wind it up it said unhelpfully 6-47.

A muscular wrist shot out of the wind-cheater and Eric said: "Quarter to twelve."

"Oh—well, he won't be back till half-past. What should I—Do you know what it's about?"

"We-ell," he grinned, showing excellent teeth, "I do and

I don't as you might say." He hesitated, rather tempted to air his entertaining knowledge but he knew that talking too much was as sure a way as any of doing yourself no good. "But better safe than sorry," he intensified the grin, making neat use of his refusal. "After all, we haven't known each other so long."

Oonagh put her head on one side and pouted. "Not even a teeny hint? At least," more practically, "you can tell me *how* urgent?"

Not life and death urgent, Eric assured her. He was to wait for a reply and he was in no hurry—now. "Tell you," he said, "I'll slip along and have a spot and a bite. Your old man can give me the doings after. No need to push myself though, is there?"

He sat down, producing cigarettes and dalliance proceeded. They exchanged names and probed warily for information.

"Something," said Oonagh looking archly at the boots, "says RAF to me. Are you, were you?"

"Once on a time," admitted Eric truthfully.

"And now you're with Hinton Brigg?"

"S'right."

Oonagh smiled at him. A hyphen cannot be heard and the significance of this one escaped her. She saw, not the Thaxley Manor garage where Eric was employed by Hinton-Brigg but acres of Works in Snaydon with HINTON BRIGG LTD. in letters of gold eight feet high. She had known other young men with Hinton Brigg and the type ran to rolls of notes and a smooth technique. Eric's technique was well up to standard.

Presently the wrist shot out again and Eric got up.

"Better push along," he said, " 'fore your old man crashes in." He moved slowly towards the table considering the next step. She was the nicest little blonde he'd seen in months and ready to come along, but though Sir Arthur would pay for one lunch for one chauffeur on duty he would not pay for two lunches, and when Eric invested money he liked to be sure of his returns.

"What do you do now?" he asked. Oonagh got off soon after half-past twelve on Saturdays. "What about meeting me for a can?" was the step finally taken. It could lead on or not, according. Oonagh paused to run through her engagements and accepted the invitation.

"Good-o," said Eric and with a brisk, purposeful step moved round the table and kissed her. "Might never get a better chance," he said with the grin full on. "See you, loveliness."

They parted, mutually delighted, and Oonagh, left alone, set about clearing up for the weekend, throwing things into drawers feeling better than she had felt for ages. Why, after all, should she bother with these flats in the School? Granted they led to Thaxley Manor and Little Campion but not one was as glamorous as Eric—this was true—and she did like a boy who got off the mark and had some pep. She giggled, thinking of Eric's speed off the mark. All the same, she wouldn't mind showing Ledenham School that she had other resources, and, the small mouth tightened, especially Alison Fielding.

Alison had not enjoyed her encounter with Oonagh and it left her with a feeling of self-distaste which she felt she hardly deserved. Fair play for Oonagh was a spent cause. It was no sort of duty to make a friend of a girl who spoke and behaved as she had done and, on the whole, it was probably better that the position was clarified. But it was impossible not to feel that she had been damaged. A fortnight ago it would have been incredible that a snowy Saturday should pass without Angus hastening to tell her to get her skis out.

"Nobody seems to be doing anything about this snow," she said to her mother when lunch was so long over that Angus clearly wasn't coming.

"Well, about five hundred boys are storming about in it," said Mrs. Fielding. "It won't be good—far too soft—but they aren't fussy."

"I'm not fussy either," Alison said sadly. "I wonder if Marthe would like to come out."

"Marthe won't be able to," her mother replied. "Frances is coming over here. Why don't you go there?"

She spoke in a slightly remote voice which Alison recognised and accepted without resentment. In private life if a neighbour comes in the daughter of the house may stay and hear all that is said but there were many occasions when the Headmaster's daughter had to make herself scarce. She was a little surprised to be given the hint in connection with Frances and the Bishop's dinner party leapt mysteriously to her mind; but there were plenty of reasons why Frances should come to School House in her official rôle of master's wife and she did not speculate.

"I'll go and see Marthe," she said.

"Would you go first and see Miss Wills?" asked her mother. "I promised yesterday to send her some books."

Miss Wills, who had been released from the hospital two days before, lived in the upper half of a small house in the village and Alison, rather to her surprise, was greeted by her at the top of the stairs.

"Why, you're up and dressed!" she cried. "How well you look. I thought I was coming to see an invalid."

"Not an invalid," said Miss Wills, "I am quite convalescent."

"Was it very painful and horrid?"

"Uncomfortable for the first few days," was the reply and she was ushered in to Miss Wills' sitting-room.

She had never been in it before and she had a suspicion that the owner suffered more from the non-clinical aspect of her illness, the intrusion of her professional life into her privacy, than from the operation itself. She looked exactly as she always looked, an austere grey figure in spectacles; the room, though it was comfortable, was austere too in its meticulous polished order and conversation was not easy.

Miss Wills was pleased, she said, to see Alison and obliged to Mrs. Fielding for the loan of the books. They went on doing their best. It was a handicap, Alison found, that of the few topics on which she could talk to Miss Wills most were for one reason or another taboo. Operations were out because one accepted affliction silently. The School was out. It came under the head of gossip and even the remark that everybody was looking forward to her return or the news that the boys were tobogganing caused a perceptible withdrawal. Alison tried books with more success and the conversation was almost becoming lively when at the sound of a passing car Miss Wills paused to listen and then glanced at the clock.

"I beg your pardon," she said. "I interrupted you—I am expecting my sister this afternoon and the roads are so treacherous I feel a little anxious." She went on to explain that her sister, who was a nurse, had a little time to spare between cases and would spend a few days with her. Alison was delighted to hear it, she had been rather oppressed by the loneliness of convalescence in that neat room.

"How very nice for you," she said warmly. "How is she coming? Not far by road, I hope?"

"Only from Leyburn," said Miss Wills. Another car came along the road. This time it stopped and she got up. "Ah! I think this must be—Mr. Selby very kindly went to Leyburn to meet my sister."

Alison had also got to her feet. "I know Mr. Selby's a friend of yours," she said boldly and wondered if there was a trace of pleasure in Miss Wills' surprise.

"A friend?" she said. "Oh no, not a *friend.* He is a very thoughtful young man. My sister knows him better than I do."

"I mustn't keep you now," said Alison regretfully. The visit had developed on unexpectedly interesting lines.

"As you are here," said Miss Wills, implying that the worst had happened anyway, "I should like my sister to meet you. Unless you are in a hurry?"

She would be very glad, said Alison promptly, to meet Miss Wills' sister and by this time the car doors had banged and noises of arrival, surprisingly loud, were in the house and on the way upstairs.

"Keep it upright, Tim dear, for *heaven's sake,"* shouted a hearty commanding voice. "That's more like it—there's a good boy—*Well,* Addie, *here* we are! Safe and sound and dying for a cup a usual—Let's look at you—"

Alison, lingering tactfully in the sitting-room heard on

the landing the sound of a smacking kiss and the loud voice and the quiet one talking simultaneously and Tim came into the room carrying a pot of hyacinths—carefully upright—and raised an eyebrow at her.

"Hullo, Miss Beak," he said and the sisters were upon them.

"—Alison Fielding," said Miss Wills and Alison's hand was grasped by a large and bountiful Wills who cried, "How do you do, dear. I've heard so much about you all—"

Each member of the Fielding family was passed surprisingly under rapid, knowledgeable review. Compliments were exchanged and the audience was over. "Now, Tim, run along, dear. I'll see you again and thanks ever so much. Good boy—"

"I am most grateful, Mr. Selby. Exceedingly kind—Must you go, Alison? My thanks to your mother—"

In a chorus of thanks and good-byes Alison and Tim were swept downstairs and paused outside to draw breath.

"Lift?" said Tim.

"I'm only going to Holly Lodge."

"Hop in." In the car he lit a cigarette and made a gesture of mopping his brow. "Not a restful woman, Nurse Wills," he said, "though she has most of the virtues."

"A bit of your past?" said Alison, who was considerably entertained.

"From the start. A difficult birth, as she never fails to tell me. My brothers behaved far better—"

Alison laughed. "Well, she did a good job."

"Actually, I believe a wonderful job," said Tim. "We owe a lot to Nurse Wills." As the car moved forward he glanced round with an amused face. "How intimate we've suddenly become," he said, "talking about difficult births. Don't let me be selfish. How was yours?"

"This quite makes up for Miss Wills' refusal to talk about her operation," said Alison. "Mine was unremarkable, so far as I know. Being number three it was probably just a routine affair."

"If it ever is—Holly Lodge, did you say?"

"Yes, but don't bother to go round." She thought he looked extraordinarily tired. "Were the roads awful?"

"It's no bother. No—they weren't so bad. Are you going to see Marthe—or just a general visit?"

"Marthe," said Alison. "Frances is out."

Looking straight ahead he said, "You see quite a lot of Marthe, don't you?"

"Yes. I like her a lot," she answered and there was a silence which she found difficult to break or to leave. "Are you coming to dance reels tonight?" she asked at last.

"Not sure," he said. "I—don't think so."

"Do come, Tim," said Alison. "I—well, it's a good sort of party. I think it would be a good idea."

Tim pulled up at Holly Lodge and turned to look at her. She was a little flushed and her eyes were anxious, afraid that she had taken a liberty and butted in to what was not her business. He smiled suddenly and his face changed to a surprising sweetness.

"You're a very nice person, Miss Beak," he said. "You're a darling. I'm afraid it isn't any good, you know, but—thank you all the same." He picked up one of her hands and slipping the fur glove half off kissed the hand and replaced the glove. "You go ahead and be happy anyway," he added unexpectedly and then quite sternly, "don't let *anything* spoil it."

"What do you mean?" Alison asked. "Why do you say that?"

"Well," he hesitated, staring out through the windscreen, "—I'm all kinds of a fool." He gave her his faint sidelong grin. "Angus will tell you—I talk too much and too soon and almost all of it would be better left unsaid anyway. But—it wasn't only that. I think now that roping Oonagh in was a major error. I thought—you know the sort of thing, another girl would be a good idea and there wasn't anybody else handy—"

"And you think she spoilt things?"

"I'm sure of it. I think she wrecked it for Marthe. She—smeared it.

"But—if you saw that, why—"

"Ah—but I didn't," he turned, speaking quickly. "I didn't spot it at all—not properly—till about the last few days. God!" he put a hand up to his head. "We've only had about a fortnight of this unspeakable term. It feels like a lifetime."

"If you still feel as you did about Marthe," said Alison, wondering if she was now saying something better left unsaid, "I don't think you should give up."

"What I feel about Marthe," said Tim vigorously, "can't be expressed. But she couldn't have been more definite. She didn't leave me a chink."

Marthe and John were taking exercise on the living-room floor when Alison joined them and Marthe pulled John backwards by a leg from under the piano before she greeted her guest. She was smiling, the baby chuckled ecstatically, Alison was sombre.

"You are very solemn," said Marthe. "Is something the

191

matter?"

"I've just been talking to Tim."

"And was that so serious?"

"Yes," said Alison. "Marthe—you're an ass."

Marthe, still holding the baby against her, sat back on her heels. "Often I am an ass," she said, "but can it be explained to me why you say it now?"

Looking down at her kneeling on the floor with the baby's fair head under her chin, Alison thought how lovely she was. When you first saw Marthe you didn't see it, you saw rather a plain, colourless girl very much withdrawn; but as you lived with her it was like living with a lake. There was a fluid changefulness about her looks and, as with the lake, the more familiar you were with her the more you saw the beauty in every change.

"You were wrong about him," she said. "Honestly you were. I don't know what you feel, but nobody will ever love you more than Tim does."

11

WHILE Alison had tea with Marthe and John telephones were busy. Oonagh, looking very sleek after a prolonged lunch with Eric—"No hurry, the old geezer can wait"—rang Mrs. Courtney.

"This is Oonagh," she began. "Listen, Annette—" a tiny pause and then a tiny laugh, "—I do call you, Annette, don't I?"

"I expect so," was the reply, resigned rather than enthusiastic.

"Well, look—it's about the Reel Club tonight. Alison can't take me because she isn't a member, so she suggested I might ask you if I could be your guest—" She waited. Was Annette a member or not? She was, but not, apparently, dying to take a guest.

"Have you done any Scottish dancing?" she asked after a noticeable delay. "The standard is pretty high."

"Well—" another laugh, "—I can get by. I do rather want to come tonight, actually, because I'm really awfully keen and a friend of mine is coming to take me out and we—well, we thought it might be a good thing to join. I haven't before," explained Oonagh, "because of transport, but now—"

Now transport was no longer a difficulty. A new boy-friend. Annette thought fast. She was sure it was a mistake to make a thing of Oonagh. The fact that she—and everyone else—disliked the girl was the worst possible reason for refusing to oblige and if the new boy-friend came up to scratch she would soon, it might be hoped, lose interest in the School. Encourage the affair by all means.

"Very well, Oonagh," she said. "Eight o'clock. You can get yourself there?"

"Oo—yes! Of course we can," the response was exultant. "Heaven! Thanks most terribly, Annette. You *are* sweet to me—"

"Cubby?" said Julie Hinton-Brigg at Thaxley. "Darling— I'm bored. This l*ousy* snow. Look—can you come over and let's go somewhere?"

"Could do," responded Cuthbert Lucreton. "There's nothing much on though. Flick, or something?"

"Well, it's a Reel Club night and I rather thought a spot of exercise wouldn't come amiss."

"Oh," no great enthusiasm. "Where is it?"

"Now where *is* it," Julie echoed. "I've got the thing somewhere—just a sec. while I—Oh, I know. Ledenham." There was a pause. "I thought," she went on cosily, "that we might snatch a bite at Molloy's and go on—just for a bit. We needn't stay if we're bored. You're not scared of the roads, are you?"

Cubby was not exactly scared of the roads, but driving on snow and ice, possibly with fog added, was not his idea of pleasure. He was, however, pursuing Julie, partly because his father was in favour of it and partly because he was as much in love with her as he was ever likely to be in love with anybody.

"Okay," he said.

Tim, as soon as he left Alison at Holly Lodge, went straight home and rang the School House number.

"Selby here, sir," he said. "I'm sorry to disturb you on Saturday, but could I have a word with you any time today?"

"That's all right," said the Headmaster, who had no leisure to be disturbed. "Just let me have a look. I'm fairly solid, I'm afraid. Would latish in the evening do—say nine? But you're probably going to dance reels, aren't you?"

"No, sir," said Tim. "Nine, then. Thank you." The problem of whether to reel or not to reel had, he felt, been decided for him; probably by fate and probably rightly.

The village of Thaxley was so small, dull and isolated that no servants would even consider the Manor unless they were provided with motor transport. It was supposed by Sir Arthur Hinton-Brigg that the respectable middle-aged Ford was driven only by the chauffeur or by the butler in accordance with the ruling laid down when the staff car was first inaugurated, but even in those earlier days everybody who could drive drove it. Several people even learnt on it for Sartha, though a terror, was quite easy to diddle.

Eric, returning from Ledenham several hours later than expected with a very thin envelope from the Headmaster, found an empurpled boss but he had no real difficulty in finding an explanation for his lateness and he managed, before he left, to get permission to use the Land Rover that evening. Standing very straight and speaking with the greatest respect he reported a defect in the car. He could put it right and, Saturday or no Saturday, he would see to it at once.

"And what I thought Sartha, sir, if you're agreeable I

195

could take it 'stead of the Ford s'evening and test it out—"

"Very well—if you're not going far," snapped Sir Arthur who wanted to read Mr. Fielding's meagre letter.

"Oh no, Sartha, thank you, sir," said Eric and left the room with a smart RAF step. It looked good to ask leave occasionally, it made for confidence between employer and employed, but he would have taken the Land Rover anyway. It was better than the Ford if you were taking a girl out—less cramped.

Eric was looking forward to the evening but he was not altogether pleased with Oonagh's idea of going to this dance. He knew nothing about Scotch dancing and though she had assured him that it was really just the same as Old Time, nothing to it, he wished that he had insisted on planning the evening himself, thereby making sure that he stayed on his own ground.

"Now where's this place we're going?" he asked when they had had a drink at the Swan and it was time to move on. "Mind I don't promise we'll stay long. I can think of better ways of enjoying ourselves than Old Time or Scotch or whatever."

"Oh goodness no, we needn't stay long," Oonagh was easy and soothing. "Through the School gates and to the—"

"*What?*" shouted Eric. "Here—what *is* this? It's not a School do is it?"

"No, no, *no,*" she laughed at him. "It's a kind of club—I told you. It just meets here sometimes."

"H'm," said Eric.

The Land Rover was parked beside the other cars outside the gym with an experienced eye to a quick get-away and they went in; Oonagh leading the way with an air of modest assurance, Eric following warily. They were a little late, most of the club was already in the changing room taking off coats and putting on gym shoes and Oonagh went straight to Annette.

"Here I am, Annette," she said sweetly, "and might I introduce—this is Eric."

"Oh hullo," said Annette and nodded in Eric's direction, "Hullo—"

Eric made no reply. He knew Mrs. Courtney. Many a time he had directed the parking of the Courtneys' car at Thaxley and many a time he had driven Sartha and Lady Hinton-Brigg to Little Campion. He saw several people whom he had met in similar circumstances and he was at a loss. If he had analysed his ideas about his place in society, which he was unlikely to do, he would have said that though he had as much right as anybody to go anywhere there were people he could enjoy himself with and people he couldn't, and his employer's friends were of the latter kind. It had never occurred to him for a moment that Oonagh was one of them, all the evidence had been against it, and yet here she was, calling them by their first names, quite at home. It only went to show that you have to be careful who you take up with.

"Alison, this is Eric," she was now saying and as this was a young, rather pretty girl whom he had never seen at Thaxley, he pulled himself together and coped.

"Hi, Alison," he said cordially but he got no further.

"*Guests?*" shouted an authoritative voice in his ear. "*Whose* guests?"

A club whose members are widely scattered and which has no geographical centre has little hope of survival unless it contains at least one fanatic. Miss Iona Macadam was the Ledshire Reel Club's fanatic and if her discipline was harsh and members found themselves dragooned to a greater zeal than they always desired they complained very little. Miss Macadam did all the work and she also demanded—and got—a standard of performance good enough to be enjoyable. So long as she was at the helm there was no danger of the Club's activities degenerating into a boisterous romp or half-hearted pushing and pulling. She looked the guests up and down in the manner of a sergeant inspecting unpromising recruits while Mrs. Courtney admitted responsibility, then she barked:

"H'm. Beginners, of course," Oonagh began her little laugh and deprecating murmur about the Gay Gordons but Miss Macadam was not listening. "Well—we'll have to do our best with them, I suppose, as they're here," she said. "Come along. We'll start with an easy one. Petronella. Hi!" very sharply, "Shoes." She pointed to Oonagh's feet. "You haven't changed."

With the exception of Annette who had withdrawn, feeling it hard that having done a Christian thing which she didn't in the least want to do she should be reproached for it by Iona Macadam, everybody Oonagh knew seemed to be standing about looking at her feet. She glared at their feet in return. Alison and Marthe and all the men wore gym shoes, Miss Macadam, Frances and others wore flat black affairs with rows of neat little peninsulas which contained holes for laces.

"I always dance in heels," she began.

"Not here you don't," said the voice of Angus firmly. "Not one step do you take on the gym floor with those."

There was a loud hoot of laughter from Miss Macadam and at the same moment Butler, the School House prefect, came helpfully forward with a selection of abandoned gym shoes. Eric, looking very sulky, had a fair choice. Oonagh had to take the smallest, dark grey in colour with peeling toe-caps and messily fringed holes. She put on the shameful things and walking flat-footed and awkward into the gym went to join Eric who took no notice of her.

"Sorry," she muttered. "This is a number one flop. Not a bit what they told me. Should we—"

"Better get partners for these people," said Miss Macadam with breezy long-suffering.

"Eric's my—"

"Can't have two duffers together. Mr. Singleton!" the commanding voice rose powerfully on the last syllable. "Take Miss—er, will you? Joy! Miss Scobie," to Eric, "will push *you* through."

Oonagh saw thin fair hair, a nervous smile and a clerical collar. "This way," said the Leyburn curate kindly.

"*Come* along," said an encouraging female voice from the level of Eric's elbow.

Oonagh, overwhelmed by the magnitude of her mistake, suffered herself to be led to the right. Eric was steered by Miss Joy Scobie to the left. He had never in his life felt such a fool and consequently he had never felt so angry. He would have walked out from the changing room leaving his new girl-friend flat if it hadn't been that it would have made him look even sillier. He was going just as soon as this first damn silly dance was finished anyway, and the only question remaining was whether he would leave Oonagh where she was or take her with him in order to wring her little neck.

He was lined up with the other men in the set, facing Miss Scobie in a row of women. The music started with a long chord, there was a lot of bowing at which he glared resentfully. Then the tune began and the four people at the top of the double line of dancers began the diamond figure and he collected himself to watch and listen, having no desire to look sillier than he must when his turn came. He was a very good dancer; he had a quick ear, a quick eye and a well co-ordinated body and by the time the pattern of the dance and the lilting tune had been completed twice he was getting the hang of it. When they had worked their way up to the top and reached the point of action he grinned at Miss Scobie, forgetting that she was a plain, flat-footed little old square with a bun, and plunged manfully in.

"Gee!" he exclaimed when it was over, warm with successful accomplishment. "That wasn't too bad."

"Very good indeed for a beginner," said Miss Scobie.

"Was it really the first time?" asked Alison who had been dancing with Butler in the same set. And when Oonagh looked across the room to resume contact with her Eric he was being coached in the figure of eight by Alison and Marthe while Angus and Butler watched and encouraged.

"Who is that fellow?" Angus asked Butler. "Do you know?" Butler did know. He had had a few minutes chat about the Hinton-Briggs' Rolls with Eric when he was waiting outside School House on Thursday and he had resumed the acquaintanceship with the perfect tact of which a well disposed school boy is a master, ignoring everything except the present moment.

"My male guest is making out better than the female," Annette Courtney remarked to Nick Vincent observing the figure of eight practice.

"Oh," said Nick, "he's your guest, is he?"

His tone was so peculiar that she glanced at him sharply. "He's Oonagh's boy-friend," she said. "What are you laughing at? Do you know who he is?"

Nick, like Butler did know. "Chauffeurs so rarely occur," he explained, "that I was interested to see what sort of chap was ferrying Sartha about for a living."

"Oh *that's* who—I thought I'd seen him somewhere— Oh, Nick!" cried Mrs. Courtney. "What *have* I done? I'll never hear the last of this—Nick—*don't tell Henry!*"

Nick's laughter would no longer be stifled. "I won't tell Henry, but you haven't a hope, you know."

She groaned. "It'll be round the School tomorrow," she agreed.

"And the county the day after that," added Nick mockingly. The Courtneys alone of the School community were assiduous in cultivating county society. Then with a change of tone, "Oh, look! Now what?"

Julie Hinton-Brigg had come tripping into the room followed by Cubby Lucreton and they saw her catch sight of Eric. Eric also saw it. Julie's eyes bulged, her mouth fell open, but she never reached the next stage, the loud exclamations of astonishment. The stare that met hers was so baleful and full of menace that she shut her mouth and flipped a hand in a gesture which mingled greeting and reassurance.

"One mark for Julie," observed Nick, unaware of the undercurrents which had led to the wave. Cubby's was the next exclamation.

"Good God! Julie—there's Sharpe! What the devil—"

"How should *I* know what the devil?" snapped Julie. "What does it matter?"

"Well I think it matters quite a lot." Cubby's reactions were slow but he always remembered that he was the future Lord Lucreton and from time to time the idea of what was due to him poured into his mind and set. To stand up and dance in the same company as the Hinton-Briggs' chauffeur, possibly even grasp that menial hand in his own, was unthinkable. "If you don't mind," he said stiffly, "we'll move on."

"Wait a minute," said Julie and left him. Dodging between dancers who were arranging themselves in sets again she reached Alison and seized her arm. "Alison," she said urgently, "where's Tim?"

"I don't know," replied Alison to whom Tim's absence was a disappointment of another kind. "He isn't coming."

"Is he in his rooms?"

"I wouldn't know."

"If it's Tim you're asking about," Angus beside Alison said coldly, "he's out. Got an appointment."

"Hell and damnation," said Julie and took off again, darting like a snipe across the room to where Oonagh stood suffering.

To Oonagh, Petronella had been no more than humiliating confusion and she had been ready to grovel as much as Eric liked and abandon Ledenham and dignity in a hasty retreat. But her punishment was different. Eric was enjoying himself. They were there for the evening.

"I say, Oonagh," said Julie arriving beside her and then

she broke off to giggle. "I say—I do like your shoes—" Oonagh was silent. Her small mouth was turned down and she was filled with hatred, but Julie having giggled at the shoes noticed nothing else. "Look," she went on hurriedly, "do *you* know where Tim is?"

Oonagh said icily that she had no idea where Tim was. The future Lord Lucreton was approaching and Julie hustled her into the changing room. Inspiration had come with desperation. What she needed was a secret agent in Ledenham, a link and a carrier of messages between Tim and herself.

"Listen," she said this time, "I've *got* to see Tim. Pop's trying to stop it but I'm simply not standing for it. But I can't phone or *anything*—will you help me? I'll give you anything—"

There was a faint reaction. "What?" said Oonagh. "Do you mean money?"

"Well—" Sir Arthur's daughter had thought more on the lines of her cultured pearls or the dance frock she had never liked.

"No. I'm afraid I really couldn't—"

Julie took a deep breath, half terrified and wholly excited. "Well—all right—" They talked fast.

"It's so terribly risky," said Oonagh.

"I don't see what risk there is for *you,*" said Julie but the thing was desperate. "I could manage thirty. I *can't* do more."

"Well—"

"And the pearls."

"All right," said Oonagh. "In notes of course. If you post it tomorrow—no, it's Sunday. Post Monday, I'll get it

Tuesday and I'll see what I can do. Mind I can't promise anything—"

"Oh God!" said Julie. "*Okay*, Cubby, coming—"

Cubby Lucreton's car shot past the Zoo, unrecognising and unrecognised, and disappeared towards Leyburn as Tim emerged to keep his appointment with the Headmaster. It was a still night and very cold, the snow creaking underfoot as he walked. From the gym he heard the sound of music and the rhythmical thud and brush of dancing feet. Hamilton House, he noticed, and wondering if Burgoyne had succeeded in booking Alison he thought of them all in there. Angus, neat and light-footed for all his size, Willie bounding like a ball—Marthe—It felt lonely trudging past on his way to see the Beak with troubles, mistakes and, he supposed, sins like Christian's bundle on his back. It also felt, in an obscure way, rather silly. In the frosty stillness, with stars pricking in the sky and that delicious tune following him he wondered why on earth he was going to see the Beak at all. He was behaving, he thought, like a pompous ass.

The light was on in the study and he went in by the School door to the Saturday evening stir of the House. A distant gramophone was playing *Petrouschka*. Somebody walking along the passage sang, undeterred; "What did Dela—*ware* boys, what did Delaware—" There were smells of coffee and cocoa, the sound of clinking china as night-caps were brewed. A loud voice in a nearby study was telling a funny story, "—so they dug the hole and loaded it on the lorry. But the lorry stalled on the hill and ran backwards and the hole fell off and the lorry fell into it—"

From further off came a sudden laugh, a boy's laugh of sheer, wholehearted amusement, and Tim grinned with involuntary sympathy as he went along and knocked on the study door.

The Headmaster was at his desk writing with great speed but, unlike Sir Arthur Hinton-Brigg, he looked up to greet the caller.

"Just finishing—sit down," he said, and in a moment as he put his pen down, "It's surprising how much there is that a temporary secretary can't—or rather mustn't—deal with."

"I believe you," was Tim's comment but he did not say it aloud and the Headmaster leant back in his chair and said conversationally as he took his glasses off:

"I've beaten Secker."

"Oh," said Tim, taken aback. "I was going to tell you, sir; I clouted his head this morning."

"So I believe. Richards came to me about the trouble he had and then I had a word with the boy's Housemaster and heard he'd tried it on with you and your reaction."

Tim wondered what sort of conversation "a word with his Housemaster" covered. Argument? Orders? Servile agreement on the part of P.-S.? He would never know. Nor would he know in what sort of terms his own behaviour had been described. He said rather woodenly:

"I know, of course, sir, that I shouldn't have smacked the boy. I probably wouldn't if I'd thought he was coming up to you. But at the time—he was so flown with himself. It seemed the only thing to do."

"It probably was," agreed the Headmaster. "It's undesirable in every way that masters in form should resort

205

to violence. It's undignified, in the end it slackens discipline and sooner or later somebody clouts an incipient mastoid or cuts a boy's eye with his spectacles. But there are occasions when it is the only thing that works and this seems to have been one of them. Don't, however, make a habit of it."

"No, sir," Tim laughed, relieved and amused, but he felt he had to explain a little further. Secker, he said, had been a nuisance all round; working badly, cutting training and constantly on the edge of insolence. "I did report him to Pearson-Smith," he concluded and stopped, not sure how he could wind this up tactfully.

"And you felt that Pearson-Smith was slow to act," the Headmaster wound up for him. "I think, you know, there's a lot to be said for a Housemaster standing by a boy as long as possible. He's *in loco parentis* as the rest of us are not and I'd rather, myself, that he gave too much benefit of too much doubt than the other way. As it is, Secker has had patience from P.-S. and violence from me—and you—and I hope we've solved him."

He thrust his spectacles on again as though making an end of the subject and Tim digested what had been said. The Beak rarely, if ever, ticked an assistant master off; but why, reflected Tim, should he? A detached, experienced view of Pearson-Smith, Secker and School discipline had been quite lightly presented to him and he was left feeling meek, respectful and very young.

Mr. Fielding, not unaware of the process of digestion, paused before moving on to the next subject, recalling the letter which was in his pocket and thinking, without looking at it, about the face of the young man opposite him.

It was quickly intelligent and impatient, honest to the point of awkwardness. Also—he had heard from Alison how Tim's afternoon had been spent—kind.

"I have had," he began dispassionately, "a letter from Sir Arthur Hinton-Brigg—"

"Already?" Tim exclaimed, startled. He had hoped to get in first with this one.

"He sent it over by hand. Now—your private affairs are no concern of mine; except if they become so by affecting your work or leading you in to misbehaviour. I don't think for a moment that you have misbehaved seriously over—"

"Sir," burst from Tim, "may I tell you the whole story?"

"Yes," said the Headmaster, "if you like. Let me say again that I don't suspect you of any kind of evil designs on Sir Arthur's daughter."

"I have no designs whatever on Sir Arthur's daughter," said Tim and described briefly and not without embarrassment his meeting with Julie at the Courtneys'; their evening at the cinema and Molloy's Steak Bar; the Sunday luncheon and finally the abortive and very disagreeable expedition of the evening before. "Of course," he concluded angrily, "I shouldn't have laughed at him or said a word—as Burgoyne faithfully pointed out to me. But honestly, sir, can one—should one—let a man get away with that sort of thing?"

"Well," the Headmaster's spectacles were off again, waving gently, "it is hard, I agree. But of course, you weren't stopping Sir Arthur. You couldn't. You were merely annoying him. There is a very calming Victorian smuggery which I often find useful: 'No gentleman *will* insult me, no other can'."

Tim looked at him and laughed suddenly. "That deserves a frame, sir," he said.

"It does, doesn't it? I can never remember where it came from—You say you didn't know about Miss Hinton-Brigg's engagement to Lucreton?"

"No, sir. I don't think she is engaged to him. If she is she shouldn't be."

"Not our affair," he was told and then the matter was summed up. "It seems to have been pure misunderstanding and I shall tell Sir Arthur so. I take it you've abandoned pursuit, if it was pursuit?"

"Yes, sir."

"Then that should be that—"

"Sir," said Tim, "may I know what Sir Arthur said?"

"I'm sorry," said the Headmaster, polite but inflexible, "no. Now—I was going to send for you anyway about your job. You've done nearly a year. How do you feel about it?"

Watching Tim he saw him whiten and Tim himself felt the blood drain away from his face; but he spoke steadily.

"If you're asking me if I want to stay, sir, of course I do. I know I haven't done too well."

"Your teaching and discipline are satisfactory. You get on well, as a rule, with boys and your help with athletics and so on is useful. In what way do you feel you have done badly? You do want to stay at Ledenham?"

Tim hesitated, frowning a little. For the second time he felt that a situation which had become distorted in his own mind had been presented to him trimmed and balanced. Of course he wanted to stay at Ledenham, not perhaps for ever, but for him as a young man nothing could be better; and he knew perfectly well that his work and his handling

208

of boys was good. But his sense of failure was still with him and he wondered how to rate it. How much did the Beak know about him after all?

"I do want to stay, sir," he said at last, "very much. But I'm bound to tell you that I think quite a lot of people would be glad to see me go. I suppose I'm quarrelsome."

"You are beginning your career," said the Headmaster. "Very few of us getting towards the end can look back on an unblemished record. There's always something we wish we hadn't done or done differently—usually quite a lot. The first year," he went on, "is not technically a probationary one as you know. But we went over this and you will remember that we do think of it as probationary when it is a man's first job. It works both ways. We may find you unsatisfactory, you may dislike us, or for some reason or another it can be a good idea to start again elsewhere. I don't think you're quarrelsome. You've been a bit of an irritant, perhaps, and you'll have to watch it, but I don't regard it as a serious thing. I have no doubt at all that you can do very well here."

The blood rushed back to Tim's face. He hadn't known what was coming. It might have been 'begin again elsewhere'; it might have been worse.

"Thank you, sir," he said. "I'm very glad—and grateful. And," he looked up with a flash of amusement and apology, "I assure you, I fully appreciate being given the benefit of the doubt."

The Headmaster laughed and rose to his feet. "Don't forget Nemesis usually finds her length in the end—witness Secker. There should be a pot of tea in the drawing-room by now. Come and have a cup."

Tim followed him along the passage and through the baize door and spent half an hour relaxing with tea and tobacco in the beneficent peace of Mrs. Fielding's drawing-room. But he was a perceptive youth and the easy, undemanding conversation of his hostess gave him time to wonder if the Beak always looked as tired as this when he eased off, and if he only imagined a look which hinted at a definite worry. Sir Arthur Hinton-Brigg's furious face leapt into his mind and his conscience ever on the alert, sat up and gave him a moment of appalled dismay. What had the unspeakable brute said? He was a Governor—He hoped to God he, Tim, hadn't started up something frightful—

He was reassured by the placidity with which both the Fieldings wished him good night, but when he had gone the Headmaster did not sit down again.

"I'll go and write to Hinton-Brigg now," he said.

"What was it all about?" asked Mrs. Fielding. "Obviously nothing serious since you brought the boy in and he looked quite easy in his mind."

"Nothing," said her husband and told her Tim's story of his encounter with the Hinton-Brigg family.

"Unfortunate," she said with a small sigh "I'm glad he's settling. I think he's a good boy and really he wasn't blameworthy over this. But, being Sartha it's—unfortunate. You'll have to have a copy of your letter. Shall I do that for you?"

"It won't be a long one," said her husband.

In his study he took the plump envelope from his pocket and glanced through Miss Foley's three pages of impassioned typescript with an expression of distaste. Then he began his reply.

"Dear Sir Arthur Hinton-Brigg," he wrote.

"Since acknowledging your letter earlier today I have had an opportunity to give some thought to its subject and I have talked to Selby.

"I am satisfied that the trouble arose through misapprehension. Selby has met your daughter three times. He had heard nothing of the engagement to which you refer—indeed I am sure it is not generally known in this part of the county—but in any case his feeling for Miss Hinton-Brigg was no deeper than that which a pretty girl arouses in any young man. I am confident, therefore, that you may set your mind at rest in the matter.

"With regard to," here Mr. Fielding paused and referred again to the letter before him. He wished profoundly that young Mr. Selby had not laughed at Sir Arthur.

"With regard to your complaint of his manner to yourself," he resumed, going rather slowly, "I can only express my regret. Selby had had a tiresome drive and some disappointment and he was both shocked and resentful at the unexpected accusations brought against him. Since I am able to assure you that these were, in fact, unfounded," concluded Mr. Fielding with raised eyebrows, "I trust that you will accept this apology and feel that an unfortunate misunderstanding may be forgotten."

He lit a cigarette and read it over. It was too short. It was far too short. But for the life of him he could think of nothing to add which would make it more palatable. He signed it quickly and peering through cigarette smoke scribbled a copy and locked it in his desk.

12

THE following day, Sunday, was one of those which stood out as an oasis in the desert of the spring term. The sun shone with some warmth in its brilliance, the snow had settled and hardened and Authority was co-operative. There was no sermon. In the absence of Hepburns calm sanctified triumph pervaded the hen-coop and matins was over in less than forty-five minutes. Lunch—cold—was again early, and soon after one o'clock the School, clad in a bizarre assortment of garments, was heading for the hills; except that in each House the week's squad of dining-hall slaves raced through their duties at an unprecedented rate of knots.

Ski-ing was nowhere very good in Ledshire but the best ground was eight or nine miles from Ledenham and a sizable party of staff, with their belongings and a few senior boys, got off in cars almost as hurriedly as the rank and file who went on foot, towing their toboggans to nearer slopes. Nick Vincent drove the School Land Rover with Alison beside him and a solidly packed load of boys and skis behind, and four members of the Zoo caused Angus' car to sit rather heavily on its springs. Several vehicles seemed to contain only excited children; those below ski-ing age, including John Henderson, were left corralled among the stay-at-homes and their young parents added an off-the-hook glee to the occasion. The Courtneys, who had no encumbrances, came by themselves in the largest car.

It was an afternoon of sheer hilarity; out of time, out of

context, out, as they say, of this world. In the extreme simplification of sunshine, snow and play ordinary life was forgotten. There were no problems or emotions, no need to watch one's words and be discreet; people slid back into a state of childhood and exuberant yells and Marthe was translated. This was her element and as though it touched a spring she was suddenly brilliantly alive as none of them had ever seen her. The cold brought colour to her face, the sea-green eyes were unveiled and sparkling and she looked like a snow nymph, perfectly at home, expert and graceful.

"Dear little hill," she cried indulgently and played with the little hill with the off-hand ease of an Olympic athlete at Sunday School sports.

"You're showing off," shouted Tim, who had not spoken to her since the day she rejected his proposal of marriage.

"What?" she shouted back, alight with laughter. "Did you say showing off? Oh—never would I do such a thing. Is this better?" and screwing her face into an expression of agonised caution she set off with precarious balance and tongue well out, clowning her way down in a series of near-disasters.

"You've come on," said Angus to Alison with kindly approval.

"I told you I had."

"Aye, but seeing's believing."

"What *I* see," panted Alison, "is you looking like the *Queen Mary* on skids."

"Weak," said Angus. "You've lost your edge among all these smooth continental types. Hook on and I'll give you a tow."

When the light failed they all went to have tea in a

nearby pub which prayed regularly for long winters with plenty of snow, and its lamp-lit interior, filled with hungry, vociferous people, was hardly nearer reality than the sunny slopes of the hills. But the day was almost over.

Alison was recalled to reality by Annette Courtney. Annette was the object of a good deal of laughter and mockery because the identity of her male guest at the Reel Club the evening before had got round. What Henry might have said to his wife in private was anybody's guess. With his standards he could hardly be expected to enjoy the joke wholeheartedly, but in public he put a good face on it and joined in. They hadn't quite made up their minds, he said, whether in future they would invite their new friend Eric to the same parties as the Hinton-Briggs or to different parties.

Never again, groaned Annette, would she oblige anybody. This was what you got for it—though she had nothing against Eric—and she turned accusingly to Alison. "It was *your* fault. You told the wretched girl to ask me to take her."

"Me?" cried Alison. "I never did such a thing."

"Oh," said Annette and paused for thought. "So it was just a little scheme, was it?" she went on in a lower voice for Alison alone. "Oh well, perhaps, at least, I've helped to consolidate Eric and that's a good thing. But you'll have to watch that girl, Alison. She's had an eye on property of yours, you know," which left Alison speechless till the general, loud talk rolled on and she forgot about it.

Some time later Nick pushed his way through the crowd to her. "Alison," he said, "I'm going to hurry on—got to get these chaps back for Chapel. You'll be all right—"

"Sure," she said easily, in no hurry to leave the party.

The party, however, was broken up by the assembled consciences. A few of the masters present always went to evening Chapel and had never intended to do otherwise; others were less regular but felt that as the boys had been with them and must go, it would be noticeable to cut on this occasion; the rest looked round to see if there would be a sufficient representation without them and then decided that after all there was nothing to stay for.

Alison had been cosily wedged in a remote corner of the room and was almost the last to leave it. When she stumbled out, rather stiff and sleepy, blinking in the sudden darkness, engines were already running and the lights of the Land Rover were well down the hill. She saw Mr. Burgoyne and Willie Munro get into the Hendersons' car which went off next. Tim appeared in a shaft of light and vanished again. In a moment it seemed that everybody was moving except Angus, whose starter was grinding unwillingly, and the Courtneys who never hurried.

"Ah!" said Annette's voice beside her, full of satisfaction. "Clever Angus. I do like a young man who can contrive. On you go. Have a nice time. You've missed Chapel anyway so there's no hurry."

"Annette," Alison, jolted right back into the world of reality and Mr. Barker, was swept by a wave of revulsion and dismay and lost her head, "—you're all wrong. There's nothing—no contriving—nothing to contrive."

"*Ha,* ha, ha," laughed Annette mockingly as she turned away.

"Look," cried Alison, "can I come with you?"

"*What?*" Annette stopped and peered at her in the dusk.

"What's all this? Don't tell me you've had a tiff with the boy-friend—Well if you have it'll be a good chance to make it up again. Go along with you, silly girl. He's got rid of the others—don't be a wet blanket."

She administered a sharp nudge and plodded off through the snow to the car and the waiting Henry. Alison, pushed as it were into Angus's arms, her mind full of implied scheming, turned and walked over to join him.

"I don't know if you intended to lift me home, Angus," she said brightly, "but it seems you're going to."

"I told Nick I would," replied Angus opening the door. "It's pretty cold, I'm afraid. Better have the rug." He handed the Cameron plaid to her and shut the door and Alison caught a glimpse of a stony, unfamiliar face in the lights as he went round in front of the car. He got in beside her and with a good deal of fuss the chains gripped and they started.

Angus's car was elderly and given to freakishness. It had some degree of steering-wander under the most favourable conditions and it was his custom to encourage it with a mixture of adjuration and cajolery in his broadest Scots. Tonight, as it bumped and sidled down the rough hill road over ruts and hillocks of snow worn to ice, he said nothing, sitting like a slab of his native granite with merciless hands on the wheel.

For years he had looked after Alison. "Angus'll bring Alison" had been taken for granted by him, by Alison herself and by everyone else. It hadn't needed a word to fix it with Nick that he'd take her home, it was sheer chance that the other Zoo men had each, independently, gone elsewhere to make room for her and it had never occurred to him that he need tell her. She would know that he was waiting for her. He had taken a considerable dunt when she refused to go with him to the Reel Club though Burgoyne's words to Munro had made it possible to patch it up with her and with himself. This was different. He could see no reason for it. And seeing Alison look horrified, almost scared, hearing her beg Annette Courtney for a lift was something from which he thought he could never recover. His friendly love for the young girl Alison, his full man's love for the woman he wanted to marry had both gone out like a light. There was nothing left in him but hurt and anger.

Alison had not been at all scared at the prospect of driving home with him, she had merely been embarrassed out of her senses by Annette's assumption of a romance which wasn't there. But she was scared now. Something perfectly appalling had happened. Sick at heart she realized that Angus must have seen and probably heard her panic-stricken fluster; they had not been close, but it was frosty and very still. She opened her mouth to explain and then glancing at the stony profile shut it again. It was not a thing one could explain and nothing could be explained to a face like that.

The car slid playfully sideways and lurched forward again. This silence must be broken somehow, she thought, and a dreadful dialogue ensued.

"That was a glorious afternoon," she said.

"Splendid, wasn't it," agreed Angus.

"No hope of another before Wednesday, I suppose."

"I'm afraid not."

"Unless Beak thinks of an extra half. Will it hold, do you

217

think?"

"It may."

"It's freezing pretty hard now."

"Yes."

Like a more eloquent comment on the frost the wheels spun on a small rise in the ground. Angus changed down, the engine roared and the car shuddering incontinently crept forward again. Angus volunteered a remark.

"Sorry about this. We'll get along faster on the main road," he said in faultless English.

"Yes," said Alison.

The hill road which led only to two farms and the tiny hamlet clustered round the pub did not appear on any motoring map. It was so narrow that two vehicles could not pass except in the places where there happened to be a gate, and under the hard-packed snow was a patchwork surface ranging from strips of tarred chips to loose gravel and boulders casually stopping up holes. There were three miles of it. Conversation was exhausted in the first, the second and third were traversed without a word—though with a variety of mechanical noises. But as it reached the main road the hill road widened as though opening welcoming arms to civilization and became two lanes, ushering the traveller to right or left. Angus bore left and they debouched on to a sheet of hard, polished ice. All the cars had skidded on it more or less; Angus's waltzed round, slithered sideways and came smartly to rest with its rump against a bank.

"Ye damned auld besom," snapped Angus. "What are you *doing?* Get *on*—" He wrenched the wheel round and set the car going again on its proper course. "Sorry," he said, reverting to English. "You're all right, are you?"

"Quite all right," said Alison and laughed a little shakily. Any skid is a shaking experience but on the whole this one and Angus's explosion had brought relief. "I almost think," she said more naturally "that you'll almost have to think of buying yourself a new car some day, Angus."

"It does me well enough," was the reply and into the silence which followed burst a shattering report. They limped to a halt.

This time Angus said nothing. He got out and went round to look at the wreckage of chain and rubber which were the remains of his rear off-tyre and Alison got out at her door and joined him.

"I suppose it got torn in the skid," she said.

"Yes," said Angus and glanced at her briefly. "I'm afraid you'll get terribly cold. I don't know if you'd rather walk on—"

Alison looked along the dark empty road and shuddered. "It's all right, Angus. I'll stay here."

"Wrap the rug round you."

"Yes—"

Angus opened the boot and from the amalgam of objects which lived in it, ropes, mackintosh, an ice-axe and, inevitably, socks, selected his tools and extracted the spare wheel, the jack and a battery lamp. It was bitterly cold but Alison hardly felt it. She wrapped the rug round her and stood back a few yards, away from the lights, and touched a depth of desolation which she had never imagined possible. Angus was working in and out of the circle of light from the lamp; his tall active figure was black against it, his hands, large and well-shaped were quick and unfumbling in the centre of it and his face and red head appeared and disappeared. Watching him Alison grew up. She had been on the edge of it, coming near in their Leyburn evening, very near at the Courtneys' party each time his arm went round her; and, of course, she had thought about it. But looking back she saw her thoughts as trifling; flutters of imagination and uncertainty. Now she simply knew that she loved Angus. It was filling her whole self and among the ingredients which she had known nothing about was an agonising compassion which saw and felt the hurt behind his stony face. What folly had possessed her that she had let Mr Barker, Oonagh, Annette or anything at all influence her? It was as if she had lost herself and a dithering idiot, full of undefined suspicions and dread of being looked at, had taken her place. She had now found herself. She was Alison and this was Angus.

A car came slowly towards them and he stood up and moved back out of its way. "All right?" yelled a voice.

"All right," he yelled back. "Watch the ice along there—" a hand waved acknowledgement and the car went cautiously on. "Pity it was going the wrong way," he said with a glance at the shrouded figure in the shadows and was back on one knee drawing the plate off. It clinked as he put it down, then he pulled the wheel off and laid it flat and Alison moved forward to look at the tyre.

"It's a pretty fair wreck, isn't it—? Shall I try to get the chain off?"

"Not much future for it. Try the chain if you like. Don't take your gloves off."

She squatted down beside him and fumbling with stiff hands, managed to free the chain as he got the spare wheel on.

"Thanks," he said. "Better put it on again, I suppose. Won't be long now—" and in a few minutes, without another word spoken, they were on their way again.

"Are you very cold?" he asked presently. "Pity you didn't go with Henry and Annette."

"Oh, Angus," said Alison. "I'm so sorry about that. I don't think I can explain it."

"Don't try," said Angus shortly. "The message got through."

"But—it didn't—" she searched desperately for words and Angus lifted a hand from the wheel in a gesture of refusal.

"I don't want to talk about it," he said and immediately went on to do so. "I know quite well what it was. I've known ever since you quoted Frances talking about chaperones."

"That had nothing to do with it," Alison said quickly. "It wasn't—I only told you as a joke—"

"You told me because I asked you what was the matter and the matter popped out. Jokingly no doubt, but you said it because you were thinking about it."

"She wasn't talking about us."

"I don't suppose she was," said Angus and went on devastatingly: "There's nothing to say about us that mightn't have been said for four years if anybody had thought it worth while. I suppose she was talking about Tim and Marthe but you—adopted it."

Alison said nothing. It was all true and it made one feel so helpless when a careless remark—and it had certainly been a very careless remark—was subjected to this sort of analysis. Angus, thoroughly wound up, went on talking.

"Frances," he said, "had plenty of men dangling after her in her time and I would say that in every case she was up on the deal. She was the one who had the fun. She then married one of the best chaps there is; but it hasn't, apparently, prevented her from joining the female caucus—"

"What do you mean?"

"I mean that it's assumed that young men have no feelings except 'the passions' and they can only be kept comparatively harmless by the united prudence of good women—"

"Nonsense!" cried Alison loudly.

"It is not nonsense," snapped Angus.

"It is nonsense. All Frances was talking about was gossip and—and publicity. She said it's hard on Marthe that everybody watched Tim running after her and then watched him ignoring her. And she's very glad nobody knew anything about her and Patsy—"

"*What?*" Angus gave a bark of laughter. "Ass! *Everybody* knew. Nick spotted it about a week after she got here." Alison was silenced. "And anyway, what the hell?" he went on angrily. "Oddly enough we're not unaware of gossip, but what do you suppose Tim felt when Marthe turned him down and he was then warned off by Frances?" They were running in to Ledenham and he reached his peroration. "I'll tell you this, Alison, if I had a girl belonging to me—a daughter or a wife—I'd send her off to Peru with Tim tomorrow and know that no harm of any kind would come to her. And you or any other girl would be equally safe with me. And," concluded Angus, pulling up with a jerk at School House, "your mother knows it if you and Frances don't."

He got out of the car and marched round to open the door for her and Alison heard in her mind her mother's voice telling not to let Mr. Barker influence her and Tim's saying urgently: "Don't let anything spoil it." She crawled out and faced him miserably.

"Will you come in and have supper?"

"No thank you. They'll have kept something for me and I want a bath. Sorry about the hold-up."

"I'm so sorry, Angus. I don't think you really understand. It isn't—"

"Oh, I think so," said Angus. "You aren't a kid any longer and of course it's bound to make a difference. Good night. I hope you haven't got cold." The car door slammed and he drove away. Alison paused to assemble herself, to thrust her state into the background and sort out her face, and then she went into the house.

She could never afterwards decide whether despair precipitated flu or flu added to her despair, but on the following morning she had a perceptible temperature and aching bones and stayed thankfully in bed. Her parents, though kind, were envious rather than sympathetic.

"I can't think of anything more desirable than a mild but lingering bout of flu," said her father when he dropped in to see her on Monday evening. "The snow's going and the mess is indescribable."

"I'm not totally bed-ridden," said Alison. "I've noticed it. What are you gloomy about?"

"Nothing particular," was the reply. "It's a gloomy time of year." He picked up *The Times Educational Supplement* which was lying on her bed. "What are you reading the Ed.

Sup. for? 'Ancillary Services—School Meals—' " he read out from the open page. "Job hunting?"

Alison groaned. It had only needed Ancillary Services. "Well," she said a little defensively, "I am job-hunting. I ought to get on with it."

"My impression was," said her father mildly, "that you didn't feel much urgency about it. But it's true," he added, "that indefinite unemployment isn't always very satisfactory; especially in winter." Turning over the pages of the paper he paused. "Have you seen this? Upton prep. wants an assistant caterer. That's the sort of thing, isn't it? And not too far away."

Alison had not seen it. "I was bogged by the Ancillary Services," she said. "When is it for?"

Mr. Fielding consulted the advertisement. "Next term or sooner. You'd better write. It's as good a start as you're likely to get, I should say."

There was no reply and after a moment he looked up. Alison had turned her head away. He saw the curve of a cheek with a tear sliding slowly over it, dark curls against the pillow and a young, defenceless neck and shoulder. A hand lay limply on the cover and he took it.

"What is it, my darling? Don't you want to go?"

"I don't want to go or stay," sobbed Alison.

"Something's gone wrong, has it?"

She nodded. "Very wrong. But," she had to make sure no blame got about and turned to him to emphasize it, "it's nobody's fault, Beak. Except mine and I didn't mean it."

The agony of youth was something Mr. Fielding never forgot and never underestimated. He understood and felt the sufferings of his young men and his boys; when it was his own young daughter it was almost unbearable and he did not believe that facile words of comfort met the case. He could not tell Alison that misunderstandings sort themselves out or that things come right in the end because quite frequently they don't. Misunderstandings can persist for a lifetime and beyond and things by no means always come right. The only comfort in such a case is felt more by experienced elders than by the victim; youth is resilient and time does heal or insulate most wounds. He held Alison's hand in a firm, warm clasp and did his best with practical advice.

"When things go wrong, don't let it show. Say nothing, look nothing, do nothing unusual. If you want help or advice or simply to talk about it you'll be safe with Mummy or with me. Otherwise—shut it away and think of it as little as you can."

"Yes," said Alison blowing her nose. "That's what I thought. It isn't very easy."

"No." He got up and bent to kiss her. Meeting her tearful eyes he saw a certain steadiness along with the misery and could not resist offering a cautious crumb of comfort. "Taking the gloomiest possible view," he said, "time the great healer does do its stuff. Good night, my darling."

"Oh my darling Beak," said Alison between a laugh and a sob. "What a glittering prospect!"

The news of Alison's illness was, inevitably, brought to the Zoo by Willie. "Poor Alison," he said tragically at dinner, "she's got flu. Isn't it a shame?"

"There," said Mr. Burgoyne to Angus. "That's your fault. Letting her stand about while you tinkered with your wreck of a vehicle. We've told you before and now perhaps

225

it'll get home. You need a new car."

Angus said bleakly that he was sorry about Alison's flu. "She might have got cold last night," he admitted, "but I can't think of a much sillier reason for getting a new car than one puncture caused by a skid."

"Skid," said Tim, "is the operative word. Other people neither skidded—much—nor got punctures. You need a new car."

"H'mph," said Angus and Mr. Lawson made one of his rare contributions.

"Unless you always arrange," he suggested helpfully, "to have another car coming along behind to pick up your stranded girlfriends."

Willie, who had been lost in thought, reached a decision. "I'll send her some flowers," he said.

"I would if I were you," said Mr. Burgoyne kindly. "Angus's stock must have slumped a bit. You cash in."

Later that night Tim went to Angus's room and found Angus as Angus had once found him doing corrections in a fog of tobacco and gloom.

"What the hell do *you* want?" was his greeting.

"I bought a bottle," said Tim. "One ought to have whisky on hand for emergencies."

"What's the emergency?"

"There isn't one right now; but when you've got whisky it's a pity not to drink it."

Angus grunted, but he relaxed a trifle and turning round to the fire, lit his pipe.

"What's up?" asked Tim, pouring out whisky.

"Nothing whatever," said Angus coldly.

Tim settled himself in the second best chair and took a

worn-looking packet of cigarettes from his pocket. "At least," he said, "you'll always have the consolation of knowing that you weren't precipitate." He listened for a moment to an unprintable flow of oratory and answered the final "you don't know what you're talking about" with: "There's only one thing that could make me feel how you look."

"Get out," said Angus, but he held his ground. He was as sure that Alison was in love with Angus as that Angus was in love with Alison and he did not propose to allow them to mess things up if he could help it. He persisted, using the method which forces information by throwing out intolerable assumptions to be contradicted, and in the end he knew quite a lot about the disastrous end to a glorious afternoon.

"Did you," he asked, "enjoy the references at dinner to stranded girl-friends and your stock slumping?"

"Cross-examination now commences," said Angus witheringly.

"And why?" examining counsel swept on, not only answering his own question but giving his interpretation of it. If, he maintained, it had been any other girl Angus would have been unmoved by the bad taste of Messrs. Burgoyne and Lawson. If, on the other hand, he had been engaged to Alison he would have been rather gratified by it. He disliked it because he didn't know where he was. And, concluded Tim, that was why Alison was thrown out by chat about chaperones and boy-friends. "If anybody linked her up with Willie—or me," he said, "she'd simply laugh like a drain."

Angus got up and stood with his elbow on the

mantelpiece staring down at the fire. His mind was not working at all well; it was grinding and churning and getting nowhere. There was something in what Tim said, certainly as far as he himself was concerned, but Tim didn't know everything. All the scenes with Alison came before him. Miss Wills' office; the kid's shriek of welcome and the easy, familiar natter. The Leyburn evening and the Courtneys' party; he knew very well where he had got to and he had been almost sure she was getting there too. And then—withdrawal. The Stoneleigh weekend—Martin Sykes, perhaps? Surely if she had wanted to be with him as he wanted to be with her she would have seen the drive home as he had seen it—a heaven-sent chance, unwangled and unobserved. She hadn't seen it like that and it seemed to him to prove what he had always feared might be the case. To Alison he was the dear old pal. At the suggestion, whoever made it, that he might move out of his class she had panicked. He remembered her voice asking, "Annette —can I come with you?" and prodded round the wound. It merely felt numb. If his love for Alison had not been killed outright it was not far from death and he would do nothing to bring it to life again.

"Get out, Tim, will you?" he said without violence. Tim who had also been staring at the fire looked up and he answered the look. "The fact is, your reasoning isn't bad but it's based on false premises—one, anyway."

"What false premise?"

"I'll admit," allowed Angus, hoping that a brief, plain statement would finally shut Tim up and at the same time close the door of his own mind on a painful error, "that I half thought I—" he stopped. No statement was, after all, possible. "Hell," he said angrily. "Clear out for God's sake."

Tim got slowly to his feet and moved to the door. Then he prudently returned to fetch the whisky and fired a parting shot. "I would never have believed," he said, "that you could be so thick."

While Tim and Angus drank whisky the Headmaster and his wife drank tea and reviewed the day.

"That's a very miserable child upstairs," said Mr. Fielding.

"Very," his wife agreed sadly.

"What's your reading of it? It's obviously 'lerv'—nothing else is so agonising. And presumably it's Angus. But how?"

"Well," said Mrs. Fielding frowning, "of course if Alison has fallen in love and he hasn't there's no blame attached. It's one of the things that can happen and can't be helped. But—they've been so lovely together, Alison and Angus. I did think they were both heading in the same direction."

The Headmaster recalled Mr. Pearson-Smith's remarks on that head at dinner the week before and recalled also his own resentment and automatic covering up. He had also, he thought, received suspiciously prompt assistance from the Chaplain in steering the conversation.

"I fancy that's a pretty general view," he replied to his wife and she looked up at him quickly.

"You've met it too, have you? I'm afraid it is and I think that may be what's wrong. People are thoughtless in this sort of thing. It really is horrid for a girl to feel she is being watched and talked about."

"Clare never seemed to bother," said her husband. "I suppose she was watched and talked about too. But of course she wasn't in love with any of them. Well—they must work it out."

"Yes," said Mrs. Fielding, "one can't help, I'm afraid. More tea?" She refilled his cup and changed the subject. "Tell me about Sartha and the Seckers."

The Headmaster grimaced hideously and then looked resigned. Sir Arthur Hinton-Brigg and the Seckers were poignant reasons for longing to retire to bed with mild but prolonged influenza. Sir Arthur, as he had anticipated, had not been mollified by his letter. He had read it at breakfast, a meal which he always took alone, and rising from the table he had stalked into the library, sent Miss Foley scuttling from the room and picked up the telephone. The Headmaster was in Chapel and the fifteen minutes which elapsed before his return call came through had not helped.

"What did he say?" asked Mrs. Fielding.

"In a nutshell," her husband replied, "he said that he didn't believe me; that I was a fool to believe Selby—if I did; and that the real situation is so serious that he is obliged to keep Julie in protective custody. He then repeated his demand for Selby's dismissal."

"Fun for the telephone exchange."

"Well—I've clarified it. I doubt if they got much."

"And the Seckers?"

"And then the Seckers—" The parents of Secker had been waiting for the Headmaster when he came out of School at 12.30. Their son had reported in his Sunday letter that he had been hit by Mr. Selby and they had come to complain.

Mrs. Fielding asked: "Did he report that you hit him too?"

"No, there's neither glory nor martyrdom in a beating.

I'm very glad, though," said Mr. Fielding with satisfaction, "that I'd given it to him. I couldn't very well have beaten him after this or it would have been assumed that the punishment was for telling his parents. I told them about it."

"What line are they taking?"

"Their line is that the School is persecuting their Brian. They know Sir Arthur Hinton-Brigg very well and he thought there was something very peculiar about the boy's being dropped from the seven-a-sides. They thought Sartha would take it big when he heard that Brian had been assaulted by Selby and then beaten by me."

"I've no doubt he will," said Mrs. Fielding coldly.

"He has," said her husband.

13

SIR ARTHUR HINTON-BRIGG and his daughter, alike in ruthless egocentricity were also alike in a direct guilelessness of method. It might have suggested a basic honesty of character but Lady Hinton-Brigg, who knew them both very well, did not esteem it a virtue. If one took it, as she did take it, that they must pursue their own ends with minds so constituted that they saw nothing except those ends it would have been easier and pleasanter all round if they had displayed some finesse. As it was the great Selby row proceeded with volleying and thunder which she found both tedious and exhausting, and which she knew was creating of itself out of nothing a situation from which it would be difficult to emerge without damage—possibly serious damage—to someone.

Julie's protective custody was a reality. Sir Arthur, his chin thrust out, shouted orders; to Pigeon that all telephone calls were to be put through to himself, to her ladyship if he was out, to Miss Foley if they were both out and all visitors were to be screened—though Mr. Lucreton might call or telephone at any time without let or hindrance; to Eric that the batteries were to be removed from Miss Julie's car and she was not to be allowed access to any other car. To his wife he issued a warning that if this method of dealing with their recalcitrant child proved insufficient she must be ready to take her abroad at a moment's notice. Julie, on her part, countered with loud hysterical sobs, protesting that she adored Tim Selby, that he adored her and nothing, neither imprisonment nor starvation nor threat of death would induce her to give him up.

To Lady Hinton-Brigg listening coldly it was clear that if her husband would stop shouting Julie's passion would die a natural death; and that, if Julie had been capable of it, a pretence of indifference would have enabled her to hoodwink her parent without difficulty.

Julie, however, would have been surprised if she had heard herself accused of lack of subtlety. The expedition to Ledenham with the not wholly unsuspecting Cubby on Saturday had not led to Tim but it had led to Oonagh and on Monday she carried out the next stage in her plot.

"Am I," she demanded, "to be shut up in the house all the time? Can't I go shopping? Am I to be treated like a criminal?"

"I'm going to Leyburn this morning," said her mother, not greatly moved. "You can come if you want to."

Lady Hinton-Brigg always went shopping in Leyburn on Monday morning and Eric took them in the Rolls as soon as he had driven Sir Arthur to Snaydon. As it was fairly early he was able to park the car conveniently in the main shopping street by the grocers' and the ladies went in. Julie immediately came out again and vanished into Woolworth's next door.

"Did you see where Miss Julie went?" asked Lady Hinton-Brigg ten minutes later. Eric told her, wondering if she knew about Woolworth's back door. "Tell her I've gone on to White's," said her ladyship casually and walked away. She did not see that Julie could get into serious mischief and she was not going to play hide and seek with her in the streets of Leyburn.

Julie, knowing the Woolworth geography, hurried through the back door and made her way by a circuitous route to the bank where she cashed a cheque for forty-five pounds. From there she hastened to the nearest cafe and in the ladies' room locked herself in and thrust thirty pounds into a large envelope beside a string of cultured pearls and two letters. She posted it and strolled back to the car, emerging from Woolworth's again with elaborate carelessness and slightly heightened colour.

"Her ladyship's gone to White's," said Eric, carrying out his instructions. His boldly handsome face was expressionless as became a well-trained servant, his words were almost correct but the net effect was not respectful. Julie got into the car and he shut the door and stood beside it waiting for Lady Hinton-Brigg who would probably have to be disentangled from her parcels. Eric admired Lady Hinton-Brigg and he rather enjoyed doing things for her, looking after her a bit.

Julie, who had not failed to notice his laconic tone, slid the window down and addressed him brightly. "Enjoy the Reel Club, Sharpe?"

"It was okay," replied Eric without turning round.

"How did you get in? Crash the gate?"

He permitted himself a faint smile. As well crash the gate at a church bazaar. "What do *you* think?" he said. "Went with a girl." The smile widened. "Liked it better than what she did, though."

Julie, running through the Reel Club members with some incredulity suddenly got it. "Oonagh!" she exclaimed and laughed "Does she know who you are?"

"She knows," said Eric, turning round sufficiently to

direct a cold stare, "that I'm Eric Sharpe and I work for Hinton-Brigg. Anything more you'd like to know?"

The stare and the tone reminded Julie bluntly that at this stage of her life she could not afford to make enemies. Allies were what she needed. She turned on her best line in frank friendliness and said she had only been joking.

"Why on earth shouldn't you go to the Reel Club if you like it?" she cried generously. "Nobody bothers about class now." The stare did not thaw and she went on a little wildly, "Oonagh's a great buddy of mine. Quite frankly," a somewhat artificial laugh, "I'm counting a lot on Oonagh at the present juncture. Possibly you know all about it. We're quite likely to rope you in before we're through, so you see you can trust me to put no spokes in wheels." She opened her bag as she spoke and casually took out the balance of the cheque, the fifteen pounds which it might be useful to have by her, and making a pretence of shuffling the bundle into tidiness put it back again. Glancing up she met Eric's eyes with a very strange expression in them. She coloured as she snapped the bag shut and he turned away and went forward to meet her mother who came along the street with her hands full of parcels.

Lady Hinton-Brigg made no comment either on her daughter's straying from her side or her return to bondage. It was not till the car was picking its way delicately among thickening traffic and slushy snow as they started for home that the subject was introduced by Julie herself.

"Darling," she said lightly, "so sorry to have given you the slip like that. The feeling of being shackled brings out the worst, I fear. Actually," she laughed, "you were very innocent and easy."

"Did you expect me to rush screaming into the street?" asked Lady Hinton-Brigg pleasantly. She lit a cigarette and settled herself in her corner. "I shall be glad, I confess, when you recover from this infatuation. We all look rather ridiculous at present, don't you think?"

Julie thrust her chin out. "It's no good," she said loudly. "Pop can shout at me till his eyes bubble and you can be as cool and amused as you like. I *mean* it. It's serious—as you'll find out."

"I'm not particularly amused," said her mother. "In fact I'm not amused at all. I'm very bored and a good deal humiliated. Don't forget that I've seen the young man and talked to him."

"Do you imagine he'd confide in you what he feels about me?"

"He was perfectly frank about his feeling for you."

There was a short silence. "Very clever," said Julie at last. "Forgive me, won't you, if I'm not frightfully impressed."

"My dear child," said Lady Hinton-Brigg speaking more warmly, "do stop being so silly and so affected. Look here, Julie," she turned to face her daughter, commanding her attention. "If you don't want to marry Cubby, don't do it; but for heaven's sake think what you're doing. You're making all this fuss and uproar about a man you've met a couple of times who doesn't care tuppence about you. I know he doesn't. I promise you. Surely you know that I only want you to sort yourself out and be happy?"

"No," said Julie. "I don't know it. What you want is a quiet life with nothing happening to send Pop up the wall."

Lady Hinton-Brigg knew as well as anyone when words were futile. She turned away and made only one other remark during the drive home to Thaxley.

"I think I'd better take you abroad for a bit."

Julie looked out at the bleak wintery landscape. She thought of her depleted bank balance and Cubby Lucreton and wavered. Then she turned her thoughts resolutely back to romance and Tim Selby, who as the days went by grew ever larger, less clear and more desirable.

"I'm not sure," she said, as though the matter was one to which she would bend her mind when the necessity arose, "whether you *could* take me abroad, as you put it. I have no intention of going," and they drove on in silence.

Sir Arthur and Lady Hinton-Brigg met for the first time that day in the drawing-room before dinner and she observed that an ominous triumph was now mingled with unabated choler. Without preamble he demanded an account of Julie's day and she gave it briefly.

"She went with me to Leyburn. Otherwise she hasn't been out."

"She was with you all the time in Leyburn?"

"She went in to Woolworth's while I was in Gregg's next door."

"H'm," the heavy face was displeased. "You should have kept her with you. Still—it wasn't long, I suppose. Any telephone calls?"

"No."

Pigeon brought in drinks. Sir Arthur poured out sherry and lit cigarettes for his wife and himself and then standing with his back to the fire became angrily expansive.

"That fellow Fielding sent a damned insolent reply to that letter of mine," he said. "Simply denied, flatly denied, every thing I said."

"Let me see it," said Lady Hinton-Brigg. He hesitated but just occasionally he responded to a quick matter-of-fact order, and when she held out a confident hand he fished Mr. Fielding's letter from his pocket and gave it to her.

Her opinion of the letter when she had read it coincided with Mr. Fielding's opinion of it when he wrote it. It was too short. Though polite and containing an apology it was not conciliatory. Yet it was difficult to see how, given the subject, it could have been contrived to please Sir Arthur.

"I don't think it's insolent," she said slowly. He began to draw himself up and she went on at once: "You complained that the boy was rude and he's apologised for that. For the rest, he's stating the case as he sees it from the evidence he has. I think myself it's correct." She held off the outburst for a moment longer by handing back the letter and added: "I saw the boy, remember. And he's made no attempt to see Julie since—"

"Do you deny," demanded Sir Arthur, "that he was out here three times in so many days? It was his fourth visit which we were fortunately able to render abortive—"

"Well—third, I think. But—"

"Do you deny that a further attempt at present would be futile in view of my precautions? Do you deny—" a dramatic hand was flung out, "—you *cannot* deny that your daughter continues to declare their mutual passion and intention to—to—to bolt, soon as we relax our vigilance."

"I don't deny it, I simply don't believe it," said Lady Hinton-Brigg. "Julie is making it up."

The out-flung hand was held, amazed, and dropped. "Then all I can say, my dear Cynthia," said Sir Arthur, "is that I disagree with you." He stalked heavily across the room and poured out a second glass of sherry. Lady Hinton-Brigg never had more than one. "Moreover," he said over his shoulder, "another and very damaging piece of information concerning the character of young Selby came into my hands this afternoon."

Lady Hinton-Brigg's hatred of loud noises and angry voices placed her at a serious disadvantage when differences of opinion arose but as her husband turned she saw that the triumph had come uppermost and she braced herself. "I'd like some more sherry please, Arthur," she said crisply.

"I beg your pardon," said Sir Arthur who never forgot that he was a gentleman and with eyebrows raised in well-bred surprise he fetched the decanter and refilled her glass. As he padded back to replace it on the tray she asked "What information?" and listened silently to his account of Tim Selby's assault on Mrs. Secker's son as reported by Mrs. Secker.

"Fielding," he concluded, back in front of the fire again, "followed this up by beating the boy the same day. The boy's only offence, so far as I can gather, being that he is the victim of persecution by certain members of the staff. But—"

"How absurd!" His wife's voice and face were so full of scorn that it halted him for a moment and she went on: "Really, Arthur, you can't swallow that. In a decent school—and of course Ledenham is a good school—a boy isn't beaten unless he deserves it. And masters just don't persecute boys. Why should they?"

Sir Arthur's colour darkened alarmingly. "Do you really," he demanded, "consider yourself qualified to enlighten *me* about public schools?" Lady Hinton-Brigg, on the whole, did, but it would not be helpful to say so and in any case she had no opportunity. He spoke for several minutes about public schools and she withdrew herself as far as she could till he reached his peroration. "Why Fielding should go to such lengths to support this cub I don't know," he confessed. "But it is my intention to expose it."

"Arthur," she said, "please leave it alone." She met his offended stare with all the earnestness at her command. "You have no standing—It really isn't your job. And I'm sure there's nothing—"

"My dear Cynthia, I am a Governor of Ledenham—"

"But you aren't."

"—I am a nominated Governor of Ledenham and when I join a body of this kind I do so with the intention of taking my full share in the work and responsibilities of that body. I will most assuredly not leave this matter alone. Indeed I have already—"

Pigeon had sounded the gong for dinner and Julie was crossing the hall with the gait she had adopted as appropriate for a victim. Lady Hinton-Brigg had been amused by it in a dry way. It reminded her of the step-pause-step-pause of the tragedy queen of melodrama, but tonight she only thought that this scene with Arthur was coming to an end and she must make one more effort to stop him. She got to her feet and cut in abruptly to his important flow.

"I have known Lord Leyburn all my life," she said, "and I've always been afraid of him. If you take him and Mr. Fielding on, Arthur, you will be defeated." Julie's hand was on the door and she finished hurriedly, "I ask you—I *beg* you to leave it alone."

When the door opened Sir Arthur was smiling. "I think," said, "that you may leave it to me."

On the following morning the packet thrust carelessly and unregistered into the post by Julie reached Oonagh. Mrs. Hepburn whose life was less colourful than she would have liked, was apt to take an embarrassing interest in her daughter's mail but Oonagh was usually able to counter it. She took the pearls and the letter addressed to herself out of the packet and stuffing the remainder into the large hand-bag she carried about with her proceeded to distract her mother's attention.

"Oh!" she gasped. "*How* lovely! The *sweetie*—Look, Mum—" and she held out the necklace.

"Pearls!" said Mrs. Hepburn. "But they look—" she took them and peered at them, "They're quite good. Whoever—"

"Julie Hinton-Brigg," Oonagh gave her little laugh. "I told you she's taken a fancy to be friends and she said she wanted me to have these. I never really thought she meant it, bless her. Yes," she had opened the letter, "she says she wishes they were real and worth a fortune but hopes I'll like wearing them all the same."

"What else is in the envelope?" asked Mrs. Hepburn suspiciously.

"Patterns," said Oonagh and went on reading Julie's letter. "Dear Oonagh," it said. "Here are the things I promised and I hope you get them all right but I still don't know how I'm going to manage but I expect I'll think of something only of course I've got to get to the bank. It would be easier to send a cheque but of course it wouldn't be safe. Everything's quite bloody. I'll have to make up something about losing the pearls as they're sure to notice and I don't know how I'm going to manage till I get my next dollop of allowance. But still—Tim is worth all I suffer. Please give him the letter I'm sending with this and make a plan with him. Tell him I'm practically *in chains* and I don't know how we'll manage, but tell him I'll be on the look-out and do anything and I think it might work on the phone if he said he was Cubby and you could say you were Iona Macadam about the Reel Club. I am counting on you to do your best and of course you should considering what I'm giving you. Love from Julie."

Oonagh maintained her pleased smile to this point without much difficulty and then she came to the postscript. "You'll have to be a bit careful about the pearls," wrote Julie with a slight stirring of the business blood of past Hintons and Briggs. "They're not really so valuable but Pop hates losing things and there's a mark to identify them with." Oonagh took the point and her small mouth was compressed as she rearranged her ideas on the subject of helping Julie's little affair along.

She took a day to think about it, carrying her bag with the £30 and the pearls in it wherever she went; and in the course of it she steamed open the letter to Tim and burnt it. It explained fully the arrangement between herself and Julie. Several matters in her life were in a state of instability. Miss Wills was reported to be progressing well so that her job in the School would shortly come to an end, and in some way which she did not altogether understand she had failed to establish herself in the School community. With the advent of Eric it had seemed as though she might as well let Ledenham slide; a job in Snaydon, near, or even in Hinton Brigg Ltd. would have many advantages. But then again, Eric was far from being a safe bet. It had taken all her ingenuity to recover the ground lost by the Reel Club mistake, for though Eric had quite enjoyed it he had not hesitated to point out that she had looked silly and it wasn't her fault that he hadn't looked silly too. It had been a near thing and he was still uncomfortably wary.

On Wednesday afternoon she had decided on her line and taking advantage of her employer's absence she went to the Zoo to call on Tim.

Heavy, cold rain was messily disposing of the remaining snow and Tim, who had spent the first part of the afternoon driving Nurse Wills to Leyburn, was in no mood for lady visitors. He made no effort to conceal his bored surprise when Oonagh appeared and his greeting was sour, but Oonagh had decided on a reasonable man-to-man approach and was not offended.

"Look," she began with great frankness, "quite honestly I don't know what you're feeling about this and if you don't want to go on with it just say. I've had a cry for help from Julie." Tim stiffened and she hurried on before he could speak, describing Julie's plight with an easy balance which would allow her to remain on the fence till she saw her way. "I'm afraid she's having hell, poor sweet," she concluded, nicely sorry about it, "and there's no doubt about what she feels for you. I mean—she's serious."

She had seated herself in Tim's best armchair but he had remained standing and he looked down at her very coldly. "My good Oonagh," he said, "you must know as well as I do that this is twaddle. Go home and tell Julie to forget it." He made a movement suggesting that the interview was over but Oonagh sat still.

"Well—" she gave a little laugh and shrugged a shoulder "—that seems clear enough. Still, she did sort of appeal to me and—well I suppose I ought to tell you she does think you're as serious as she is."

"She isn't serious and she knows I'm not. Dammit—she's engaged to this Lucreton fellow."

"That's not true, you know. It's all Sartha's idea. She'd run away with you tomorrow, Tim. She would really."

Tim laughed involuntarily. "Not her. And there's absolutely nothing of Young Lochinvar about me."

"Pardon?"

"Let it pass. The episode is closed, Oonagh, and there's no future for a romantic plot, if you were thinking on those lines." He looked at her as he spoke and to her dismay she felt that her expression had slipped. His eyes sharpened. "Are you up to some thing?" he asked. "Because, if so, kindly stop it. What *is* all this?"

Oonagh laughed and clutching her large hand-bag struggled up from the sagging depths of the chair. "It's nothing on earth," she cried, "beyond a mild pity for poor Julie. She's rather a dim-wit, I agree, but one can't help feeling sorry for her. No plot, Tim, I assure you."

"I hope not," said Tim.

"Forget it," said Oonagh, and resuming her good-natured smile as she buttoned her coat: "Don't hold it against me, will you?"

Tim said: "Oh, of course not," and moved towards the door. "I suppose," he added with perfunctory politeness, "your job in the School is nearly finished. Have you enjoyed it?"

"Oh yes," she responded readily. "I've a tremendous admiration for the Beak, of course, and it's great fun being behind the scenes and knowing all the secrets."

"It must be," Tim's words were inoffensive but his expression was ironic and Oonagh was stung.

"Have you heard yet," she asked, "about Patsy Henderson? He's going to be Headmaster of Upton."

"*What?*" Tim spun round, politeness swept away.

"Oh yes," she was drawing on her gloves, dropping her inside knowledge airily. "He's been asked to—"

"Oonagh," snapped Tim and gripped her arm painfully, "do you realize what you're doing? Nobody's heard a whisper of this. If it's true it's *secret*—"

"Well—you needn't bite," protested Oonagh. "I know it's secret but I'm not broadcasting it. I'm only telling you—"

"You've no right to tell anyone. It's dishonest. You're trusted to hold your tongue about what you hear."

"Well—I wasn't—" she hesitated and looked at him uneasily, "I mean—I didn't promise—I mean it just happened that—" her voice died away under his angry eyes and after a pause he turned her round to the door and let go of her arm.

"Off you go," he said, "and for God's sake keep your silly little mouth shut. I shall have to think what to do."

"Tim!" she cried. "What do you mean? You're not going to say anything? What a fuss—I only told you. Honestly I won't tell another soul if you're in such a state—"

"What's that worth?" demanded Tim and repeated, "I'll have to think about it."

She tried pleading and tears, mockery and threats and

finally went away. Twenty minutes later Tim walked along the road to Holly Lodge. It had been so much a habit to walk straight in and knock on the living-room door that it was not till he saw Frances and the baby in the room with Patsy that he remembered it was a habit no longer.

"Sorry to barge in on you like this," he said a little awkwardly. "Could I speak to you for a minute, Patsy?"

"Sure," said Patsy and as Tim hesitated, "Is it private?"

"Well—not from Frances, I imagine. The fact is I've heard something which I shouldn't have heard." He told his story quickly, standing at a distance from them, near the door, as a boy does who comes in on business and doesn't like to intrude further than he must. Patsy stood in his characteristic position leaning against the mantelpiece, Frances, with a dismayed face, sat near him and out of the corner of his eye Tim could see the absorbed back of the baby whose whole self was concentrated on something out of sight. "I don't know if it's serious," he concluded, "but I thought I'd better let you know."

"Thanks Tim," said Patsy. "Glad you did. It's not too good as a matter of fact, because I swore I'd keep it dark. I haven't been offered the job. The present chap's retirement hasn't been announced yet and they've merely asked a preliminary question or two. Nobody's meant to know about it except the Beak and Mrs. Beak and ourselves. Not even Nick," he added "—and not even my parents."

"But how on earth," burst from Frances, "did the wretched girl *get* it? Surely Uncle Hugh wouldn't dictate that letter he wrote to the Bishop?"

Patsy said: "I'm sure he didn't. In fact he said so." He looked puzzled and Tim remembered Oonagh stammering:

"I didn't promise—I just happened—"

"A bit of snoopery, I fancy," he said. "Well—I'll leave it with you." He looked at Patsy. "Your little secret's safe with me, but I don't know what else may happen to it."

"No," said Patsy. "I think we'll have to take it to the Beak, you know. Better both go."

"If you think I'm needed," said Tim. "Let me know—Oh, hullo, John."

The baby, having finished with whatever had been engaging him, had caught sight of a grey flannel leg and grasping it firmly was struggling to his feet. He managed it and in his triumph sat down again with an expression of exquisite chagrin. Tim, since his errand was done, was anxious to get away but he was unable to resist a look of angry appeal.

"Hard cheese," he said solemnly and postponing his escape held out a finger. "Try again."

Frances got up from her chair. "Stay and have tea, Tim," she said. "Marthe's just bringing it."

"Thank you, Frances," he said, "but—"

"Please stay," said Frances.

"He'll do what he's told, of course," said Patsy and heaved himself upright. "I'll go and ring the Beak now."

Frances went out of the room and he followed her. Tim played with the baby, thinking of the last time he had been in the house and listening for some sound of Marthe. He didn't know whether he was glad or sorry to be there; whether the palpitations he was now suffering were better or worse than the hopeless ache he had been getting used to. John was again roughly vertical. One hand clung to a trouser leg, with the other he clutched a finger and, wavering slightly, concentrated on the problem of balance. It was touch and go for a minute, then he was steady and his flushed, anxious face began a cautious beam of triumph. Tim laughed and Marthe came in.

"Sh!" said Tim holding up his free hand in warning. "Don't disturb."

"Someone else is showing off today, I think," she said and John sat down heavily.

"O-oh," said Tim and Marthe in a descending groan.

"O-oh," echoed John, disgusted, and Tim meeting Marthe's smile decided that the palpitations were worth it.

"The Beak," said Patsy coming back from the telephone, "is out somewhere. Higgins doesn't know when he'll be back. Have to try again."

Earlier in the day the Headmaster had held a brief and cryptic telephone conversation with the Clerk to the Governors. Mr. Craig was a man who feared the worst and he had a deep, rather hollow voice which could sound as gloomy as anything in nature.

"I think," he said mournfully, "that we'd better meet."

"Yes," agreed Mr. Fielding who had opened his post. "I'll come in this afternoon," and while Tim told the Hendersons about Oonagh's revelation he was drinking a cup of weak tea in the Clerk's office and examining the steps taken by Sir Arthur Hinton-Brigg.

He had been informed of the steps that morning in a curt letter from Sir Arthur who was, he said, gravely concerned by his, the Headmaster's, attitude in the matter of his, Sir Arthur's, complaint against Mr. Selby. Since then he had been shocked to hear from a parent who appealed to him as

248

a nominated Governor of the School that the same master had violently attacked her son, striking him repeatedly on the head. And finally he had heard from this parent that on the attack being reported to him the Headmaster had admitted that he himself had beaten this unfortunate boy later on the same day. "It is almost incredible," concluded Sir Arthur, "that such a case of brutality can occur in a school of the standing of Ledenham. As one of those who share responsibility for the School I am taking steps to ensure that the matter is brought to the notice of the Governors."

"This is mine," said the Headmaster passing it to the Clerk. "What did you get?"

"A—" moaned Mr. Craig, "well, not much. I was only told that he was circulating the information to all the Governors."

"He didn't send the circular billets to you?"

"A—no. Sent them direct. But Tommy Ward looked in and showed me his. A—I took a copy."

He pushed across a smeary photostat and Mr. Fielding read it. The accusations were there and the Governors were advised to investigate a situation which Sir Arthur Hinton-Brigg regarded as exceedingly grave.

"This is libellous," said Mr. Fielding.

The Clerk sighed. "Yes. Both yourself and Selby . . . Actions would certainly lie, I should say. But . . ."

Mr. Fielding looked at him with sudden amusement, almost glee. "You don't happen to know who Selby's father is, do you?" he asked. "No—neither does Hinton-Brigg probably. He's the Q.C."

"Quentin Selby?" Mr. Craig paused for a moment with

open mouth and then smiled. "Really?"

"Now this," the Headmaster tapped the paper in front of him. "What is to be done?"

"Nothing can be done till the Chairman gets home," said the Clerk. "He's gone to join Lady Leyburn at Nice. He won't be back for a month. And then," he spoke with gloomy relish, "there will have to be some discussion—with yourself and probably the Bishop. Ward, too, possibly—Then of course if it is decided to have a meeting proper notice must be given."

Mr. Fielding did not share his legal friend's fondness for delay. "I don't think we can wait, Craig," he said decisively. "It's too messy. You'll have to send this out to the Chairman. Write tonight—so will I. Oh—you might make me a copy of this letter."

"Right," said Mr. Craig taking it. "Miss Wills not back yet, is she? Awkward."

"Very," agreed Mr. Fielding.

14

WITH the snow melting a lot of mess came into the House. They couldn't help it, in and out all the time, and Higgins did not resent it unduly. He got going again on the School entrance and, since the Headmaster was out, he accompanied the leisurely sweeps of the mop with a vocal number.

"Meh-mo-rees," he warbled in an edgy tenor, "Meh-mo-rees—Dreams of lerv so true-oo—O'er the sea—of meh-moree I'm drifting back to—" He broke off to listen to the telephone ringing in the secretary's office. It had been going on for some time. It was still going on; too long for the Swooner, as the boys called her, to be in the you-know-where. He leant his mop against the wall and tramped along to the office which was empty, untidy and deserted looking. Proper mess, thought Higgins, and she'd nipped out and never even alerted him for the phone.

"School House," he said into the telephone and drew the messages-pad towards him. "No, sir, he's out. Right, sir, I'll see he gets it." He put down the telephone and glanced at the clock. It had stopped and he paused for calculation and then wrote: "4.15 approx. Sir, Mr. Henderson rung. Will be obliged to be rung back on return."

On return the Headmaster went straight to his study and picked up the telephone. It was dumb. Still holding it he put a finger on the secretary's bell. No reply. He went through to the deserted office, observing that it was not yet 5 o'clock and used the telephone on the secretary's table.

"Pearson-Smith?" he said. "I would like you to come

251

round if you can—Yes—now." His letters, ready for signing, were on the table and beside them Higgins' courteous message. Frowning and irritated, Mr. Fielding switched the telephone through to the study and rang Patsy Henderson up from his own desk. His eyebrows went up when Patsy said: "Selby and I would like to see you, sir," but he replied merely: "Certainly. In about three-quarters of an hour," and turned to his letters. They needed a good deal of correction; he put aside two which could not be sent as they were and rang for Higgins.

"Post," he said, handing him the bundle. "When did Miss Hepburn go?"

"I don't know, sir," Higgins sounded shocked and at the same time self-righteous. "She was gone some while before I took that call and she never came back 'cause I was mopping."

"Did she tell you she was going?"

"No, sir. I just happened to hear the phone 'cause I was mopping."

"All right," said the Headmaster and Higgins withdrew as Mr. Pearson-Smith arrived.

When the door was shut and his caller seated Mr. Fielding began at once: "There's a follow-up to the Seckers' call, P.-S., and I think you must be in on it." It was his instinct, when trouble arose, to confine it always to the fewest possible people and the fewest possible words. Since he presided responsibly over a community of roughly six hundred souls, troubles, varying in kind and importance, were his lot and he was an expert, but this particular trouble was not under his own control. Sir Arthur Hinton-Brigg did not share his belief in economy and restraint and it seemed to him that it would probably be necessary for most of the commonroom to know what was afoot, at least enough to be prepared to meet a flank attack. To Pearson-Smith, who was, as Secker's housemaster, already involved, he showed Sir Arthur's letters to himself and the Governors.

When Mr. Pearson-Smith was moved he looked dyspeptic. His long Sherlock Holmes face was grey and his nose was red when he finished reading. "*Good God!*" he said and stared at his Headmaster who obeying his instinct allowed himself a wry smile and spoke matter-of-factly.

"A good example of inflation, isn't it? I don't think we need take it too seriously, you know. It's a nuisance."

"But I *saw* the Seckers," exploded Mr. Pearson-Smith. "The day they were here. I saw them before you did—or after. I *told* them the boy had been troublesome—" He looked angrily at the Headmaster. "You know very well, Headmaster, that I find young Selby—tiresome. He's not a fellow I like and I think he was wrong to smack the boy. But I realized afterwards that Secker had, in fact, asked for it and so I told the parents." He waved Sir Arthur's letter and quoted: "Striking him repeatedly on the head— Nonsense! He got one box on the ears. Brutality? Tchah!"

"Yes," said the Headmaster soothingly. "Very silly."

"It's the woman—the mother. The father wasn't so unreasonable."

Mr. Fielding agreed. Fathers, in his experience, seldom were so unreasonable, and Mr. Pearson-Smith, simmering, turned to the letter addressed to the Governors. "I don't know about all this first part—Pursuing his daughter? I don't believe it." He was recovering a little and almost

253

returned to his usual manner. "It's common knowledge that that Danish girl of the Hendersons has Selby's heart."

The Headmaster with his finger on the pulse of the meeting sat up ready to proceed. "I know nothing about Selby's heart," he said, "except that, like you, I'm sure Miss Hinton-Brigg has no lien on it. Now, I don't think there is any action to be taken but our attitude should be—"

The outburst being over they talked usefully and Mr. Pearson-Smith was on his feet preparing to depart when Patsy and Tim appeared.

"Come in," the Headmaster said to their looks of polite enquiry. "We've just finished. That's all, P.-S., isn't it? We've got our line."

"Yes," said Mr. Pearson-Smith. "Thank you," but he did not go. He hesitated and then, looking dyspeptic again, said: "I think, Headmaster, that in the presence of yourself and Henderson I should say to Selby that I hold him blameless with regard to Secker. I—in fact I supported him when I saw the parents and I shall continue to do so."

Tim had heard nothing of the Secker parents. His jaw dropped. "Er—" he began and the Headmaster moved in.

"That's excellent," he said. "Most satisfactory. Thank you very much, P.-S.—Good night." Mr. Pearson-Smith, greatly embarrassed, went away and he turned to the two younger men and told them to sit down. "This is a tiresome development," he went on cheerfully, "but I think we shall clear it up without much trouble. Of course these allegations won't stand up for a minute—" He caught sight of two puzzled faces and stopped, feeling as though he had missed a step.

"I don't understand, sir," said Tim worriedly.

"Developments? Have the Seckers—"

"I'm sorry," said the Headmaster and paused. Sometimes on busy days he became oppressed by the sound of his own voice. He now seemed to hear it grinding out, of its own accord, bright professional platitudes, in this case, unfortunately, from the wrong sound-track. "Ours is a full life," he said apologetically, and to Tim, "There is a Secker development, Selby, which I've been discussing with Pearson-Smith. I'm afraid I assumed it had reached you and you'd co-opted Henderson and come to talk about it . . . What can I do for you both?"

Patsy answered: "I'm afraid this is a new headache, sir. Mine. Your secretary confided to Selby this afternoon that I'm going to be Headmaster of Upton."

"But," said the Headmaster of Ledenham, "how did she get it?" expressing no surprise, Tim noticed, that having got it Oonagh should talk. "I received one letter," he went on slowly, recalling the matter as he spoke, "and wrote one—in longhand; made a copy, also in longhand, and locked it up. Blotting-paper? No—it's an overrated source. They—the Bishop's letter and the copy of my reply are in the safe file and the key is on my ring. Wait—" He shut his eyes and they waited. In a moment he opened them again and said: "Yes. I remember. I was reading the Bishop's letter and several things happened at once—telephone and so on. She was standing by the desk. Did you terrify her, Selby?"

"I did my best, sir," said Tim. "I don't know how far I was successful."

"I'm not much concerned for myself," said Patsy, "but it might worry the Upton chaps. Ought I to let them know there's been a leak, sir?"

The Headmaster said: "No. I hope we can seal it. Leave it with me and I'll try it anyhow. I'm sorry, Henderson."

"You couldn't possibly have prevented it, sir. Natural hazard."

"I should probably have got somebody more reliable from the start. An outsider—But this girl was here and I thought she couldn't do much harm if I was careful. Which," added Mr. Fielding ruefully, "I was, but not sufficiently it seems. Now—as you're here—this Secker business."

Patsy got up to go. "You won't want me any longer, sir?"

"Well," he glanced at Tim, "it has blown up so far that a good many people must know about it. I don't know if you'd rather talk privately, Selby?"

"No, sir," said poor Tim, wondering what was coming and Mr. Fielding smiled.

"I thought when you both came in," he said, "that co-opting Henderson was a good idea. He has a calming influence . . ." and Patsy laughed and sat down again.

Half an hour later when they got up to go Tim said: "Sir, wouldn't it be better if I just—went?"

"Most certainly not," was the reply, instant and authoritative. "You would merely disarm me." He looked kindly at the young man's shocked face and added: "I think I can assure you that there will be nothing worse than unpleasantness which will pass. What about your parents?"

Tim thought for a moment and then laughed suddenly. "My mother wouldn't be safe," he said. "She'd be as bad as Mrs. Secker. My father ought to know, perhaps. I'm not sure."

"I should tell him," said Mr. Fielding thinking of his own

sons. "Now," he glanced at his watch, "I will go and have a talk with Miss Hepburn in the presence of *her* unreasonable mother."

Patsy and Tim walked away from School House in silence. Tim's mind felt as though it had been involved in an earthquake or a hurricane and as they walked one aspect of one of the various shocks occurred to him which he had overlooked at the time the shock was administered.

"I can't imagine this place without you in it," he said. "As a matter of fact I thought you were lined up for P.-S's House." Having said it he wondered if it would have been better to make no reference to his accidental knowledge but Patsy merely glanced at him with mild amusement.

"Lord bless you," said his easy voice, "you can't imagine me in that job, can you?"

Tim, startled, thought about it and could imagine it very well. "Why not?" he asked.

"Not my dish," said Patsy. "I am lined up for the House and that's as far out of my rut as I'm going."

"Aren't you keen on the other thing?"

"No. I sometimes think I'm too comfortable here, but I don't let it worry me."

They had reached the Zoo and Tim's thoughts reverted to the Hinton-Brigg menace. "I've got some whisky," he said. "Will you come in and have some?"

"Good idea," said Patsy.

Tim's room had a strong family likeness to the one which had been Patsy's before it was occupied by Angus, and Patsy looked very comfortably at home standing against the mantelpiece filling his pipe. He was twelve years ahead of Tim in age and experience but he never gave the

257

impression of looking down and though Tim had both liked and admired him it was only now, as he was getting out bottle and glasses, that it struck him how much further on than himself Patsy was. The presence of the tall lounging figure was wonderfully comforting. It was so easy and balanced; it had the kind of assurance which gave no thought to assurance and to a very young man, by nature impetuous, who was going through an acutely painful and difficult phase of young man's troubles it proclaimed a security, remote but infinitely desirable.

He put a glass on the mantelpiece and Patsy said "Thanks" through clouds of smoke. Tim sat down with his own drink and a cigarette and came to a decision.

"If you don't mind," he said, "I'd like to tell you how this damned Hinton-Brigg lunacy blew up. There was really nothing to it, you know."

"I never supposed there was," said Patsy. "A chap usually runs around with a girl or two and you couldn't possibly foresee Sartha. He's unique in my experience."

"You know him, do you?"

"Come across him a bit in the county cricket. Quite a good cricketer in his day but a swab from birth by all accounts."

This was enjoyable but Tim had no time at present to discuss Sir Arthur. He returned to Julie. "I sort of dashed at her," he explained, "because Marthe turned me down. I'd have done better, perhaps, to talk to you about that before." He scowled at the fire. "I wanted—I still want Marthe to marry me. She was definite enough—I don't know if I'd have a chance if—if I tried again."

Patsy glanced at him and smoked for a moment in

258

silence. "I don't know," he said. "There was no reason, really, why you should have talked to me. I'm not much of a hand at that sort of thing and though we're responsible for Marthe's well-being while she's with us, we've no *locus standi.*"

"I suppose not."

There was a silence and into it came the mournful sound of a flute. Patsy cocked an interested head.

" 'Where e'er you walk'," he observed. "I thought 'Sheep may safely graze' was his piece."

"It was till Secker killed it for him," said Tim. "He's never played it since and he was getting on quite well. How glad I am that I clouted that oaf."

"Yes," said Patsy. "Well—time may heal the wound— Richards' I mean." He finished his drink and stood upright saying that he must get back and see what Frances was doing. But he paused before he went with direct friendly eyes on Tim. "You know," he said, "Marthe's only about nineteen and she's a long way from home."

Tim said: "Yes—I know."

"She seemed quite pleased to see you this afternoon, I thought," continued Mr. Henderson moderately. "If I were you, Tim, I should re-embark. But only if you make up your mind to a long and up-hill wooing. Keep off love altogether till you can go to Norway and see her with her own people."

"Oh God!" exclaimed Tim getting to his feet. "What a fool I've been! Poor Marthe—"

Patsy laughed. "Well—yes," he agreed. "But also poor Tim. It's hell . . . I wouldn't worry about this turn up," he added, turning to Tim's secondary trouble. "The Beak'll sort it out. I wonder how he's getting on with Miss H."

Tim had been quite successful in terrifying Oonagh, but at first her predominating emotion was astonishment. Apart from a natural desire to prove inside knowledge and wipe that smug look off his face, Oonagh told herself that she had merely been acting on a kindly impulse to do him a good turn by putting him ahead with a juicy bit of news. She was so shattered by his reaction that when she left the Zoo she was at a loss. To go back to her office, perhaps face a Beak already informed, or to go home to her mother's inquisitive eyes seemed equally impossible, and she turned away to the village and walked about, staring blankly at its rather limited window displays.

Presently it occurred to her that it would be as well to clear her feet of Julie Hinton-Brigg. Furthermore it would be convenient to ring up from a call-box. And if she did it now she would probably miss Sir Arthur.

But Sir Arthur was not tied to office hours and when the telephone rang he was having tea with his wife and daughter. Lady Hinton-Brigg who was nearest the telephone took it up and said: "Thaxley Manor."

"Oh," said a slightly flurried voice, "this is Alison Fielding speaking. Could I speak to Julie, please?"

"Hold on," said Lady Hinton-Brigg and put her hand over the mouthpiece. "Alison Fielding wants you, Julie."

"*Alison Fielding?*" To anybody but her father Julie's surprise would have made it clear that she had nothing to hope for from Alison, but as she was getting up from her chair Sir Arthur said: "Stop!" and got up himself. Everybody living in Ledenham was suspect in his view and anyone named Fielding was anathema. He strode across and took the telephone from his wife.

"Miss Hinton-Brigg," he told it, "regrets that she is obliged to refuse further communication with you," and he put it down and returned to his chair. Julie, with open mouth, stared at him for a moment then burst into tears and fled from the room.

"Arthur," said Lady Hinton-Brigg, "the Fieldings are well-known and popular in the county. You are making us a laughing-stock. Worse. You're disgracing yourself—and me."

"I think, my dear Cynthia," replied Sir Arthur, "that you will do best to leave the matter to me."

In the call-box at Ledenham Oonagh gaped at the abruptly silenced instrument with wide eyes and dropped jaw. Her inside information did not extend far enough for her to suspect that Sir Arthur might dislike the name of Fielding and she could not imagine how she had given herself or been given away. Had Julie said something idiotic? Or did Lady Hinton-Brigg know Alison well enough to recognise that the voice was not hers? She might never know the explanation, but it was clear that telephonic communication was off.

She walked home, confused and troubled, wondering as she went if a timely attack of flu would solve her problems. But she expected Eric that evening and decided to postpone it. A headache would serve and it could develop or recover as circumstances required. "I'll just have a cup of tea and aspirin, and lie down for a bit," she told her mother, and brushing questions and suggestions aside she went upstairs and shut herself in her bedroom.

She was still in it when Mr. Fielding arrived and Mrs. Hepburn's greeting held a perceptible tinge of reproach. "I'm afraid you can't possibly see her now—she's lying down. A really blinding headache, poor child. I know she wouldn't give up till she simply couldn't help it and she hasn't been in long."

"I believe she left the office before 4 o'clock," said Mr. Fielding, "but that isn't what I am concerned with now. If she is in bed, Mrs. Hepburn, perhaps you would take me up and let me have a word with her in your presence. I have daughters of my own," he added pleasantly but without any suggestion of giving way, "and it is important."

Mrs. Hepburn, rather shaken, pushed open a door. "If you'll wait in the lounge," she said, "I'll speak to Oonagh."

Waiting among the plywood panelling and dainty pinks of the room which smelt a little stuffily of Mrs. Hepburn and Oonagh, Mr. Fielding was informed by sounds from above that his temporary secretary had locked herself in. The nearer voice was urgent, the more distant one bleated protestingly and he considered the implications of a refusal to come out, but in a few minutes Mrs. Hepburn returned with Oonagh, fully dressed and very sulky, behind her.

"A most miserable child," announced Mrs. Hepburn, hamming her motherliness, "but she's got herself up and come to say she's sorry."

Neither lady was of a type that appealed to Mr. Fielding but Oonagh was young and feminine and in the way of discipline he was not accustomed to girls.

"Oonagh knows," he said gently, "that it is a more serious matter than leaving her work early."

"I had a frightful headache," whined Oonagh, putting off

the crux of the interview. From somewhere the words "Official Secrets Act" had leapt into her mind and the gentleness of Mr. Fielding was far more terrifying than the roughness of Mr. Selby. "I know I should have told Higgins but I forgot. I—"

"All right," Mr. Fielding interrupted her and came to the point. She had read a confidential letter which she was not meant to read and she had talked about it.

"I can't see that it's so desperate," she cried defensively. "It's not life and death or selling information to the enemy. I only told Tim Selby. I thought he'd be interested and everybody will know soon anyway."

"Oh—is it the Henderson appointment?" said Mrs. Hepburn, enlightened. "Yes—well doesn't it seem rather a fuss about—I mean these things always are known, aren't they, long before the official announcement?"

There was an uncomfortable silence. Her daughter's face was scarlet and the Headmaster's was less gentle.

"One unfortunate and rather serious aspect of the matter, Mrs. Hepburn," he said, "is that the information spread by your daughter is incorrect. But the real point is that she knows perfectly well what her duty to her employer is. It was stressed by me and it must have been stressed in her training that all information, trifling or important, which comes to a secretary through her job is secret. Breaking that rule is the most serious crime she can commit."

Oonagh burst into tears. She sank into a chair sobbing: "I didn't mean—I'd no idea—I never thought—I won't go back—it isn't fair—"

"But," cried Mrs. Hepburn aghast, "you can't—Everybody knows," she turned on the Headmaster, "everybody knows she is doing the job while Miss Wills is away. What will people say if she leaves before Miss Wills is back? What about a reference?"

Mr. Fielding had very little doubt what people would say but as he thought about the girl's future he was oppressed by the feeling that he himself was greatly to blame. An irresponsible Ledenham girl was a bad appointment, even for a few weeks. An outsider, however irresponsible, would have nobody to confide in, no interest in what she heard or read. He had put too much temptation in Oonagh's way, giving her an irresistible chance to show off, and he must save her from the consequences if she would allow herself to be saved.

"I quite agree," he said to Mrs. Hepburn, "that it would be damaging if she left now. She has had a pretty severe lesson and I'm going to leave it to herself." He turned to Oonagh and compelled her to look at him. "Are you prepared to go on with your job sensibly and honestly till Miss Wills comes back?" Oonagh wept anew. "Think about it for a minute," he said.

Mrs. Hepburn chattered of references, other jobs, over-work and strain. Oonagh, buried in her handkerchief, thought about it and plumped for repentance.

"Oh—yes," she said and looked up with tear-filled eyes at her employer. "How—how good you are to me. I'm so terribly sorry. It was so thoughtless and silly. I promise I'll do my very best—I'll never be able to repay your kindness—"

"Very well," said Mr. Fielding and went away, greatly revolted.

One way and another Oonagh had had a severe shaking

and her pale face and a lingering pinkness about the eyes led Eric, when they were seated in the saloon bar of the Swan that evening, to enquire unflatteringly if she was sickening for something.

"Oh no," she said with a brave little smile, "just a terribly heavy day. Quite honestly, I'm a wee bit worried. Do you often see Julie?"

Eric was amused. He was not deliberately deceiving Oonagh about his job, she could take it or leave it, but it was part of his tough creed to give no information about himself. If it had been the other way round he would have found out all about her quick enough and he was surprised that the penny hadn't dropped before now. But he did not dislike her simple-mindedness. He saw Julie most days, he said. "Why?"

"Well," said Oonagh, "you know this business about her and Tim Selby?"

"The school-teacher?"

"That's right. Well of course," Oonagh was very casual at this point, "I know Tim quite well. Not my dish, I may add, but still—Tastes differ. Anyway Julie, being more or less in chains, yelled for help." A nice touch occurred to her here and she added: "I didn't like to tell you at the time, but that was why I *had* to go to that foul Reel Club, actually. I'd promised to see her there." She glanced up but it was difficult to tell how it had gone. There was no response in the bright brown eyes staring at her through the smoke and she reverted to the main theme feeling rather discouraged. "Well—I saw Tim today and the thing's dead. Not a flicker. I don't see how I can do anything more but I've got to tell her. Could you get a letter to her?"

Eric stirred and felt for his cigarettes. "Ring up, why don't you?" he asked, holding out the packet.

"I did, but her father wouldn't let me speak to her. Thanks."

"How come Sartha connects you with it?"

"Oh, he doesn't," said Oonagh quickly and then stopped. It was all too complicated, too difficult to remember what she had planned to say or foresee where a careless word might lead. "Quite frankly," she went on with a laugh, "I wasn't *going* to be connected with it. I didn't give my name."

"What name did you give?"

"Oh—I forget."

"Come on," said Eric.

Oonagh, considerably startled, tried a gay, "Who do you think *you* are?" but it failed. He simply sat waiting to be told till she told him.

"Funny," he said after a long pause. The whole thing was funny, he thought. Between Pigeon's facetious reports and his own observation he was fairly well abreast and it was his opinion, and Pigeon's too, that the teacher had never been all that keen and had switched off without a backward glance. Sartha and Julie, however, were still keeping steam up and Eric's mind groped about his own errand to School House through the snow; the sudden eruption of Alison Fielding into the picture; Julie in Leyburn coming out of Woolworth's; now Oonagh.

"I suppose I could get a letter to her," he said at last. "Got it written?"

"Yes," said Oonagh and took it out of her large bag which still held the packet of bank-notes. She felt Eric's eyes on the bag and snapped it shut. "Here it is," she said and handed him the letter.

Eric examined the envelope back and front and then, without saying anything, put it in his pocket and went across to the bar to get more drinks. Oonagh peered after him. He was not hurrying as he usually did but standing at one end of the bar counter, allowing later comers to get their orders ahead of him. She sagged in her chair and yawned, nervous and very tired, and let her eyes close for a minute. When she opened them Eric was coming back, carrying her gin and orange and his own pint and looking purposeful.

"Look," he said, when he had sat down again beside her, "I want to read this," and he took the letter out of his pocket.

"*What?*" the exclamation came out in a screech and she turned it as well as she could into a laugh. "Oh no, Eric! Have a heart! After all it's got all poor Julie's secrets in it—" She made a grab for it but he twitched it easily out of her reach and made no response to her attempts at playfulness.

"It's like this, see," he proceeded, "there's a hell of a lot of honky-tonk about this business. Sartha's up to something, young Julie's up to something, and you can't kid me *you're* not pretty deep in. Well—I'm not sticking my neck out. I've got my job to think of." There were no half-measures about Eric. Either he told nothing or he told all and in this case he told all with devastating candour. He told the wilting Oonagh about his job, his theories about getting on in the world and his moral standards. Finally he wound up: "So that's the way it is. You let me see what's written in this here and I'll think about it. If I don't see it—" he made

267

a graphic gesture, "—caput. I'm through."

"I don't know what you mean," quavered Oonagh. "Do you mean if I let you read it you'll promise—"

"I'm only making one promise," said Eric. "If I don't read it I take you home right now and I'm off. Just as you say— it's all the same to me. I like you all right, I'm not saying I don't, but no girl's going to get *me* airborne. I like to keep my feet on the floor and see where I'm going."

She hesitated but her resistance was lowered by the experiences of the day and the tough, uncompromising attitude adopted by Eric was having a strange effect on her. She resented him, she was afraid of him; above all she longed to cast herself and her troubles on to his sturdy chest and let him cope, and it was so uncertain that the chest would receive her.

"Okay," she said with a heart-rending sniff. "Go on."

Eric glanced at her as he took the envelope and at once tore it open and read the letter. "Gawd!" he said. "Of all the dopes—"

The saloon bar of the Swan was a discouraging apartment, decorated in bilious cream and chocolate and with horse-brasses poorly polished, but the beer was good and it was filling up. Oonagh was already in tears and on the verge of loud, uncontrollable sobbing.

"We'll get out o' here," said Eric hurriedly, and seizing the hand-bag and her oddments of gloves and scarf he bundled her out, not omitting to give the barman a nod and a "G'night," and through the rain to the Land Rover.

He drove a mile or two away from Ledenham with Oonagh crying wholeheartedly beside him and when he stopped the car she cast herself uninvited against his shoulder and poured out the story of her day. He felt rather sorry for her and switching the engine on again left it running with the heater at full blast.

"That'll do now," he said. "Stop it, can't you? Go on— mop yourself up." He stared moodily through the windscreen while she did what she could with her sodden face. Then he delivered his ultimatum. He couldn't do with any funny business. If she wanted to see him again she must leave it to him to get a censored letter to Julie which would get her, Oonagh, clear. "You can tell her all what you said about the teacher," he added. "Sooner she gets it in her silly head that's off the better."

"What about the money?" asked Oonagh miserably.

Eric was realistic. "Well—depends. If she says anything she'll have to have it. Don't want no trouble. But she deserves to lose it—might teach her something and she'll not miss it all that. See how it goes. Better give back the necklace though."

Oonagh did not hesitate. "All right," she said, taking off the pearls. "I'll leave everything to you, Eric," and she handed them over, gazing at him with meek docility.

The dashboard light was dim and though the tears had blurred her face they had left it looking soft and young. Eric regarded it sternly but not with complete condemnation. She was, he thought, proper dumb and a bit of a twister, but in his view girls were all much the same. It didn't matter, so long as they made no mistake about who was boss.

"It'll be a long time before I'm ready to think of going steady," he said warningly. "But I don't mind seeing how it goes," and he gathered her to him with an expert grip.

15

THE HEADMASTER'S routine had been modified in several respects because of the absence of Miss Wills, in some cases deliberately, in others almost unconsciously, and somewhere between came his hurried breakfasts. It was desirable to have longer in his study before Chapel so that his post could be weeded before being exposed to the eyes of his temporary secretary. On the morning following his own and Oonagh's trying day he felt that some reform in punctuality might be expected, and since four Governors had sent him copies of Sir Arthur Hinton-Brigg's manifesto with comments, and others had written describing at length its contents and their own reactions, his post was both explosive and bulky. He consumed his meal hastily, raised his eyebrows at his wife as he gathered up the mass of paper and crossing the hall at a brisk pace butted his way through the baize door.

Outside his study, which was locked at night, stood Miss Wills, a neat grey figure with tidily netted hair, ready for work. He stopped with a jerk and stood still. Miss Wills said:

"Good morning, Mr. Fielding. I thought it best to come a little earlier than usual so that you might know of my return before going out to Chapel."

Mr. Fielding, as he told his wife later, was not sure whether he would burst into tears or clasp the unyielding form of his secretary to his bosom. What he did was to unlock the door of the study, try to usher her in and fail— she preferred to follow—and demand an explanation of her presence.

"It's too soon," he said. "You can't possibly be ready for work yet. What does the doctor say?"

"Thank you, Mr. Fielding," said Miss Wills. "I am quite ready. I spoke to Dr. Miles on the telephone and he has no objection provided that I follow a few simple instructions which will cause no inconvenience."

"But why suddenly today?" he asked looking sharply at her as the coincidence of timing struck him. Miss Wills, gazing obstinately at his shoes, admitted under pressure that she had heard there had been a little difficulty. With Miss Hepburn. Mr. Selby had informed her of it. Mr. Selby had told her nothing of the nature of the difficulty. Finally, Mr. Selby had kindly said that until she had fully recovered her strength and the weather had become more clement he would drive her from her home to School House in the morning and back again in the evening. "I will rest a little, if you have no objection," concluded Miss Wills, "after lunch."

"Very well," said Mr. Fielding. "I am very glad to have you back. Your lunch will be taken upstairs to the old nursery and you will lie down on its very comfortable day-bed for an hour afterwards every day."

"Half an hour will be quite sufficient," said Miss Wills.

"Those are my orders," retorted her employer asserting himself. He glanced at his watch and heaved an inward sigh of relief that he could shuffle all this paper into safe keeping and that he need no longer keep a nervous thought on the telephone. Then he remembered awkwardness and at the same moment Miss Wills asked:

"And Miss Hepburn?"

"Yes," he said. "We shall have to think about her. It would be a little hard to pack her off without notice. Could you use her for a few days?"

"No doubt she may be usefully employed," said Miss Wills without enthusiasm.

Mr. Fielding was shrugging himself into his gown and made no reply. He picked up his cap and paused before he left the room to select a copy of Sir Arthur's manifesto from the pile of papers. "Look after these," he said, indicating the pile, "and I'd like you to read this. We're having a bit of melodrama," and he hurried away to Chapel.

After a good night's sleep Oonagh felt rather less enthusiasm for repentance and she was not so concerned as her mother about references and the future. Though Eric was determined not to pledge himself before he had had plenty of time to make up his mind, she was fairly confident that her future was secure. It was true that compared, say, to Angus Cameron, the Hinton-Briggs' chauffeur was not a great match; and it was also true that Eric would be a bossy husband who might not hesitate to raise a hand to his wife if he thought an occasion demanded it. But she was prepared to regard his present menial position as a rung in a ladder which he would certainly ascend and in her view men ought to be bossy. It was part of masculine virility. Altogether, so far as she was concerned, they couldn't start going steady too soon and she was not without hope that it might be sooner than he intended for she held two strong cards; her superior gentility—provided she didn't plug it—and the inherent respectability which would shortly lead the lusty Eric to look upon marriage in a favourable light.

272

With these thoughts in her mind she was neither so humble nor so punctual as Mr. Fielding had anticipated and he was back in his study after Chapel when she walked into the office and found Miss Wills seated at the table.

"Good morning, dear," said Miss Wills, bland and condescending. "This is quite a surprise, isn't it?" Oonagh was temporarily dumb so she went on truthfully: "It was only yesterday that Dr. Miles said I might—"

"I don't believe it," cried Oonagh breathlessly. "It's a frame-up. It's the dirtiest bit of work I ever heard of. He *said* I was to come back and then he was in such a fuss—"

Miss Wills raised a hand. "Hush, Oonagh. You don't know what you are saying. The Headmaster himself did not know I was coming and he said at once that you must not be sent away without notice. Now—go and speak to the Headmaster. You're very late. He is in the study."

Flushed and sullen Oonagh marched to the study and faced Mr. Fielding. She did not believe that Miss Wills' return sooner than she was expected was a coincidence, and neither Miss Wills nor the Headmaster said that it was, but she could not, at the moment, find anything of which she could complain.

"I am very glad to have Miss Wills back," said Mr. Fielding frankly, "but I suggest that you stay on for a further week. It will lighten the work for her, and," he looked at her directly, "it will be better for you."

"I don't think—I don't want to stay on with Miss Wills here," muttered Oonagh.

"I think you should, however," he said. "I should tell you that Miss Wills knows nothing about yesterday's incident. I am offering you a chance, as I said that I would, to finish

273

your job here with credit. You should take advantage of it."

Oonagh hesitated but her confidence had evaporated somewhat with the reminder that she had, in fact, slipped up rather badly and she was a good deal in awe of the Beak. She said: "Very well, Mr. Fielding," in a subdued voice and returned unwillingly to the office.

Miss Wills was encouraging. "*Come* along, dear," she said kindly. "Take your things off and let us get to work." With nostrils slightly distended she looked round the room. "We shall have to rearrange things a little and we may as well tidy up thoroughly as we do it."

They worked almost in silence. Miss Wills made no comment as chocolate, magazines, dingy pieces of cotton-wool and spilt powder were disentangled and cleared from drawers. She dealt with disordered files looking only soberly pleased to be handling them again, but Oonagh clicked about the room, smouldering with resentment, slamming or banging everything she touched.

At the end of an hour she stopped. "I'm through," she announced suddenly. "I can't stick this," and taking no notice of Miss Wills' protests or reasoning she put on her coat and left.

There was an unpleasant scene with her mother when she walked in to the house before the morning had, for Mrs. Hepburn, well begun.

"Do you mean to say," came the first inevitable question pitched to a scream, "that after all he said last night that man has turned you off without notice?"

"I've told you," snapped Oonagh. "I'm damned if I'm going to stay and be pushed around by that old cat."

"What will people think? Walking out like that you've

put yourself wrong. Just given them an excuse to drop you."

Oonagh shrugged her shoulders and stated briefly what the Ledenham people could do with themselves. Her mother stared at her, puzzled and inimical.

"You've been stupid all round, in my opinion," she said sourly. "You were keen enough on them up till the last day or two. All these young men—you seemed to be getting on all right. What about Angus Cameron? I thought you said—"

"Angus Cameron's Alison Fielding's boy," said Oonagh. "At least that's her idea and the Headmaster's daughter has the guns. But she can have him so far's I'm concerned."

It was airily said but also defiantly and Mrs. Hepburn took a deep breath. "Oonagh," she said solemnly, "who *is* Eric?"

Oonagh told her and the Hepburn balloon went up.

At the moment of Oonagh's departure the Headmaster was in School instructing the Mathematical VIth in Divinity and it was not till he returned to his study that the news was broken to him. He was not altogether surprised. The Misses Wills and Hepburn were unlikely to pull well in double harness and he regretted it only because he disliked untidy endings and he had not been allowed to work off his own feeling of guilt. He would tell the Bursar to pay the girl's salary to the end of the following week and if she asked for his help in finding another job he would do what he honestly could for her. Higgins appeared with his midmorning coffee and lighting a cigarette he dismissed Oonagh from his mind and turned it to the Hinton-Brigg crisis.

275

He was not deluded by its fundamental absurdity. Like Lady Hinton-Brigg he knew that persistence in folly can of itself produce a damaging situation and he already had proof that the process had begun. Ledenham's Governors came to it, as Governors always do, from a variety of sources. The Mayor and Council of Snaydon most unfortunately in this case, nominated one, the town of Leyburn nominated another, Ledshire County Council a third. There were representatives from the universities and the old boys of the School. The Bishop was an *ex-officio* member and others were co-opted by the Governing Body itself, one of these being Lord Leyburn and another Lord Lucreton, who had been brought in at a time when it was thought desirable to add business acumen to the Board.

Surveying his Governors from what might be called the crisis angle the Headmaster, who knew them all well, saw them as individuals. In the normal course of School affairs they were corporate; well led by an experienced Chairman and well content to leave the School to the management of an experienced and established Headmaster. Outside the normal their individuality as men with other interests more important to them than Ledenham asserted itself. On the desk were two communications from two busy men. The Cambridge University representative wrote: "Who on earth is this Brigg?" His Oxford colleague, even more economically, had merely embellished Sir Arthur's letter with a large question mark and put it in the post. From the last of the distant Governors, a lofty and decorative soldier, there was nothing—he was probably abroad, and, in fact, unless the crisis grew to proportions which were unthinkable the local Governors would deal with it. Mr. Fielding thought of the Bishop, a gentle, far from militant cleric and of the Old Boy, Tommy Ward who, like Henry Courtney, resented to some extent every change made in the School. The County Councillor had been elected in a passing flurry of Labour enthusiasm and was disappointed that he had less direct authority over the Headmaster than he had expected and the Leyburn nominee supplied Thaxley Manor with fish and would be in a dilemma.

He gathered his crisis letters together. When a Governing Body received specific complaints against its Headmaster and an assistant master it could hardly ignore them. It was a pity Lord Leyburn was in Nice; he would very likely have to cut his holiday short. In the meantime replies to all the letters, to the laconic dons, the faintly reproachful Vicar of Leyburn and the baffled baronet on the far side of the county, could be little more than acknowledgements. Time, prudence and the unbelievable nature of the case were all against lengthy attempts at explanation.

He rang the bell. Miss Wills clumped quietly in, notebook and pencil in hand, and he looked at her with pleasure thinking that in about half an hour he would have forgotten that she had ever been away. Here she was, exactly the same impersonal machine as she had always been—or was she?

"Have you read this letter of Sir Arthur Hinton-Brigg's?" he asked, indicating the papers on the desk before him.

Yes, she said, she had read it.

"What do you make of it?" It was very rare, indeed almost unprecedented for any comment to be made by either of them on the business they handled but she, like the commonroom, must be prepared to meet developments and he was curious to know if he had noticed something less detached than her customary discretion or merely imagined it.

He had not imagined it. "I think it could be very serious, Mr. Fielding," she said, unmistakably distressed. "And it is very wicked. I could never have believed that a man in Sir Arthur Hinton-Brigg's position would be so irresponsible and—and, well, one can only say spiteful." The Headmaster agreed that it was surprising and she looked at him earnestly and went on: "I would not, of course, have spoken of the matter if you had not done so first, but I must say I am concerned on Mr. Selby's account."

"You know him, I believe, fairly well, don't you?" said Mr. Fielding.

"No," said Miss Wills, "I would not say that I *know* him. My acquaintance with him is slight. My sister has been with the family on several occasions and for that reason Mr. Selby made himself known to me when he came." She paused, looking extremely forbidding and added: "He may have been impertinent to Sir Arthur Hinton-Brigg; it is not for me to say. But the family has been very well brought up. I do not believe that he has been guilty of any more serious offence."

The Headmaster said: "I'm sure he hasn't. It was unfortunate that he allowed himself to be provoked," he added and caught sight of a shrewd pair of eyes.

"Very unfortunate," Miss Wills agreed primly. She made the slightest of gestures towards the papers on the desk. "It might be difficult," she said, "to save Mr. Selby's career at Ledenham."

"I hope it won't come to anything like that," said the Headmaster, "but it may certainly be troublesome." He thrust on his spectacles and reached for his papers. Miss Wills opened her pad and held her pencil poised. From small, even ludicrous incidents large events may spring and they both knew that though it was improbable it was not impossible that Tim Selby's flirtatious fancy for Julie Hinton-Brigg might bring to an end not only his own but also the Headmaster's career at Ledenham.

Alison stayed in bed on Monday and most of Tuesday. On Wednesday she was up, not much the worse for her flu but unwilling to face the world, and she kept out of sight and sadly wrote a letter of application for the post of assistant caterer at Upton preparatory school. On Thursday she appeared at hall lunch where the conversation was devoted to Mr. Cameron and his seven-a-sides.

Everybody asked her kindly if she was all right again and passed on. The snow had almost disappeared but the question now was how soon the fields would be playable.

"Mr. Cameron says Old Level's no good yet, sir," was thrown by Butler to Nick Vincent across her front. Nick, returning the ball, said that he wouldn't expect it.

"Mr. Cameron says the drainage there's slow—"

"We're going to do some passing practice on the outer field. Get us moving again anyway—"

"You'll wreck it."

"No, Mr. Cameron says it can take it—"

"Sir, Mr. Cameron's going to give Dixon a trial on the wing—"

"Dixon? Too heavy—"

"*Fanatics,*" groaned the prefect who despised games. "Custard, Miss Fielding?" Alison looked up and received across the table a jug of custard and a sweet, rather too innocent smile. "Are you going out to watch Mr. Cameron's passing practice?"

Alison was accustomed enough to her position. Lunching in hall was lunching in public and it was at all times necessary to be mentally alert. She was able to manage a convincing laugh.

"What? In *this* wind?" she said and Nick came in, adding that though seven-a-sides undoubtedly had audience appeal there was a limit to the discomfort audiences were prepared to endure. But it was a jolt and she was unpleasantly aware of tension around her, some of it disapproving, some merely inquisitive, and aware too that Nick had come deliberately to her rescue.

As they walked along the passage together from the hall he said cheerfully, "Angus seems to have come up in the betting. I believe I started favourite and Burgoyne and Munro found some backers after the Reel Club."

"I'd no idea I was so interesting," said Alison.

"Of course you're interesting," said Nick. "Clare was engaged to every bachelor in turn, sometimes several of us at once. She never minded. You don't either, do you?"

Alison said, "Of course not," but she thought her sister's case was hardly comparable to her own. Clare had had her Nevill, whom nobody in Ledenham either saw or heard of till they were engaged, and it was easy enough for her to be indifferent to Mr. Barker. There was, however, only one way to take Mr. Barker and she smiled gaily at Nick, with she hoped, a convincing display of being amused.

In the afternoon she ventured out into the cold wind for a bracing convalescent walk but ill-luck went with her. Angus and Willie appeared from the Zoo, running towards the playing-fields, but only Willie veered from his route to enquire and commiserate while Angus raised a hand without looking at her and ran on. And in the post office she met Annette.

"Oh—you're out!" was Mrs. Courtney's greeting. "What relief. I've been feeling entirely responsible for your cold or whatever it was. I was sure you'd have pneumonia *and* rheumatic fever when I heard about that puncture."

Alison with another easy laugh said she didn't think the puncture had much to do with it. It had been flu—mild.

"Then that's all right," said Annette and drew her to a remote corner of the post office, which was scheduled for reconstruction and rather dark. "What was it all about?" she asked. "You hadn't really quarrelled with Angus, had you?"

Her tone was friendly, indeed it was genuinely concerned, an easy laughter, even if Alison had been able to force it again, was hardly appropriate.

"Oh no," she said. "No quarrel at all," and groping she found a sort of explanation. "Actually, it was simply muddle. Nobody had told me who was going to lift me home. I just knew Nick had gone on."

"I see," Annette's observant, rather prominent eyes were upon her and her tone accepted the explanation without believing a word of it. "Well—you mustn't quarrel with Angus. You were a perfectly sweet pair at that party of ours—as clear a case as I ever saw—and I couldn't bear it if it didn't happen."

"Oh, Annette," protested Alison gallantly, making grateful use of Nick. "I've already been assigned to Nick, Willie and Burg as well as Angus—"

"I dare say," said Annette, "but we all know what we know," and before she turned away she said seriously: "Don't, for heaven' sake, Alison, take any notice of any rumours you may hear about Angus and that horrible Oonagh. I'm *absolutely positive* there was never anything in it."

Alison's next port of call was Holly Lodge where she found Frances alone with a pile of mending. Marthe had taken John for an airing, she said, and Patsy had gone to look at Angus' sevens.

"I've applied for a job," said Alison.

"Have you? I didn't think you were looking for one yet."

"I wasn't exactly. This turned up. It's at Upton."

"*Upton?*" Frances looked up.

"Not the main School—the prep. Why not?"

"No reason at all why not. It's quite a good place, and near. What sort of job?"

Alison described what she knew of the job briefly. She wanted it known that she was applying for jobs but she had no desire to dwell on the subject and went on to change it. "Miss Wills is back, did you know? So Oonagh is no longer with us."

"Oh," said Frances. "I heard about Miss Wills but I didn't know Oonagh had gone. Good riddance, really." She paused for a moment, her eyes on her darning and then said rather uncertainly; "Alison, I don't know whether I should tell you this but I'd hate you to hear it from anyone else and you might. Patsy was asked if he'd like to be considered for the Headship of Upton and Oonagh got hold of it and let it out. That's why Miss Wills scurried back. Tim did it. Oonagh told him and of course we can't be sure she won't tell other people and start off a lot of rumours—"

It took a minute or two for this to be brought into comprehensive form and then Alison, echoing Tim, cried: "I can't imagine Ledenham without you and Patsy."

"Oh, we're not *going,*" said Frances. "I thought about it a bit, but Patsy hardly even did that. We'll be taking over the P.-S.'s House in another year or so and that's just what he wants. I can't imagine living anywhere but Ledenham either, though it's bound to change, of course."

"Why should it change? What do you mean?"

"Well, when Uncle Hugh and Aunt Hester go it won't be the—" she caught sight of Alison's face and cried: "It's all right. I only mean Uncle Hugh will retire sooner or later—"

But Alison, who could remember no home but Ledenham said: "I never once thought of it," and wept.

"Alison *darling,*" Frances dropped her work and rushed to put her arms round her shaken cousin. "Dear love, what have I done? I don't mean *soon*—They're going great guns—Alison, it'll be *years.* You'll be married and settled— in Ledenham, as like as not—long before—"

Alison lifted a scarlet, outraged face. "Don't say another word," she snapped and Frances sat back on her heels.

"All right," she said, after a pause. "I won't."

There was a short silence. Frances returned to her needle and Alison blew her nose and tidied her face up.

"A brief shower," she announced presently, "now over. Flu is a very insidious thing."

"Yes," Frances kept her eyes on her work. "Put your feet up. We'll take you home after tea."

"I think I'll go home now," said Alison.

She was longing for home, for the warm seclusion of the old nursery, and as she put on her coat and said good-bye to Frances she was miserably aware that, whether because of the insidious flu germ or not, her strength was not at present equal to going about the Ledenham world which no longer held Angus as a friend and ally. But as she reached the Holly Lodge gate it occurred to her that just as she had mistimed her exit from School House and coincided with Angus on his way to the field so she had mistimed her return. He would now be on his way back to the Zoo and she could cope with no more aloof waves.

She turned wearily to the left, leaving the Zoo and the School gates behind her, to go home by what was known in nursery days as the short, dull walk. It would take her as far as the Leyburn road, back along the main street of the village and by the direct approach from the street to the School. It would also take her, she remembered gloomily as she trudged along, past the Hepburns'. Ledenham was suddenly full of hazards, and this, it appeared, was a day when on which the hazards were out in force. As she turned into the road which held the Hepburns' cottage a figure in a spectacular three-quarter length coat of white leather approached it from the village. As she looked curiously at this unfamiliar garment the wearer raised her head and Alison, with a sinking heart, walked on to meet Mrs. Hepburn.

About ten minutes later Tim Selby, returning from a hasty shopping expedition to Leyburn, drove past the

Hepburns' house and saw Alison Fielding parting from Mrs. Hepburn at the gate. She walked away quickly and he accelerated and pulled up with a warning toot beside her.

"Taxi, ma'am," he hailed her and Alison turned a sheet-white face and tried and failed to reply. Tim thought 'a faint' and before the thought had reached his conscious mind he was out of the car beside her. "In you get," he said, opening the door with one hand and keeping a firm grasp of her arm with the other. "Right. Now put your head down—far as you can."

"I'm all right," said Alison. "I'm not going to—" her teeth began to chatter and she stopped.

Tim said: "Shall I take you to Frances?" but she shook her head. "Sit quiet for a minute, then," he said and took one of her hands and rubbed it gently.

"B-better," she said after a moment. "Could you just take me home?"

"Okay," said Tim and started the car. "What is it, Miss Beak? Did you come over queer?"

"No. I—" she shook her head again. "I—can't tell you."

He drove on slowly, thinking that a few extra minutes would give her time to steady herself and while the sensitive part of his mind felt her nervous and emotional shock his astuteness had little difficulty in deducing the cause of it. He had not been told what the Beak had decided about Oonagh, but he knew from Willie, whose business had taken him to the secretary's office before lunch, that Oonagh was not in it. He could make a guess at the Hepburn mood and it was hard that Alison should have taken the rap when he, who was really responsible, could have coped with it so much more easily.

"You should never allow anything said by ill-bred persons to affect you, Alison," he said and adapted her father's quotation: "No lady *will* insult me, no other can."

She had glanced round, startled, and there was a little sound, nearly laughter, as she turned away again. "I'm so feeble," she said. "When anybody's really nasty I just fold up."

"Raise the eyebrows, lift the chin and murmur *'canaille'*. Then quote the above pomposity—which was quoted to me, masculine gender, by your revered papa."

"Was it? The things he gets hold of——" said Alison. "Well, I don't know about insults, I just feel I'll never be clean again."

"No no, Miss Beak, draw it mild," said Tim firmly. "Don't you be downed." He stopped the car at School House and went round to open the door for her. "All right? Knees normal or shall I give the populace a treat by carrying you in?"

"No, thank you—I'll manage," said Alison hurriedly. "I'm perfectly all right. I'll get to the angry stage in a minute and think of all the things I might have said back. Thank you, Tim. I'm ashamed of the fuss."

"You needn't be that. Anybody would be shaken by an enraged Hepburn and you stood your ground. I'd have run for it." She laughed and he resisted an impulse to plant a platonic kiss on the unusually pale cheek, she was being so good about it. Instead he smiled at her and offered a final bit of advice. "You go and have a good wash and forget it."

Alison followed the first part of his advice. She went straight upstairs and took her things off and washed copiously. Then she did her hair and her face and feeling at least outwardly purified but extraordinarily tired, she sat down by the fire in the old nursery and deliberately recalled the scene with Mrs. Hepburn to see what, after all, it amounted to.

It was a terribly crippling weakness to be born with this lack of resistance to abuse. What had actually been said she could hardly remember. It was what one would expect, what she had almost been prepared by Annette to hear; bitter accusations of running after Angus, of using her position as her father's daughter—The horror was the ugliness. The hatred in the mean face and the squalor in the words. And the attack had come upon her when she was already so sorely beset.

"Oh *gosh!*" said Alison. She put her head down on the familiar arm of the sofa and shut her eyes. The boys at lunch—Angus running past without a look—Annette, Frances. Angus again—that unspeakable drive on Sunday.

The door opened and shut again quietly. She lifted a startled head and saw Angus himself coming across the room.

"*Angus!*" she jumped up. "How did you—"

"Tim told me," said Angus coming on. He stood before her and put his hands on her shoulders. "He told me what happened—that damned woman. Alison," he hesitated. Speech was too difficult. Where could he begin? There was all the confusion of misunderstanding, of hurt and anger to be explained; and the blinding realization, when Tim told him about the episode of the afternoon and Alison's shaking, that none of it mattered a damn. There was all he had always felt for her, and all he felt for her now— "Alison," he said again. "I couldn't stay away. What

287

happens to you happens to me—"

"Oh, Angus," cried Alison, "I wanted you so *badly*."

As they looked at each other Mrs. Hepburn and all the ramifications of Mr. Barker bowed themselves out. They were Angus and Alison who had always been a pair and now were one. Angus saw his girl transfigured, all lovely and all woman, and Alison looked up at a face which was almost as different from the familiar friendly one as the stony aloofness of the afternoon, with all Angus's honest, loving heart in its tenderness.

"It's not just that I love you," he said, holding her closely and with one hand raising her face for the kiss that was coming, "though, as a matter of fact, I do. You're part of me."

"Your rib," said Alison.

Presently they were seated, still one, on the sofa and a little spasmodic conversation took place. Alison said: "I've applied for a job."

"Tell them you're suited," said Angus and with the utmost readiness she dismissed Ancillary Services from her mind for ever.

"What," asked Angus, remembering dizzily that he had recently been furiously angry, "did that auld braxy yowe say to you?"

"*Angus!*"

"I'm not swearing. I could do far better than that if I was trying."

"Well—I really forget what she said," said Alison truthfully.

"Just as well," said Angus and their peace was shattered by the clamour of the School bell.

"Help! Are you in?" cried Alison.

"Yes, by God." He stared into space for a concentrated moment and then relaxed. "It's all right. My gown's in commonroom. I'll make it."

The bell clanked relentlessly. The mathematical Upper VIth converged upon its classroom. Its master caught up his girl and kissed her and moved reluctantly to the door.

"Come back to supper," she said. "Oh, blast—we've got a lecturer. Trees. Never mind, Angus. Come."

"I'll come," he assured her and paused with his hand on the door. "Have you heard anything from the Beak about this Tim Secker—Hinton-Brigg mix-up?"

"No," said Alison. "What—"

"I think Tim's in a hell of a mess," said Angus.

16

THAT EVENING at dinner in the School House a distinguished visiting lecturer and Mr. Burgoyne, who was Ledenham's ecological expert, looked benignly at the two young people who smiled so vividly at each other and so vaguely at everyone else. After the meal Mr. Burgoyne, raising an eyebrow at his Headmaster, took the visitor in tow and departed to drink beer in the Zoo, leaving the Fieldings to welcome what Mrs. Fielding called "my sixth and largest child" into the family.

"They've always had what you might call a liking for each other," said Mr. Higgins over a cup of cocoa in the kitchen.

"Well, they have, but you never know," said his wife who liked a bit of drama. "There's many a slip—"

"Ah, no." Higgins went for sentiment every time. "No. Not when you remember how they took to each other from the first."

"I've always said," said Matron, calling on another matron and blinking back a tear, "those two were made for each other—"

And in the Head of House study the aesthetic prefect said, "Sucks! Hand over—" and took half-a-crown from the reluctant Butler.

In School next morning Mr. Cameron was greeted with cheers by every set he taught, an experience which he bore with stoical calm. At lunch in School House Butler caught the eye of the Headmaster before he said grace and in the briefest possible speech offered Miss Fielding and Mr.

Cameron the House's congratulations and good wishes.

"Thank you," said Alison.

"Benedictus—" began her father and everybody sat down, comfortable in the knowledge that the proper thing had been done and there was no need for further action in the matter.

"Well, my love," said Nick, following the Fieldings into the drawing-room after lunch, "they got pretty near the bone yesterday, didn't they?" He put an arm round her shoulders and kissed her. "It's supposed to be rather impolite to congratulate the lady, but I do. He's a grand chap, is Angus—"

"Yes," said Alison.

"—and you're alpha double plus. But—" with his arm still round her he turned to her mother, "isn't it *dull*, Mrs. Beak? Settled, you might say, at the age of seventeen."

"Isn't it," agreed Mrs. Fielding. "Quite unstartling. I don't think she's ever even noticed another young man."

"And what could be more beautiful and romantic?" demanded Alison with spirit.

"Nothing," her father said promptly. "However it happens is always the most beautiful and romantic way it could have happened."

Nick laughed, but he said: "I must say this way is particularly nice for Angus," and Alison looked at him affectionately.

"As soon as I'm established," she said, "I must see about getting *you* off, my dear. It's high time."

It was true that the element of surprise was absent from the engagement between Miss Fielding and Mr. Cameron, except in the principals themselves. Everybody was delighted but everybody had seen it coming for years and as headline news it was never a screamer and it was eclipsed almost at once by the Selby crisis.

In the absence abroad of Lord Leyburn it fell to the lot of the Vice-Chairman to decide whether or not to set in motion the machinery for the Governors' enquiry demanded by Sir Arthur Hinton-Brigg. Colonel Tommy Ward acted with the greatest reluctance. He had been Vice-Chairman for some years but as Lord Leyburn seldom left home and was never ill no responsibility had ever before devolved upon him and he was sorely troubled. On the one hand was the Headmaster, accused of, really, God knew what, and though he sometimes felt that there were too many changes everywhere nowadays he regarded Mr. Fielding himself with respect and had a lingering awe, left over from his school days, for his status. On the other hand there was Hinton-Brigg accusing; a man he dined with and met on every county occasion, a trying man in many ways but too successful and too powerful, surely, to have any imaginable axe to grind.

The Clerk gave him very little comfort. There was no precedent on which they could act, he said gloomily. He thought they could: (*a*) take no notice; (*b*) summon a special meeting; (*c*) leave it alone till the May meeting; (*d*) try to sort it out privately. He did not think the Headmaster would agree to either the third or fourth alternatives.

"Oh dear," said the Colonel.

"The allegations have been made, you see."

"Yes. Yes, of course." Poor Colonel Ward gnawed his moustache and gazed into space with puzzled eyes. He tried a feeler. "I can't see that Hinton-Brigg would make these complaints without some foundation. No smoke without fire—" He paused hopefully but there was no response. The Clerk merely said it was not for him to express an opinion, though he did not believe personally in "no smoke without fire" as a basis for suspicion. You had to see what the fire was before you could interpret the smoke. Having handed back the responsibility he waited patiently till the Vice-Chairman, sighing heavily, decided that a special meeting was necessary and mustered the courage to instruct him to summon it.

"Will all these people have to come?" he demanded irritably when the step had been taken. "Hinton-Brigg, this man Secker, young Selby—"

"I think they should be told they may attend," said Mr. Craig. "The meeting will decide whether to see them or not. The Headmaster doesn't mean to bring Selby in unless you ask for him, but he would like to know if Selby's father may be present if he wishes. The accusations against the young man are quite serious."

"Yes," said the Colonel with more decision, "I think the father should certainly be present if he wants to be. I should, if it were George."

There had never been the slightest hope that the matter would not become generally known; too many people were involved and Sir Arthur Hinton-Brigg in the van was by nature loud-mouthed. By Friday afternoon Tim was aware of discomfort in the commonroom. The prevailing feeling was indignant and sympathetic but many of his colleagues found the situation too awkward for them. Nothing quite like it had ever happened before, they didn't know what to say or where to look and the effect on the victim was much the same as if they condemned him.

"Pay no attention," said Mr. Burgoyne when he had explained the phenomenon to his unhappy young colleague. "And I'm damned," he added with unusual energy, "if we let it spoil Angus's moment. Tomorrow evening we'll have a party. Got a pencil, Munro? Make a list."

"Yes," said Willie bravely. "Right—"

It was on Friday, too, that Mr. Secker, this time unaccompanied, called on the Headmaster. He wished, he said, to withdraw the complaint against Mr. Selby.

"Actually," he explained, looking very hot, "it was my wife who saw Hinton-Brigg. Women get upset—So I'll—er, just withdraw this damned nonsense. I don't know if I should take Brian away till it blows over."

"Well," said the Headmaster, "both decisions are yours, of course, but the complaint made in your name has reached the Governors. For Selby's sake—and mine—there will have to be an enquiry. As for Brian, I must tell you that if you take him away now I don't think he *could* come back. It would be more than any boy could face."

"Hell," said Mr. Secker unhappily.

On Saturday morning a boy in Mr. Pearson-Smith's House received a letter. "What's all this," asked his father in Snaydon, "about Selby assaulting Brian Secker? The town's full of it. Is it true that Selby has been sacked?"

"Coo!" said the boy with starting eyes and bolted to find an audience.

Tim was, on the whole, liked, or rather he was not disliked, which is as much as any schoolmaster can expect, and even Secker's friends and followers, some of whom had

294

witnessed the assault, were of the opinion that Secker had asked for it. But the strongest reaction was outrage. The School was perfectly capable of managing its own affairs. Parents, apart from occasional visits and discussions about careers if unavoidable, should keep out. Butting in on matters which were the School's business was intolerable. And if parents were intruders the Governors, those shadowy background figures, were more so, while Sir Arthur Hinton-Brigg, who was neither parent nor Governor, was merely a subject for raised eyebrows and cold incredulity.

On Saturday morning Tim was conscious of a curious alertness in his sets and it dawned on him with some alarm that they were being nice to him. Everybody was very interested in what he said, helpful questions were asked and the atmosphere was genial. In the lower VIth set Secker sat with a wooden face, while his fellows wore a watchful air. Secker had not seen his father when he called on the Headmaster the day before. He had had an interview with his Housemaster who warned him that when the news reached the School he, Secker, might have a good deal to bear. The only thing to do, said Mr. Pearson-Smith kindly, was to stick it like a man and remember that it would pass. Secker did have a good deal to bear. It was not agreeable to be known as the man who told his mother. But it was, in a way, fortunate for him that his mother had taken what he told her to such a high level. Public opinion was too much concerned with Sir Arthur, the Beak and Selby to spend much time on him except in one particular and there it was adamant. Secker had made enough of a fool of himself and done enough damage. Those around him now saw to it that he behaved and backed up Selby in the only way open to him by regularity, docility and strenuous endeavour in athletic training.

On Saturday afternoon an owner-driven Bentley arrived at School House and Lord Lucreton brought business acumen to bear on the crisis. Unlike Sir Arthur Hinton-Brigg, Lord Lucreton had won his wealth and his title for himself. He was a quick-moving man with an alert scarlet face whose hair was so brushed as to suggest horns to the imaginative eye while the imaginative ear was reminded of the Trumpet Voluntary by his brazen, assertive but mainly good-humoured voice.

"Active School you've got this afternoon," he began genially, waving a hand at the well-populated playing-fields. "How many head of stock do you carry per acre?"

About eight and a half head per acre of playing-field, Mr. Fielding thought, and they stood for a moment by the study window looking out indulgently at the School's activity.

"Young Selby out there?" demanded Lord Lucreton who believed in the sudden pounce and the Headmaster, recognising the technique, smiled.

"Out of sight," he said. "Over on the running track," and he added blandly: "He's a very good coach."

"Really?" said Lord Lucreton.

They turned away from the window and sat down facing each other; the Headmaster in the high chair behind his desk, since he never sat anywhere else in his study, Lord Lucreton in the comfortable leather armchair in which Sir Arthur Hinton-Brigg had battled with post-luncheon drowsiness a week or two before. It was a good chair, nicely placed so that the occupant was not troubled by the light, not so low that he felt imprisoned, and the visitor was provided with an acceptable cigar and all the courteous attention due to him. He sat back in the chair and smoked for a moment in silence and the Headmaster sitting sideways and relaxed, lit a cigarette and waited.

"It's a great pity," Lord Lucreton began at last; "that this unfortunate affair had been allowed to reach the proportions of what can only be called a row."

"It's a great pity it began at all," said the Headmaster.

"Of course it is. But then young men do, from time to time, lose their heads and misbehave. I may as well say at once that I wish you could have seen your way to smoothing the thing over at the start. A man in Hinton-Brigg's position," Lord Lucreton waved his cigar in a gesture which, so to speak, accepted Sir Arthur and all that he was, "—a man in that position may have his foibles—who hasn't?—but when he makes a complaint he has a right to be taken seriously."

"Certainly," said the Headmaster. "He made three complaints and I took them all seriously."

Lord Lucreton looked amused. "I saw your letter," he said. "You didn't exactly grovel. And a little tactful grovelling does frequently avert trouble."

"True. But in this case the only grovelling which would have satisfied Sir Arthur was the instant dismissal of Selby. An unreasonable demand, in my opinion, and one that I was not prepared to meet."

"Hinton-Brigg, of course, was a good deal inflamed at the time."

"And that being so, I don't see how he could have been placated."

Lord Lucreton eased the ash gently off his cigar and sat up a little straighter in his chair, replacing the amused expression by one which was more forceful.

"This youth," he said, "has been in the School for less than a year, I gather. I don't know the ins and outs of Hinton-Brigg's complaints against him and I don't want to know. I'm not interested. It is a fact, however, that he has contrived to annoy, to get across, an influential man who is a nominated Governor of the School and a complaint has been made against him by the parents of a boy. I should have thought that in these circumstances if dismissal was too severe, you and he might both feel that a new start elsewhere would be desirable. It would do him no harm—or very little. He's young. Ten to one he'll move on anyway and there are plenty of schoolmasters—for a school like this."

The Headmaster was silent for a moment, but he did not change his position and went on smoking unhurriedly. This was the line he had expected and he quite understood what was left unsaid. Sir Arthur Hinton-Brigg was a fool but he was also Chairman of Hinton Brigg Ltd. Lord Lucreton was a clever man, he was in no respect a fool, and since this matter had unfortunately arisen he thought it desirable that it should be settled smoothly and without fuss; but he was determined that fuss or no fuss it must be settled so that his industrial brother suffered no loss of face. Assistant masters were in his view expendable assets and so, in the end, was the Headmaster. There was never any difficulty in finding good recruits for the Ledenham commonroom and plenty of able men would be glad to step into the Headmaster's shoes. Sir Arthur Hinton-Brigg was different; on his stability much depended. If he died it would not matter but if he were discredited wide and complex industrial concerns would be affected and Lord Lucreton would therefore support him till the danger was past and his balance restored. The fate of one young man, the alleged persecution of a troublesome boy were incidental and of no interest. The root of the matter, now laid bare, was whether the Headmaster was willing to modify a School decision to suit two powerful Governors or not.

Mr. Fielding was aware of the danger of making enemies of Lucreton and Hinton-Brigg, but he had been aware of it from the outset and he thought that his position was not quite so dangerous as they supposed. He did not, however, feel called upon to show his cards in advance.

"I don't know," he said mildly, "that we can do much good by discussing it now. The enquiry is laid on and nothing will be decided till——"

"There's one thing you may not have heard," Lord Lucreton's brassy voice cut in. "Hinton-Brigg has evidence that Selby has had a considerable sum of money from his daughter." He saw the Headmaster look utterly astonished and went on: "It puts rather a different complexion on it, doesn't it?"

"How much?"

"What? Oh—thirty or forty pounds, I believe. I must say I don't see how you can get round that one. It——" He broke off. The Headmaster had leant back in his chair and was laughing with pure, unforced amusement.

"Forgive me," he said glancing at the scarlet, unamused face of his visitor. "Schoolmasters are notoriously underpaid, of course, but our young men are really pretty comfortable and Selby, as it happens, is very well off indeed. He inherited a considerable income."

It was Lord Lucreton's turn to look astonished and he enquired with sharp asperity why a man with private means should be slaving in a school. Selby was slaving in a school, the Headmaster replied, because that was the job he had chosen to do and he added:

"He is, or he will be, a genuine and valuable schoolmaster and they're not so plentiful as you might suppose. Lord Lucreton—" he turned so that he was sitting squarely at his desk and met Lord Lucreton's shrewd and now rather hostile eyes, "—the meeting has been called to enquire into these complaints and I can do nothing except wait for it. But I have no desire to be obstructive. I agree that one should avert trouble whenever it is possible and I think I should tell you that Selby's father is the Q.C."

"What?" snapped Lord Lucreton. "Quentin Selby?"

"That's the chap. I've heard nothing from him myself, but I think it's not unlikely that he will attend the enquiry. After all," said Mr. Fielding, "these accusations are damaging. If they were made against a son of mine I should want to look into it."

There was a short silence, a very busy one. Lord Lucreton was engaged in a process of adjustment and Mr. Fielding reflected upon the prevalent conception of schoolmasters as unfortunates without position, means or backing who have failed to find a real job.

"Yes," said Lord Lucreton at last and glancing at his watch he got briskly to his feet. "Well," he was loudly genial again, "a useful talk. We'll do what we can to soft-pedal this business. Pity if it got out of hand."

"A great pity," agreed Mr. Fielding politely. "It was very good of you to come—"

The Bentley drove away, honking musically from time to time to clear the road of boys returning to Houses from the playing-fields and passing Tim Selby who, to his own surprise, was accompanied by Mr. Pearson-Smith.

Mr. Pearson-Smith was doing the right thing. Resenting the intrusion of outsiders into the running of the School as hotly as any boy, he had been jolted out of his touchiness and forced by native honesty to admit that Selby was no worse than other young men; and in any case he would have given his support, both in public and in private, to any colleague against any outsider. The elderly man giving support and the young man receiving it were not, however, congenial, and conversation was going heavily when Pearson-Smith broke off to peer after the Bentley.

"That's Lord Lucreton," he said.

"Who's he?" asked Tim indifferently and then, recollecting, "Oh—father of Cubby."

"Cubby?" Mr. Pearson-Smith looked vague. "There is a son I believe. He—Lucreton is a Governor. I wonder—" he stopped. His eyes slid round doubtfully and then making up his mind, apparently, to speak out, he went on: "I expect he's been seeing the Headmaster about this enquiry. A very good thing. I'm glad he's taken the trouble. He'll have been given the rights of the case and he's an influential man. Well—" he glanced round again, "—G'bye. Come and have a drink after Chapel tomorrow if you've nothing better to do."

"Thank you very much," said Tim and their ways parted.

Outside the Zoo Angus's car was standing with a group of people round it; Angus himself and Alison on the point of getting in, Mr. Burgoyne, Willie and Marthe looking on.

"Hullo," said Tim. "Where are you off to? You haven't forgotten the party, have you?"

Of course they hadn't, they said. They were just going in to Leyburn—a bit of shopping. Everybody smiled indulgently and Mr. Burgoyne, who was leaning comfortably against a gate-post, explained.

"They're a bit shy but there's no use trying to keep these things dark. They're off to buy the ring."

"Oh," Tim added himself to the audience, appropriating the other gate-post, and gazed at his large, supremely contented friend. "Sunshine on the Grampians," he observed. "Been to the bank?"

"Cheque job," said Angus.

"Humiliating if it bounced."

"It's all right," said Mr. Burgoyne. "He's gone into it carefully and Alison's tastes are simple."

"This is a very personal conversation," said Alison and pointedly opened the passenger's door.

"All friends here," said Mr. Burgoyne soothingly and Angus, his hand on the driver's door, paused and looked over the car at Tim.

"Talking of friends," he said, "have you heard that you've had a lot of money from Julie Hinton-Brigg?"

Tim said: "*What?*" and before he had taken it in or anyone else spoke, Marthe, with a small smile at Alison and a general glance of vague farewell, walked away. He took in this latest unsavoury rumour and her departure together and it was a moment before he asked, "Where did that come from?"

"Me," said Alison, "through Annette. She came charging in when I was having coffee with Frances this morning and she was livid. She's just had it on the 'phone from somebody in Snaydon."

"Hell," said Tim, feeling sick.

"How on earth could it *start?*" asked Willie, much distressed.

"I don't think there's any clue," Alison replied. "Don't *bother,* Tim. It's too silly—"

"There might be a clue," said Angus and Burgoyne, pushing himself off the gate-post added:

"You had a caller the other day. An emissary."

"Yes," said Tim. A picture flashed into his mind of Oonagh in his study clutching an enormous hand-bag.

"The whole thing's just bloody silly," said Angus crossly. "Come on, Alison."

They drove away and the three who were left went silently into the house.

"I resent this," remarked Mr. Burgoyne, "extremely. I don't think," he looked at Tim, "that it's serious—in any way. But it's messy and it's a damned nuisance."

"I can't understand it," said Willie sadly.

"Don't take it to heart," said Tim. "Forget it. There's this party—"

From time to time the Zoo gave a sherry party for the purpose of working off accumulated debts of hospitality and did it very well, but they regarded the sherry party as such with disfavour. It was a brief, tiring period of uproar, limited in length by the necessity of eating an evening meal, and when pleasure was their object they preferred the after-dinner party. Then they laid in vast quantities of beer, reasonable quantities of such other liquids as occurred to them, and the party went on as long as anybody felt like keeping it up, overflowing into all the studies and with conversation getting better and better as the night went on.

The engagement party for Angus and Alison was a special effort. It was held, or at any rate it began, in Mr. Burgoyne's study which was opposite Willie Munro's on the ground floor, and a great deal of trouble had been taken. The whole establishment had undergone a ruthless tidying up. Extra glasses were borrowed from Annette Courtney and Frances Henderson and with the assistance of these ladies flowers were arranged and attractive savoury snacks emerged from the kitchen. Over Mr. Burgoyne's mantelpiece hung a magnificent garland with entwined initials in a vast heart, and Mr. Richards' gramophone was placed in the hall with a borrowed record of Mendelssohn's Wedding March. Mr. Burgoyne himself wore a fez which had come mysteriously into his possession. He wore it as he might have hoisted a flag. Its signal was read and understood by initiates and apart from its significance, its announcement that this was a fez sort of party, its appearance instantly—if obscurely—promoted gaiety and ease.

Angus had been sent out for dinner with instructions to return with his betrothed at nine sharp. The rest of the Zoo's inmates had a hurried meal of soup and pork-pie and were all ready, as unnaturally tidy as their rooms, when guests began to arrive soon after half-past eight. They were all men accustomed to living communally in school, university and the services. In spite of minor irritations they got on well together and any major event in the life of one was felt to some degree by all. They were all angry and troubled on Tim's account, but they were all concerned that his misfortune, happening now, must inevitably dim the glory of their engagement for Angus and Alison, and they put their backs into the job of making the party as good as it would have been if the horizon had been cloudless.

The guests, all members of the School, shared their feeling and as they came in, exclaiming, congratulating, welcoming the fez, there was an atmosphere which was warmer and more aware of its intimacy than usual. Tim, who was at all times perceptive and at this time hyper-sensitive, felt it painfully. These were the people he knew best in Ledenham, the friends who were close enough and sufficiently like himself to have avoided mistakes in dealing with his ludicrous predicament, but though he was grateful for it their friendly loyalty was uncomfortable. He was in a jam. The presence of twenty or thirty people being nice about it multiplied it in proportion. And in the midst was Marthe.

He was in the hall, alone as it happened, when she came in with Frances and Patsy.

"We've been leaving John at School House with Aunt Hester," Frances reported, "and the A.s are all set with their eyes on the clock. I say! The garland! Smashing—And Burg's got his fez on. What a party—"

It was characteristic of Frances that the estrangement with Tim being over was as though it had never been. They had had a brush, they had made it up and he was in trouble and needing his friends. Her look and smile said it all without heaviness and Patsy dropped a hand on his shoulder.

"What have you done with that money?" he asked. "Blued it?"

Tim said: "Not yet. I'm thinking of an extended pub-crawl."

"I'll join you," said Patsy. "Get a nice lot of beer for a hundred quid."

"A hundred?"

"That's Annette's story."

"Nothing less would be worth scandalling about, would it?" said Frances and Tim laughed and shrugged it off.

"Ladies' cloaks in Willie's room," he said. "Shall I take them for you or do you want to use the clean comb he has thoughtfully provided?"

Frances said "Later, perhaps," Marthe said nothing and Tim took their coats into Willie's desperately neat room and gave himself a moment to reassemble his gaiety.

He lit a cigarette and thought about trouble. He was—officially—in trouble. Over him hung accusations into which enquiry was to be made and the outcome could be that the short distance he had travelled in his profession would be washed out. And it didn't matter. In twenty years or even ten, he would have forgotten about it, or remember it only occasionally with sour amusement. But Marthe walking away this afternoon, her unsmiling face as he took her coat—that was a different kind of trouble.

The door was flung open, more guests surged into the hall and smiling cheerfully he went to meet them, to take coats from other girls, to do his stuff in the party.

At nine o'clock sharp Angus arrived with his betrothed,

who was wearing a very nice ring. Pandemonium broke out. Delia beat the gong, clashing horribly with Mr. Richards' gramophone rendering Mendelssohn, and since the Zoo was spreading itself a slightly ragged salute was fired as Messrs. Vincent, Munro, Lawson and Selby almost simultaneously opened bottles of champagne.

Angus and Alison, too happy and too much at home to be at all embarrassed, stood below the garland closely surrounded by well-wishing friends raising champagne glasses and shouting. Only Mr. Richards switching off his gramophone in the hall heard the door bell ring. In a moment he appeared at the door of Mr. Burgoyne's room with a face so dismayed that the shouting stopped abruptly.

"Er—" he began unhappily, but everyone was staring at him and words failed him. He moved aside and Julie Hinton-Brigg walked into the room.

17

JULIE had been somewhat lowered in the course of the week. Her easy success in outwitting her mother had sustained her for a time but the complete uneventfulness of the days which followed was hard to bear and her father's handling of the telephone call purporting to be from Alison Fielding was a shock. It never occurred to her to doubt that it was Alison and even her limited vision perceived that if her affairs led her father to be as rude as that to all the acquaintances he might suspect of complicity, life in Ledshire would become impossible. She waited to hear from Oonagh, she hoped to hear from Tim and meanwhile she stayed under observation at home and nobody came near her. Cubby, feeling that he had been made use of in the matter of the Reel Club, resented it and withdrew. One or two friends who were not black-listed such as George Ward, the son of Colonel Tommy, were curiously surprised when she rang them up and after some hesitation declared themselves absolutely booked solid. It dawned on her slowly and horrifyingly that her name was mud. And it began, too, to dawn that if Tim had wanted to get in touch with her he would have managed to do it.

On Thursday she almost gave up. If she could have thought of a formula which would bring the whole affair to an end she would have used it, but no formula presented itself. She could hardly announce her readiness to be engaged to Cubby since Cubby had apparently lost interest in her. Her protestations of undying love for Tim Selby were too recent for indifference to be accepted now and the best line which occurred to her, a request, unelaborated, to be taken abroad, seemed impossible in the face of her mother's pale detachment and her father's glaring antagonism. After a dinner during which Sir Arthur complained, Lady Hinton-Brigg made an occasional monosyllabic response and Julie herself remained silent, she trailed miserably upstairs and found on the table in her sitting-room a small parcel.

She pounced on it, her spirits and enthusiasm soaring. Then they sagged again. Her pearls and a very short letter. It seemed better, wrote Oonagh under the influence of Eric, to send the pearls back, though it was terribly sweet of Julie to have given them to her. And she was terribly sorry but she had seen Tim and quite honestly, she hated saying this, but it was better to be perfectly frank and as far as he was concerned it was all washed up. "I tried *everything*," concluded Oonagh spaciously, "but really you'd better wipe him off," and she added with unmistakable finality that there was nothing more she could do. No mention was made of the £30.

Julie set her jaw and breathed fast and angrily through the nose. Wipe Tim off, advised Oonagh and Julie who had been on the point of doing so was damned if she would. As for the rest the explanation was simple. Oonagh had got the money and done nothing to earn it.

She spent Friday endeavouring to see Eric. Eric spent the day avoiding her and his was the easier task. On Saturday morning came the letter from the bank.

Julie's correspondence like her telephone calls had been screened since her imprisonment but both had proved disappointing. Now came Sir Arthur's reward for persistence. He tore the envelope open, mastered its contents with satisfying horror and marched upstairs.

"Perhaps you can explain," he said majestically to his wife, "how your daughter was able to cash a cheque for £45—overdrawing her account, as you see—in the course of a minute or two in Woolworth's?"

Lady Hinton-Brigg, fully dressed, was eating a light breakfast by her sitting-room fire and she looked at her husband with resentment, but she read the letter in which the bank manager pointed out politely to Julie that in cashing her cheque for £45 she had overdrawn her account by nearly £20.

"Is there *nobody,*" Sir Arthur was demanding, "whom I can trust? You have made light of this entanglement from the first. You have withheld the support, the loyalty which I have a right to expect from you. And now we find this—" he took the bank manager's letter from her in order to gesticulate with it, "—this unspeakable young cad getting money from her—"

Lady Hinton-Brigg was surprised into an exclamation. "Getting money from her? Why should she give money to Mr. Selby? It is quite *impossible!*"

"Who else?"

"I don't know. She may still have it. I suppose she could have posted it to someone on Monday, but why—"

"Quite so," Sir Arthur dropped rhetoric and became icily courteous. "Perhaps you would be good enough to fetch Julie—doubtless she is still in bed. I shall see what explanation she has to offer."

He stood on the white sheepskin rug, his massive bulk screening the bright morning fire and in perilous proximity to the gilt and enamel French clock and the delicate china ornaments on the mantelpiece; incongruous in the elegant feminine room because there was no feeling either in himself or his wife to make him at home in it. Lady Hinton-Brigg glanced at him with distaste and hesitated. If they had their row here the room would jangle for the rest of the day. But it had to happen and she got up and went to fetch Julie who presently appeared in a dressing-gown with rumpled curls and sleepy eyes.

"Good morning, Julie," said her father. "Read that." He held out the letter and she took it, looking startled. Sir Arthur with out-thrust chin watched her read it while Lady Hinton-Brigg sat down and lit a cigarette, giving up hope of her cold coffee and half-finished toast.

"Damn," said Julie airily.

Her father said: "I should be glad of an explanation," and she thrust her own chin out and retorted:

"Quite simple. I cashed a cheque for more than I'd got."

But this, of course, would not do. Sir Arthur's voice rose as he commanded her to tell him what she had done with the money and she jibbed and dodged with stubborn defiance till her mother cut in.

"Julie," she said incisively, "did you or did you not give this money to Mr. Selby?"

Julie gaped. "Mr. Selby? Tim? Of course not. What on earth would I do that for?"

"I don't know. What *did* you do with it?"

"We know what she did with it," said Sir Arthur and he was convinced that he did. A further ten minutes went by while he tried to make Julie confess that the money had been sent to Tim and she refused to say what she had done with it. They had reached deadlock when Pigeon appeared to announce Lord Lucreton on the telephone.

"I'll take it downstairs," snapped Sir Arthur and paused only to tell his wife: "You will take her abroad as soon as it can be arranged," before striding out of the room.

"It's a pity," said Julie, laughing rather breathlessly, "that we're not R.C. You could pack me off to a convent."

"I wonder if you've ever thought for a moment of the harm you may have done this boy," said her mother. "If your father gets his way he will be dismissed from Ledenham and seriously discredited. I am sure you know better than anyone that the whole affair has been—made up by you." The girl looked blank and she went on levelly: "It's a considerable responsibility, isn't it? I should think about it if I were you."

"I don't believe it," cried Julie. "It's got nothing to do with his job. It's doing *me* a lot of harm. Nobody thinks of that. But I'm sticking to him—"

The day dragged itself on. After talking to Lord Lucreton, Sir Arthur had himself driven to Snaydon and reappeared after lunch looking smug and expectant. During tea Lord Lucreton rang up again and when Sir Arthur returned from taking the call in his study the smugness had given place to a bolting look of incredulity.

"The Lucretons want us to go over for a drink after dinner," he said to his wife.

"Julie too?" she asked, wondering what had shaken him.

"Er—no. No. Lucreton didn't include her—" Both parents eyed their child and she went on turning over the pages of a shiny magazine. "Pigeon and Miss Foley will both be here," said Sir Arthur and she raised her eyes and returned his stare with cold dislike.

Presently she got up and without a word trailed listlessly out of the room, but now she was putting on an act and behind it her brain buzzed furiously. If she was to be defeated, and she recognized that defeat was almost inevitable, she was not just going to give in. Nobody, thought Julie, had ever been so badly treated. Her parents, her friends, the servants, Oonagh, even Tim himself—they were enemies or they were indifferent, but she was not quite so meek and helpless as they supposed.

On her way to her room she extracted the key of the garage from her mother's hand-bag and awaited the hour.

"Saturday," said Sir Arthur at dinner. "Sharpe will be going off duty, I suppose."

"I believe so, Sartha," breathed Pigeon.

"Very well. Tell him to bring her ladyship's car round. I'll drive it."

"Very good, Sartha." Eric had gone off duty several hours ago but there was no need for Sir Arthur to know that. Pigeon brought the Rover to the door and left it there with plenty of time in hand to emerge decorously from his pantry and help his employer into his coat.

Sir Arthur always fought his cars. The Rover, which by courtesy belonged to Lady Hinton-Brigg but which she was never allowed to drive when her husband accompanied her in it, departed with a grinding of gears. Pigeon thinking contemptuously that it took real talent to make such a hash of a lovely bit of machinery, closed the door and turned to stare at Julie who was crossing the hall. Miss Foley appeared from her room behind the library and stared too, one hand fidgeting with a long necklace of what looked like irregular lumps of toffee.

"Are you going to be upstairs, miss?" asked Pigeon.

"Yes," said Julie, maintaining her wilting attitude with an effort.

"What about a little game, dear?" suggested Miss Foley with real kindness. "Halma?" She smiled ingratiatingly. Julie closed her eyes and shuddered slightly.

"No thank you, Miss Foley," she said and went upstairs with bowed head and her best tragic gait. Miss Foley gazed after her, wondering if girls ever go into declines now; Pigeon shrugged his shoulders and both vanished to their respective parts of the house.

Twenty minutes later things went well for Julie. She crept downstairs carrying her shoes and a torch, prepared to make her escape by the drawing-room window. But that proved unnecessary. Miss Foley, whose leisure hours were devoted to the collection of material for a biography of Sir Arthur Hinton-Brigg, was typing energetically. Exploration in the direction of the kitchen was rewarded by the guffaws of Pigeon and the high trilling laughter of Mrs. Pigeon sounding through the uproar of the telly. Julie walked out of the back door and pausing to put her shoes on sprinted across the yard to the garage.

Sir Arthur and Lady Hinton-Brigg had the Rover, Eric had the Land Rover. In the garage stood the staff Ford, Julie's own little car, lifeless without its batteries, and the Rolls Royce complete with ignition key. Julie hesitated for one moment and chose the Rolls. She had never, of course, been allowed to drive it but she did not have much difficulty. With its engine running almost soundlessly she backed it out and set off confidently down the service drive which did not pass the house. Since there was a fair light from the moon she decided not to turn the lights on till she reached the public road; someone might look out of a window and anyhow it was in the best escape traditions. But though she knew the road well she knew less about the size of the car. Half-way along the road was an open gateway, rather narrow, and into her quiet getaway came a hideous noise as the off-side length of the car scraped the stone gate-post.

"Lord!" gasped Julie with starting eyes, but she was committed now and she switched on the lights and put her foot down.

No other mishap marred the drive to Ledenham. The roads were quiet and when she got over her rather nervous unfamiliarity the exquisite response and docility of the car was a delight, the first real pleasure she had had, she felt, since that ghastly Friday, a fortnight ago, when her father began creating about Tim. It was not till she reached the outskirts of Ledenham that she considered what she was going to do there and by then her ferocity had waned. All she wanted to do was to go on driving the Rolls and she had to slow down and remind herself of her purpose. She would see Tim and discover from himself whether the affair was washed up or not, and she would see Oonagh, tell her what she thought of her and get her money back— if it was there to be got—by physical force if necessary. She had no idea where the Hepburns' house was but she knew the Zoo and drew up behind a line of cars parked outside it.

It was clear that the Zoo was *en fête*. Not only were there the cars, every window was lit and from it came sounds of music, cheers and laughter. Julie hesitated, she had not imagined herself making an entrance to a party, but the thought of Tim, and Oonagh too, very likely, enjoying themselves in there while she suffered alone stiffened her resolution and revived her wrath. She rang the bell and walked in, brushing Mr. Richards aside.

There was a sudden silence and for a moment everybody was still, Alison and Angus standing under the huge, absurd heart and a room full of startled people holding glasses of champagne. Julie looked round and saw Tim on the far side of the room.

"Hullo all," she said, "sorry to crash in. I wanted a word with Tim." She stood in the doorway, a smartly dressed little figure with a suggestion of sturdiness which always prevented her from achieving elegance and a pretty, obstinately wilful face; and to everyone in the room she appeared more or less as an enemy.

The moment of stillness was the briefest of pauses. Tim put down the bottle he was carrying and moved towards her, Alison and Angus also moved forward and Annette Courtney said "No!" very sharply and hurrying across the room took her by the arm.

"Stay where you are, Tim," she said. "I'll look after this. Out, Julie. You've done quite enough harm."

Julie grasped the handle of the door and held on. "Harm? What harm have I done?" she demanded. "Don't be stupid, Annette. Let go. Tim—I've got to speak to you."

"Yes," said Tim sternly, "but not here, I think."

Annette cried: "Tim—no. You mustn't—" Patsy Henderson said quietly: "I'd have a witness if I were you," and there was another horrified pause.

"*Idiotic!*" cried Julie scornfully and let go of the door,

flinging it from her. "Well—if you're scared have all the witnesses you want. *I* don't mind."

She turned and walked out of the room and without any arrangement five people followed her. Tim, feeling both angry and ridiculous, Alison and Angus because they had been involved and knew Julie, Annette who knew the Hinton-Briggs and trusted nobody's worldly wisdom but her own and Henry Courtney in support or pursuit of his wife.

Julie addressed Tim as if they were alone. "I haven't heard a word from you for more than a fortnight," she said. "Oonagh Hepburn says you're through. Are you?"

"Of course," said Tim. "It wasn't the sort of thing to go on, was it? And when your people objected and told me of your engagement to Lucreton that naturally finished it."

She said: "I wasn't—I'm not engaged. And," she paused, staring at him with a look of puzzlement, "—why did you defy Pop if you weren't serious?"

"Defy him?" Tim almost laughed. "I didn't defy him. Your mother politely and he rudely said 'get out' and I said 'okay' politely and rudely respectively."

"Then what's all the hoo-ha about?" asked Julie.

"I thought you might tell me that," Tim began but Annette's voice, warm with indignation, interrupted him. More than anyone else in the Ledenham community she was in touch with county people and county gossip and the story of Julie's passionate attachment and her imprisonment had reached her in various forms from various sources.

"*You* played it up," she said to Julie. "*You've* been threatening to run away—keeping it boiling with a lot of lies—"

"Well," Julie defended herself, "I thought if he'd defied Pop he must be frightfully in love. I—"

"What about this money?" asked Angus.

She coloured. "Oh—that. That's all nonsense of course."

Angus said: "I don't think that's good enough," Annette cried: "Very strange nonsense," and Henry, clearing his throat contributed an urbane smile and man of the world reasonableness.

"I think, Julie, my dear, that there's a tremendous amount of misunderstanding in all this," he said. "We must clear it up. It's one of those cases when everybody has meant well but—er—wires have got crossed—that sort of thing. Annette, why don't we take Julie home and have a talk with Arthur and Cynthia? Pool our bits of knowledge—"

"Yes," said Annette, longing for battle.

"No," said Julie.

She stood facing the five people in the cold, linoleum-covered hall of the Zoo and Alison's heart was suddenly moved. She had been as angry as anybody with Julie, she still was, but she had known her for so long, she could remember her when she was small, and it might be that while she stood there, stubborn and defiant, she was feeling about Tim as Alison herself had felt about Angus before that wonderful moment when he appeared in the old nursery.

"Julie," she said and slid her left hand through Julie's stiff right arm, "honestly you've no idea what a mix-up it is. I'm so sorry but it's no good and you *must* stop the fuss."

Julie caught sight of the ring on her hand and pointed to it. "Engaged?" she said. "To him?" indicating Angus. Alison

318

nodded and she laughed. "Nobody ever tells the truth in Ledenham it seems."

She looked at Tim and then her eyes appraised their surroundings; the linoleumed stairs, the worn paint, the glimpse through the open door of Willie's study tidied for the party but bleak with porridge-coloured walls, team photographs and scout trophies. Alison's new diamonds were small. She recalled the docile power of the Rolls and shaking Alison off she said: "You needn't worry. I'll clear it up," and made for the door, nonchalant and unhurried.

Tim reached it in time to open it for her. "I'll see you to your car," he said and added with his eyes on hers: "It'll be a very good thing if you can clear it. It's quite a mess. It hasn't meant a thing to you, has it?"

"Not a thing," said Julie carelessly and she believed it as she had lately believed in her grand passion. Something else had turned up as her mother had foreseen. She went out without looking at any of them but Tim went with her and the others rather uncertainly followed, the Courtneys exchanging a muttered conversation as to whether they should escort her back to Thaxley or not.

"We couldn't really say much," said Henry.

"Well I think we should make it an excuse to go and say *everything,*" retorted Annette and stopped suddenly.

Behind the Rolls, which itself was surprising enough outside the Zoo, a Land Rover had drawn in so hurriedly that it was hardly off the road and its engine was still running. Eric in his knitted cap and fleece-lined jacket was inspecting the car, incandescent with fury and swearing volubly, and Oonagh, wide-eyed, stood by.

"Coming along this bloody road," shouted Eric to

whoever it might concern, "and I sees my Rolls—bloody great scratch on her—who the—what the—" He caught sight of Julie. "Oh—it's you. Might of known. How the hell did you—"

"Oonagh!" shrieked Julie and sprang. She seized the flabbergasted Oonagh by the shoulders and shook her vigorously. "Where's my money? You didn't do a dam' thing and you've the flaming nerve to freeze on to thirty pounds—"

"Oo-oh!" cried Oonagh.

"Here!" roared Eric.

"Ah!" said Mrs. Courtney.

Pandemonium broke out. Julie went on shaking and demanding repayment. Oonagh gasped and shrieked. Eric started forward and Angus's hand closed inexorably on the sheepskin collar.

"Stop it, Julie," snapped Tim.

"Julie, my *dear*," pleaded Mr. Courtney and they parted the two girls but not before Julie got home with a ringing slap.

"*That'll* teach you," she panted, "swindling—"

"*Quiet!*" said Angus. He, Henry, Tim and Alison glanced automatically up and down the road. Fortunately it was late enough for all boys to be in Houses. "Now," he said, "sort yourselves out and go home."

"I'm driving my Rolls," said Eric. "I don't want it damaged no more. You get in the back, miss—"

"Don't talk to me like that," snapped Miss Hinton-Brigg. "What are you doing with the Land Rover? Better get it safely home and think up something to say for yourself." She got into the Rolls and slammed the door, backed it

320

smartly into the Land Rover's bumper and drove away. Eric leapt for the Land Rover, scooping up Oonagh as an afterthought, and shot off in pursuit.

Julie had a start and under the magnificent bonnet of the Rolls there was plenty of speed but Eric was a much better driver and she had an uncomfortable picture of the Land Rover shooting ahead and forcing her to stop. It was still surprisingly early and her parents would not be home from the Lucretons' for some time. She turned away from Thaxley. After all she would probably never have a chance to drive the Rolls again and thirty or forty miles would make no difference to the offence of driving it at all.

About an hour later she drove into the yard at Thaxley and found Eric waiting for her with Pigeon beside him looking avid and Mrs. Pigeon and Miss Foley hovering in the background. Eric with a large torch sprang at the car and began to examine it as a mother might examine a child recovered from kidnappers.

"There's nothing wrong with it except a scratch," said Julie getting out.

"We'll see, but it's plenty," retorted Eric grimly. "Scratch, my God! Wing's crumpled," he ran a sorrowful hand along the scratch, "need a new door panel—whole side's mucked up. See here—" he called in Pigeon who peered and felt it with him, shaking his head and making moaning sounds of agreement.

Julie looked at it. It was shocking, that scraped ugliness on the shining paint, but she still felt the exhilaration of her drive and she was ready to take on anybody.

"Really, Sharpe," she said crisply, "what a fuss! It'll go in for repair and come back as good as new and nobody's blaming you."

"Nobody'd dam' well better try blaming me," said Eric.

"I don't know what Sartha will say, I'm sure," said Pigeon. "What came over you to do a thing like that, miss?"

"If he half kills you it'll be okay with me," added Eric.

An immense feeling of power flowed into Julie. For the last fortnight she had been in a position so weak that anybody could trample her underfoot but she was through with weakness. In a few pithy words she told Pigeon that what Sir Arthur thought was none of his business and ordered him off so sharply that, taken aback, he withdrew some yards.

"As for you, Sharpe," she turned on Eric, "we'll see what he thinks about you using the Land Rover. *And* your girl-friend getting money from me on false pretences."

"Now see here," Eric began a threatening advance but she stood her ground. He must have known all about it, she said. He brought back the pearls and the letter. Eric paused and Pigeon made no move. The situation had changed so suddenly that they were baffled, deprived equally of weapons and armour. What had happened about the teacher, they wondered, groping. Was he on or was he off?

"I'll go in," said Julie grandly. As she walked away the sound of Sir Arthur changing gear at the lodge gates was clearly heard. It was his habit if he reached home before midnight to leave his car at the front door for somebody else to put away and his approach was the signal for general rapid movement. Julie and Eric were both determined to get in first, Pigeon was determined not to miss anything and the ladies, equally curious but more timorous, made for well-tried vantage points which allowed them to hear without being seen.

322

Julie took a short cut through the house but Eric had a useful turn of speed and she arrived to hear him embarking a little breathlessly on his report.

" 'Scuse me, Sartha, Miss Julie's had the Rolls out and marked it. Something shocking, sir. I—"

Sir Arthur struggled out of the driving seat, Lady Hinton-Brigg slid neatly out on the passenger's side and came round.

"Actually," said Julie airily from the door step, "it's nothing but a scratch. Sharpe," she looked meaningly at Eric, "is scared you'll blame him but I'm quite ready to admit liability."

"How did you get *at* it?" demanded Sir Arthur safely upright and finding his voice. "Was the garage unlocked? The car itself? Where was Pigeon?" Pigeon, hovering near the door backed hastily. "You all knew my orders—"

"The garage was locked. I snitched the key," said Julie, but the car had not been locked and nothing could save Eric. Sir Arthur thrust his bulk back into the Rover.

"Get in," he snapped. "I'll look at it," and started the car with a punishing jerk almost before Eric had joined him.

Lady Hinton-Brigg walked past her daughter into the house. Her level gaze noted the two women, who had not been quite quick enough, and rested briefly on Pigeon who came forward officiously.

"You needn't wait," she said and went into the drawing-room followed by Julie, who in her turn glanced at Pigeon and closed the door. Pigeon retreated. Her ladyship could, without a word, make him feel uneasy.

In the drawing-room her ladyship, making her daughter feel uneasy, went slowly to the fire and sat down. She lit a cigarette and inhaled deeply.

"Too bad about the car," said Julie. "It only happened because I was making my getaway without lights."

"I suppose you went to Ledenham hunting that unfortunate young man," said her mother.

Julie's colour rose but she held on to her nonchalance. "Yes, of course I did. Pity I didn't see him before and we needn't have had all the fuss. It's finished."

"I told you from the beginning that he cared nothing for you."

"But you'd have said that anyway."

"No," Lady Hinton-Brigg considered it honestly. "No, I wouldn't."

"Well," said Julie letting it pass, "it was better to find out for myself. If Pop hadn't—"

The door was flung open and Pop was with them, tramping heavily across the room. "Now," he began and Lady Hinton-Brigg braced herself for the storm.

But there were two new factors in this storm. A new toughness and confidence in Julie who, since she had driven the Rolls, knew exactly what she wanted from life; and in Sir Arthur a slight discomfort which puzzled him. He knew that he could not be wrong, that he was invulnerable, yet since Lord Lucreton had told him whose son it was who had been so insolent to him he had been conscious of Sir Quentin Selby, Q.C. like a gremlin on his shoulder.

Lady Hinton-Brigg, tense and nervous, began to see that in some curious fashion her husband and daughter had changed places. Julie's obstinacy had acquired an edge, Sir Arthur was plunging and floundering. Much of Lord

324

Lucreton's conversation that evening had been aimed at Lady Hinton-Brigg and it had found its mark. Sir Quentin Selby was to her a great deal worse than a gremlin. Lord Lucreton had dwelt significantly on his reputation and the thought of her husband's probable performance against so formidable a foe made her shudder. She sat up in her chair. Neither Sir Arthur nor Julie took any notice of her.

"Drop it, Pop," Julie was saying. "It's all your fault making such a bru-ha-ha without knowing the facts. I don't care if I never see Tim again. You've nothing to complain of."

"You're wrong," said her father. "I have very serious complaints against him. And against Fielding—"

Lady Hinton-Brigg got up. "I am going to bed," she said shortly. If, after all these years, she now abandoned compliance and asserted herself, could she do any good? She walked wearily upstairs considering her weapons and her strength. They seemed very slight. There was no chink in Arthur's armour. He was impervious; and as she went into her room and shut the door she thought that, in fact, she had adopted the only line which was possible.

She had never imagined that Mr. Fielding's position was in danger and she was no longer greatly concerned for young Tim Selby. With Sir Quentin Selby in the field it was her husband taking Julie and herself with him—who was running for the rocks. A case of libel, Lord Lucreton had hinted at it—

But there was nothing she could do except what she had always done, smoothing things over, covering up and making the most of what she had.

18

WHEN Julie and Eric in their respective vehicles had driven away the road outside the Zoo had a moment of silence and then the five people who were left turned back, rather dazed, to the house. Mrs. Courtney was the first to speak.

"Henry, we should go after them," she said.

"No, darling, we could do no good," was the reply and though she argued, yearning to join in the chase to Thaxley Manor and demolish all the Hinton-Briggs, Henry took a more realistic view and was, for once, immovable. He would have enjoyed taking grief-stricken, subdued Julie home and saying a few wise helpful words to grateful parents but he had no stomach for a brawl.

Behind them Tim, walking with Alison and Angus, mopped his brow and said: "I can think of no comment except a weak smile."

A muffled explosion of disgust came from Angus and from Alison a half-guilty giggle.

"I couldn't have done it myself," she said, "owing to my inhibitions, but Oonagh had that smack coming to her. Well—now we know about the money."

"Pretty squalid," said Angus.

"Forget it," said Tim who felt that he never could forget it. "There's a party—Got your poise in order?"

It might have been difficult to save the party after so shattering an interruption but Mr. Burgoyne's sangfroid was equal to it. "Well? What occurred?" he asked loudly as they trooped in and since it is the avoidance of a delicate subject which taxes social poise a suitably brief and inaccurate account of the late scene did all that was required.

The Zoo offered its guests a variety of entertainments and allowed those who preferred it to entertain themselves. Mr. Burgoyne's room containing the drinks remained the centre, but the dining-room with its furniture stacked provided a modest dance floor, highbrows climbed the stairs to listen to Bartok with Mr. Richards and in other parts of the house people argued violently about translating the Bible, protest-marchers and the exploration of space.

It was late and the party had begun to thin out when Tim, after a casual, conversational dance with Alison, met Marthe who had been dancing with Angus and, face to face with her for the first time that evening, decided to have it out. If she was going to treat him in this offensively aloof manner he had, he thought, a right to know why.

"Come and dance," he said rather peremptorily and with no sign of either pleasure or displeasure, she went with him, while Angus and Alison, restored to each other, looked delighted and drifted away.

It was a long time since he had danced with Marthe, not since before the Christmas holidays, and he had not taken her hand since the day when he returned to Ledenham and asked her to marry him. They danced in silence for some time because he found himself unable to speak and Marthe, apparently, had nothing to say. The face so near his might have been a mile away. It was composed and remote and the black lashes allowed him no glimpse of the eyes. It takes two to have things out, Tim discovered, and nobody ever looked less like taking part. Angry and sore he wondered why he loved her so desperately, but whatever the reason or reasons might be the fact remained and he felt an obscure, half-amused pride in her, she was holding out on him with such tenacity and politeness.

There were two other couples in the room—Willie, to everyone's relief, was having a very nice time with the doctor's daughter—and for a little he let himself forget everything except that he was dancing with Marthe. They danced together very well and till emotion made their relationship difficult they had enjoyed it enormously. Now a sort of peace came upon them and he felt some of the defensive stiffness leave the slight body. She too forgetting everything except the pleasure of dancing and he had a sudden surge of hope. Their bodies were so harmonious, so long as they went on like this, dancing without saying a word, it seemed as though they understood each other completely. And almost, it seemed, loved each other completely.

The record came to an end. The other couples went away in search of drinks and Tim quickly started the gramophone again and held out his hand. But the spell was broken. Warmth had come into Marthe's face but it disappeared and she, so to speak, suffered his arm to go round her and began dancing again only because it would have meant a fuss if she had refused. After all, bodily harmony was not enough.

"I've always heard," said Tim bitterly, "that the Norwegian Resistance was the toughest in the war. I believe it."

Marthe glanced up. Surprise, puzzlement, a flash of amusement showed fleetingly in her eyes and then the veil descended again "They were very brave and had strong purpose, I think," she said sedately and did not enquire why the subject had been introduced at this juncture.

Tim persisted. "I suppose you know that I'm in a bit of a jam. Of course there's no reason why you should be interested or—friendly about it, but it seems that you're even less friendly than you were. I'd like to know why."

"I'm very sorry you are in a jam," said Marthe after a pause. "I thought better not to say anything. It is not good for strangers to intrude. I hope," she added politely, "that soon it will be finished."

"Thank you so much," responded Tim, equally polite. "How kind." The eyes looked up again with a flash of resentment so now they were both angry. They proceeded for a few steps in silence, like two pieces of wood, then he said: "Do you believe these things that are being said about me? You sound as if you do."

"I know very little about it. Only from hearing Frances and one or two other people talking."

"That should be plenty. Marthe—" the record went on but he stopped dancing and stood facing her, "—come clean. I mind about this very much. I don't think I've done anything seriously wrong. If you think I have you ought to give me a chance to explain what I *have* done. You've heard people talking, you've heard nothing from me. Do you think it's fair to condemn me unheard?"

"It is not for me," began Marthe but he stopped her.

"Don't, for God's sake take that line," he said impatiently. "You know quite well what I feel about you. It matters to me like hell what you think."

Marthe hesitated and then, at last, looked up and spoke

directly to him instead of addressing the air around them. She said: "Since you ask like this, Tim, I must answer. Your friends all sympathise with you very much. They are angry with this Sir, the father of Julie and they blame Julie too, but never you."

"Well?"

"Well—I don't know everything that happens but it seems to me that a father has some right to be angry if you make his daughter in love with you without meaning anything. And if you are rude to him also he may be annoyed, but that is not so serious."

Tim had asked for it. He had now got it. The record ended and sounds of the party reached them, voices loud in cheerful argument and a burst of laughter. He flipped the record over and started the machine again as cover, then he said "Listen" to Marthe and told her coldly the full story of himself in connection with Julie Hinton-Brigg. "There was never the slightest chance of either of us falling in love," he concluded. "She was bored and I—well, you had ditched me, Frances warned me off and I was as sore as hell."

The music, unheeded, throbbed and wailed. Marthe stood frowning at the floor.

"Say something," said Tim.

"I don't know what there is for me to say," she replied. He waited grimly, determined that she should make some comment, or at least some sign that she had heard what he said whether she believed it or not, and this being so she raised her head and went on: "I don't think, as you say, that you have done anything very wrong, but it is that you are a little like Oonagh. Always there must be the boy-friend or the girl-friend, whether it is somebody you like or not. If you do this, then I think some sort of trouble comes some time—soon or late. And for me—"

"For you?" Tim prompted her.

"For me, I have no right to say it is wrong. Usually there is nothing wrong in it. It is just something I don't like. Friends I like, I hope like every girl that I'll have a lover some day, but this," she moved a shoulder in a small shrug which expressed ineffable scorn, "this, I think, is cheap."

She had finished. The gramophone throbbed on and Tim finding it suddenly unbearably irritating went and lifted the needle and switched it off.

"You're perfectly right, of course," he said into the silence. "All of us, I imagine—Oonagh and myself included—prefer the real thing both in love and friendship. If it's denied us we're not all strong enough to eschew what substitutes may offer." He opened the door. "Let me get you a drink."

"I have offended you," said Marthe regretfully. "I am sorry but you made me say it."

"Quite true," said Tim, "and it's better—I suppose—to have it said."

She looked at him oddly and then went before him out of the room to rejoin the party.

It had been agreed almost without a word between the witnesses of Julie's attack on Oonagh that nothing should be said about the destination of the mysterious sum of money. Public opinion had already decided that there had never been any money. The hundred pounds or forty or fifteen alleged to have been received by Tim was, it was thought, merely something else cooked up by Sartha or

331

proof of how wild rumour could get, and the witnesses had found the truth so distasteful that they felt it better to leave public opinion to its own solution. But as Alison and Angus walked home very slowly from the Zoo to School House she said:

"I think Beak ought to know about Julie coming and the money."

Angus agreed reluctantly. "I suppose so. In fact—yes, he must know," and then he went on: "What's it all about? Did the silly creature think Oonagh would persuade Tim to marry her? I don't get it."

"I don't know," said Alison, "but I think she meant it when she said she'd clear it up. I think there really was a muddle and she's had enough of it."

"About time. She's had her fun, if it was fun, and Tim's left waiting to see what the rap's going to amount to."

Alison sighed. It was a real pain to her that when she was so happy herself others were unhappy. For Julie she had no sympathy, it was clear enough that no genuine feeling was involved, and she could feel no great concern over Oonagh even if she was in for trouble about the money, but she grieved for Tim.

Angus was less moved. He thought Tim was a bit of an ass in some ways, almost bound to have run into trouble of some kind before settling down to adult life, and he had very little doubt that the row handled by the Beak, would fizzle out when it came to the enquiry. "And," he added, "of course he did make a pass of sorts at the wretched girl."

"Yes," said Alison. "He's a really nice person though. Basically, I mean—anybody can be an ass at times. He's too good to be landed in trouble by a squirt like Julie and you

332

know, Angus, the worst thing is that I think it's put him back with Marthe."

"Had he made any advance, do you think?"

"Well—I thought it looked a little more promising, but she's very frozen again now."

They reached School House and went in to the hall. "You can't do anything about it, you know," said Angus. He was very sorry for Tim and would have been delighted if Marthe had returned his affection and they had been as happy as Alison and himself, but he pointed out that people have to work these things out for themselves and Tim would get over it. "After all," he said, "I was terribly in love with Frances for a week or so and gosh! How glad I am that she brushed me off and fell for Patsy."

"Shall I brush you off and see if the reaction is as good?" asked Alison comfortably encircled by his arms.

"No," he said, "if I lost you now it would kill me. As a matter of fact I don't know if I'd ever have recovered from you if, say, Oonagh's Sykes story had been true. It had gone deep, you see."

Though it was late there was still a light in the study and when Angus had gone Alison went along to see her father and tell him the story of Julie's dramatic appearance. He listened giving it all his attention and thought about it.

"I can't explain the money," said Alison. "Even Julie couldn't have been silly enough to think she could tempt Tim with rich bribes, and what did she think Oonagh could do?"

Mr. Fielding had a shrewd idea of the explanation. He knew about Julie's imprisonment and could imagine her determination to make contact with Tim somehow. "But

333

it's not our concern," he said. "We can now prove, if necessary, that it wasn't sent to Selby and that's all that matters to us."

"Are you worried about this business?" Alison asked rather diffidently. Questions about School affairs were not encouraged. But her father answered quite readily.

"No," he said. "Not really. There's always a certain risk that things will go in a direction you don't expect. Governors are individuals and bound to be a bit incalculable with all their different view-points. But as a rule," he smiled at her sober face, "they get the right end of the stick. How was the party?"

Alison described the Zoo's gifted hospitality, the garland, the champagne and Mr. Burgoyne's fez and he was amused by the melodrama of Julie's arrival and raised his eyebrows when she told him, rather guiltily about the slap. "We thought that really must be kept dark," she said.

"Certainly not a thing to get about," he agreed and then with a change of tone: "What about Selby? Is he bothered, do you think?"

"Well, yes. I think he is a bit," said Alison.

She sounded hesitant and he said: "You like him, don't you?"

"Yes," she said at once. "I do like him—very much. Angus does too. He thinks he's a bit—well, flibberty, but that's nothing."

"Not very much certainly," her father qualified it, "so long as he doesn't keep on." He got up and began collecting the papers on his desk, sorting them out with practised neatness and Alison who had been considering what her duty was said:

334

"I don't know if you know, but I believe you ought to and it isn't gossip or tale-telling. He—Tim—is very miserable about Marthe. He'd never even have seen Julie if she hadn't turned him down. Did you know?"

"I did hear something," he said. "Nothing definite. He's had a real knock, has he? Come on, darling. Let's go."

Alison felt that neither her father nor Angus fully appreciated all that Tim was suffering and she spoke firmly. "A very bad knock," she said. "I'm very sad about it."

"Are you?" he smiled at her and put an arm round her as they crossed the hall towards the stairs. "Well—don't overdo it. Persons who are engaged to be married are excused sadness. Selby will get over it you know. One does if one has to, as I think I observed to you a day or two ago. Anyhow there's nothing you can do about it. By the way," he paused as they reached the top of the stairs, "did you withdraw from the Upton job?"

"Yes—pronto," she laughed and blushed remembering her despair as she wrote the letter of application. But she was not altogether convinced that there was nothing she could do about Tim.

In the days before the enquiry was held Ledenham thought about very little else. It would have been desirable, in the Headmaster's opinion, if the School had known nothing about it but it was one of those things which could not be kept secret since the basic fact that there was a row on had reached the public ear. Speculation was continuous and there was a flourishing crop of rumours but there was nothing to be done about it. It was impossible to rationalize speculation by making all the facts known and equally impossible to quieten rumour by prophecy about the outcome of the enquiry. The Headmaster accordingly pursued his normal imperturbable course and as far as could be seen gave no thought to the matter. Tim's sets continued to treat him kindly, Secker, much subdued, sweated manfully on the track and in the gym, becoming a better and more disciplined athlete in the process, while Tim himself, keeping an eye on the Beak, maintained a creditable air of unconcern.

Mrs. Fielding, like her husband, went about looking as serene as usual but unlike him she was subjected to some discussion and pumping. "Is the Headmaster *worried* about this wretched business?" asked the bolder ladies hopefully. "Oh, I don't think so," was the reply and she made it with a faint suggestion of surprise which usually, as Alison noticed with mild glee, held them.

But Matron was not to be held. She was frequently found to take the same view as the boys in controversial matters and she shared to the full their resentment at outsiders, in which category the Governors were included, butting in.

"Why do schools have to have Governors?" she demanded crossly. "What good do they do?"

It was hardly the moment, Mrs. Fielding felt, to explain that public schools are so named because they are governed by a Body of independent members of the public, but she pointed out mildly that Governors have their uses and that the Ledenham Governors had always shown themselves helpful and reliable.

"Well if you ask me, Mrs. Fielding," said Matron, unconvinced, "the School should be left to the Headmaster. He understands it," and she went on her way muttering:

"That Secker—just wanted his ears boxing—"

While Matron boiled and scolded Miss Wills remained quietly discreet. Her convalescent routine held. Every morning Tim drove her to School House, every afternoon he drove her home and they talked about the weather and the approach of spring. Her lunch was taken upstairs to the old nursery and she rested obediently but though as a consequence of her coming through to the private side Mrs. Fielding saw more of her than she had ever done before no reference was made to the crisis. Both, however, were very conscious of it and Mrs. Fielding suspected that Miss Wills was worrying a good deal.

"You can't get away from it," she said to her husband. "Whether people talk or don't talk, whether they look at you or avoid looking—I wish Lord Leyburn was at home."

The Headmaster laughed and told her to take no notice of Mr. Barker but he admitted that he too would have been glad to see or hear from his Chairman. Lord Leyburn was lost. He and Lady Leyburn were assumed to be in the South of France but no replies had been received to the letters written to him at Nice and his son was only able to say vaguely that they were very likely moving about.

It was, perhaps, because everyone concerned with the enquiry was more than anything wondering why they were having it that they kept aloof from each other beforehand. Colonel Ward consulted the Clerk several times about the actual form the meeting should take and the Clerk, sighing heavily, gave him replies which he found depressing and less helpful than he had a right to expect. The fact was, the Clerk said, it was impossible to foresee how the thing would go. The only way was to approach it with a flexible mind. The Colonel, whose mind was not flexible, fell into a state of dread and slept badly. The Headmaster, he thought, as he turned and tossed, was as bad as the Clerk. He simply lay low and said nothing and telephone calls elicited only soothing noises.

Leyburn Castle, once the home of the Earls of Leyburn, was now a kind of county headquarters. It housed the library, a picture gallery and a museum; balls were held in it, also concerts and plays, whist drives and meetings various. Upstairs in what used to be the Earl's bedroom, now furnished with a large table and chairs of a boardroom nature, a somewhat scratch team of Ledenham Governors assembled on a Friday afternoon. Sir Arthur Hinton-Brigg arrived in company with Lord Lucreton. The Headmaster brought with him an alert and extremely dapper man whom nobody had ever seen before.

The Clerk looked round dismally. He had no experience of meetings in the absence of Lord Leyburn, and he wished he was not going to have it now. Everything, he suspected, depended on him. None of the distant Governors were present, the Bishop was visiting the Holy Land and all the less intelligent and calculable were there in force. He heard the bright-eyed Sir Quentin Selby ask the Headmaster in a low voice if they opened with prayer and saw the Headmaster's quick grin, and frowning a little at the flippant tone he whispered to the Vice-Chairman, who cleared his throat nervously and rapped on the table harder than he had intended.

"Er—gentlemen," said Colonel Ward, "I—we—that is, it will be best if the members of the Governing Body have a few minutes to discuss this—this unfortunate matter before the—a—enquiry, the *formal* enquiry begins. If you, Sir Arthur," he gave a little bow, "and —er," another bow in the direction of the dapper man—

"Sir Quentin Selby, Colonel Ward," said the Headmaster.

"Ah—er, how do you do," both gentlemen bowed. "If you would be good enough to withdraw, we won't keep you more than a few minutes." The Clerk whispered again and he added hurriedly: "The Headmaster will leave the room or remain, as he chooses." The Headmaster said easily that they would probably get on better without him at this stage and ushered the two knights into the Earl's late dressing-room. He introduced them. Sir Quentin talked urbanely about the castle and the view. Sir Arthur prowled round the room, empurpled and silent.

In the other room Colonel Ward, after a few halting words, handed the meeting over to the Clerk who laid the matter for enquiry before it. It fell, he said, into two parts.

I. Sir Arthur Hinton-Brigg, who, as they all knew, was nominated by the Mayor and Council of Snaydon to the vacancy on the Board occasioned by the death of Canon Harris, made complaint (a) of improper behaviour towards his daughter by a Ledenham assistant master, Timothy Quentin Selby, and of insolence from Mr. Selby to himself when he remonstrated with him and ordered him not to see Miss Hinton-Brigg again; (b) of carelessness on the part of the Headmaster when this matter was reported to him.

II. Sir Arthur Hinton-Brigg also conveyed to the Governing Body a complaint alleged to have been made to him by the parents of a boy at present in the School.

There was an interruption at this point.

"Mr. Chairman," said Lord Lucreton, "I must take

339

exception to the word 'alleged'. There is no intention, is there, to doubt Sir Arthur's statement that this complaint was made?"

"Oh—er—no," said the Colonel.

"I used the word," explained the Clerk respectfully, "because, though the complaint was undoubtedly made, it could not properly be made to Sir Arthur Hinton-Brigg since he is not yet a member of the Board and has no standing. I will withdraw the word 'alleged', sir," he looked at Colonel Ward, "if you instruct me to do so."

"I submit, Mr. Chairman," said Lord Lucreton, "that it is misleading. I accept the Clerk's explanation, but the word should be withdrawn."

The Chairman decided that the word was, perhaps, misleading and the Clerk withdrew it, reflecting gloomily that Lucreton was out to make trouble. He concluded his statement, reading in a flat voice the accusations made, rather hysterically, by Mrs. Secker and passed on with inaccurate enthusiasm by Sir Arthur.

"Dear me!" explained the Vicar. "That seems most— Struck the boy repeatedly on the head, you say?"

"And the Headmaster followed up with a full-dress beating," Lord Lucreton added briskly. "One allows for upset mothers, of course, but it seems to me there is something here which needs looking into."

"There's never been anything of the sort before," somebody said unhappily. "I can't really—there must be a muddle somewhere—"

The Clerk looked at him gratefully and proceeded, with permission, to read aloud a letter received from Mr. Secker withdrawing the complaint *in toto.*

340

"Strange," said the Vicar.

"Very strange," said Lord Lucreton significantly.

"Not really," said Colonel Ward with unexpected decision. "It was his wife—Mrs. Secker went and complained to Sir Arthur."

There was a discreet ripple of masculine amusement and the Clerk followed it quickly by reading letters from two of the distant Governors. They apologised for their inability to attend the special meeting and expressed the opinion that the only course open to the Governors was to refuse to make enquiry into business brought before them by someone who had no right to bring it, and which was in any case Headmaster's business.

But he had no real hope that this most reasonable line would be adopted and it was not. Colonel Ward himself felt unhappily that such complaints could not be ignored, Lord Lucreton was determined that the Chairman of Hinton Brigg Ltd. should not be so lightly brushed off and all round the table there were doubts and worried faces. Discussion went on for what seemed to the three gentlemen in the dressing-room a very long time. They gave up making conversation and instead listened to the murmur of voices, the unmistakable brazen notes of Lord Lucreton dominating it, in the other room. At last the sad face of the Clerk appeared to them.

"If you would come now," he murmured, and as they filed in he looked at the Headmaster coming last and turned his thumb down.

"The Governors are agreed," said Colonel Ward, "that the complaints brought before them must—that is they require careful investigation."

"Will you allow me, Mr. Chairman," said the Headmaster, "to point out to the Governors that this matter is one in which the issue is confidence or no confidence in me?"

There was a short, startled silence. "Oh—surely," began the Chairman, "it isn't quite—There's no question of—"

"Rather an extreme view," suggested Lord Lucreton genially.

"I don't think so." The Headmaster spoke quietly, almost as genially but the Clerk, who had his imaginative moments, thought of a drawn sword. Mr. Fielding glanced round the table. He had been Headmaster of Ledenham for a long time. He had weathered all sorts of storms, serious storms some of them, and his time had been one of prosperity and well-doing for the School, devotion and satisfaction for himself. Out of nothing this particular crisis had come upon him but he was under no illusion; he was fighting for all that mattered to him as a schoolmaster. He explained it, as much as he thought necessary and as much as they would understand. The appointment and dismissal of assistant masters, the discipline of the School, that was to say discipline of masters and other staff as well as of the boys, were his job, laid down in the terms of his appointment. Either the Governors must abide by this or they must, if they no longer had confidence in him, proceed accordingly. They had the machinery to do so. What he was not prepared to do was to impair his own authority and that of all future Headmasters of Ledenham —indeed to some extent of headmasters everywhere—by allowing the Governors to usurp authority and take decisions which were properly his. "You must, in fact," he concluded, "allow me to run the School or find someone else to do it. You can't do my job for me."

This, the crux of the matter, though he had spoken of it to nobody but his wife, was understood by most members of the School commonroom, who would, they hoped, take the same risk themselves if circumstances ever made it necessary. And it was also understood by Miss Wills. Such decisions would never be required of her, her responsibilities were narrow and she worked under the direct authority of one man, but she knew enough about schools and the job of running them to know that the Headmaster would resign rather than hand over Tim Selby or any other of his responsibilities to a collection of men who were, in the last resort, strangers and laymen. She also knew that a few of the strangers and laymen saw themselves in a different light, as men of wide experience and diffused wisdom whose mission it was to guide the steps of the man who was only an expert in his job, and she was therefore worried.

The meeting took place in the afternoon and the Headmaster had lunch in hall as usual and drove off immediately afterwards. Miss Wills picked at her own meal upstairs, rested dutifully and returned to her office when it was time to return; but there routine broke down. For once in her life she could not concentrate on her work and so restless and fidgety did she feel that she even considered briefly going in search of Mrs. Fielding to see how she was getting on. She rejected it at once. It was, she supposed, a sign that she had not fully recovered her strength and she had drawn herself up and turned her wavering attention to the typewriter when the telephone rang.

"The Headmaster's secretary," she said to it as usual.

"Ha, you're back," shouted the telephone cordially. "Glad you're better. Is the Headmaster—"

Miss Wills gasped and grabbed for her self-possession. "Lord Leyburn," she said as calmly as she could, "the Headmaster has already gone. The meeting began at two-thirty—"

"Meeting?" shouted Lord Leyburn. "What meeting?"

There was a period of confusion but it was short. Lord and Lady Leyburn had, as their son expected, been moving about the shores of the Mediterranean. The letters from the Clerk, the Headmaster and the Vice-Chairman telling him of Sir Arthur's attack had just caught up with him and he had very crossly flown home to deal with it. He had heard nothing of the meeting.

"Got it up very quick, didn't they?" he grumbled. "Why couldn't they wait?"

"There has been so much talk," Miss Wills explained and he said:

"Oh, there has, has there? H'mph. Well, just give me the dope, will you—expect you've got it all—and I'll get along."

Miss Wills had it all neatly filed in her mind and she was very skilled in selecting the facts which were important and presenting them clearly and economically. It was only five or six minutes later that Lord Leyburn, well briefed, got into his car. He opened the door and walked into the meeting in the silence which followed the Headmaster's statement: "You must allow me to run the School or find someone else to do it."

19

"AFTERNOON," barked Lord Leyburn, coldly surveying the startled faces gaping at him. "Apologise for being late. Unavoidable."

Exclamations broke out. Men rose hurriedly to their feet. "We didn't expect—heard nothing from you, m'lord—letters gone astray—" sounded from all round the table. No explanations were vouchsafed them. Lord Leyburn, looking like an aggressive terrier, stumped towards the Chair.

"I see," he said, "that the Vice-Chairman has very properly opened the meeting. No doubt you would prefer that he should remain in the Chair? I am perfectly willing for him to—Very well. Thank you." Colonel Ward, who was already standing, backed hastily away. The Chairman sat down.

His sharp protruberant eyes passed deliberately over the company, noting which Governors were there and which were absent; he glanced at the Headmaster's impassive face, dwelt with something like astonishment on Sir Arthur Hinton-Brigg and came to rest on Sir Quentin Selby.

Sir Quentin was presented to him and he bowed courteously. "Ah yes," he said. "It's your son who's being accused of all this seduction—or abduction, was it? —and laying violent hands on somebody's boy."

"I hope," said Sir Quentin, "that you have no objection to my being present at this meeting, m'lord? The—a—acting Chairman was kind enough to—"

"No objection at all," said Lord Leyburn. "Very natural that you should wish to attend. And permission was also given to Sir Arthur Hinton-Brigg, I presume? Or are you present by invitation, Sir Arthur?"

There was a gulp from Colonel Ward and the Clerk looked uneasy. It was dawning upon them both that they had allowed themselves, as people so often did, to be mesmerized by Sir Arthur. Why, when all was said and done, was he there?

"Naturally," he was replying for himself, "I was invited— that is, it was assumed that I should be present. My presence is necessary." The Chairman grunted and leaning his stocky body forward placed his elbows on the table and clasped his hands.

"Well, gentlemen," he looked at them more amiably, whereupon the Clerk, who knew him very well, stiffened and the Headmaster, who knew him even better, remained absolutely motionless and blank. The amiable gaze was held for a moment with a growing flavour of amusement, very dry. "Well, gentlemen, I'm afraid, you know, that you're all off-side."

There was an uneasy stir and a few puzzled faces. Sir Quentin Selby grinned delightedly and was instantly solemn again.

"We must plead, my lord," said the Vicar stiffly, "that in your absence we did what seemed best. Had we known that you were to be home so soon we should naturally have postponed—"

"Oh, I don't mean that," Lord Leyburn interrupted him.

"Then," said Lord Lucreton, "are you suggesting that we are out of order?"

The two peers looked at each other, a large peer who had achieved his peerage and a small peer who had inherited

346

his, equally aggressive and equally tough.

"As I said," said the small one, "you're off-side. What are you doing here?" More than one voice started to tell him what they were doing but it was his intention to tell them. "Sir Arthur Hinton-Brigg," he said, "had a complaint to make about a master in the School. His proper course, if he was convinced that the matter was sufficiently serious, was to make his complaint to the Headmaster."

"I did complain to the Headmaster—"

"So I understand. What," he turned to Mr. Fielding, "did you do about it?"

Mr. Fielding replied that he had made enquiries and satisfied himself that the matter was one of misunderstanding. He had replied to Sir Arthur to that effect. Sir Arthur sat in glum silence but Lord Lucreton came in again. There had been a feeling, he said, that the Headmaster, if he might say so with all due respect, had taken the matter rather too lightly. Sir Arthur, he knew, had felt this at the time and Governors had later had the same impression. The Vicar put in a grave observation about the seriousness of any complaint of misbehaviour on the part of young masters and the Governor who supplied Thaxley Manor with fish added that it wasn't likely Sartha would complain without he had a reason.

Lord Leyburn turned briskly to the plaintiff. "What exactly was the nature of the young man's misbehaviour?" he asked.

Sir Arthur did his best but he was handicapped by the fact that the misbehaviour was difficult to define with any precision. *Lèse majestie,* perhaps, was as near as one could get and that could hardly be used. Also the danger to his daughter, or rather to his plans for her, had fizzled out and he was not unaffected by pressure brought to bear upon him recently. He did his best but it was bluster. Lord Leyburn gazed at him steadily with eyebrows rising. Lord Lucreton looked down at the table; Sir Arthur was never an easy man to support. Most of the faces round the table were puzzled, somewhat embarrassed, and even Sir Arthur began to feel that the meeting was not wholeheartedly with him.

"I submit, my lord," he plunged angrily into his peroration, "that the young man misbehaved grossly and that I have just cause for my complaint of negligence against the Headmaster." With his chin thrust out he glared at the meeting and moving on from Lord Leyburn's steady stare encountered the bright eyes of Sir Quentin Selby. "I submit," he repeated a little wildly, "that it is the duty of the Governors to uphold my request that Mr. Selby be dismissed from the School on the grounds that he has misbehaved and is unacceptable in the district."

"I confess," said Lord Leyburn after a prolonged pause, "that I am still in the dark as to the offence of which you complain."

"Surely—" began Lord Lucreton looking up quickly—

"My lord, I protest," shouted Sir Arthur, dangerously blue.

"May I, m'lord," said Sir Quentin Selby meekly, "be allowed to ask Sir Arthur Hinton-Brigg two questions?"

"Mr. Chairman, this gentleman has no status in this meeting," Lord Lucreton interposed sharply. "I object."

"How can you?" asked the Chairman. "If Sir Quentin has no status Sir Arthur has no status either. The whole meeting is irregular. If you, Sir Arthur, were dissatisfied with the Headmaster's decision your remedy, in my opinion, was to go to law with Mr. Selby. No member of the public has any right to demand the dismissal of one of our masters and your complaint, so far as I can follow you, has nothing to do with the School."

Sir Arthur became icily grand. "Let me remind your lordship that I am hardly a member of the public. I have been lately nominated a member of this Board—"

"You have been nominated," replied his lordship, "but it is for the Board to decide in May whether or not to accept the nomination. Sir Quentin?"

Sir Quentin smiled. "Thank you, m'lord. Just two questions, Sir Arthur. How often had my son met your daughter before you put an end to the acquaintance?"

"I really forget," snapped Sir Arthur. "I can hardly be expected to remember such details—"

"Oh, I don't mind about details. Let me put it like this. Had they been meeting frequently, perhaps secretly, for some considerable time, or is my information that they had met three times substantially correct?" Sir Arthur said reluctantly that he believed they had met only a few times, but—"Thank you," said Sir Quentin and proceeded to his next question. "What reasons had you for objecting to the friendship between these young people?" He glanced round the table and added: "I ask this because I have never heard anything to suggest that my son is a man of other than good character."

There was no immediate reply. Sir Arthur found himself in a position of some delicacy. His main reason, the engagement between Julie and Cubby could hardly be given, especially in the presence of Cubby's father, since it

349

was not, as yet, a certainty; and the ineligibility of Sir Quentin Selby's son was unconvincing.

He lifted his head. "My reasons, sir," he said firmly, "were based on your son's underhand behaviour. There was evidence, confirmed by his insolence to me, that he—that they—In short I had reason to believe that he was leading my daughter into a clandestine affair. Possibly an elopement."

"But why," the Vicar leant forward, earnest and baffled, "should he? I mean, the young man has a good position at Ledenham. Why should he endanger it by a clandestine marriage with Miss Hinton-Brigg?"

"Did he ever try to see her after you kicked him out?" asked the Chairman crudely.

"I dare say he tried," Sir Arthur smiled unpleasantly. "I made it very difficult for him."

"My lord," said the Headmaster crisply, "I have to inform the Governors that Mr. Selby assured me that his relations with Miss Hinton-Brigg were no more than a pleasant social friendship and he made no attempt to see her again when he knew that her father objected to it."

"Pardon me," said the fish-supplying Governor helpfully, "wasn't there something, Sartha, about the young man getting money off the young lady?"

All round the table people looked up quickly and Sir Quentin was suddenly alert, poised, as it were, for action.

"Ah," said Sir Arthur, "I had reason to believe that was so. I fancy, however, that there was some confusion—My daughter certainly gave a large sum of money to someone in connection with the affair, but whether Mr. Selby— There is some doubt—"

"My lord," said the Headmaster, "I know where that money went. I know that Sir Arthur has been informed and I have here a letter from witnesses who heard it—discussed between Miss Hinton-Brigg and the person who received it. Mr. Selby had no knowledge of it, as there is ample evidence to prove."

"Thank you," said Lord Leyburn and went on quickly before silence could fall or further helpful discussion break out. The second matter for enquiry. The complaint by parents that their son had been maltreated by Mr. Selby and—persecuted was the word, wasn't it? by the School generally.

"Er," said the Clerk and produced Mr. Secker's letter.

"Well, that clears *that* up," observed Lord Leyburn briskly. He looked at his fellow Governors and gave them a sudden grin of companionable amusement. "I think," he said to them, "that we'll ask the visitors, if we may call them so, to leave us now."

The Clerk got up and opened the door which led to the anteroom. Sir Quentin and Sir Arthur withdrew. The Headmaster was signalled to stay where he was.

"Have we," began the Vicar severely, "really got the truth of the matter? Because if we have I am at a loss to know why we have been called."

Colonel Ward, clearly very unhappy, said the accusations had seemed serious. Nobody, he became a little resentful, could have known that Secker would withdraw what had been presented to them as a genuine complaint. And they had thought that when Sir Arthur Hinton-Brigg had complained to the Governors—in writing—the thing had to be looked into. He looked at the Headmaster pleadingly

351

and Mr. Fielding responded. It had been his opinion, he said, that since every Governor had received the complaints they must meet to decide what to do about it, and he had thought an early meeting desirable because it had been impossible to prevent the matter becoming known throughout the district and the School.

The Chairman said: "Quite so," and thought about it for a few minutes. Lord Lucreton was also deep in thought and their eyes met briefly and without antagonism.

For many reasons, some of which they shared and all of which they both understood, it was not desirable that Sir Arthur should lose face. That doubt should be thrown upon him was inevitable and provided that it was limited it would do no harm; but he must not be allowed to look a fool to the public and above all he must not be involved in a libel case. They wished that Sir Quentin's facial control was less perfect. There was no doubt that an action for libel would lie and it would have been useful to have some clue as to what was going on in his famous legal mind.

The Headmaster, the Vicar, the Clerk and perhaps one or two others were following their thoughts.

"I don't think," hazarded the Headmaster, "that anyone wants to do more than bring the thing to an end as quickly as possible and forget it."

Lord Leyburn looked at him. "I dare say," he said, "you could bring an action yourself, if you felt like it."

"If it cost me the confidence of my Governors I should certainly have to think about it. If the complaints are dismissed I see no reason why it shouldn't be allowed to die."

"And the same applies to young Selby, presumably?"

"I can't answer for Sir Quentin, of course. I don't believe lawyers are any fonder of going to law than the rest of us."

"Seems to me," said the fishmonger coming along at his own pace, "it's all been a bit of a muddle, like. Likely this young chap was a bit cheeky to Sartha, my lord, and Sartha wouldn't put up with it. Well, being what he is it's hardly right as he should."

"No," agreed Lord Leyburn. "But if the boy was accused of something he hadn't done and turned out of the house he'd naturally resent it, you know."

"He did," the Headmaster's tone was dry. "He admitted that he ought not to have opened his mouth and I conveyed an apology to Sir Arthur. I did not think the offence warranted anything further."

"Is it necessary to put a motion, my lord?" asked the Vicar who had another meeting that afternoon.

"What I would like to suggest," said the Chairman, "is that this meeting be regarded as informal and that no records should appear. In my opinion the matter is purely Headmaster's business and he has dealt with it to my entire satisfaction."

The meeting agreed promptly and with profound relief and he said: "Then I think that concludes our business," and pushed his chair back.

"There's just one thing," said a new voice. The baronet from the other side of the county was habitually silent and had not been heard at all during the afternoon but he was now, though embarrassed, determined. "In the matter," he said, "of this fellow's nomination to the Board. I'm against it." There was a pause and feeling strongly he went on: "In my view—mind, I don't intend to say anything about it

353

outside this room, but in my view the chap's an ass. If he's up for election in May I'll vote against."

"Might be a bit awkward after this," suggested Colonel Ward.

"A little uncomfortable," the Vicar thought.

Hope rose in the assembled bosoms.

"The Governors will have the opportunity to vote for or against at the election in May," said Lord Leyburn.

"Not good enough," said the baronet emboldened. "Might slip in. He should be tipped off not to stand."

The Clerk began an anxious, "I don't think—" but Lord Lucreton got briskly to his feet.

"It's very unlikely," he said in his trumpet tones, "that Sir Arthur will consider joining the Board after this very unfortunate episode. I entirely agree that the sooner it's forgotten the better, but I will just say that in my opinion a little more co-operation at the beginning would have prevented the annoyance. However," he glanced from the Chairman to the Headmaster and his scarlet face crinkled in an impish grin, "it may be that, not for the first time, a man has been taken by his daughter for a ride."

In the release of laughter people got to their feet and the meeting was over. Most of them made for the door with the alacrity of boys let out of school. Lord Leyburn stumped off to the dressing-room of his ancestors to perform an unpleasant duty and the Headmaster, the Clerk and Colonel Ward drew together.

"Clever devil, Lucreton," said the Colonel respectfully. "Neat, you know, the way he wound it up. I mean he knows as well as anybody what Hinton-Brigg is, but the way he put it—well it sort of covered it up. Well," he heaved a sigh, "that's over, thank God."

Sir Quentin Selby, dismissed from the dressing-room while Lord Leyburn performed his unpleasant duty, appeared and the Headmaster went to join him. He was looking amused and said: "I needn't have wasted my time. You had it all very nicely buttoned up."

"Don't you believe it," said the Headmaster. "How the Chairman got here, fully briefed, I have yet to find out, but I assure you it wouldn't have been at all the same thing without him. Even with him you were invaluable."

"How so?"

"You struck terror to the heart of Lord Lucreton. I fancy he's still a little uneasy."

Sir Quentin smiled. "He may be. I don't believe Hinton-Brigg, even now, realizes how far he's laid himself open, but Lucreton's got it all right."

"Do you intend to take it up?" asked the Headmaster and the smile became a grin. The elder Selby looked round and spoke in a lowered voice.

"Not bloody likely," he said and then as Lord Leyburn came in he raised his voice again and said seriously: "I should be against taking any steps provided the matter is closed here."

"I think," said Lord Leyburn, "that you may be assured that the matter is closed." He turned to the Headmaster with an abrupt change of expression. "By God, Fielding," he said, "that woman Wills is a marvel."

While the meeting went on Tim worked hard on the running track and tried to pretend that he was giving all his mind to it. He had had a rather hurried lunch with his

355

father at Ledenham's Trust House during which he had suffered a stiff cross-examination and clearing of the mind. He had felt it to be impossible that anybody who had not actually encountered Sir Arthur Hinton-Brigg would believe in him, but Sir Quentin had met plenty of foolish men in his day and was seldom surprised.

"It's not really your show at all now," he told Tim. "Fielding has decided to back you and it's between him and the Governors. You won't go unless he does and they're not likely to let that happen. But you'll have to learn to keep your mouth shut."

"Yes, yes, yes," groaned Tim in no way cheered that he and the Headmaster stood together since there remained the possibility that, together they might fall, and having seen his father driven off to Leyburn in his hired car he sought relief in violent exercise.

Mrs. Fielding rarely felt the need for escape but she felt it on this occasion and driving away with a brisk air of keeping an appointment she took to the hills. Matron went about her duties with a belligerent face and snapped at the boys. Alison, since Angus was busy, went to find company and support at Holly Lodge.

Frances, who took her line from Patsy and had been boosted by him at lunch, was calmly confident but sympathetic and ready to talk. Marthe was not ready to talk. She was rather silent and remote, which it seemed had lately become a habit with her and when Frances went out with the baby, leaving the two girls together, Alison felt crossly that if Marthe wanted to sit in silence she wasn't going to cajole her out of it.

Marthe, however, seemed unconscious of the crossness.

They had not been alone together since Alison's engagement and she turned to the subject at once with her startling smile and a recovery of warmth which was completely disarming.

"I didn't know anybody could be so happy as you look," she said. "It is as if you have a great lamp burning inside you. How long have you known you love Angus?"

"I know now I've always loved Angus," said Alison. "I haven't known I was in love with him for very long."

With anxious politeness Marthe asked: "Do you mind talking about it? I would be very sorry to annoy you—to intrude, but I have no sisters and I never had a friend engaged before. Of course I am interested."

Alison laughed. "I'm interested myself. It's really quite difficult to remember my manners and not bore everybody by talking about it endlessly. You're a godsend. Where shall we begin?"

"At the beginning?" suggested Marthe.

It would have been impossible for either of them to talk about the intimate details of the engagement. What Angus said to Alison and what Alison said then was, like the revelation of the first kiss, between those two alone. But there was plenty to say.

"Were you ever in love with anyone else?" Marthe wanted to know.

"No. I really never had much chance," was the candid reply. "But Angus was. He was awfully in love with Frances when she came up here first. A lot of people were."

"Was he?" Marthe was surprised. "And do you—forgive me—do you mind?"

"Of course I don't mind. It was all over before I knew

him properly. I expect he's had lots of minor in-loves as well. He'd be a bit odd," said Alison, "if he hadn't."

"But you didn't."

"Well, no. At least only the usual swoon about the occasional heart-throb. But it's different for men. Richard," Alison smiled indulgently as she thought of her brother, "is always falling in love and out again."

Marthe looked doubtful, as if she didn't quite believe this and wouldn't approve if she did, and Alison felt suddenly that the moment was important and there was a job for her to do. She hoped she could do it and searched a little nervously for the right thing to say and the words in which to say it.

"Most people do a bit of experimental falling in love," she began, "but I think men *have* to. You see they have to take the initiative. The woman's rôle is responsive." She hesitated, faintly embarrassed and then went on with determination. "I knew I was in love with Angus but I didn't know the half of it till he came and told me. A rather horrible thing happened to me—I don't want to talk about it—and Tim knew about it. He was terribly good to me himself, then he went and told Angus and Angus came rushing round and everything came right in a minute." She looked sternly at Marthe when this enlightening statement was concluded and added: "I'll love Tim all my life because of what he did for me that day."

"I don't quite see—Angus would soon have asked you anyway," said Marthe.

"Well, I expect he would, but I don't know. We'd got in a muddle, we might have gone on for ages—even lost each other altogether. And that wasn't all Tim did."

358

There was quite a long silence. Alison had a sense of failure and was somewhat resentful. She had not expected any specific response from Marthe, but the complete lack of any response at all made her feel that she had laid bare her soul—at some cost—only to have it turned into an exhibition of rather foolish enthusiasm. She stood up abruptly and said that she would go home. "I want to be there when my father comes home and hear what happened."

"Oh, yes, I expect you do," said Marthe politely. She stood up too and their eyes met. Alison's were angry and suddenly they were in the throes of a sharp quarrel.

"I suppose," snapped Alison, "that it doesn't matter in the least to you what happens to Tim. He's one of the best people I know and he loves you terribly and you just couldn't care less. You're just damned cold and snooty and you think he isn't good enough for you."

"You don't know *what* I think," retorted Marthe, no longer cold. "Nobody can know what other people feel and think."

"They can see what you do and how you look."

"And what is wrong with how I look?"

"I think you are the only person in Ledenham who looks as if all this—this beastliness was Tim's fault. And you're the person he loves so it isn't very nice for him. *Do* you think he was to blame?"

"Well," Marthe's face was flushed but she kept her head up, "I think what I always think, that Tim likes being in love with girls—"

"Boloney," said Alison rudely. "He wasn't a bit in love with Julie."

359

"Then if he plays that he is her father is right to be angry. She may be hurt by such play."

"You don't know Julie."

"Perhaps. But all the same you can't say that it is good."

Alison felt as she had sometimes felt in the past when at war with one of her brothers. She took a deep breath and hit as hard as she could.

"How lovely to be you," she said. "So sure of your own rightness that you can't love or even be kind to anybody who isn't perfect."

Marthe stood still. The colour which had come into her face ebbed away leaving it very white. She looked as shaken as Alison herself had felt when Tim picked her up after the scene with Mrs. Hepburn, but Alison did not see it. She rushed out of the house and breathing fast hurried along the road.

Opposite the Zoo she was arrested by a piercing whistle.

"Pardon the crudity," said Angus, grinning from his study window. "I was just coming to look for you. Come on up."

He met her at the top of the stairs and seeing her face swept her hastily into his room. "My darling, what is it?" The Governors' enquiry, which had never been far from anybody's thoughts all day, came horrifyingly to his mind. "Have you heard—has it gone wrong?"

"Terribly wrong," said Alison whose rage had left her with only one thing in her mind and that in a confused and tattered condition. But Angus's concern pulled her together and she embarked on explanations.

"Why did you lash out at poor Marthe?" he asked as clarity began to emerge.

"She *asked* for it. Taking this high moral line—blaming Tim—"

"Losh, you're fierce," said Angus. "Poor Marthe. She's quite right, you know. Tim started it."

"Julie started it. I saw her do it. In fact I aided and abetted."

"Well, maybe she did, but he was an ass all the same."

Alison meditated. Was she enraged by Marthe and not enraged by Angus saying the same thing because she loved Angus more than Marthe? Were their attitudes in the matter of Tim's sinfulness really the same or really different? And was the difference merely one of terminology? One of them using his native language, the other doing her best in a foreign tongue. She put the question to Angus and then answered it herself.

"Marthe condemns him," she said. "You just say Tim's been an ass and it doesn't make any difference to being friends with him."

"Oh, well," said Angus vaguely, "chaps go their own way."

They walked over to School House to have tea together before Angus went in to afternoon School and found the Headmaster back and the atmosphere greatly relaxed.

Nothing, the Headmaster thought, could have been more satisfactory, if the nuisance had to come upon them, than that it should have ended as it had done in a fizzling out. Nobody had triumphed, there was no drama to be wrung from it and that was just as it should be.

"So the pike, or whatever the chaser is, has been removed from the pool," was his wife's comment, "and you can swim about at your own pace till the time comes to retire. Mind you pass Lord Leyburn's bouquet on to Miss Wills."

Mr. Fielding duly passed it on, in suitable form, and like the news of the result of the enquiry it was received primly. "Lord Leyburn is very kind," said Miss Wills, just as she said: "It was, of course, the only decision they could properly take," about the meeting.

"All the same," said the Headmaster firmly, "we owe you a great deal. The Chairman would have had a very difficult job if you hadn't briefed him." He smiled at her. "You have repaid a thousandfold young Selby's services as a chauffeur."

Miss Wills replied that she had merely done her duty but her face relaxed its sternness very slightly. "I am glad," she admitted, "that the matter is satisfactorily concluded. Do you intend to make a statement to the School?"

But the Headmaster had decided against statements. He told Tim and Mr. Clayton and let it filter. This was sufficient and the effect was a general flatness throughout the School. "Of course," said Matron tartly to a boy who wanted someone to discuss it with him, "we always knew the Governors only wanted telling by the Headmaster. That was all the enquiry was," and many people shared her feeling that their undoubted anxiety had been unnecessary; a foolish panic which they intended to forget as quickly as possible.

At Thaxley Manor Lady Hinton-Brigg and Julie waited for the husband and father with as much restlessness and rather more trepidation than their Ledenham counterparts. Mrs. Fielding faced the possibility, as even remote possibilities have to be faced, of the meeting going so far wrong that her husband's career would come to a premature end but there was never any danger that she would have to feel ashamed of him. Lady Hinton-Brigg, with nothing material at stake, sat in her charming upstairs sitting-room in the house where she was born, enduring humiliation and dreading more humiliation to come. What, she wondered painfully, was Arthur saying? If he lost this battle, or if, as usual, he triumphed how long could they go on living on tolerable terms with their neighbours? People never, of course, said anything, but this time it was impossible to escape the feeling. She was wholly withdrawn from Mrs. Fielding, who was a pleasant acquaintance of an occasional kind. Annette Courtney was as near to an intimate friend as she ever had and she had neither seen nor heard from Annette until, on the morning after Julie's escapade with the Rolls, she had telephoned to give her a cold description of the scene and confirm what Julie had already told her parents about the destination of the £30.

"I ought to tell you," Mrs. Courtney had concluded, "that Henry and I have sent a statement to the Headmaster which can be used if necessary."

"I see," said Lady Hinton-Brigg and indeed she had seen. The fact that Arthur now knew the truth was not enough.

Remembering this conversation she got up to mend the fire and light another cigarette and started violently as the door opened.

"It's only me," said Julie. She sounded subdued and came across the room with a dragging gait which set her mother's teeth on edge.

"Must you droop like that?" she asked sharply.

"Sorry," said Julie, injured. "This waiting is getting me down. Do you want me to go away?"

Lady Hinton-Brigg did but she didn't say so and Julie sat down to relieve her worry by passing it on. "What do you think will happen? I think it's going to be pretty good hell whoever wins, you know. I mean if Tim gets sacked our name'll stink. All these Ledenham people will talk and they were really livid. Then if Pop loses he'll be up the wall. It's not going to be much fun either way."

"It's a pity you didn't think of all this before you brought it on us," said her mother.

"Well, but how could I have known it would *be* like this?"

"You were given plenty of warnings."

"Oh, warnings," a shrug of the shoulders dismissed warnings. Nobody, in Julie's view, took any notice of those. "What shall we do?" she went on. "Honestly I think we'll have to get away for a bit. Couldn't we go on a cruise or something till it blows over?"

"What about Cubby?"

Lady Hinton-Brigg was so far in her daughter's confidence as to be aware that Cubby's stock had risen. The revelation of the Rolls had been passed on and Julie's consequent decision to marry Cubby and have a Rolls, or the nearest she could get to it, of her own. Either her father or Lord Lucreton, she thought, would probably give her one for a wedding present. Or they could club together if they felt stingy. She now, however, looked pensive.

"Cubby," she confessed, "seems a bit static lately. If we go on a cruise couldn't he come too?"

364

"There's the car," said Lady Hinton-Brigg starting to her feet. They hurried downstairs to find that there were two cars and Lord Lucreton preceding Sir Arthur into the hall.

"Ah, Cynthia," shouted Lord Lucreton at his most genial. "Just begging a cuppa tea to set me on. How are you?" The Lucretons and the Hinton-Briggs were recognized to be inevitably great friends and in token of the friendship Lord Lucreton kissed Lady Hinton-Brigg's cheek whenever they met or parted while Sir Arthur, returning the compliment, pecked Lady Lucreton.

Lady Hinton-Brigg held up her cheek automatically and looked past the embrace at her husband who was very dark in colour and very glum. She smiled vaguely at her friend, assuring him of tea, and hurried the party into the drawing-room. "What?" she began, but Lord Lucreton was before her.

"Well, young woman," he greeted Julie, pinching her cheek, "you're a little pest, aren't you? A dozen busy men have spent the afternoon clearing up after you."

Julie gaped and as she took in what he had said resentment filled her heart. But she thought of the Rolls and achieved a weak, moderately repentant smile.

"But you managed to clear it up?" said Lady Hinton-Brigg who had no objection to Julie bearing her full share of blame.

"Oh, yes. Of course we did. No trouble." He was immensely cheerful and so quick off the mark that Sir Arthur hadn't a chance. The boy, he went on easily, was all right. Safe in his job, bless his silly heart, and the whole thing had been taken out and aired, given a good shaking and folded up. Lady Hinton-Brigg said that it was very

365

satisfactory and made no sign of registering the fact that Arthur had certainly been defeated and probably made a fool of himself. It was not the first time that Lord Lucreton had acted as a face-saver. Julie, who was not well versed in diplomacy, was round-eyed and puzzled.

"Cigarettes, Julie," said her mother with a look which got her moving and asked lightly who had taken the Chair.

"Leyburn turned up," Lord Lucreton was still doing the talking. "We didn't think he'd be home in time, but it was a very good thing. Tommy Ward," he made a funny face, "dear chap, but not, shall we say, as clear-headed as some. Actually," his voice dropped confidentially, "he'd got things in a pretty fair muddle, but we won't say anything about that."

"Leyburn," said Sir Arthur, who could not be kept silent indefinitely, "is a very arrogant fellow. He has his position, of course, but I must say he takes rather too much upon himself and—"

"Oh, he's tough, old Leyburn," the trumpet tones broke in agreeably, "but he does get results." There was a hearty laugh. "Bit everybody, tore no end of a strip off me and pulverized poor Ward—you got off lightly, Arthur—but when it's all over you find he's got it buttoned. Of course Ledenham's his baby. It suits me. I don't mind going along to a meeting now and again but I'm not all that interested. If he likes to do all the work let him, is my line. I've other things to do myself—same like you," he nodded to Sir Arthur, one important man to another.

Sir Arthur was not perfectly soothed, but he was doing as well as could be expected. He managed an important smile, if rather a sour one. "The old man did make some sort of apology," he said, "I'll give him that. He agreed, I fancy, with you, Luke, that Fielding had been grossly negligent, to say nothing of his incivility to me personally but—"

"But nobody wanted to make an issue of it," Lord Lucreton concluded smoothly.

Sir Arthur agreed a little doubtfully and went on: "He asked me what I felt about the nomination. I disappointed him there, I'm afraid. I said I thought I had already spent enough time on the School and Fielding isn't a man I care to work with. But he had to accept it. They only want figureheads there, you know—Leyburn runs it—and when I join a Board I do so with the object of taking my full share of the work and responsibilities of that Board. I am too busy a man, too much of a man of ideas, if I may say so, to waste my time—"

They allowed him to talk for a reasonable time while Lord Lucreton disposed efficiently of a hearty tea. When he had finished he got briskly to his feet, his mission nearly completed.

"As a matter of fact, you know, Arthur," he said seriously, "I'm glad to hear you aren't taking on any more at present. You've had quite a winter," he ran over a few of the Hinton-Brigg undertakings which had not driven the Chairman of the company very hard and concluded significantly: "and there's plenty more coming up. Why don't you get away for a decent holiday? Cynthia—what about persuading him to take you for a cruise?"

"Oo !" cried Julie prettily. "*Heaven!* Yes, Pop. Do!"

Sir Arthur passed a hand over his brow and smiling made light of his weariness. "Ah, well," he said, "one carries on. So many people depend—But perhaps—" An idea occurred to him. "A cruise would be very pleasant but I don't know that Cynthia and I would be very amusing companions for Julie. Julie," he turned to her with a compelling smile, "why don't you ask Lord Lucreton if he could spare Cuthbert to come with us?"

Lord Lucreton had long ago weighed the advantages and disadvantages of the Hinton-Brigg girl as a wife for his son. All he had to do now was to laugh genially, give her a rather kinder pinch and cry:

"Splendid! *He'll* keep her out of mischief."

20

THE day of the Governors' meeting was the first on which there was a genuine, convincing feeling of spring but nobody paid much attention to it. Tim was vaguely aware of it as he toiled conscientiously on the track and it had, to a great extent, inspired Angus to hail his beloved from his window with a vulgar wolf whistle, but on the whole Ledenham's thoughts were confined to Leyburn Castle.

Tim was just out of his bath when he was summoned to the Headmaster's study and he listened very soberly to what Mr. Fielding had to tell him. "So it can now be forgotten," was the conclusion to an extremely economical statement, "and I'm sure you feel as I do, the least said and the sooner forgotten the better."

"Yes, sir," said Tim flatly.

The Headmaster regarded him with considerable sympathy. The boy, he thought, was feeling much as he felt himself. The whole crisis had been so unreal and so disagreeable that one was left with a sense of degradation. It was dishonest kind of danger to threaten an honest man and it was not justice so much as Lord Leyburn's practised ability which had brought them safely through it. He knew that this was not the only reason for the young man's downcast face but it was the only one to which they could refer; and though Tim was young and inexperienced he was intelligent enough and more than sensitive enough to recognise it for what it was.

"It's been an unpleasant business," he said without much emphasis. "I'm putting it behind me. You do the same. It's surprising how soon such things fade—if you let them."

"Yes, sir," said Tim again and this time he looked up and tried to express some of the gratitude he felt, not only for the solid backing the Beak had given a raw, unstable young assistant and the forbearance which had never told him what a nuisance he had been, but also for the companionable implication that they had the same feelings about it.

The Beak received it and then put it aside and took a new direction with what was a grin rather than a smile. "Your father," he said, "confined himself to a couple of awkward questions. I was very glad he was there and sorry we couldn't see more of him. Persuade him to come and talk to the Sixth some day. Are you seeing him again?"

"I'm going to pick him up after School, sir," said Tim, "and have a meal with him before he catches his train."

The Headmaster nodded amiable dismissal and Tim, walking slowly back to the Zoo and tea, investigated his emotions. The load which he had got used to carrying had rolled off his shoulders and as he, so to speak, straightened and became conscious of relief he became conscious too of the feeling of spring. But this, instead of exhilarating him brought depression, for now that danger was past the light mild breeze, the airy clouds, all the genial promise reminded him that the danger had never really mattered. Marthe, who did matter, was as far or further away than ever.

He turned out of the gates and saw Frances coming along the road from Holly Lodge, pushing the baby in his pram and walking quickly. She waved an imperative summons and he went to meet her. "Well?" she said anxiously. "Have you heard?"

"All well," said Tim. "The Beak didn't spread himself so I don't know what occurred but I gather I'm over the hump. I may get a bit more from my father."

Frances was delighted and said so, though, like everyone else, she now wondered what she had been worrying about. But she did not linger over the subject. "You haven't seen Marthe, have you?" she asked.

"No. Why?"

"Well," she looked apologetic, as if she suspected herself of fussing, "I'm wondering where she is. Alison was with her when I took John out and when we went in just now there was a note just saying she'd gone out and not to worry."

"Isn't she still with Alison?" Tim began and then remembered he had seen Alison in the distance with Angus. "No—she isn't. But there are lots of places. She may have remembered she's been asked out to tea, or gone for a walk."

"Yes, she may have gone for a walk," Frances agreed without conviction, "but she doesn't drop in to places and if she'd been asked to tea she wouldn't have forgotten. I wouldn't bother—she knows I don't want her to feel she's got to tell me where she's going—only she always has. And—" she hesitated, "I don't know—there was something about the note. A sort of fluster—"

Tim was very still. "I have no clue at all," he said. "I don't know of anything to bother her and I've no idea where she might go."

"I expect I'm fussing about nothing," said Frances. She turned the pram round. "I'll go home. Patsy'll be in soon."

Patsy and Nick, who came in with him to have tea, were at first more interested in the result of the enquiry than in Marthe's disappearance, but when tea was over and John played with and put to bed they allowed that it was a little unexpected.

"She's never done it before," repeated Frances, who was now really unhappy. "I think I'll ring Alison. She was—oh, gosh, how horrible!—she was the last person to see her."

"Easy," said Patsy, but he agreed that Alison might now be rung up without an appearance of fuss.

When Alison came to the telephone and was asked if she knew where Marthe was she didn't reply at once. "Are you there?" asked Frances impatiently. "Did Marthe say anything about going out? Do you know *anything?*"

"I—I don't know," stammered Alison. "I'll come round—"

Afternoon School was over. Tim, who was in a hurry since he had to meet his father earlier than was quite easy, raced back to the Zoo, rang Holly Lodge and was waiting for Angus when he came in.

"Marthe lost?" exclaimed Angus. He looked unexpectedly concerned and Tim said:

"You don't know anything about her, do you? Did Alison—"

"No," said Angus slowly. "I've no idea where she might be."

"Well," Tim hurried on, "there's no real reason to flap. I mean she wasn't upset or anything so far as we know. Angus—I've got to go now. I'll ring up from Snaydon. Will you—?"

"I'll go along," said Angus and Tim, comforted by his

solidity, ran out of the house and drove away fast.

As Angus followed him Alison came hurrying through the gates, wide-eyed and rather pale. "Angus," she said, "do you—have you heard—"

Angus, large and reassuringly calm, took her arm and led her at a moderate pace towards Holly Lodge saying: "Canny, lass. What in the world are you imagining? Yes, I know you lashed out at her but you don't think Marthe's soft enough to do anything daft because of a quarrel, do you?"

The arm he held relaxed a little. "It does sound a bit silly," Alison admitted. "But—I *was* savage."

"Was she savage too? Or meek and tearful ?"

"Oh—savage too. I got in the last, worst crack, though."

"Well she was fighting in a foreign language," Angus pointed out. "She's probably walking it off, cursing at all she could have said in Norwegian."

The atmosphere at Holly Lodge was reasonable. Frances was uneasy but controlling it. Patsy and Nick had decided not to be uneasy before, say, the arrival of the last bus from Leyburn at half-past ten.

"About ninety-nine per cent of those reported lost," Nick stated, "turn up peacefully having obeyed a sudden impulse and gone to the pictures. The fact that Marthe hasn't done it before means nothing. There has to be a first time and," he nodded amiably at Alison, "your slanging match probably set her off. Marilyn Monroe, or whoever it is, will be a soothing diversion after the infuriated Miss Fielding."

"Thank you very much," said Alison, but she was less relieved than he intended. They didn't know what the quarrel had been about.

"People do get lost on the hills sometimes," Frances echoed her thoughts uncomfortably.

"Marthe was brought up among real hills," said Angus. "She's not the kind of mug that gets lost."

Patsy heaved himself to his feet. "What about a drink?" he suggested. "If we loosen Alison's tongue we might get the dope about the enquiry."

Tim, pushing his car along on the way to Snaydon, thought about Marthe reluctantly. Even if she had disappeared, so to speak, seriously, he kept reminding himself that it had nothing to do with him. Not once only had she told him where he got off and, if she should be in any sort of trouble, he would be the last man she wanted to help her out of it. He dismissed her from his mind but as often as he did so she returned, promptly and with such a sensation of crisis and agitation that as he drove he was searching for her along the roads, then in the streets of Snaydon and almost forgot the purpose of his journey.

Sir Quentin had had tea with an acquaintance in Snaydon at whose house Tim picked him up. The acquaintance was a legal brother and Sir Quentin emerged with an amused face and a racy selection of scandalous stories about Sir Arthur Hinton-Brigg.

"Do have him up for libel," begged the acquaintance. "You'll be the most popular man in the north of England."

"Not even for that," was the reply. "But don't tell him I said so. No, thank you very much, we won't bring the boy in. I want to talk to him and I haven't much time."

With neat proficiency Sir Quentin got himself out of the house and joined his son. "An amusing chap," he remarked of his host. "Probably ask you in now he knows you exist. We may as well go along to the Station Hotel, Tim. It's no worse than usual and it's convenient. You're very glum. What's the matter with you?"

Tim, weaving his way through the exceedingly confused traffic of Snaydon, said there was nothing the matter.

"Have you been fussing about this schemozzle?" asked his father.

"No, not really. Glad it's cleared up, of course. It leaves rather a stink."

"You feel befouled, do you?" Tim nodded, his eyes on the traffic. "Well—that'll soon pass. Curious business. Extraordinary the inflated egotism you find in some of these stupid men with a lot of money. They're insulated from the pricks and it grows and grows—"

Sir Quentin was a rapid talker. His memory, vocabulary and opinions were always ready to his hand and by the time they had driven from the suburbs of Snaydon to the station in its centre Tim had been half amused and half aghast by a full description of the enquiry.

"So it could have gone wrong?" he said. "Wrong enough for the Beak to resign—"

"Oh, I wouldn't say that." Sir Quentin could hardly see himself defeated by Sir Arthur Hinton-Brigg. "But it could have meant a fight, you know. You may as well park in the station yard—it's no distance. Both you and Fielding could have him for libel, but that's better avoided."

"God, yes," said Tim with all his heart and drew his car neatly into the parking ground.

They walked away from the station, the father and son alike in build and movement and sufficiently alike in mind to be congenial and at ease with each other. But though Sir Quentin was describing the course and personalities of the meeting with all his usual wit and virtuosity the subject was so distasteful to Tim that he let it flow past him, listening only enough to make some sort of comment if required. The rest of his thoughts were with Marthe. He was still feeling the sense of crisis which must be some curious trick of imagination or reaction from his own worry. He was still idiotically searching for her. He would ring the Hendersons as soon as they got to the hotel—

"—don't you agree?" his father's voice suddenly penetrated.

"I—" he began guiltily and saw Marthe walking along on the other side of the street. A sharp exclamation startled Sir Quentin. "Wait, Dad," said Tim and plunged recklessly into the traffic.

Sir Quentin stood still. He saw his son, safely across the road, running with a nice turn of speed. He saw him overtake a thin dark girl and grasp her purposefully by the arm. With slightly raised eyebrows he strolled on towards the hotel.

"Marthe," said Tim and when she turned a startled face he saw he had been right about the crisis. She was very pale; she was young and tender and a long way from home, and she was at a loss. Tim forgot that she had turned him down. He forgot that she considered him blameworthy in the Hinton-Brigg affair, he almost forgot that he was in love with her. He slid the hand which grasped her through her arm and held it against him with no desire except to comfort. "What are you doing in this hole all by yourself?" he asked.

"I had—had something I wanted to do," she said.

"Frances was wondering where you'd got to." He spoke lightly, not wanting to worry her about it but she looked more miserable than ever.

"Was she? But I left a little letter. I was not going to be very late. There is a bus—"

"Never mind the bus," said Tim. "We'll ring them up and I'll take you home. My father's here—we'll have dinner with him and see him on to his train."

"Oh," she stood still. "I don't think—I think I should go on this bus. I don't want—" but he was much stronger than she was and one can't start a struggle in a street.

"Come on," he said turning her round. "You'll like my old man. He had a lot to do with Norwegians in the war." He raised an eyebrow at her. "That's how I knew about Norwegian Resistance."

She smiled faintly and then asked: "Did he come because of this thing—enquiring? I think Frances said so."

"He did."

"And was it—is it all right?"

"It's all over and perfectly all right. We're all going to forget it as fast as we can."

"Yes," said Marthe. "It is best to forget it." She looked up to add: "I am very glad it is all right."

Sir Quentin was naturally interested but he was looking very placid smoking a cigarette in the vestibule of the hotel when Tim, still holding Marthe's arm, brought her in.

"Let me introduce you to Marthe Jensen," said Tim whose glumness was no longer noticeable. "You'll like this—she's Norwegian and she's going to have dinner with us."

"Norwegian? Certainly I'm delighted," Sir Quentin smiling and taking her hand looked as if he meant it, and when he raised a comical eyebrow as Tim frequently did and spoke, rather haltingly, in her own language Marthe laughed and was transformed.

"That, however, will do," he reverted to English when they had exchanged a few sentences. "I was never good and now I'm very bad. We'll talk about Norway in English. Tim, we haven't too much time. Let's get clean—"

Tim looked at Marthe. "You wouldn't run away, would you?"

"No," she said. "I promise."

"Why," Sir Quentin asked mildly as the two gentlemen went towards the washroom, "should the lady run away?"

"Well," said Tim, "she doesn't approve of me. I had to bring her along by force." They butted their way through a swing door and he added abruptly: "Something's up. I don't know what, but I don't want her to bolt off and get on a bus by herself."

"She's quite extraordinarily beautiful," observed Sir Quentin and Tim looked at him with a sudden grin.

"I've noticed before," he said, "that our tastes march."

The light had gone from Marthe's face when they joined company again but Sir Quentin was skilful and, since he was pleased with her, very kind. He talked about Norway. He had been involved in the Resistance training, he told her, and he had made friends with whom he had exchanged visits after the war so that he knew something of the country.

Tim, watching Marthe's response, was greatly depressed. He had never seen her so at ease or so brilliantly alive and he was dismayed to think how much she must have felt herself a foreigner and a stranger among them all at Ledenham, how homesick she must have been that merely talking about her own country with someone who knew it slightly could make her look like this. It wasn't so good, he thought, that on top of the strangeness and the homesickness she had had to cope with an obtuse and persistent suitor. Nevertheless he intended to find out what the crisis was about and stand by.

After dinner they walked back to the station with Sir Quentin and saw him to his train. Tim said: "Thanks for coming. Pity it was so easy, really, but I'm no less obliged. Give Mother my love. How did you stop her coming too?"

"Marital authority," said the father.

"Oh yeah?" said the son.

Sir Quentin, pointedly deaf, turned to Marthe. "It's unthinkable," he said, "that you should leave England without seeing London. Let Tim drive you south at the end of term and stay with us for a little. My wife would be delighted."

Marthe coloured. "It is very kind, but—" she hesitated, "— I think I shall leave England before the end of term. I think very soon now."

That was a pity, Sir Quentin said easily, but no doubt she would have other opportunities to see the capital, and then they were waving as the train pulled out and left them alone on the platform.

Tim hooked his arm in Marthe's again and they walked back to the yard where his car was parked making a desultory kind of conversation so that the tension which lay in wait for them should be kept at bay. Marthe said that she had enjoyed her dinner and liked Sir Quentin who was very kind. Tim explained about his mother who was tiny and very pretty and ruled her famous husband and three tall sons with benign effortless despotism.

"It sounds nice, your family," said Marthe. "Your father coming up here to be with you—to defend you—"

"Not bad," Tim agreed and cashed in. If they could talk about his people they could talk about hers and exchange of family information eased and warmed the atmosphere till they were through Snaydon's traffic and on the open road. Then he asked: "What happened this afternoon? Why did you suddenly rush off to Snaydon?"

There was no reply for a moment and he wondered if she was going to refuse to talk, but at last it came reluctantly. "I want very much to go home," she said. "I wanted to think about it and I came to Snaydon to ask when I could make the journey."

"Did you find out?"

"Oh yes. It is not difficult to go soon. I will write to my parents and tell them what I want to do."

"But," Tim insisted, "what cracked you off today?"

Marthe moved uneasily and he glanced round at her. She was frowning and miserable and he turned the car into a side road and pulled up. "Now we can talk," he said. "We must all have failed very badly if you feel you can't bear to stay any longer. Frances and Alison, Patsy, Nick—How have they gone wrong?"

"But they haven't," cried Marthe. "They haven't failed—I've failed. I—Alison said—"

"Alison?" Tim cut sharply into her stammering. "What did Alison say?"

"Oh—" she made a gesture of hopelessness. "How difficult—I forget all the English I know. Wait."

Tim waited. He offered her a cigarette and though she smoked very little she took it thankfully and when, after some minutes, she began to speak again her tone was more conversational.

"I am not nearly so clever as I think," she said unexpectedly. "When I don't understand I don't know it—I am quite pleased with my misunderstanding. So I make mistakes and then, very cleverly, I make more mistakes thinking I am putting things right." Her dry, rueful voice made Tim laugh and she smiled and then turned to face him with some embarrassment but with direct honesty. "I want to say I am sorry. One of my mistakes was about you and—and this Julie. I had no right to—"

"Oh, Marthe." Tim felt sand-bagged. He wanted to burst into tears and could only hold out a hand to her. Marthe hesitated and then put hers into it and immediately there was the comfort, the comprehension that physical contact brought them. "You were perfectly right about Julie," he said. "It wasn't good. It was cheap and stoopid and it didn't mean a thing. But it didn't mean a thing to her either."

"No," said Marthe. "That is what Alison said."

"But that can't be all," Tim said after a pause. Marthe apparently thought it was and he gave her hand a sharp squeeze. "Come on. Open up. Did you and Alison quarrel?"

"Yes, we quarrelled," she opened up at last. "And first I was very angry and then I thought she was right and I was sorry. I do nothing in Ledenham except quarrel so it's better if I go away. And now I've frightened Frances." She kept her composure and left her hand in his but she had an air of feeling herself defeated. Her dark head was bent and in the feeble light from the dashboard her face was reticent and unhelpful. Tim was somewhat at a loss. He knew Alison was a partisan. She had been wholly on his side in the row and she made no secret of her hope that he would get Marthe after all. But she should have known better than to try and push Marthe into it. Nobody had any right to play that sort of game with any girl, least of all with her. If she was ever to love him she would have to come to it in her own time and her own way. Her hand gave him some hope. He could not believe that the touch of it could mean everything to him if the touch of his meant nothing to her. But his own efforts to persuade her had come to a sticky end. Alison's, it seemed were going to drive her out of the country.

"Are you still angry with Alison?" he asked.

She shook her head emphatically. "Oh no. It was for a moment only."

"Well, you may be sure she got over it just as quickly. Marthe—don't throw in your hand." She looked puzzled and he hurried on: "Don't go away before your time. It would be so miserable. Frances would feel it was her fault, Alison would feel it was hers. And I would know, really, that it would be mine. But I promise I won't bother you. Can't you forget the mistakes and stay?"

A man may be successfully resisted when he is pleading his own cause however well he does it. When he genuinely sets his cause aside and is thinking only of her there is nothing for a girl to resist. The remote, composed Marthe looked wildly at Tim and with a small despairing moan, covered her face with her hands and wept. Tim sat still for a moment and then slid his arm round her shoulders and was not repulsed. But steering wheel, gear lever and all the other impediments which Eric knew so well caused him no inconvenience since there would be no masterful embraces. He held Marthe as he had held Alison in her hour of need, patted her a little and stared out through the windscreen with a sober face. In the silence, with her beside him and no longer hostile, the thoughts and emotions which had been so restless and incoherent a kaleidoscope lately began to make a pattern. Whatever Marthe's feelings were or might become her instinct had been right when it led her to reject not only his proposal of marriage but also the kind of relationship which had been his idea of leading up to it. He had a vision of Patsy Henderson; the look of security and self-knowledge which had stirred his respect and envy. Angus too, steady and purposeful in his immense happiness. There was a hell of a lot more in marriage besides love-making when you took a proper look at it, thought Tim sombrely, and he had some way to go before he could be ready to make a go of it.

Marthe straightened and fishing in her pocket for a handkerchief dried her eyes and blew her nose delicately.

"Better?" he asked her and she glanced at him and nodded.

"Of course I won't go home before it is time," she said. "Will you please not say to Frances why I went to Snaydon?"

"No, said Tim. "I won't tell anyone."

"I am ashamed that I have worried her—and all of you. "I don't know," her voice was puzzled, "what was the matter with me."

"Spring, perhaps," suggested Tim with a faint grin. "It had a reputation for upsetting the balance. Induces moods and strange fancies."

"Oh," Marthe thought about it and then turned, her face alight with amusement. "Well—for me, I think it has passed."

"For me too, I hope," said Tim and withdrawing his arm he started the car and drove back to Ledenham at a leisurely speed.

Next morning Ledenham woke up to the realization, twenty-four hours delayed, that winter was over. There was no doubt about it. There had been fine days earlier in the term but they had deceived nobody; they were winter days fine enough to remind one what spring is like, this was the real thing. Upstairs in School House Matron's cap was jaunty. She looked calmly at the empty sickrooms and, except for one emergency bed, she folded up the blankets with moth-balls. Downstairs Higgins plied his mop with the more vigour because from now on they wouldn't be tracking in dirt as soon as he got his floors nice and when the Headmaster had gone over to School he let himself go. "I'll sing thee so-hongs of Arabee," roared Higgins in greeting to the spring and Miss Wills, wearing her medium-weight grey cardigan, heard it from her office almost with pleasure.

With the sunshine, the genial look of the river and the excited birds the spirits of the School soared. There was a good deal of folly but it was of a good-tempered kind and the flat feeling that they had allowed themselves to worry over something that didn't rate worry gave way to a just relief that a cloud had passed.

"Might get in some beer and a few thirsty souls to drink it," suggested Mr. Burgoyne at lunch in the Zoo. "After all," he gazed blandly at Tim, "we still have you. I suppose it's something to celebrate. Not a real do like last time of course."

"Oh well, hardly," said Willie. "That was an engagement," and he simpered a little. He was getting on very well with the doctor's daughter and just possibly the next engagement party—

"Would the Beak come, do you think?" Tim was saying. "We wouldn't say anything but it would be nice to drink a silent thanksgiving for recent deliverance."

"Yes," said Mr. Burgoyne at once. "We'll ask him—and Mrs. Beak, of course. Good idea."

The Headmaster and Mrs. Fielding accepted the invitation to drop in for a drink at the Zoo with pleasure. Though no reference was made to the recent cloud on that occasion, and very little at any time, they were not unaware that the School was glad it was safely past. The atmosphere of relaxed cheerfulness was, the Headmaster admitted later, gratifying. If the School had hoped that this row would see him out there was no sign of it.

They did not stay very long at the party, knowing their place, but took themselves away with accustomed skill leaving it, so to speak, to put its feet up. Mr. Burgoyne, remarking that one thing to be said for the Beak was that he was an easy man to entertain, drew forth his fez from behind a row of books and putting it on settled down with Messrs. Henderson and Vincent in a favourable position near the beer.

"Calm water all round, I think," remarked Nick surveying the company. "Peace perfect peace with Briggses far away. Did you discover what drove Marthe to bolt to Snaydon?"

"Never asked," was Patsy's reply.

Mr. Burgoyne grinned. "Don't tell me Frances didn't find out?"

"No."

"Well, whatever it was it seems to have passed," said Nick. His eyes rested on Marthe for a moment and moved on to Tim who was not far away. "Would you say an understanding has been reached?"

"No," said Patsy again. "At least—Frances thinks they've agreed to forget the past."

"All passion spent?"

"In abeyance anyway."

"Thank God for that," said Mr. Burgoyne piously. "We've enough passion on our hands. Look at Willie." They looked indulgently at Willie, going well. "I don't know about you, Nick, but just occasionally I feel uneasy. I look at these enthusiastic young chaps and I ask myself, am I still single because I like it or am I one of the unwanted?"

"And what's the reply?"

"No reply, so far."

"Have some more beer," said Patsy kindly.

Nick, with an air of resignation, said that his days of carefree bachelorhood were probably numbered. "Alison intends to get me off as soon as she has a base to work from. She'll deal with you next, Burg, and then there's Richards—"

"He has his art."

"Fat lot of good that'll do him." Nick, looking across the room at Alison, caught her eye and sent her a grin and a wink. "She's so happy herself she can't bear it if everybody isn't in the same state of bliss." He laughed suddenly. "I wonder if Oonagh's fixed up with the likely-looking shuvver. She seems to have passed from our lives."

Patsy took his pipe from his mouth to remark with unexpected cordiality that he wished Oonagh well. She had told nobody but Tim about the Upton flutter. "If the shuvver is what she wants," he said, "I hope she gets him."

A few miles from Ledenham in the Hinton-Briggs' Land Rover Oonagh was doing her best. It was the first time she had seen Eric since he had practically thrown her out of the car and dashed in pursuit of Julie and his Rolls and there was a good deal of catching up to be done. She began carefully by saying that she had heard Tim Selby wasn't going to be sacked after all. Did Eric know how Julie was feeling about it?

Eric said he reckoned she'd stopped thinking about it. She was always hanging about the garage talking about the Rolls and he reckoned she was after the Lucreton bloke again. The Rolls had talked louder than the teacher, he said shrewdly, and a Rolls costs a packet of money. "They're going away," he concluded. "Whole boiling *and* young Lucreton, according to Pigeon. Going on a cruise."

"Nice to be some people," said Oonagh. "Not," she added hastily, "that I'm all that keen on cruises and that. What did Sartha say about the Rolls?"

Eric became reserved. "Not so much. Matter of fact," he loosened up again, "he soon forgot about it. He copped quite a packet, I'd say, at that meeting they had." He retailed all that Pigeon had managed to overhear. "That's why they're clearing out, see."

"Not for ever, though?" Oonagh was wide-eyed.

"Oh no. Three or four months." There was a pause. "You never heard any more about that money, did you?"

"No."

"Reckon," said Eric cautiously, "they've forgotten that too. Or else her ladyship told young Julie she'd better wave it good-bye."

By tacit consent they dropped the subject. It was one of those things better left undisturbed.

"What'll you do while they're away?" asked Oonagh, very casually.

Eric took his time about his reply. He fished for his cigarettes and they both lit up. "Well, I could have just stayed hanging around with the Pigeons and old Foley, but what I reckoned, it's a chance. I got a month's wages due me anyway so I asks Sartha what about a job in the Works after."

"And what did he—"

He proceeded at his own infuriating pace. He had got a reference from Sartha and he'd get a job okay. Big money when he got cracking. Oonagh knew that any display of enthusiasm would be as much as her place was worth.

"Nice work," she said brightly and took a calculated risk. "You won't have this," indicating the Land Rover, "to run your girl friends round in, though."

"Well," said Eric, "I'm keeping an eye on the cars till they come back. But what I was thinking, whyn't you get a job in Snaydon?"

"I'd love a job in Snaydon, quite honestly," said Oonagh. "But of course it depends if anybody in Snaydon wants a secretary, doesn't it?" She looked at him with a gay smile but Eric did not return it.

"I don't see," he said, "that it'd hurt you to go in a shop for a while if you can't get a job as a typist."

Oonagh took a long wavering breath. "That's true," she said. Eric threw his cigarette away and turned to her purposefully. As his arm went round her she remembered Ledenham School, its eligible bachelors and social opportunities long enough to say: "Queer, isn't it, to think I'd never have got to know you if old Wills hadn't got appendicitis?" but Eric was not inspired by wonder and she let it pass without regret.

As the Headmaster and his wife strolled homeward from the Zoo, leaving the gaiety behind them without too much feeling of deprivation, Mrs. Fielding sniffed the mild air and felt, like Matron, that they were in the straight. To her experienced senses came the assurance—though one never quite dared to accept it—that the spring term had once more been vanquished.

"I had no idea," remarked her husband before she had found sufficiently non-committal words to convey the thought without tempting providence, "that that child Marthe was so lovely. I must say I see Selby's point."

"She's always had lovely moments," replied Mrs. Fielding, letting the term go, "but she was looking happier, I thought. More at ease."

"Does that mean that Selby has succeeded in his suit or abandoned it?"

"Well, if he'd succeeded I think we'd have heard. Perhaps he's postponed it." Mr. Fielding murmured that if so it would show a welcome sign of common sense and she went on quickly: "Of course they're too young, but if he wants her I hope he'll get her in due course. He's really a very nice boy and he's growing up fast."

"About time."

"I hate old heads on young shoulders."

The Headmaster smiled. "It's a serious defect in you, considering the position you occupy," he observed, "that you invariably favour the attractive near-rakes. I myself rate a man solely on merit."

"Men, perhaps," retorted Mrs. Fielding. "What about Oonagh?"

"Oh, you're adding Oonagh to the arsenal, are you? Well—you have to admit I ran the School for more than a fortnight without Miss Wills."

"*Ran* it?" she raised her eyebrows. "I suppose you could say you ran it. It shook a bit."

"But consider the nature of the events and the calm which now prevails."

There was nobody about. Mrs. Fielding took his arm and patted it kindly. "You didn't do so badly," she said and went on more soberly: "I'd have hated to retire before we're ripe for retirement. I don't see why we shouldn't go on for years yet. Do you?"

"Not at the moment," said the Headmaster cautiously.